Murder Most
Medieval

Murder Most Medieval

Noble Tales of Ignoble Demises

Edited by Martin H. Greenberg
and John Helfers

Cumberland House
Nashville, Tennessee

Published by Cumberland House Publishing, Inc., 431 Harding Industrial Drive, Nashville, Tennessee 37211

Cover design by Gore Studio, Inc.

Library of Congress Cataloging-in-Publication Data

Murder most medieval : noble tales of ignoble demises / edited by Martin H. Greenberg and John Helfers.
     p. cm.
   ISBN 1-58182-087-9 (alk. paper)
     1. Detective and mystery stories, American. 2. Detective and mystery stories, English. 3. Historical fiction, American. 4. Historical fiction, English. 5. Middle Ages—Fiction. I. Greenberg, Martin Harry. II. Helfers, John.

PS374.D4 M86 2000
813'.087208358—dc21
00-021470

Printed in the United States of America
1 2 3 4 5 6 7 8 9 — 05 04 03 02 01 00

Contents

Introduction

John Helfers

There's no doubt that the medieval period (A.D. 750–1500) was a time of great hardship. After the fall of the Roman Empire, most of Europe and the British Isles remained mired in the Dark Ages. Nobles controlled the land, the Catholic Church attempted to rule the royalty, and the peasants owned nothing. Add to this the human devastation caused by the Black Plague, which killed as much as one-third of the population of Europe, and the outlook for humanity appeared very grim. Would Europe fall apart as nobles bickered and battled for lands and crowns? Not likely. The aristocracy and the Church made sure no one overstepped their bounds. Would the continent remain stuck in these medieval ways forever? No. In the fifteenth century, Johann Gutenberg and the Renaissance put an end to the Middle Ages.

During this era mankind continued doing what it had always done: living and dying. The former was difficult (one of every three babies died within six months of birth), and the latter was all too easy (because of plague, starvation, and war, among other factors). But humanity, like the cockroach, is exceedingly easy to kill but very difficult to exterminate. Even with plagues, starvation, and war, mankind was growing, expanding, even learning. One lesson people learned very well was how to survive.

Survival was what everyone fought for in one form or another. Everybody struggled to survive: from kings and queens, who fought to hold their crowns and their countries; to the Church, which fought to maintain control over the masses; to the nobles, who fought to retain their lands and way of life; to the merchants, who fought for trade routes and business; to the peasants, who fought simply to stay alive. Most people would do anything to ensure their survival, to keep what was theirs and perhaps gain a little bit more when the opportunity presented itself. They would conspire for it. They would lie for it. They would steal for it. They would even kill for it.

Which brings us to the theme for this anthology. Of the crimes man commits against his fellow man, murder is the basest one of all. Depriving another human being of life simply to gain what they have, to protect what the murderer has, or to protect one's reputation, is an act that shocks and appalls society, regardless of motive. Even in cases of self-defense, no matter how justifiable, there is a certain amount of wonder about the person who can be pushed no farther, believing that the only way to save themselves is by committing murder.

It is certainly conceivable that there would be people who lived in the Middle Ages who felt this way. Peasant women, subject to a lord's whim if he fancied one, were sometimes treated as badly or worse by their own husbands. Lords spent their whole lives scrabbling for a piece of land and the tenants to make it profitable, or at least livable. Kings did not know which to fear more—their enemies abroad or the ones in their own court—so they hid their treachery behind false smiles and promises of allegiance.

The following stories examine the medieval world—a world of dirt and struggle—and the men and women who lived and died in it. Murder is committed in these stories for many of the same reasons that murder is committed today. And, as always, there were men and women in medieval times who crusaded against the lawlessness that, at times, threatened to overwhelm the land. Peter Tremayne's Celtic detective Sister Fidelma makes an appearance here, solving a twenty-year-old crime of passion. The noble highwayman Robin Hood, as written by Clayton Emery, is also found within these pages, solving a mystery of witchcraft and heresy, with the help of the indomitable Marian. And, of course, what collection of medieval murder mysteries would be complete without a tale from the late, lamented grande dame of historical mystery, Ellis Peters, and her soldier-turned-sleuthing-monk, Brother Cadfael?

From Gillian Linscott's tale of a lord whose survival needs necessitate starting a war, to Margaret Frazer's story of political intrigue and deception at King Henry's court, we are pleased to bring you thirteen tales of murder most foul, murder most malicious, murder most malevolent. So turn the page and prepare to be swept back through time into a world of intrigue, danger, and history—to a time when death was all too common, and murder was a crime committed by everyone from kings to peasants—a time of murder most medieval.

Murder Most Medieval

Like a Dog Returning . . . A Sister Fidelma Mystery

Peter Tremayne

I t's very beautiful," Sister Fidelma said softly.
"Beautiful?" Abbot Ogán's voice was an expression of disbelief. "Beautiful? It is beyond compare. Worth a High King's
honor price and even more."

Fidelma frowned slightly and turned toward the enthusiastic speaker, a question forming on her lips. Then she realized
that the middle-aged abbot was not looking at the small marble
statuette of the young girl in the robes of a religieuse, which
had caught her eye as she had entered the chapel of the abbey.
Instead, he was looking beyond the statuette, which stood at
the entrance to a small alcove. In the recess, on a small altar,
stood an ornate reliquary box worked in precious metals and
gemstones.

Fidelma regarded the reliquary critically for a moment.

"It is, indeed, a valuable object," she admitted. But the reliquary box was not unusual in her experience. She had seen many such boxes in her travels, all equally as valuable.

"Valuable? It is breathtaking, and inside it is the original *Confessio* penned in the hand of Patrick himself." Abbot Ogán was clearly annoyed at her lack of homage before the reliquary.

Fidelma was unimpressed and not bothered at all by his look of disfavor.

"Who is the young girl whose statuette guards the entrance to the alcove?" she demanded, turning the conversation to what she considered to be the object of greater interest. Somehow the artist had brought the young religieuse to life, endowing her with a vibrancy that burst through the lines of the cold stone: It seemed that she would leap from the pedestal and greet the worshippers in the tiny abbey church with outstretched hands.

The abbot reluctantly turned from his contemplation of his community's most famous treasure—the reliquary of Saint Patrick. His face darkened slightly.

"That is a likeness of Sister Una," he said shortly.

Fidelma put her head to one side to examine it from every angle. She could not get over the extraordinary vitality of the piece. It was almost as if the artist had been in love with his model and only thus able to draw forth some inner feeling into the cold marble.

"Who was the sculptor?" she asked.

The abbot sniffed, clearly not approving of the interest she was showing.

"One of our brethren, Duarcán."

"And why is her statuette in this chapel? I thought only the holy saints could achieve such honor?"

The corner of Abbot Ogán's mouth turned down. He hesitated and then, observing the determination on Fidelma's face, asked, "Have you not heard of the story of Sister Una?"

Fidelma grimaced irritably. It was surely obvious that she would not be asking the question had she heard the story. The abbot continued: "She was killed on this very spot some twenty years ago."

"What happened?" Fidelma's eyes had widened with greater interest.

"Sister Una entered the chapel when someone was attempting to steal the holy reliquary. The thief struck her down and fled but without the reliquary."

"Was the thief caught?"

"He was overtaken."

"How did the Brehons judge him?"

"Sister Una was very beloved by our local community." The abbot's features were set in deep lines, and there appeared a defensive note in his voice. "Before the culprit could be secured and taken before a Brehon for judgment, the people hanged him from a tree. This small marble statuette was erected in the chapel in Una's honor to guard the reliquary for all eternity."

"Who was the thief and murderer?"

The abbot again hesitated. He clearly was unhappy at her interest.

"A man who worked in the abbey gardens. Not one of our community."

"A sad tale."

"Sad enough," the abbot agreed shortly.

"Did you know Sister Una?"

"I was a young novitiate in the abbey at the time, but I hardly knew her." The abbot turned, clearing his throat as if in dismissal of the memories. "And now . . . I believe that you are staying with us until the morning?"

"I will be continuing my journey back to Cashel in the morning," Fidelma confirmed.

"Stay here then and I will send Brother Liag, our hostel keeper, to you. He will show you to the dormitory of the religieuse. We eat after Vespers. You will forgive me leaving you here. There are matters I must now attend to."

Fidelma watched as he hurried along the aisle and vanished beyond the doors of the chapel. As they banged shut behind him, her eyes were drawn back once again to the extraordinary statuette. It held a curious fascination for her. The artist had, indeed, given the poor Sister Una life and, for a while, she was lost in examining the lines of the fine workmanship.

There was a sound behind her: a shuffle of sandals and an exaggerated cough.

She turned. A religieux had entered and stood a little distance off with his arms folded inside his robe. He was balding and wore a doleful expression.

"Sister Fidelma? I am the hostel keeper, Brother Liag."

Fidelma inclined her head toward him. Yet her gaze was still reluctant to leave the intriguing statuette. The newcomer had observed her interest.

"I knew her."

Brother Liag spoke softly and yet there was a curious emotion in his voice that caught her attention immediately.

"Yes?" she encouraged after a pause.

"She was so full of life and love for everyone. The community worshipped her."

"As did you?" Fidelma interpreted the controlled emotion of his voice.

"As did I," Brother Liag confirmed sadly.

"It is an unhappy story. I have heard it from your abbot."

Did a curious expression flit across his features? She was not sure in the gloomy light.

"Did you also know the man who killed her?" she pressed when it seemed that he was saying no more.

"I did."

"I gather he worked in the gardens of the abbey?"

"Tanaí?"

"Was that his name?"

"That was the man who was lynched by the community for the crime," Brother Liag affirmed.

Fidelma exhaled softly as she gazed at the marble face of the young girl.

"What a miserable waste," she observed, almost to herself.

"Grievous."

"What sort of man was this Tanaí? How did he think that he, a gardener, could steal that precious reliquary and sell it—for presumably he did it for mercenary gain?"

"That was the theory."

Fidelma glanced quickly at him.

"You do not agree?"

Brother Liag returned her gaze and his expression had not changed. It was still mournful.

"I think that we share the same thought, Sister. The only way such an object could be sold for gain is by its destruction. Where and to whom could such a priceless treasure be sold? The selling of jewels pried from the box might be sold individually. The value of the box itself and the greater value of that which is contained in it would be entirely lost. There would be no market for anything so invaluable. Who would purchase such a treasure?"

"Yet if Tanaí was merely a laborer in the garden here, he might not have considered that aspect of the theft. He might simply have seen a precious jeweled box and been overcome by greed."

The hostel keeper smiled for the first time, more a motion of his facial muscles than indicative of any feeling.

"It is true that Tanaí worked here as a gardener. He was an intelligent man. He had been an apothecary and herbalist. One day he mixed a wrong prescription and one of his patients died. He answered before the Brehons for manslaughter and was fined. The Brehons said it was an accident, and there was no guilt of intent involved—only the guilt of error. But Tanaí was conscientious and, although he could have continued to practice as a herbalist, he withdrew here to the abbey and did penance by returning to study the plants and herbs, living a life of penury and self-sacrifice."

Fidelma glanced at Liag cynically.

"Until he coveted the reliquary; for what you are telling me is that he was intelligent enough to know its real value. Maybe he thought he would find someone who would endanger their immortal soul for possession of it?"

Brother Liag sighed deeply.

"That is what everyone has thought these last twenty years."

"You sound as though you still do not agree?" she commented quickly.

Brother Liag was hesitant, and then he sighed reflectively: "The point that I was making is that he was intelligent enough to know that he could never sell the reliquary, if that was his motive.

There are some questions to which I have never found satisfactory answers. Tanaí had removed himself to the monastery with his wife and young daughter because he felt he must do penance for a mistake. That strikes me as the action of a man of moral principle. He worked in the abbey gardens in a position of trust for five years. Never had there been a whisper of anyone's distrusting him. He could have been appointed apothecary of the abbey for the old abbot—he died many years ago now—who had several times urged him to take the position, saying that he had paid for his mistake more than enough.

"Why did he have such a sudden mental aberration? For over five years he was in a position in which he could have stolen the reliquary or, indeed, any one of the several treasures of the abbey. Why did he attempt the theft at that point? And to kill Una! He was never a violent man, in spite of the mistake that led to the manslaughter charge. The killing of poor Sister Una was so out of character."

"What actually connected him with the attempted theft in the first place?" Fidelma asked. "The abbot said that he fled without the reliquary."

Brother Liag inclined his head.

"The reliquary was untouched. Sister Una had disturbed the thief before he could touch it, and she was killed while trying to raise the alarm."

"Where was Tanaí caught?"

"Trying to enter the abbot's rooms." Brother Liag shot her a keen glance. "The community caught up with him at the entrance and dragged him to the nearest tree. God forgive all of us. But Sister Una was so beloved by all of the community that common sense was displaced by rage."

"The abbot's rooms? That is a strange place for a man to run to when he has apparently just committed murder," murmured Fidelma.

"A question that was raised afterward. Abbot Ogán, who was one of the community, a young brother at the time, pointed out that Tanaí must have known that he would be caught and was trying to throw himself on the old abbot's mercy and seek sanctuary."

"I suppose that it is plausible," Fidelma conceded. "What happened to Tanaí's family?"

"His wife died of shock soon after, and his young daughter was raised by the Sisters of the abbey out of charity."

Fidelma was perplexed.

"There is something here that I do not understand. If Tanaí was found at the abbot's rooms, if the only witness was killed and the reliquary had not been touched, and there was no eyewitness, what was there to link Tanaí with the crime? Indeed, how do you know that theft was even the motive for the murder?"

Brother Liag shrugged.

"What else could have been the motive for killing poor Sister Una? Anyway, everyone was crying that it was Tanaí who did the deed and that he had been seen running from the chapel. I presumed that this was without question since everyone was shouting it."

"How much time had passed between the time the crime was committed and when Tanaí was found?"

Brother Liag shifted his weight as he thought over the matter, trying to stretch his memory back two decades.

"I can't really recall. I know it was some amount of time."

"An hour?"

"No, well under an hour."

"A few minutes?"

"More than that. Perhaps fifteen minutes."

"So who identified Tanaí as the culprit?"

Brother Liag gestured helplessly.

"But everyone was shouting that . . . I saw Brother Ogán, the abbot as he now is. In fact, it was Ogán who was foremost in the hue and cry; but there was Brother Librén, the rechtaire . . . the steward of the abbey. Everyone was shouting and looking for Tanaí . . . I have no idea who identified him first."

"I see," Fidelma replied with a sigh. "Why do you now have doubts of Tanaí's guilt?"

Brother Liag appeared slightly uncomfortable.

"I know that this community has his death on its conscience because he was unjustly killed by the anger of the mob and not by legal process. That is enough to lay the burden of guilt on us.

There is always doubt if a man has not had a proper chance to defend himself."

Fidelma thought for a moment.

"Well, on the facts as you relate them, you have a right to be suspicious of the guilt of Tanaí. Had I been judging him at the time, I would have acquitted him on grounds that there was insufficient evidence. Unless other witnesses could have been produced. However, there is little one can do after twenty years."

Brother Liag gave a troubled sigh.

"I know. But it is frightening to consider that if Tanaí was not guilty, then all this time the real murderer of Sister Una has dwelt within these walls nursing this dark secret."

"We all live cheek by jowl with people who nurse dark secrets," Fidelma pointed out. "Now, perhaps you'll show me to my room?"

After the evening Angelus bell and a frugal meal in the refectory of the abbey, Fidelma found herself almost automatically making her way to the chapel to once again examine the marble statuette of Sister Una. She disliked unsolved mysteries; they kept nagging at her mind until she had made some resolution of the problem. The face of Sister Una, alive in the marble, seemed to be pleading, as if demanding a resolution to this now-ancient murder.

Fidelma was standing before the statuette when, for the second time, a voice interrupted her meditation.

"He didn't do it, you know."

The voice was a soft feminine one. Fidelma quickly glanced around and saw a religieuse standing nearby. She was, so far as Fidelma could place her, somewhere in her thirties. The face could have been attractive, but even in the softening candlelight it seemed bitter and careworn.

"To whom do you refer?" Fidelma asked.

"To Tanaí, my father. My name is Muiríol."

Fidelma turned to her and examined the woman carefully.

"So you are the daughter of the gardener who was hanged for the killing of Sister Una." It was a statement rather than a question.

"Unjustly so, for, as I say, he did not do it."

"How can you be so sure?"

"Because I was here at the time and he was my father."

"Daughters are not the best witnesses to their father's deeds. I would need more than a statement of belief. You were surely young at that time?"

"I was twelve years old. Do you think that day is not impressed on my mind? I was with him in the abbey gardens, for I used to often play there. I remember seeing Sister Una passing to the chapel. She greeted us and asked my father a question about his work. Then she passed on into the chapel."

Muiríol paused and swallowed slightly. Her dark eyes never left Fidelma's face. There was a haunted look in them as if again seeing the scene—a vivid scene that appeared to torment her.

"Go on," Fidelma encouraged softly.

"A few minutes after she passed into the chapel, there came a scream. My father told me to remain where I was and ran to the chapel. He disappeared inside. Others of the community had heard the scream, and some came into the garden to inquire what it portended. There came shouting from the chapel, a man's voice was raised."

"Was it your father's voice?"

"I did not think so at the time. But time often confuses some details."

"Your memory appears clear enough."

"It is the truth, I tell you," she replied defensively.

"What happened then?"

"I saw my father emerge from the chapel. A voice was crying—'Tanaí has murdered Una!'—or words to that effect. I saw my father running. Later I realized that he was running to the abbot's rooms in fear for his life. But there was an outcry, and the people were angry. I did not know what had happened. I was taken to our rooms by one of the religieuse and remained there until my mother, prostrate with grief, was carried inside. She had seen my father being . . ." Her voice caught and she paused a second before continuing. "She had seen my father being lynched outside the abbot's rooms. She never recovered and died soon afterward."

There was a silence between them for a while.

"From what you tell me, your father could not have killed Una," Fidelma finally observed. "Did you never tell your story?"

Muiríol nodded.

"I told it to the old abbot, but I was not believed."

"But did you tell it to the Brehon who investigated the matter?"

"The matter was kept secret within the abbey for years until the old abbot died. The abbot felt guilty that the lynching had taken place with members of the community involved, and he wished to conceal it. So it was not reported to the Brehons. That was why the religious here were kind to me and raised me as one of the community. After the old abbot had died, no one bothered about the story of Una and my father."

"Knowing this, why did you remain in the abbey?"

The girl shrugged.

"One day, so I hoped, I would find the guilty one. Someone in this abbey killed Sister Una and was also responsible for my father's death."

"So you wished your father's name to be cleared?"

Muiríol grimaced.

"That was my original purpose. Twenty years have passed. Is anyone still interested?"

"Justice is always interested in justice."

"Isn't there a saying that there is little difference between justice and injustice?"

"If I believed that I would not be an advocate of the courts," Fidelma returned.

FIDELMA WAS IRRITATED. SHE could not sleep. Her mind was filled with the thoughts of young Sister Una's death. She turned and twisted for an age, but sleep would not come to her. She sat up and judged it was long past midnight.

Finally, she rose from her bed, put on her robe, and decided to go down to the abbey gardens to walk in the cool of the summer night. The only way to the garden that she knew of led through the chapel.

She heard the sound almost immediately as she opened the door into the chapel—a low groaning sound followed by a thwack as if of leather on a soft substance. The groan rose in a new note of pain.

Then she heard a voice: "*Mea culpa, mea culpa, mea maxima culpa!*"

Her eyes narrowed at familiarity of the masculine voice. She peered into the gloom to seek out the penitent.

A figure was kneeling before the marble statuette of Sister Una, head almost to the ground. The back was bare where the robe was stripped down to the waist. In one hand was a broad leather belt that, every so often, the figure would strike his back with, drawing blood, as she saw by the candlelight. Then the groan would issue a second or so after the impact of the leather on the flesh. The words of contrition were mumbled in Latin.

Fidelma strode forward.

"Explain this, Abbot Ogán!" she demanded coldly.

The abbot froze for a moment and then slowly straightened himself up, still kneeling on the chapel floor.

"This is a private penitence," he replied harshly, trying to summon anger to disguise his shock at being thus discovered. "You have no right to be here."

Fidelma was unperturbed at his animosity.

"On the contrary. As a *dálaigh* of the Brehon courts, no doors are barred to me, Abbot Ogán, especially when it is deemed that a crime has been committed."

The abbot rose from his knees, pulling his robe around his shoulders. Fidelma had noticed that his back was scarred. It was of no concern to her that the abbot practiced flagellation: many mystics of the Church did, although she found such practices distasteful in the extreme. The scars, obvious even in the candlelight, indicated that the abbot had practiced the self-abuse for many years.

Ogán was defensive before her hard scrutiny.

"What crime?" he blustered.

With a slight forward motion of her head, Fidelma indicated the statuette of Sister Una.

"You seem to be expressing some guilt for her death. Were you guilty of it?"

The last sentence was suddenly sharp.

Abbot Ogán blinked rapidly at the tone.

"I was responsible, for had I been in the chapel at that time she would not have been alone to confront Tanaí."

Fidelma's brows came together.

"I do not follow."

"It was my task on the day she was killed to clean the chapel. I had delayed my task out of simple sloth and indolence."

"I see. So you were not here when you should have been. If you feel guilt then that is within you. So when did you become involved in leading the hue and cry after Tanaí?"

A frown passed the abbot's face.

"Who said I did?" he asked cautiously.

"Are you saying that you did not?"

"I . . . I came on the crowd as he escaped across the garden. Everyone was shouting. They caught and hanged Tanaí from the tree outside the old abbot's quarters. That was when I first knew about her death and realized my guilt, for if I had been here . . ."

"An 'if' will empty the oceans," Fidelma snapped. "So you did not witness the event? You did not identify Tanaí as the murderer and would-be thief?"

Abbot Ogán shook his head.

"Everyone was proclaiming that Tanaí was the guilty one."

"But someone must have done so first. Who first identified Tanaí as the culprit?"

The abbot again shook his head in bewilderment.

"Perhaps a few of those who were there that day and who have remained in the abbey might recall more than I do."

"Who might they be?"

"Brother Liag, Brother Librén, Brother Duarcán, and Brother Donngal. Everyone else who was here at the time has either died or moved on."

"You have neglected to mention Tanaí's daughter, Sister Muiríol," observed Fidelma.

The abbot shrugged.

"*And* Sister Muiríol. But she was only twelve years old at the time. No one took any notice of her, for like any loyal daughter, she swore her father was innocent."

Fidelma paused for a moment and looked once again at the vibrant features on the statuette. An idea suddenly occurred to her.

"Tell me, Ogán, were any of the community in love with Una?"

The abbot looked bewildered and then pursed his lips sourly.

"I suppose that we all were," he said shortly.

"I think you know what I mean."

Celibacy was not forbidden among the religious of the Church in Ireland. Most houses, like this abbey, were often mixed communities in which the religious, male and female, lived and brought up their children in the service of the new religion.

Fidelma noted that Ogán's chin jutted out a little more.

"I believe that some of the brethren were emotionally and physically enamored of her. She was a very attractive woman, as you may have noticed, because this statuette is an excellent likeness."

"Were you, yourself, in love with her?"

The abbot scowled.

"I was not alone in my feelings."

"That was not my question."

"I admit it. There was a time when I thought we could have been together under God's holy ordinances. Why are you asking such questions? It has nothing to do with her murder."

"Does it not?"

Abbot Ogán's eyes narrowed at her tone.

"What are you accusing me of?"

"You will know when I am accusing you. At the moment I am simply asking questions."

"Una was killed protecting the holy reliquary when Tanaí attempted to steal it. There is nothing else to consider."

"How can you be so sure? There were no witnesses. The reliquary was not even stolen."

"I do not understand," frowned the abbot.

"You mentioned that you were not alone in your love for Una," she went on, ignoring his implied question. "Is there anyone else in the abbey today who fell into that category?"

The abbot thought for a moment.

"Liag, of course. And Duarcán."

"Did Una show particular affection for any one person?"

Ogán scowled for a moment, and then he shrugged in dismissive fashion.

"It was rumored that she and Liag would be married. I thought they were going to leave the abbey and set up a school together."

"And you mentioned Brother Duarcán. Is that the same Duarcán who sculpted this statuette? You mentioned that name when I asked you earlier who the artist was."

The abbot nodded reluctantly.

"It is the same man," he confirmed. "I think he was very jealous of Liag. After he sculpted the statuette, he refused to undertake any more work of a similar nature. A waste of a great talent."

"It is late," Fidelma sighed. "Before I leave the abbey tomorrow morning, I would like to speak with Brother Duarcán. Where will I find him?"

"He will be in the abbey kitchens. He now works cleaning and cooking for the community."

The next morning, Fidelma found Duarcán, a tall dark man, washing kitchen utensils. He glanced up as she approached him and paused in his task. He smiled nervously.

"You are Fidelma of Cashel. I have heard of you."

Fidelma inclined her head in acknowledgment.

"Then you will have also heard, perhaps, that I am an advocate of the Brehon Court?"

"I have."

"I understand that you were in love with Sister Una."

The man flushed. He laid down the pot he was cleaning and turned to her, clasping his hands loosely before him.

"I'll not deny it," he said quietly.

"I am given to understand that she did not return your sentiments?"

Duarcán's mouth tightened at the corners.

"That is not so. We were going to be married."

Fidelma raised an eyebrow.

"What of the story that she was going to marry Liag and set up a school with him?"

"Brother Liag is a liar to tell you that. It is not so. That was *our* plan; mine and Una's."

Fidelma examined his expression carefully. His eyes met hers with a frankness that she found hard to doubt.

"I am told that you were a good sculptor once and that you executed the exquisite statuette of Una in the chapel. Is that so?"

"It is."

"Why are you now wasting your talent?"

"Wasting? My talent died after I had given Una life in marble. I have nothing else to give. I exist, waiting for the time that I can rejoin Una in spirit."

The dramatic words were rendered without drama, offhanded, as someone speaks of a mere statement of fact about the condition of the weather.

"Do you recall where you were when Una was killed?" pressed Fidelma.

"Do you think that I would forget the events of that day?" There was a controlled passion in his voice. "Yes, I recall. I was in my studio that overlooked the gardens. I was the abbey's stonemason and sculptor. Una had been with me that morning, and we were planning to see the old abbot—he is now dead—to tell him of our decision to marry and leave the abbey. When Una left me, I saw her walk toward the chapel."

"So you saw her cross abbey gardens?"

Duarcán nodded.

"And you saw her go to the door of the chapel?"

"No. Not as far as that. The door was obscured by the shrubs and trees of the garden."

"What did you see then?"

"Tanaí and his daughter were in the garden. Tanaí was doing some work. I saw Una pass by, pausing momentarily to speak with them. Then she went on. A few moments later, I was looking out, and I saw Tanaí rise and move off rapidly after Una.

There was something suspicious about the way he moved. Rapidly, I mean, purposefully."

"Did you hear anything?"

"Hear anything?" He frowned and shook his head. "I was intent on cutting some stone at the time. I do not even know what made me glance out the window. It was the sight, shortly afterward, of people running through the garden that caught my attention rather than the noise. It caused me to go to the door, and that was when I was told that Una had been killed; that Tanaí had tried to steal the reliquary and had killed her."

"Who told you that?"

"Brother Liag."

Fidelma looked thoughtfully at him for a while.

"Did it ever occur to you that if Tanaí was going to steal the reliquary, he would hardly have waited for Una to pass by on her way to the chapel and then attempt to steal it while she was actually there?"

Duarcán stared at her as if he had difficulty following her logic.

"But, Brother Liag said . . ."

Fidelma raised an eyebrow.

"Yes? What did he say?"

"Well, it became common knowledge that is what happened."

"Was it at your instigation that the statuette was placed in the chapel?"

Duarcán frowned.

"Not exactly. In those long, lonely days and nights that followed, I felt compelled to recreate her likeness in marble from fear that it would be lost in the mists of receding memories. One day, Brother Ogán, as he then was, came to my studio and saw the finished statuette. It was he who persuaded the old abbot that it should be placed in the chapel where it has stood ever since. After that, I did no more work as a stonemason nor sculptor. I now merely work in the kitchens."

Sister Fidelma drew a deep sigh.

"I think I am beginning to understand now," she said.

Duarcán looked at her suspiciously.

"Understand? What?"

"The cause of Una's death and the person responsible. Where can I find Brother Liag?"

Duarcán's face filled with surprise.

"I saw him pass on his way to the chapel a moment or so ago . . . Are you saying . . . ?"

But Fidelma was gone, hurrying toward the chapel. Inside, she saw Brother Liag talking with the abbot.

"Sister Fidelma," Brother Liag seemed surprised to see her. "I thought that you had already started your journey back to Cashel."

"There was some unfinished business. Just one question. Cast your mind back twenty years to the events surrounding Una and Tanaí's death. There was tumult in the abbey gardens, shouting and so forth. You passed by the door of Duarcán's studio, and he came out to see what was amiss. You told him what had happened. That Una had been killed; that Tanaí had committed the deed, and you also told him the reason—that Tanaí had attempted to steal the reliquary and was prevented by Una."

Brother Liag frowned, trying to recall, and then he slowly and reluctantly nodded.

"I seem to recollect that I did so."

"This was before Tanaí had been caught. It was a short time after the community had heard Una's last scream, and Tanaí was even then being chased across the gardens. How did you know so soon, all these details?"

Brother Liag stared at her, his face going suddenly pale.

Abbot Ogán exhaled loudly.

"Liag, did you . . . ?"

He left the question unfinished, for Liag was returning the abbot's look in horror as a further recollection came to him.

Fidelma's lips compressed for a moment in satisfaction as she turned to the abbot.

"You told Liag your version in the garden. You were heard to cry that Tanaí was the murderer. Your and Liag's versions differ so much that one of you was lying.

"The truth, Ogán, was that you were in love with Una, not Liag. When you found that Una was going away with Duarcán, that love turned to hatred. Sometimes what is thought as love is merely the desire to possess, and thus it and hate become two sides of the same coin. Was it here, in this chapel, that Una told you of her love and her decision to leave the abbey? Did you then strike her down in your jealous rage? Her scream of terror as you struck was heard by Tanaí, who came rushing into the chapel . . . too late. He was not running to the abbot for sanctuary, but to tell the abbot what he had seen. You raised the alarm, denouncing Tanaí as the murderer, and the first person you told was Liag. The death of both Una and Tanaí are your responsibility, Ogán."

The abbot stood, head bowed.

When he spoke it was in a dull, expressionless tone.

"Do you not think that I haven't wished for this moment over the years? I loved Una. Truly loved her. I was overcome with a mad rage that I instantly regretted. Once Duarcán's statuette had been placed here, I returned each night to seek her forgiveness . . ."

"Your contrition could have been more readily believed had you made this confession twenty years ago. I would place yourself in the hands of Brother Liag; prepare to answer for your crimes."

Brother Liag was regarding the abbot in disgust.

"Some of us knew that you were secretly flagellating yourself before her statuette. Little did we realize you were merely as a dog, as the Book of Proverbs says; a dog returning to its own vomit. There is no pity for you."

The Country of the Blind

Doug Allyn

I 've never much cared for my own singing. Oh, I carry a tune well enough, and my tenor won't scare hogs from a trough, but as a minstrel, I would rate my talent as slightly above adequate. Which is a pity, since I sing for my living nowadays.

As a young soldier I sang for fun, bellowing ballads with my mates on battlements or around war fires, amusing each other and showing our bravery, though I usually sang loudest when I was most afraid.

The minstrel who taught me the finer points of the singer's art had a truly fine voice, dark and rich as brown ale. Arnim O'Beck was no barracks room balladeer; he was a Meistersinger, honored with a medallion by the Minstrel Guild at York.

An amiable charmer, Arnim could easily have won a permanent position in a noble house, but he preferred the itinerant life of the road, trading doggerel tunes in taverns for wine and the favors of women.

My friend ended dead in a cage of iron, dangling above the village gate of Grahmsby-on-Tweed with ravens picking his poor bones. I hadn't bawled since my old ma died, but I shed tears for Arnim, though I knew damned well he would have laughed to see it. In truth, he ended as we'd both known he would.

19

But it wasn't only for my friend that I cried. I was a soldier long years before I became a singer. Death has brushed past me many times to hack down my friends or brothers-in-arms.

I mourned them, but I never felt their passing had dimmed the light of the world. A soldier's life counts for little, even in battle. His place in the line will be filled.

But when a minstrel like Arnim dies, we lose his voice and all the songs in his memory. And in these dark times, with the Lionheart abroad, Prince John on his throne, and the Five Kings contending in Scotland, this sorry world needs songs to remind us of ancient honor all the more.

My friend the Meistersinger knew more ballads of love and sagas of heroes than any minstrel I've ever known.

But even he was not the best singer I ever heard. . . .

I'D BEEN WAITING OUT a gray week of Scottish drizzle, singing for sausages in a God-cursed log hovel of an alehouse at the rim of the Bewcastle wastes. If the muddy little village had a name, I never heard it nor did I inquire. I was more concerned with getting out of it alive.

The tumbledown tavern had too many customers. Clearly there was no work to be found in the few seedy wattle and daub huts of the town, yet a half dozen hard-bitten road wolves were drinking ale in the corner away from the fire. They claimed to be a crew of thatchers, but their battle scars and poorly hidden dirks revealed them for what they were: soldiers who'd lost their positions. Or deserted them. Men whose only skill was killing.

Bandits.

Ordinarily, outlaws pose no problem for me. Everyone knows singers seldom have a penny, and brigands enjoy a good song as readily as honest folk. If I culled the gallows-bait from my audiences, I'd sing to damned skimpy crowds indeed. But along the Scottish borderlands, thieves are more desperate. And as ill luck would have it, I had some money. And they knew it.

I'd earned a small purse of silver performing at a fest in the previous town. One of the border rats jostled me, purposely I think. Hearing the clink of coins, he hastily turned away. But not before I glimpsed my death in his eyes.

And so we played a game of patience, whiling away the hours, waiting for the rain to end. And with it, my life and possibly the innkeeper's. Cutthroats like this lot would leave no witness to sing them to a gallows tree.

My best hope was sleep. Theirs. And so I strummed my lute softly, murmuring every soothing lullaby I could remember. And praying they would nod off long enough to give me a running start.

And then I heard it. I was humming a wordless tune when an angel's voice joined my own in perfect harmony, singing high and clear as any Gregorian gelding.

Startled, I stopped playing, but the melody continued. For a moment I thought it was a voice from heaven calling me to my final journey. Then the innkeeper, a burly oaf with a black bush of a beard, cursed sharply and ended the song.

"Who was that singing?" I asked.

"My evil luck," he groused. "A nun."

"A nun? In this place?"

"Well, an apprentice nun anyway, a novice or whatever they're called. There were a fire at the abbey at Lachlan Cul, twenty mile north. Most died, but one aud bitch nun stumbled here with her charge before death took her, saddling me with yon useless girl."

"She has a wonderful voice."

"It's nought to me. I've no ear for song, and my customers don't care much for hymns. She's heaven's curse on me, I swear. She's blind, no good for work, nor much inclined to it neither."

"Bring her out, I would like to hear her sing more."

"Nay," he muttered, glancing sidelong at the louts in the corner. "That's a bad lot there. I'll not risk harm coming to a nun under my roof. My luck's foul enough as 'tis."

"I'm sure you're wrong about those fellows," I said a bit louder. "I have plenty of money, and they've not troubled me. Buy them an ale, and bring the girl out to sing for us. I'll pay." I tossed a coin on the counter, snapping the thieves to full alert.

The innkeeper eyed me as though I'd grown a second head, but he snatched up the coin readily enough. Brushing aside the ratty blanket that separated his quarters from the tavern, he thrust a scrawny sparrow of a girl into the room. Sixteen or so, she was clad in a grimy peasant's shift, slender as a riding crop with a narrow face, her eyes wrapped in a gauze bandage.

"What's your name, girl?"

"Noelle," she said, turning her face to the sound of my voice. The landlord was right to worry. She was no beauty, but she'd pass for fair with the grime wiped away.

"Noelle? You're French?"

"No, the sisters told me I was born at Yuletide."

"Ah, and so you were named Noelle for Christmas, and your holiday gift was your lovely voice."

"You're the singer, aren't you?" she asked with surprising directness. She hadn't the mousy manner of a nun. "What are you called?"

"Tallifer, miss. Of Shrewsbury and York; minstrel, poet, and storyteller."

"I've been listening to you. You seem to know a great many songs."

"I've picked up a tune or two in my travels. Most aren't fit for the ears of a nun, I'm afraid. Nor is it proper for you to stay at an alehouse. There is an abbey a few days to the west. I'll escort you there if you like."

"Hold on," the innkeeper began, "I shan't let—"

"Come now, friend, the girl can't remain here, and I need a good deed to redeem my misspent life. I'll pay for the privilege." Pulling the purse from beneath my jerkin, I spilled the coins in a heap on the table. "Consider this as heaven's reward for your kindness to this poor waif. Have we a bargain?"

Stunned, the innkeeper stared at me, than hastily glanced at the crew in the corner. Their eyes were locked on the silver like hounds pointing a hare.

"There's no point in haggling," I continued. "Search me if you like, but I haven't one penny more. Come girl, we'd best be going."

"But it's still raining," the innkeeper protested, eyeing the outlaws, afraid of being left alone with them. "Surely you'll wait for better weather?"

"Nay, I've no money to pay for your hospitality now, and I wouldn't dream of imposing further. Has she any belongings?"

"Belongings? Nay, she—"

"This will do for a cloak then," I said, ripping the blanket from the doorway, draping it about her. Snatching up my lute, I paused at the door long enough for a 'God bless all here,' then I dragged the girl out into the drizzle. But after a few paces she pulled free of my grasp, whirling to face me, her narrow jaw thrust forward.

"Kill me here. Please."

"What?"

"If you mean to dishonor me, then kill me now where I can be buried decently. Sister Adela warned me about men like you."

"And rightly so, but I'm no one to fear. I'm old enough to be your father, girl. I was a soldier once, and I swear my oath to God I mean you no harm. Unfortunately, I can't swear the same for that lot back there. We've got to get away from here and quickly, or we'll both be dead."

"Then stop pulling me along like a puppy. I can walk. Fetch me a slender stick."

Cursing, I hastily cut an alder limb, and she used it as a cane to feel for obstructions in her path. Though she stumbled occasionally, she had no trouble maintaining my pace. Coltish legs, young and supple.

We marched steadily through the afternoon, moving north on a rutted cart track through the forest. Tiring as dusk approached, I began casting about for shelter.

"Why are we slowing?" Noelle asked.

"It'll be dark soon."

"Darkness is nothing to me. Continue on if you like."

"No need. The rain will wash out our tracks, and they may not follow us at all. If I can find a copse of cedar—"

"That way." She pointed off to our left. "There's a cedar grove over there."

She was right. Peering through the misty drizzle, I spied a stand of cedars some twenty yards off the path.

"How could you know that?"

"Scent. We've passed cedars several times in the last hour, though the wood around us is mostly alder, yew, and ash. Each has their own savor. Gathering osier wands for baskets was my task at the abbey. I often did it alone."

Taking her hand, I threaded my way through the brush to a cedar copse with a soft bed of leaves beneath and heavy boughs above that kept it relatively dry. I cut a few fronds to make our beds, then used flint and steel to kindle a small fire.

Leaving Noelle to warm herself, I scouted about and found a dead ash tree with a straight limb as thick as my wrist. Twenty minutes whittling with my dirk produced a usable quarterstaff, a peasant's pike.

Returning to the fire, I was greeted by the heavenly scent of roasting meat. Noelle was holding two thick blood sausages over the fire on the end of a stick, sizzling fat dripping into the flames.

"You came well prepared," I observed, sliding a sausage off the spit, blowing on it til it cooled enough to chew.

"In the country of the blind, one learns to cope."

"But surely you were well treated at the convent?"

"They were kind, but their lives were so . . . stifling. I was always pestering new novitiates for songs they knew and news of the outside world. Have you traveled far?"

"Too far. From London to Skye and back again many times, first as a soldier, now a singer."

"Would you sing something for me? A song of some faraway place?"

"Is France distant enough?" Sliding my lute from its sheep-skin bag, I tuned it and began the "Song of Roland," a war ballad from the days of mighty Charlemagne. In the streets or a strong-hold, I sing it lustily, but huddled near the fire as dusk settled on the wood, I sang softly. For Noelle only.

A dozen verses into the ballad, she raised her hand.

"Stop a moment, please." And then she sang it back to me, echoing my every word, every inflection in her crystalline angel's voice, ending the refrain at the same place I had.

"Sing on, girl. Your voice does wonders for that song."

"I can't. I've ne'er heard that tune before, and I can only memorize a dozen or so verses at a time. But at the end I'll remember it all."

"Truly? You can learn an entire ballad with one hearing?"

"There are no books or signposts in my country. Memory is everything. Sister Adela said Homer was blind, yet he sang ballads of ten thousand verses."

"Homer?"

"A poet, a Greek I think."

"I know who Homer was. I was bodyguard to the young Duke of York during his schooldays at London. I'm just surprised that nuns study Homer."

"I'm not a nun. I was a ward of the convent, a lodger. I had my own quarters and Sister Adela to teach me and help me get about."

"How long were you there?"

"Always," she said simply. "My whole life."

"But no bairns are born in convents. Where are your parents? Your home?"

"The convent was my home," she said, with a flash of anger. "They had other guests, an idiot girl and a boy so deformed he had to be wheeled about in a barrow. If I had parents, I know nothing of them, nor care to. In the country of the blind all men are handsome, all ladies lovely."

"But all is in darkness?"

"Not all, I can see the changes 'tween day and night readily enough and some colors and shapes, though not clearly. I wear this ribbon to spare confusion and let my other senses compensate. That's how I knew the cedar was near. And that someone is coming now."

"What? Where?"

"Behind us, on the track we left."

"I hear nothing."

"Sight is no help in the dark. He's on horseback, moving slowly."

"I hadn't counted on horses," I said, rising, seizing my cudgel. "The louts from the inn—"

"No," Noelle said positively. "There were no horses at that place. And I hear only one animal now."

And then I heard it as well, the soft *tlot, tlot* of hooves on the muddy trail. Then they stopped.

Silence. Only the drip of the rain.

"Hellooo, the fire," a voice called. "I'm a traveler, wet and in need of direction. I have food to share. May I approach?"

"Come ahead, and welcome," I replied, moving into the shadows.

He walked in warily, leading his animal, a plowhorse from the look of it. Our visitor had much the same look. Heavily built, stooped from farm work, his face was obscured by the cowl of his rough woolen cloak. He appeared to be unarmed, though with his cloak pulled tight I couldn't be sure. I stepped out to face him, quarterstaff in hand.

"God bless all here," he said, glancing about. "I'm John of Menteith, a reeve for Lord Duart. No need for that stick, friend. I mean no man harm."

"You're far from Menteith," I said.

"Aye," he nodded, warming his hands at the fire, "I'm bound for the fair at Grahmsby. Hope to trade this sorry nag for a bullock and a few cups of ale. Who might you folk be?"

"Tallifer of York," I said. "Traveling to Strathclyde with my daughter."

"A blind girl, by chance?"

Sweeping off his cloak, he revealed a sword, a crude blade, standard issue at any barracks.

His bush of a beard split in a gap-toothed grin. "Drop the stick, fellow, or I'll cleave you in two."

If he expected me to wet myself or scamper off, he was disappointed. I've seen blades before; I've even faced one or two with nought in my hand but sweat. I had a stout cudgel and Menteith had the look of a farmer, big but clumsy. I waited.

So did he. His eyes flicked from me to Noelle and back again. He licked his lips, unnerved by our stillness, gathering himself. Then with a roar, he lunged at me, swinging his blade like a field sickle.

He'd have done better with a sickle. Jabbing the cudgel butt between his shins, I sent him sprawling into the fire. He moved quickly for a big man, though. Rolling with the fall, he scrambled clear of the flames, crouching on the far side, panting.

Unable to tell what was amiss, Noelle stood frozen as Menteith began sidling around the fire toward her. I thought he meant to seize her as a shield. I was wrong. Eyes wild, he charged again, this time at Noelle!

He was almost on her, blade raised high to hack her down, when I rammed the pole hard into his gut, doubling him over. Gasping, he staggered back, slashing at me. A mistake. Blocking a blow with one end of my staff, I swept the other around full force, catching him squarely on his bull neck just below the ear.

He stared at me a moment, surprised. Then his eyes rolled up like a hog on a hook, and he toppled backward into the fire. I stood over him, taut as a drawn bow, ready to finish him if he moved. But even the flames couldn't rouse him.

Kicking the blade out of his fist, I prodded him out of the fire with my staff.

"Tallifer? What's happened?"

"Our guest had no manners, and it worked out poorly for him. Do you have any idea who he might be?"

"I've ne'er heard his voice before. Why?"

"He seems an unlikely thief. He was armed with a yeoman's blade, but he was no soldier."

"He said he was a reeve, perhaps he spoke true. He smells of cattle."

"He fought like one, all bull, no skill. He was definitely seeking us, though. He knew you were blind though he could see neither of us clearly."

"I don't understand."

"Nor do I, yet. I'll persuade him to explain when he wakes."

But he didn't wake. As I stripped off his belt to tie his hands, his head flopped unnaturally. I checked his pupils. Dead as a goose on Saint Margaret's Day.

"God's bodkin," I said softly.

"What is it?"

"The bastard's dead. Damn me, I didn't think I hit him that hard. And damn him for an inconsiderate lout. Not only does he keep his secrets, I'll have to haul his useless carcass into the wood. We don't want him found near our camp."

After dragging his dead weight for what seemed like a mile, I used his sword to dig a shallow grave, rolled the reeve in it, and threw his blade in after him. Weapons are outlawed for common folk in Scotland and the sword surely hadn't done the reeve much good. His purse held a few shillings, fair payment for a burial.

I slept poorly, restless from the fight and the death of the reeve. As a soldier I was no hero. I fought for my life and my friends, killed when I had to but took no satisfaction in it. In battle I was always afraid. And afterward, though I survived, I knew how easily it could have been me bleeding out while my enemies divided my gear and had a drink on my luck.

The reeve's death was doubly troubling, though. He was no vagrant bandit. Only a fool travels this country at night, yet he'd arrived at our camp well after dark. He must have been hunting us though I couldn't imagine why.

Had the cutthroats from the inn set him on us? Unlikely. Why hire out work they could easily do themselves?

Odder still, in the midst of the fight, he'd lunged at Noelle when she was clearly no threat. It made no sense. Unless she was the one he came for, and I was just in his way. But who would kill a blind nun?

"Tallifer? Are you awake?"

"Yes."

The fire had burned to embers, and her face was only a vague shape in the shadows. As all faces were in her world.

"I've been thinking. You can't leave me at an abbey."

"Why not?"

"Without money to pay for my lodging, they won't accept me."

"How were your expenses paid before?"

"I don't know, by a kinsman, I suppose. It was a private arrangement with the abbess and she was lost in the fire. I have an idea, though."

"Such as?"

"Take me with you," she said in a rush. "I can earn my way. I sing fairly well and you can teach me to—"

"It's out of the question. Life on the road is too hard; it's nothing for a girl."

"All roads are hard in the country of the blind. I heard you breathing heavily this afternoon, when I could have walked another day without tiring. I can carry burdens, wash clothes. I'll be your woman if you want."

"My what? Good lord, Noelle, what do you know of being a woman?"

"The novitiates seldom talked of anything else, and I know a few songs of love."

"I know songs about dragons, girl, but I can't breathe fire. And I'm much too old for you anyway."

"I wouldn't know."

"Yes, you would. Trust me on that."

"You don't want me? Am I too plain, then? Or does my blindness offend you?"

"Neither, but—"

"Then what is it? You've saved my life twice. Why did you bother if you mean to cast me off?"

"Noelle—"

"A minstrel came to the abbey once. He had a little dog who danced when he played the fife. I can't dance, but I can sing a bit. And I promise to be no more trouble than a little dog. Please, Tallifer."

"Enough!" I said, throwing up my hands. "The sun is rising and we'd best be away from here. We'll talk more of this later."

But we didn't talk. We sang instead. We took turns riding the reeve's mount, entertaining each other, with Noelle memorizing each ballad I sang, then vastly improving it with her marvelous voice.

I skirted the next few hamlets, afraid the reeve's horse might be recognized. But in the first town of any size, I found a tailor and squandered our inheritance to buy Noelle a decent traveling garment.

After the measurements, Noelle and the tailor's wife disappeared into the family quarters for a final fitting. I waited with the tailor, exchanging news of the road and the town. And then Noelle stepped out.

The dress wasn't fancy. It had no need to be. In pale blue woolsey, and with her face scrubbed and shining, my grimy foundling was transformed. And I was lost.

The tailor's wife had replaced her blindfold with a blue ribbon that matched the dress. She was a vision as lovely as the damsels of a thousand ballads. But no mirror could ever tell her so.

My throat swelled and I could not speak. Mistaking my silence for displeasure, the tailor's wife frowned.

"If the color is too dark—"

"No," I managed. "It's perfect. Wonderful. No man ever had a more lovely—daughter."

And so it seemed. Born restless, I've never had a family of my own nor much felt the lack. Yet after a few weeks with Noelle I could scarce remember life without her.

As summer faded into autumn, we worked our way southwest toward the border, singing for our supper. And prospering.

My performances have always been well received, but Noelle brought freshness and sparkle to songs I'd sung half my life, her youth and zest a sprightly contrast to my darker presence.

Audiences responded to her and she to them, basking in the applause like a blossom in the sun. The waif from the convent was fast becoming an assured young beauty. And though she never raised the subject of being more than a daughter to me again, neither was she interested in the young bloods who lingered after our performances to chat her up.

She was always courteous but never a whit more than polite as she dismissed them. When I asked why she showed no curiosity about boys, she replied that they were exactly that. Boys. For now, the music and freedom of her new life were more than enough. She'd never been happier.

Nor had I. The last large town we worked was Strathclyde, a performance in the laird's manor house for his family and kinsmen that was well received. Afterward, his steward offered us a year's position in his household as resident artists.

A month earlier I'd have leapt at the chance, but no more.

I've always felt comfortable amongst Scots. Their rough humor and love of battle songs suits both my art and my temperament, but Noelle was changing that.

As her talent and skills improved, I noted the magical effect her singing had on village folk and was certain she could charm larger, more worldly audiences south of the Roman walls just as easily. Newcastle, York, perhaps even in London itself.

For the first time in years I allowed myself to consider the future. We could become master minstrels, winning acclaim and moving in finer circles than either of us had known before.

But to reach that future, we'd have to survive the present. There are always rumors of war in the Scottish hills, but I was seeing more combatants than usual, not only Scots and their Irish cousins, but also hard-bitten mercenaries from France and Flanders.

In earlier years I would have been pleased at the chance to entertain soldiers far from home with fat purses and dim futures. Lonely troops are an amiable audience, easily pleased and generous with applause and coins.

But I had a daughter to worry about now. So after politely declining the steward's offer, we began working our way south toward the border and England. Perhaps we could even journey to my family home at Shrewsbury after long years.

Traveling was a pure pleasure now, singing through the lowlands, describing the folk and the scenery to a girl who savored every phrase like fine wine. My sole regret was that Noelle remained in her country of the blind and I could do nothing to light her way out.

But there is little difference between a lass born sightless and a fool befuddled by dreams. Though I recall those days as the happiest I've ever known, in some ways I was more blind than my newfound daughter.

THE FIRST FROSTS OF autumn found us moving steadily south and into trouble. We were entering the country of the true border lords now, nobles with holdings and kinsmen on both sides of the river Tweed and loyalties as changeable as the lowland winds. Arnim once described the Scottish border as a smudged line drawn in blood that never dries.

Perhaps someone was preparing to alter the mark once again.

As we neared the Liddesdale, traveling from one small hamlet to another, we often took to the wood to avoid troops, well mounted and heavily armed. Skirmishes between Norman knights on the Tyne or the Rede and restive Scots along the Liddel Water are common in a land where cattle raids are lauded in song. Still, with war in the air, crossing the border would be dangerous. We might be hanged as spies by one side or another.

But our luck held. As we approached Redheugh, I spotted a familiar wagon in a camp outside the town wall, a bright crimson cart with a Welsh dragon painted boldly on its sides.

After changing from our traveling garments into performing clothes, I led Noelle on our mount into a world unfamiliar to most folk, a traveling circus.

Most minstrels, especially in the north, ply their trade alone or in small family groups. But a few singers earn enough renown to gather a larger assemblage, a troupe of musicians, jugglers, and acrobats whose appearance at a town is reason enough to declare a feast day.

One such is Owyn Phyffe, Bard of Wales and the Western World as he calls himself. A small, compactly built dandy, blond-bearded and handsome as the devil's cousin, Owyn is a famed performer on both sides of the border and on the continent as well. A son and grandson of Welsh minstrels, he's a master of the craft. And well aware of it.

His camp was a hive of activity, cookfires being doused and horses hitched for travel. I found Owyn strolling about, noting every detail of the preparation without actually soiling his hands. He dressed more like a young lord than a singer, in a claret velvet doublet and breeches of fine doeskin. His muslin shirt had loose Italian sleeves. And not just for fashion.

Owyn carries a dirk up one sleeve or the other, perhaps both, and I once saw him slit a man's throat so deftly that the rogue's soul was in hell before his heart knew it was dead. Owyn dresses like a popinjay, but he's not a man to take lightly.

Our paths had crossed a number of times over the years, usually on friendly terms. Or so I hoped, because I needed him now.

He scowled theatrically as I approached leading the mount.

"God's eyes, I believe I spy Tallifer, the croaking frog of York. I can't tell which is uglier, you or that broken-down horse. Here to beg a crust of bread, I suppose."

"Not at all. In the last town, folk told me of a perky little Welsh girl who dresses like a fop and calls herself Owyn Phyffe the poet. Is she about?"

"Aye, she's about, about to thrash you for your loud mouth," Owyn said, grinning, seizing my arm in a grip of surprising strength for a small man. "How are you, Tallifer?"

"Not as well as you. The years have been kind to you."

"You were always a poor liar. How goes the road?"

"We've been doing quite handsomely. We've played Ormiston, Stobs, and a half dozen rat-bitten hamlets between, to very good response."

"We?"

"May I introduce my daughter, Noelle, the finest singer in this land or any other."

"I'm sure she is," Owyn snorted, then read the danger in my eyes and hastily amended his tone. "Because, as I said, your father is an inept liar, my dear. Honest to a fault."

Taking her hand, he kissed it with a casual grace I could only envy, favoring her with the smile that melted hearts on two continents. If he noted her blindness, he gave no sign. Owyn is nought if not nimble-witted.

"I would gladly offer you the hospitality of my camp, Tallifer, but we're making ready to leave."

"I see that. Well, there's no point in our playing yon town now. A performance by Owyn the Bard is impossible for lesser minstrels to follow."

"Even shameless flattery is sometimes a Gospel truth," Owyn grinned wryly. "Do we meet by chance, Tallifer, or can I be of some service to you and your . . . daughter?"

"We meet by God's own grace, Welshman. Over the past weeks the roads have grown crowded with soldiers. I'm hoping we can travel with your troupe across the border. I can pay."

"Don't be an ass, come with us and be welcome. We're not bound directly for the border, though. I've an agreement to perform

in Garriston for Lord DuBoyne on All Saints Day. Do you still want
to come?"

"Why shouldn't we?"

"Because the soldiers you've been seeing likely belong to
DuBoyne or his enemies. Whatever the trouble is, we're wandering merrily into the heart of it, singing all the way."

"We're still safer traveling with you than on our own."

"That may be," Owyn conceded grimly. "But I wouldn't take
much comfort in it. The sooner we're south of the Tweed, the
happier I'll be, and devil take the hindmost."

Owyn's company traveled steadily for the next few days,
stopping only at night to rest the animals. If anything, we
encountered more soldiers than before, but with wagons, we
couldn't cede the road. Troops simply marched around us.

Owyn's fame is such that even warriors who hadn't seen him
perform greeted us cheerfully. After chatting with one grizzled
guards' captain at length, though, the Welshman's gloom was
palpable.

"What's wrong?" I asked, goading my mount to match pace
with Owyn's. Noelle was riding on one of the wagons with
Owyn's wife, or perhaps his mistress. His two companions looked
much alike to me, small, dark women, with raven hair. Sisters perhaps? Some things you don't ask.

"Everything's wrong," Owyn said glumly. "You were a soldier
once, Tallifer, have you noted anything odd about the troops
we've encountered?"

"Mostly Scots, supplemented by a few mercenaries. Why?"

"I was talking about their direction."

I considered that a moment. "We haven't met any for the
past few days," I said. "They've all been overtaking us."

"Exactly," Owyn sighed. "They're traveling the same way we
are, and the only holding on this road is Lord DuBoyne's. But
when I offered to buy the captain of that last lot an ale at the fes-
tivities, he declined. He said he wouldn't be there."

"So?"

"So there's nowhere else for him to be, you dolt, only Garriston. And if he's not bound for Garriston to celebrate . . ." He left
the thought dangling.

"Sweet Jesus," I said softly.

"Exactly so," Owyn agreed.

"Perhaps they'll delay the bloodletting until after the holiday."

"That would be Christian of them," Owyn grunted, "though I'm told good Christian crusaders in the Holy Land disembowel children then rummage in their guts for swallowed gems."

"You're growing gloomy with age, Owyn."

"Even trees grow wiser with time. And I wouldn't worry much about old age, Tallifer. We're neither of us likely to see it."

Arriving at Garriston on the fourth day did little to lift Phyffe's spirits. It was a raw border town on a branch of the Tweed, surrounded by a high earthen wall braced with logs. Its gate was open but well guarded. Noelle was riding at the front of the train with Owyn as I trudged along beside.

"What do you think, Tallifer?" he asked, leaning on his pommel, looking over the town.

"It seems a small place to hire such a large troupe."

"So it does. The DuBoyne family steward paid us a handsome advance without a quibble, though."

"Is it a pretty town?" Noelle asked. "It feels lucky to me."

Owyn shot a quizzical glance at me, then shook his head.

"Oh, to live in the country of the blind, where every swamp's an Eden. Aye, girl, it's a fine town with gilded towers and flags on every parapet. But perhaps you'd better stay in the camp, while your father and I taste the stew we've got ourselves into."

Leaving instructions with his wives to camp upstream from Garriston near a wood, Owyn, myself, and Piers LeDoux, the leader of the Flemish jugglers, rode in together. In such a backwater, well-dressed mounted men are seen so rarely we were treated like gentry. The gate guards passed us through with a salute, saying the manor's steward could be found in the marketplace.

An old town, Garriston was probably a hamlet centuries before the Norman conquest. Houses were wattle and daub, set at haphazard angles to the mud streets. It was a market day and the air was abustle with the shouts of tinkers and peddlers, the squeal of hogs at butchering, hammers ringing at a smithy, and, beneath it all, the thunderous grumbling of a mill wheel.

A month earlier I wouldn't have noted the noise, but after traveling with Noelle I found myself listening more, trying to savor the world as she did.

A stronghold loomed over the north end of the town. Crude, but stoutly built in the Norman style, the square blockhouse sat atop a hill with corners outset so archers could sweep its walls. And even in peaceful daylight, sentries manned its towers.

The street wound into an open-air market in the town square, with kiosks for pottery, hides, and leatherwork, an ale-house, and a crude stone chapel. Owyn spied the DuBoyne family steward, Gillespie Kenedi, looking over beeves for the feast day.

Heavyset, with a pig's narrow eyes and a face ruddy from too much food, too little labor, Kenedi wore the fur-trimmed finery of his station and its airs as well. He was trailed by a rat-faced bailiff who bobbed his head in agreement whenever his master spoke. Or farted, probably.

Kenedi talked only with Owyn, considering the Fleming and myself beneath notice. But as the haggling progressed, he kept glancing my way, as though he might know me from somewhere.

When their bargain was struck, Owyn and the steward shook hands on it, then Kenedi beckoned to me.

"You there! Where did you get that horse you're holding?"

"From a crofter north of Orniston."

"And how did the crofter come by it?"

"As I recall, he said he traded a bullock for it. Why?"

"It resembles one of our plowhorses that went missing some time ago."

"I'm sure Tallifer acquired the horse fairly," Owyn put in. "If you have a problem, it's with the man who took it from you."

"Unless you believe I'm that man," I said, facing Kenedi squarely, waiting. But he was more beef than spirit.

"Perhaps I'm mistaken," he said, glancing away. "One spavined nag looks much like another. I'll let it pass, for now." He turned and bustled off with his bailiff scurrying after.

"Nicely done," Owyn sighed. "It's always good business to antagonize one's host before getting paid. So? Did you really get the horse at Orniston?"

I didn't answer. Which was answer enough.

AS DUSK SETTLED ON our camp like a warm cloak, townsfolk and crofters from nearby farms began gathering to us. Dressed in what passed for their best, carrying candles in hollowed gourds or rutabaga hulls to light their way, they brought whatever small gifts they could afford, a flask of ale, bread or a few pickled eggs, walnuts, even a fowl or two.

Drawn by the noise, Noelle came out of the women's tent. I led her to a place near the fire as Owyn entertained the gathering throng, singing in Italian love songs to folk who barely understood English. And winning their hearts.

"What's afoot, Tallifer?" Noelle whispered. "What is all this?"

"We were hired to perform tomorrow at the DuBoyne castle for All Saints Day. But among Celtic peoples, tonight is a much older celebration called All Hallomas Eve, or Samhain, the festival of the dead."

"The dead? But I hear laughter and the music is gay."

"Life is so hard for borderland peasants that death isn't much feared. For the rest of us, Samhain is for remembering those who are gone. And to celebrate that we're not among them yet."

"Owyn is a fine singer, isn't he?"

"Aye, he's very good. He's an attractive man, too, don't you think?"

"Owyn?" she snorted. "You must be joking. He's a snake. His glib tongue and smooth hands put me in mind of the serpent of Eden. And you should hear what his wives say about his love-making."

"You shouldn't listen to such things."

"What do you think women talk about when we're alone? They asked me about you as well. About what we really are to each other. They noted we bear little resemblance."

"What did you tell them?"

"The absolute truth, of course. That you are the only father I've ever known and that you never speak of my poor mother."

"Very poetic. And ever so slightly misleading."

"Thank you. I have a good teacher. What's happening now?"

"Piers and the Flemish acrobats are putting on a tumbling show. It's not so fine as they will do for the nobility, but it suits this lot. Some of the women are cracking walnuts to read the future."

"Can they foresee it? Truly?"

"Certainly. A peasant's future is his past, and any fool who trusts a walnut has no future at all."

The crowd continued to swell with folk from the town, tradesmen, manor servants, even a fat priest who mingled with his flock quaffing ale as heartily as the rest. The steward too made an appearance with his rat-shadow of a bailiff, standing apart from the rest, aloof.

"Horses," Noelle said quietly.

"What?"

"I hear horsemen coming. Many. Moving slowly."

For a moment I thought she was mistaken, but then I saw them, moving out of the woods in a body toward our fires. A mounted troop, battle-weary from fighting by the look of them. Their horses were lathered and played out, and the men weren't much better, slumped in their saddles, exhausted, some wounded.

Their leader was young, less than twenty, but he was no boy. Dressed in mail with a black breastplate, he sat on his horse like a centaur. His armor was spattered with blood, not his own, and a broken arrow was stuck in his saddle.

A shaggy mane of dark hair obscured his eyes, but as he scanned the camp, I doubt he missed a thing. Including Noelle. His glance lingered only a moment, but I've seen the look before. In battle. We'd been marked.

"God's eyes," Owyn said, sidling over to us. "Here's trouble if I ever saw it."

"Who are they?"

"Milord DuBoyne's men. That's his eldest son, Logan. Black Logan he's called, both for his look and his sins."

"What sins?"

"Cattle raiding's a national sport in Scotland, but instead of beating or ransoming the thieves Logan hangs them, then guts them to make easy feeding for the ravens."

"I can see why he'd be unpopular with cattle thieves, but that's hardly cause for sackcloth and ashes."

"He's a hotspur, gives battle or extracts a tax from anyone found on DuBoyne lands, even neighbors. He's killed three men in single combat and God knows how many more in frays. There's already a ballad about him."

"He seems a bit young for a song."

"The legend is that after two babes were stillborn, his mother made a Christmas wish for a healthy son. Instead, the devil sent a demon child who sprang full-grown from the womb, called for his armor, and rode off to fight the Ramsays. Villagers hide their children when he passes."

"They hide from thunder as well." I spoke lightly, but in truth I was growing concerned. Black Logan was conferring with Kenedi, and both of them were glancing our way.

"Perhaps you'd better take Noelle . . ." I began. Too late. The steward was bustling toward us, looking altogether too pleased.

"I'm told this girl is with you, minstrel," he said without preamble. "How much for her?"

"What?"

"The girl. Young DuBoyne wishes to buy her for the night. He's willing to pay, but don't think you can—"

And then he was on the ground, stunned, his lip split open. It happened so quickly I didn't even realize I'd hit him.

"Damn," Owyn said softly. "Now we're in for it."

Logan strode angrily to us, his hand on his sword. "What madness is this? You struck my father's steward!"

"He asked my daughter's price and paid a small part of it. Are you here for the rest?"

He blinked, eyeing me more in surprise than anger. "Are you offering me a challenge, commoner?"

"He asked the price, I'm simply telling you what it is. Your life. Or mine. Is that plain enough?"

It was a near thing. Young or not, he was a warrior chief with a small army at his back. I was but a cat's whisker from death. He cocked his head, reading my eyes.

"Do you know who I am?" he asked quietly.

"I only know I'm not your man, nor do I owe that hog on the ground any fealty."

"I'm Sir Logan DuBoyne—"

"He's lying!" Noelle snapped, pulling free of Owyn's grasp.

"What?" DuBoyne and I said together.

"Any DuBoyne would be noble," she continued coldly. "At the convent they said I could tell the nobility by their scent and fine manners. You smell like a horse and show your breeding by insulting my father who was a soldier before you were born. Yet you claim to be a knight? I think not."

For a moment, I thought he might butcher us both. His eyes darkened, and I could see why the villagers hid their children. But the rage passed. He shook his head slowly, as if waking from a dream.

"You were convent raised, miss? Then clearly I've . . . misunderstood this situation. I apologize. I've fought two skirmishes today, and I'm not as young as I used to be. I meant no offense to you. But as for you," he said, turning to me, "if you ever lay hands on a man of mine again, I'll see your head on a pike."

Reaching down, he hauled Kenedi to his feet. "Come on, Gillespie, let's find some ale."

"The bastard struck me!" Kenedi said, outraged.

"He saved your life," DuBoyne said, leading him off. "The girl would have cut our hearts out."

"You idiot," Owyn said angrily, spinning me around. "You could have gotten us all killed!"

"And if she were yours? Would you have sold her?"

For a moment I thought I'd pushed him too far. But Owyn is nothing if not agile. "Sweet Jesus, Tallifer. You may not be the world's greatest singer, but by God you're never dull. And you, girl, you've enjoyed my hospitality long enough. It's time to earn your keep. Come, sing for us. If I'm to be slaughtered defending your honor, you'd better be worth it."

I wanted to fetch my lute to accompany her but I was afraid to risk letting her out of my sight, even for a moment. Black Logan was prowling the camp, talking with pedlars and travelers. And glancing my way from time to time.

It didn't bode well. Most men with black reputations have earned them. His own people shied from him as if he wore a leper's bell and I knew that if he snatched up Noelle, none but me would oppose him.

And so I watched tensely as Owyn led Noelle into the ring of firelight, introduced her, then stepped back. It was an impossible situation. Drunken revelers were bellowing jests, laughing, groping their women. A clown troupe juggling lions with their manes ablaze wouldn't satisfy this lot.

Yet, as that slip of a girl began to sing, the crowd gradually fell silent, listening. She sang a simple French lullaby in a voice so pure and true that my heart swelled with longing, not for Noelle but for all I'd lost in my life. And would lose.

When she finished there was a long moment of stone silence, then the crowd erupted with a roar of applause and cheers. They called for more and she gave it, singing a rousing Irish war ballad I'd taught her and then a love song that would have misted the eyes of a bronze idol.

I was as transfixed as the rest, until I realized that Black Logan was standing a few paces to my left. He was eyeing Noelle like a lion at mealtime, but if her song moved him he gave no sign, not even applauding when she finished. He turned to me instead.

"I didn't know the girl was blind."

"What difference does it make?"

"I don't know. But it does. I've asked around the camp. Folk say you truly were a soldier once. Whom did you serve?"

"I was a yeoman for the Duke of York, bodyguard to his son for a time. Later I fought for Sir Ranaulf de Picard."

"At Aln Ford?"

"I was there, and at a hundred other scuffles you've never heard of."

"Then you must know troops. Whose men did you pass on the road here? How were they armed?"

"I was a soldier once and now I'm a singer. But a spy? That I've never been."

"Minstrel, you're trying my patience at a bad time. My father's health is failing, and his neighbors and enemies have begun raiding our stock and gouging taxes from our people. When I answer their aggression with my own they whine to Edinburgh, branding me an outlaw. My father has invited some of those same neighbors to the feast in hopes of a truce, but I know they've brought troops with them. Perhaps they fear treachery. Perhaps they plan it. Either way, you'd best tell me what you've seen."

"Suppose we compromise, and I tell you what I didn't see instead? We saw no heavy cavalry on the road, nor any siege engines, nor did we encounter any supply trains. The soldiers were carrying a few days' provisions, no more."

"Then they aren't planning a siege; they're escort troops only. Good. How many men did you see, and whose were they?"

"I took no count, and I don't know the liveries of this land well enough to identify them."

"And wouldn't if you could?"

"They did us no harm, DuBoyne. We've no quarrel with them."

"Nor with me. Yet." The camp erupted in a roar as Noelle finished her song, with Owyn standing beside her leading the cheers.

"Your daughter sings well."

"Yes, she does."

He started to say something else but his voice was drowned by the throng as Owyn led Noelle back to me. DuBoyne turned and stalked off to rejoin his men.

"Tallifer, did you hear?" Noelle's face was shining and Owyn's grin was as broad as the Rede.

"You were in wonderful voice, Noelle, and they knew it. What was that French lullaby? I've never heard it before."

"A woman sang it to me when I was small. I don't know why it came back to me tonight. Was I foolish to sing it?"

"*Au contraire, cherie,* it was brilliant," Owyn countered. "By singing softly, you made them quiet down to hear. You won many hearts tonight, little Noelle, including mine."

"All of it?" she asked sweetly. "Or just the parts your wives aren't using at the moment?"

"Get back to your tent, imp," Owyn snorted. "I swear, if you weren't so pretty I might believe you really are Tallifer's child.

Your tongue's as sharp as his." Laughing, Noelle set off, but Owyn grasped my arm before I could follow.

"What did Black Logan want? More trouble?"

"He has trouble of his own." I quickly sketched the situation DuBoyne had described.

"I've heard the old laird's mind is failing," Owyn nodded. "And vultures gather early along the borders. Do you think there will be quarreling at the feast?"

"I hope not. That boy may be young, but he's already a seasoned fighter. I half believe that nonsense about him leaping from his mother's womb to his saddle and riding off to fight the Ramsays."

"He won't have far to ride tomorrow," Owyn sighed. "The Ramsays are among the honored guests. A baker's dozen of them. And that captain I spoke to yesterday, the one who's probably watching us from the hills at this moment? He was a Ramsay man."

"Damn it, you should have warned me away from this, Owyn."

"I tried to, remember? Besides, Noelle likes it here. Thinks the blasted place is lucky."

"She may be right. But good luck or bad, I wonder?"

THE EVENING FEAST OF All Saints Day was a rich one, probably to atone for the carousing and deviltry of the night before. It was also a display of wealth and power by the laird of Garriston, Alisdair DuBoyne. Food and drink were laid on with a will, steaming platters of venison and hare and partridge, wooden bowls of savory bean porridge spiced with leeks and garlic; mulled wine, ale, or mead, depending on the station of the guest.

The great hall, though, was great in name only, a rude barn of a room, smoky from the sconces and cooking fires, its walls draped with faded tapestries probably hung when the DuBoynes first came to this fief a generation ago.

Seated at the center of the linen-draped high table, flanked
by his wife and two sons, Laird DuBoyne was even older than I'd
expected, seventy or beyond, I guessed. Tall and skeletal with a
scanty gray beard, it was said he'd once been a formidable warrior, but his dueling days were long past. He seemed apathetic, as
though the juice of life had already bled from him and only the
husk remained.

His wife was at least a generation younger. Dressed in green
velvet, she was willowy as a doe, a striking woman with aquiline
features and chestnut hair beneath a white silken cap. Her
youngest son, Godfrey, nine or so, had her fairness and fine features, while his brother, Black Logan, with his dark beard and
burning eyes, sat like a chained wolf at the table, seeing everything, equally ready for a toast or a fight.

Kenedi, the stocky steward, and his wife sat at the far end of
the high table beside the chubby priest I'd seen at the Samhain
fest. Father Fennan, someone had said, was a local man who'd
risen from the peasantry to become both parish priest and chaplain to the DuBoynes.

Two lower tables, also decked in fine linen, extended from
the corners of the high table to form a rough horseshoe shape,
which was appropriate since the guests were probably more
familiar with war saddles than silver forks.

Three family groups of DuBoyne's neighbors, the Ramsays,
Duarts, and Harden clans, nearly thirty of them, were seated in
declining order of status. A hard-eyed crew, wary as bandits,
they'd brought no women or children with them. Nor had they
worn finery to honor their hosts, dressing in coarse woolens
instead, clothes more suited to battle than a banquet.

Randal Ramsay was senior among them. A red-bearded
descendent of Norse raiders, Ramsay conversed courteously with
his host and the other guests but kept a watchful eye on Logan,
an attention the younger man returned.

In England, strict protocols of station would have been
observed, but along the borders the Scots and their English
cousins act more like soldiers in allied armies, jests and jibes
flying back and forth between high and low tables. But I noted

the exchanges were surprisingly mild and politely offered, lest harmless banter explode into bloodshed.

Owyn delayed beginning the entertainment as long as he dared. Scots at table can be a damned surly audience, and the tension in DuBoyne's hall was as thick as the scent of roasting meat. Later, with full bellies and well oiled with ale, DuBoyne's guests might be more receptive.

Not so. When Piers LeDoux and his troupe of Flemish acrobats opened the performance, their energetic efforts received the barest modicum of applause.

After a juggler and a Gypsy woman who ate fire fared equally poorly, Owyn took the bull by the horns and strode to the center of the room. He stood silently for a bit, commanding attention by his presence alone. Then, instead of singing, he began to recite a faerie story of Wales and then ghostly doings in the Highlands and Ireland, delivering the tales with such verve and drama that even the bloodthirsty warriors at the low table leaned forward to hear.

It was a masterful performance. Owyn entranced the DuBoynes and their restive neighbors alike, holding them spellbound for the better part of an hour. He finished to rousing cheers and applause, the first enthusiastic response of the night.

"Match that if you can," Owyn whispered with a grin as he passed us in the doorway.

The minstrelsy is a free-spirited life, but it has protocols of its own. As Noelle and I had joined Owyn's troupe last, we were scheduled to perform last, the toughest position of all.

Ordinarily, I warmed up a crowd with a few rowdy ballads before bringing on Noelle, but after the way she won over the revelers at the Samhain, I simply introduced her and began strumming my lute, softly, softly, hoping the crowd would quiet.

Facing her unseen audience, Noelle sang the French lullaby, even more beautifully than the previous night. And with the same wondrous effect. The room fell utterly silent, every eye fixed on Noelle as she poured all the pain and longing of her blighted life and our own into that song. Angels on high couldn't have sung it one whit better. My eyes grew misty as I played the accompaniment, and I wasn't alone.

As I glanced about, reading the room, I noted Randal Ramsay's fierceness had softened, Lady DuBoyne was crying silently, while her husband . . . was up and moving. Laird DuBoyne was shuffling past the low table, coming toward us.

Unaware of his approach, Noelle sang on. I couldn't guess his intentions, but he seemed anguished and angry. Brushing past me, the old man seized Noelle's arm, startling her to silence.

"My dear, this is not fitting. You sing as beautifully as ever, but it's not proper for my lady wife to—"

"Let go of me!" Noelle shouted, pulling away. "Tallifer!"

"Come back to the table, milady, we'll—"

"Milord Alisdair!" Lady DuBoyne's voice snapped like a whip, cutting off her husband's ramblings. He stared up at her, shocked, then turned back to Noelle, eyeing her in wonder.

"I . . . but you're not my lady," he said slowly. "I thought . . . Your voice sounds much like hers did. Long ago. I'm sorry. I've ruined your song . . ."

And then Black Logan was at his father's side. Firmly disengaging his hand from Noelle's arm, he led Laird DuBoyne from the room. But at the door, the old man stopped, turning back to stare at Noelle in confusion.

"Who are you?" he asked, his voice barely a whisper. "Who are you?"

With surprising gentleness, Logan ushered him out, leaving us in stunned silence.

"What was all that?" Lord Ramsay said, rising. "Is our host going mad, then?"

"He had a bit too much wine, that's all," Lady DuBoyne said coldly. "It's a celebration, Ramsay, and you're falling behind. Continue the music, minstrel. Play on!"

And I did. Striking up a merry Scottish reel on my lute, I played as though the strings were on fire. To no avail. The spell of Noelle's song was shattered, and the guests were only interested in discussing their host's behavior with one another.

Owyn led Noelle quietly out of the hall, then after letting
me twist in the wind alone for a time, he called the rest of the
company back for a final song and bow before we all beat a hasty
retreat to a smattering of applause.

Noelle was waiting for us in the outer hall. "Tallifer, what
happened? Who was that man?"

"Our host, my lark," Owyn said. "The man who is supposed
to pay me tomorrow. Assuming he doesn't mistake me for a tree
and have me cut down."

"Is that what happened?" I asked. "He mistook her for someone else?"

"For his lady, I believe. There's a vague resemblance, and a
man addled by age could mistake them. Still, if DuBoyne's neighbors came to take his measure, they just saw the ghost of a man
who's still alive, but only barely. I don't like the feel of this a
damned bit. We're breaking camp at first light, I—"

"Good sirs, hold a moment, please." It was the pudgy priest,
red-faced and puffing as he hurried after us. "I'm Father Fennan,
Mr. Phyffe, chaplain to the DuBoyne family. Milady DuBoyne
would like a word. And with these other two as well, the blind
girl and her father."

"It's late," I said. "Noelle should—"

"It's not that late and I want to be ten miles south of here
tomorrow," Owyn interrupted. "Lead on, Father."

"You must be a busy man," Noelle said, as we followed the
friar. "From what I hear of Black Logan, he badly needs a priest.
Or is it already too late for him?"

"It's never too late for salvation, miss," Father Fennan said,
eyeing her curiously. "You sang in French very well. Where did
you learn?"

"I know only the one song. I grew up in the convent at Lachlan Cul and must have heard it there."

"I see," Fennan said curtly. Too curtly, I thought. Either the
song or the mention of the convent seemed to trouble him. I
knew the feeling. Everything about this place was worrying me.

We followed the priest down a shadowed corridor lit by gut-
tering sconces, arriving at a windowless room at the west corner

of the fortress. Vellum scrolls and ledgers filled pigeonhole racks against the walls.

"A library?" Noelle asked. "Linseed and charcoal. I love the ink scent. It smells like knowledge."

"Nay, it's a counting room," I whispered. Though such a place was normally a steward's lair, Lady DuBoyne was seated alone at his desk with a ledger open before her.

"According to Kenedi's accounts, this was the sum agreed on," she said brusquely, pushing a purse of coins toward Owyn. "Count it if you like."

"That won't be necessary, milady," Owyn said, touching his forelock. "I'm only sorry that—"

"Our business is concluded, Mr. Phyffe. Wait outside with Father Fennan, please. I want a private word with these two."

"As you say, milady." Giving a perfunctory bow, Owyn followed the priest out. Fennan swung the oaken door closed as he left.

Lady DuBoyne eyed me a moment, lips pursed, then pushed a small purse toward me. "This is for you, minstrel. And your daughter."

"I don't understand."

"It's money for travel, the farther the better. And for your silence. My husband is no longer young and has no head for wine, but he's still my husband. I will not have him ridiculed."

"I saw nothing to laugh at, milady, and Noelle saw nothing at all. You need not pay us."

"The girl is truly blind then? I thought the ribbon might be an artifice. Come closer, child. You have a beautiful voice."

"Thank you. Do you know me, lady?"

"I beg your pardon?"

"Have we met? You seem . . . familiar to me, though I can't say why. Have you ever visited the convent at Lachlan Cul?"

"No, and I'm sure we've never met. You're very lovely. I'd remember."

"I must be mistaken, then. Forgive me, the country where I live is a land of shadows. It's confusing sometimes. But Tallifer is right, there's no need to buy our silence."

"Then consider it a payment for your song."

"The song was for any who listened, not for you alone. You needn't pay for it and you have nothing to fear from us. We'll not trouble you again."

She turned and started for the door so hastily I had to grab her arm to save her from injury. I glanced back to make our good-byes, but Lady DuBoyne didn't notice. She was leaning forward on the desk, her face buried in her hands.

"Well?" Owyn said when we joined him in the hall. "What did she want?"

"Not much," I said. "She asked us to be discreet."

"Discretion is always wise," Father Fennan agreed. "We live in fearsome times."

"That lady has nought to fear," Noelle said sharply. "Her son has a ballad of his own already. Tell me, Father, did Logan fight those battles or just bribe minstrels to praise his name?"

"Hardly," the priest said, surprised. "As his confessor, I assure you the song doesn't tell half the carnage he's wrought, and he despises it. He once struck a guardsman unconscious for singing it."

"I'm surprised he didn't hang the poor devil," Noelle snapped. "This is an unlucky town for singing, gentlemen. We'd best be away from here."

Owyn glanced at me, arching an eyebrow. I shrugged. I had no idea why Noelle was so angry. Or why Lady DuBoyne had broken down. Women have always been an alien race to me, as fascinating as cats and no more predictable.

Noelle was right about one thing, though: Garriston was unlucky for us. The sooner we saw the back of it, the better.

Pleading the lateness of the hour, the priest led us to the chapel, which had its own exit through the town wall. He seemed uneasy, eager to have us gone.

"Good luck and Godspeed," he called, as he strained at the heavy door. "And remember, discretion!" The armored door clanged shut like the gates of hell.

"Paid to the last penny," Owyn said somberly, hefting his purse. "A successful engagement, I suppose. At least we finished with a profit."

But we weren't finished with Garriston, nor it with us. We'd scarcely retired to our tents when a commotion arose from

behind the city walls. Shouting, men running. A raid? Trouble
between the DuBoynes and their guests?

I was pulling on my boots when horsemen thundered into
our camp followed by foot soldiers on the run, shouting for us to
come out, tearing open the tents and wagons. My first thought
was to reach Noelle, but I was seized as soon as I showed myself.

"Hold him! He's one of them!" The rat-eyed bailiff who'd
been with Kenedi the first day was on horseback, armed with a
poniard, directing the search. Owyn stalked boldly out to
demand an explanation, but the bailiff ordered him seized as well.
Then they dragged Noelle out and marched the three of us back
to the stronghold under guard, directly to the great hall.

The linens were gone now and the high table was occupied
by the steward, Kenedi, Black Logan, his younger brother Godfrey, and the heads of the guest families, Randal Ramsay, Nicol
Duart, and Ian Harden. Red-eyed, disheveled, and still half-drunk
from the feast, they were in an evil mood, eyeing us like wolves
'round a wounded calf.

Armed guards ringed the room and blood was in the air, real
blood. A body was laid out on a trestle table in the center of the
room covered by a sodden sheet, bleeding gore onto the flagstones.

"What is the meaning of this?" Owyn said coldly. "Why have
we been unlawfully seized?"

"You've been brought to answer, Mr. Phyffe," Randal Ramsay
said coldly. "For murder."

"Whose murder?"

"See for yourself." The squat soldier holding Noelle thrust
her forward, banging her into the corpse. She recoiled, and as he
reached for her again, I pulled free and tackled the lout from
behind, slamming his face into the floor! Once, twice, and then
the others were on me, dragging me off him, kicking me down.

"Enough!" Black Logan's bark stopped the beating instantly.
"This is a court, not a damned alehouse brawl!"

"What kind of court?" Owyn said coolly. "I see no townsmen
here to act as a jury."

"This isn't a hallmote hearing for selling bad ale, Phyffe,"
Ramsay said. "As the crime is against a peer of the realm, only his
equals can sit as judges."

Jerking his arm free of his guard, Owyn strode boldly to the table with the corpse. Noelle helped me to stand as Owyn drew the sheet back. His mouth narrowed, but he gave no other sign.

"Who's been killed?" Noelle whispered to me. "Is it the steward?"

"God rest him," Owyn said quietly, gazing at the corpse. "Father Fennan seemed a good man, but he was only a parish priest, unlettered and coarse of speech. I doubt he was of noble birth."

"Fennan was not the only one attacked," Ramsay said. "The laird of Garriston also lies wounded and is unlikely to—"

"He's not dead yet," Logan snapped. "He's survived worse."

"When he was younger, perhaps," Ramsay countered, "but he's been failing for some time. No one of sound mind would have loosed you to ravage the countryside!"

"Gentlemen, please," Owyn interrupted. "Could you save your private quarrel for a more convenient time? My friends and I have been hauled from our beds to no good purpose I can discern. There are any number of folk here with cause to harm Laird Alisdair while we have none. If you wish us to testify, let's get on with it."

His sheer audacity stunned the room to silence.

"Testify?" Gillespie Kenedi sputtered. "You are charged with the crime!"

"On what basis?"

"You are the only strangers here, and you were last seen with the priest. Money was found in your tent."

"Money paid to me by the lady of the manor for the night's performance," Owyn replied. "As to the priest, when last we saw him he was alive and well. He saw us out through a portal at the rear of the chapel and bolted it behind us. Once outside the walls, we could not return, and since you found me abed with my wife who will swear I never left once I'd arrived—"

"Your *wife* will swear," Kenedi sneered.

For a moment Owyn stood silent, his eyes locked on the steward's until Kenedi looked away. "Gentlemen, I have been falsely charged with murder. I have answered that charge with truth. I can have six free men in this room in half an hour to vouch for my word. But there is a simpler way. You have impugned my wife's honor, Mr. Kenedi. Suppose we put the question to the test in the courtyard? With any weapons you choose."

It was a bold move, and pure bluff. Owyn was a lover, not a fighter. Though lightning quick with a dirk, he had no real skill with weapons. But he was a master at reading audiences. The Scottish lords, tired and surly, brightened at the idea of a trial by combat. And he read Kenedi correctly as well. The steward had the arrogance of his high office, but no belly for a fight.

"No offense was intended to your wife," Kenedi muttered.

"Then you accept my word and my explanation?" Owyn pressed.

"Yours, yes. But what about the other minstrel? Who was he abed with? His daughter?"

Owyn glanced at me, warning me with his eyes to control my anger. But he wasn't the only one who could read people. Owyn was about to lie for me and I couldn't let him. Nothing but the truth could save us now.

"My daughter was with Owyn's family," I said. "I was quite alone."

"Then you could have returned," Kenedi said intently. "The gate guard has admitted he drowsed off. You could easily have passed by him to commit the crime."

"To what end? I have no quarrel with anyone here."

"You were sent by Lord Alisdair's enemies," Kenedi countered. "You arrived on a stolen horse. My bailiff can testify that the horse came from Garriston."

"No need. I accept your word that the horse came from Garriston. Was the reeve who rode it a Garriston man also?"

The question surprised him. It surprised me as well, but there was no turning back now. Murder had been done, and someone would pay for it before first light. Denials were useless. I had neither witnesses nor friends to vouchsafe my word. I had only my road-weary wits and the glimmer of an idea.

"Aye," Kenedi conceded, "the reeve was from Garriston. Why?"

"Because he attacked me in a wood on the way to Orniston. I buried him there." That woke them up.

"You admit you killed the reeve?" Kenedi said.

"In self-defense, yes."

"Why would a reeve attack you?" Black Logan asked. "Did you quarrel?"

"No, we hardly spoke. And he seemed more interested in killing Noelle than me."

"Same question: Why would he attack your daughter?"

"Much as it pains me to admit it, Noelle is not my daughter. She was a resident at the convent at Lachlan Cul until recently, when it burned."

"All was lost," Noelle put in. "A sister was taking me to her family when she died of injuries. Tallifer saved me."

"A touching tale but irrelevant," Kenedi sneered. "After killing the reeve, you likely came to Garriston for revenge."

"If I'd known the lout came from Garriston, I would hardly have ridden his horse here. Chance brought us to this place, or perhaps fate."

"An ill fate," Kenedi snorted. "You rode here on the horse of a murdered man yet claim you know nothing of the attacks on our laird and his chaplain?"

"I didn't say that. I had no part in what happened tonight, but I believe we may have caused it."

"Don't bandy words, minstrel," Randal Ramsay demanded. "What are you saying?"

"I think what happened tonight was the echo of another crime, one that occurred many years ago."

"What crime?" Logan asked.

"Before I answer, I have a question of my own." Turning to Noelle, I quietly asked her something that had troubled me. Then I turned back to the court. "Gentlemen, I believe the explanation lies in a ballad I heard when I came to this town—"

"What nonsense is this?" Kenedi sputtered. "You stand accused of murder—"

"Let him talk," Randal Ramsay interrupted. "His life is in the balance. But bear in mind, minstrel, if we don't care for your tale, you'll never tell another. Go on."

"The song is one you all know, the "Ballad of Black Logan," the boy warrior. Like most songs, it's part fancy, part truth.

"For example, it speaks of his birth at Christmas. Is this true? Was he born at Yuletide?"

"What difference—?" Kenedi began.

"Aye, it's true enough," Nicol Duart offered. The lanky clan chief had a buzzard's hook nose, and the same implacable eyes. "It was a damned black Christmas for this country. But the rest is a lie. Young Logan never leapt from his crib to raid Lord Randal's lands. He were at least a year old before he turned outlaw." The third lord, Ian Harden, guffawed. Neither Logan nor Ramsay smiled.

"Then the ballad is partly true. And the rest of it, the myth of a bairn riding off to war, is to explain a thing seen but not understood."

"What was seen?" Logan demanded.

"Here is what I believe happened. Seventeen years ago; a young wife who'd lost two stillborn children feared she might be put aside if she didn't deliver her lord an heir. So when she was expecting again, she arranged to obtain a male child. When her own child came, a frail girl born blind, she replaced it with the other and sent her true daughter off to a convent. At Lachlan Cul.

"The boy became a fearsome warrior. But his size at birth did not go unremarked, and a local legend sprang up to explain it. A ballad that grew with his exploits."

"You lying dog," Logan said coldly. "You dare insult my family by—"

"Hold, hold, young Logan," Ramsay said, his face split by a broad grin. "Perhaps you haven't fully grasped the implications. If the minstrel's tale is a lie, his life is forfeit. But at least part of his story *is* true. And if the rest is, then you have no right to threaten anyone, nor even to a seat at this table. Any fool can see you don't favor your father, and the girl looks so like Lady DuBoyne that her own husband mistook her earlier tonight."

"My father is not well—"

"*If* he is your father."

"By God, Ramsay, step into the courtyard, and we'll see which of us doesn't know his father!"

"I don't brawl in the street with common louts, boy. We'll hear the rest of this before I consider your offer. What of it, minstrel? Have you any proof of your tale?"

"Lady DuBoyne knows the truth of it," I said.

"My mother is keeping vigil with her dying husband," Logan snarled. "Anyone who dares disturb her grief for this nonsense will deal with me first."

"I admit it's inconsiderate to trouble the lady now, but neither is it fair to condemn me without asking the one person who knows the truth."

"We needn't hear any more," Kenedi snapped. "The minstrel has admitted to killing a reeve from this town. As steward of Garriston and head of this court, I say we condemn him for that murder and dismiss the rest of this nonsense as a pack of lies told to save himself. We can hang him straightaway unless . . . any of you gentlemen truly wish to dispute the birthright of Lord DuBoyne's son and heir?"

The Scottish lords exchanged glances, and I read my fate in their eyes. Death. They couldn't risk challenging Logan in his own hall with his men about. They might raise the matter another time but that would be far too late for me.

"Well, gentlemen?" Kenedi said. "Shall we put it to a vote?"

"No," Logan said, his face carved from oak, unreadable. "We've gathered to resolve the murder of a priest and assault on my . . . on the laird of Garriston, not the death of a reeve many miles away. If we condemn the minstrel for killing the reeve, the rest remains unresolved and I will not have any stain on my name nor any question of my rights of inheritance. But I see a way to settle this. We'll send my younger brother Godfrey to ask Lady DuBoyne the truth of the minstrel's tale. If she denies it, he stands condemned out of his own mouth. Unless any man here doubts the lady's honor?"

"The minstrel's the one who'll be dancing the hangman's hornpipe if she misleads us," Ramsay noted dryly. "He may have a misgiving or two."

I considered that a moment. "No, as it stands, only a few know the truth of what happened, and the lady is the one most likely to tell it. I agree to the test. Send the boy."

"So be it," Ramsay said, eyeing me curiously. "Duart will accompany the lad to vouch that all is done properly."

"Agreed," Logan nodded, "with one stipulation. If my mother denies Tallifer's lies, he will not hang. One of you will loan him a blade, and we'll settle our differences in the courtyard. If he kills me, you can hang him afterward."

"Or gift him with silver and a fast horse," Ramsay growled. "Duart, take the boy to speak with his mother. And listen well to her answer."

The whey-faced youth and the burly border lord exited, and I resigned myself to wait. Perhaps for the rest of my life.

The reply came sooner than I expected. A stir arose at the back of the room, which grew to an uproar. Logan bolted to his feet, his face ashen. "Help him to a chair, forgodsake!"

I turned. Lord Alisdair had tottered into the hall, supported by Godfrey and Duart. He looked even more ancient than before, as though he might fade to smoke any moment. His muslin night-shirt was bloodstained, hanging loosely over a poultice.

A servant fetched him a chair and Alisdair eased painfully down, but as he looked about him, his eyes were bright and alert.

"Milord," Logan said, "you should not be here."

"Miss a trial for my own murder?" Alisdair asked, his voice barely a whisper. "Not likely. Is this the man accused of the attack?" He gestured weakly at me. "Well, sir, speak up. What have you to say for yourself?"

"Me? Nothing!" I said, dumbfounded. "You know damned well I didn't attack you!"

"I fear not. I sleep like the dead nowadays, especially after wine. Someone jammed a pillow over my face, and when I struggled against it I was stabbed. And woke in the arms of my wife. A most agreeable surprise. I expected to wake in hell."

"Sir," Ramsay said, "perhaps your lady can better answer our questions. You should be resting."

"I'll be at rest soon enough, Ramsay," DuBoyne said. "And my lady is at chapel, praying for my soul. Prematurely, I hope. I've survived cuts before; God willing, I'll survive this. Nothing like a good bleeding to clear a man's senses. And his wife's as well. As I lay a-dying, my lady confessed to a deception long ago, a wondrous tale of a child put aside and another put in its place."

"My God, it is true then?" Ramsay breathed. "Black Logan is not your son?"

"My family tree is no concern of yours, Ramsay, only the murder of my priest."

"But surely they are related!"

"Perhaps, but . . ." DuBoyne winced, swallowing. "It is the minstrel's life and his tale. Let him finish it. If he can."

"As you say, lord," I said. "The exchange of the children took place years ago. But when word came of the fire at Lachlan Cul, a reeve was sent to end the threat the girl represented. He failed. Later, when we arrived, someone realized who she was."

"Who?" Ramsay asked.

"The priest knew, for one. As milady's confessor, he would have heard the tale long since. But only one person stood to lose everything if the truth came out. Not the lady. Her deception was done for love of her husband, and she has borne him a second son since."

"Only Logan stood to lose all," Ramsay said, turning to the youth. Black Logan met his stare but made no reply.

"True, Logan had everything to lose," I agreed, "and he's surely capable of any slaughter necessary to protect himself or his family. But only if he knew the truth of his birth. And he didn't."

"How can you know that?" Ramsay countered.

"Because I'm still alive. A moment ago, the steward could have hanged me for the death of the reeve. Logan prevented it, something a guilty man would never have done."

"Who then?" Ramsay demanded.

"Only one other person had everything to lose if the truth came out. The one who arranged the original substitution. A foundling child couldn't come from this village, too many would know. Who can travel his lord's lands at will to deal with peasants who might sell a babe? And later, when word of the fire came, who could send a reeve to do murder?"

Ramsay swiveled slowly in his seat, to face Kenedi.

"It's a lie," Kenedi breathed.

"Is it? If Lord Alisdair learned the truth he might forgive his wife, and even the foundling boy who came here through no fault of his own. But he would never forgive the man who betrayed him for money by arranging the deception. His steward."

"But killing his lord wouldn't save his position," Logan said coolly. "Surely the lady would guess what happened and confess the truth."

"Only if she knew there'd been a murder. Lord Alisdair said he woke beneath a pillow. If he'd smothered, everyone would believe he died in his sleep. But when the priest surprised him, Kenedi lashed out in desperation."

"All lies," Kenedi said, "a tale told at bedtime. There's not one shred of proof."

"Actually, there is," I said. "When Noelle and I were first brought into this room, she asked if you'd been killed, Kenedi. Tell him why, girl."

"When the soldier pushed me against the body, I smelled linseed and charcoal. Ink," Noelle said, stepping forward. "The scent was unmistakable."

"And the priest was unlettered," I finished. "As are most of us here. Only you have the gift of literacy, Kenedi. And the smell of ink on your hands. Only you."

"It's not true."

"Do you dare say my daughter lies?" Lord Alisdair asked weakly. "If I were hale I'd kill for that alone. But as things are. . . . Logan, see to him."

"Wait," Ramsay interjected. "If Logan is not your blood, he has no standing in this court, no right to be here at all."

"Sir," Alisdair said, rising unsteadily, "the offense was against me and mine in my own hall, so the justice will be mine as well. Gentlemen, I invited you here to celebrate All Saints Day in a spirit of fellowship. The banquet and the . . . entertainment are finished now. And I am very tired."

Ramsay started to object, but a glance at Logan changed his mind. We were still in DuBoyne's hall, surrounded by DuBoyne's men.

"As you wish, milord," Ramsay said, rising. "My friends and I thank you for the fest and pray for your speedy recovery. For all our sakes."

Ramsay stalked from the hall with Harden and Duart close behind, joined by their clansmen at the rear. At Logan's nod, a guardsman led the steward away.

Their departure sapped the fire from DuBoyne. Wincing, he sagged back in the chair. Logan eyed him but didn't approach.

"Where is the girl?" DuBoyne asked quietly. "The one who claims to be my daughter?"

Warily, Noelle stepped forward. DuBoyne raised his head to observe her, then nodded slowly.

"So it is true. You look very like my lady wife did once. A great, great relief."

"Relief?" Logan echoed.

"Aye, that I wasn't completely bereft of my senses last night when I mistook them. And a relief that so late in my life, my daughter has been returned to me."

"And relief that I am no son of yours?"

"That too, in a way. In truth, a part of me has always known you weren't mine, Logan. My young wife lost two sickly babes before the miraculous birth of a strapping lad the size of a yearling colt, a boy who looked not at all like me. I feared she'd taken a lover to get the son I couldn't give her. I'm relieved to be wrong.

"But if you're not my blood, you're still my creation, the son I wanted. And needed. My daughter's birthright will be worthless if our land is lost. Fiefs are bestowed in Edinburgh or London, but they can only be held by arms. Your arms, Logan. You remain lord here in all but name, and for now that is enough. I'm tired, boy. Help me to my bed. Perhaps my daughter can join us later. We have much to talk of, lost years to make up for."

As Logan led the old man out, I touched Noelle's hand.

"I must be going as well, Owyn will be breaking camp. But you needn't stay here unless you choose to. We'll find a way to—"

"No," she said, stopping my lips with her fingertips. "I have always known I belonged somewhere and for good or ill, I've found that place. In the country of the blind, places are much alike, only people are different. Besides, if I go with you, I may end up as Owyn's third wife."

"There are worse fates. It won't take long for that young border wolf to realize he can reclaim his inheritance by marrying the lord's newfound daughter."

"And is he truly such a monster?"

"No, but . . . why are you smiling? My God, Noelle. You've thought through this already, haven't you?"

"At the convent, the young girls talked of little but love, love, love. I can never have love at first sight, but I know Logan wanted me before he knew who I was."

"He wanted to *buy* you! And you said he smelled of horses."

"I suspect he will always smell of horses. I like horses."

"The poor devil," I said, shaking my head in wonder. "He has no chance."

"Perhaps I'm his fate. He may only own his armor now, but he has a song. And you've said I'm a fair singer."

"You have the loveliest voice I've ever heard, Noelle, on my honor. I shall miss you greatly."

"We'll sing together again, whenever the wind or the road bring you to me. Perhaps one day we can sing to my children."

"We will. I promise."

We said our good-byes in the great hall, and I took to the road, leaving my foundling child with strangers. And yet I did not fear for her. She grew up in a harsher land than any can imagine and flourished there. She would have no trouble coping with her new situation, of that I was certain.

And she would have Black Logan. But not because of her family or position. Love at first sight is more than a legend or a girlish fancy. It happens rarely, but it does happen.

I'd seen Logan's face at the Samhain as he listened to Noelle's wondrous voice. He had the look of a starving wolf at a feast, a turmoil of hunger, love, and lust.

I remember that terrible yearning all too well. I felt it for a woman once myself, long years ago.

But that is another tale . . .

Cold as Fire

Lillian Stewart Carl

G eoffrey knew only too well what happened to a bearer of bad news. Nevertheless, he had bad news to bear. The sergeant-at-arms spat sympathetically onto the mucky cobblestones before the castle gate. "So you're off to tell the archbishop the sheriff's arrested one of his men, eh?"

"Yes," Geoffrey replied.

"The archbishop thinks his men are above the law of the land, I'm thinking."

"Whatever I'm thinking, I know enough to keep to myself." Geoffrey wrapped his cloak around his body as though it were armor and trudged down from the castle into the town.

The towers of the cathedral looked like blunted swords against the frost-gray November sky, dominating the rooftops of Canterbury as its archbishop dominated the political squabbles of England. Geoffrey didn't know and refused to guess whether Thomas of London was defending the honor of God or his own pride. Posts as archiepiscopal clerks weren't that easy to come by, but Geoffrey's merchant father had found him one, just as Gilbert Becket had done for his Thomas some twenty-odd years before. With discretion, Geoffrey could rise high—not that he had ambitions toward an archbishopric.

But then, Thomas had had no ambitions toward an archbishopric either. It was his friendship with King Henry that caused his swift if controversial rise in power, and his sudden transition—his sudden conversion—from secular to sacred.

Geoffrey made his way along Castle Street, skirting the foulest of the puddles. Merchants flocked toward the well-dressed young man. Beggars called piteously. A woman brushed against him, her loosely draped cloak affording him a glimpse of her wares. Normally, he'd have gaped at her, but not today. Waving them away like flies, he walked on past the gate of the bishop's palace, through the yard, beneath the portico, and into the great hall.

The air was warm and close, filled with the scents of meats, peas, beans, and bread. Smoke eddied between the carved beams that braced the ceiling. There was Thomas, just rising from his dinner. He was surrounded by clerks and scholars as usual and yet, as usual, he stood aloof, set apart as much by height and bearing as by rank. His profile was as sharp as a hunting bird's, and his golden-brown eyes as keen.

Geoffrey shoved his way through the gathered men. "My lord, I bring news from the castle."

"Yes?"

Geoffrey felt like a field mouse beneath that gaze. "Johanna Frelonde of Estursete, a tenant on your manor, has been found dead."

"Johanna," Thomas repeated. "A widow. She paid five marks a year for the privilege of remaining single. Edward, find out whether she had children who will inherit and then arrange a mass for her soul."

One of the other clerks nodded. Servants began to clear the tables. Geoffrey quickly seized half a loaf of bread.

"Give the extra food to the poor," the archbishop directed.

Geoffrey, remembering the outstretched hands and empty eyes he'd ignored on Castle Street, put the bread back down. "There's more, my lord. Johanna was murdered."

"Murdered? By whom?"

"Some say by Father Baldwin de Lucy."

"What?"

The word was so short and sharp Geoffrey fell back a step. Everyone else fell back two. "He and Johanna were heard arguing.

Within the hour Wulfstan, the village smith, found Baldwin
kneeling over her body."

"Where is Baldwin now?"

"The sheriff had him taken to the castle, to be held there
until the king's justiciar arrives in two days' time."

A gasp ran around the circle of men. Thomas's face went
hard and tight, but his eyes blazed. "Baldwin de Lucy is a priest. It
is for us, his peers, to judge him and, if necessary, punish him. He
must not—he will not—be tried in a secular court."

It was for just such words and more that Henry had stripped
Thomas of his secular honors last month, and the two former
friends were now enemies. Was it fortune or choice, Geoffrey
asked himself, that drew such a fine line between love and hate? "I
just came from Baldwin, my lord. He—he's not sensible. He's
babbling of *Dies Irae*, the day of wrath. Judgment day."

"He said nothing of Johanna?"

"He muttered of witchcraft, of *maleficium*, and said Johanna
will be consumed by fire for her sins."

"So shall we all," Prior Wibert muttered from the edge of the
group, "unless we beg for forgiveness."

"Baldwin's gone mad," Edward offered. "He's been possessed
by a demon. He can't be held accountable."

Thomas's mouth crooked upward. "Madness is in the defini-
tion, isn't it? Perhaps it's Johanna who was mad. And to dismiss
Baldwin's crime—if indeed he committed one—by saying it's the
work of madness is much too easy."

"I reminded Baldwin that he can take an oath he's innocent,"
Geoffrey said. "But he refused, rambling on about innocence and
guilt and how the two are different sides of the same coin."

"An oath, no matter who supports Baldwin when he makes it,
might not be enough to satisfy the justiciar," Wibert added.

"Nor the king." Thomas set his jaw and Geoffrey remembered he'd once been a warrior, too. "But we mustn't sing the
Magnificat at Matins. You, Geoffrey, find out whether Baldwin is
indeed the murderer. If he is, well then, I shall deal with him. And
the king's justiciar."

"Me?" asked Geoffrey, and added belatedly, "Yes, my lord."
But the archbishop had already turned away.

Men said that when Thomas of London was making his way up the social ladder, and even when he'd reached the pinnacle of Chancellor of England, he was known for charm and grace. But now he was an archbishop, on Henry's no doubt much-regretted whim, true, but an archbishop still. Now his charm was abrading to haughtiness. As archbishop of Canterbury, he no longer had to court his betters. He had no betters—save only God Himself.

A CHILL SPRINKLING OF rain wetted Geoffrey's head as he left the palace and turned toward the northwestern part of the town. Evening came on quickly this time of year, and with the thick, heavy clouds, the night would be dark. But he already had reason to hurry.

In the dim, dank interior of Saint Peter's church, the candles standing to either side of the bier and its cloth-covered body seemed bright as bonfires. Beyond them the shadows were so thick that Geoffrey didn't see the old woman crouching by a pillar until she moved and spoke. "You've come to see Johanna, have you?"

"Oh—ah, yes, mother, I have. Geoffrey of Norwich, on the archbishop's business."

"And I'm Edith, Johanna's godmother." The old woman shuffled forward and turned back the cloth. "There she is, then. Poor soul, I remember her as a lass gathering reeds by the Stour in the spring. Odd, isn't it, how when you look back it always seems to be spring."

Geoffrey had so few years to look back on he had yet to assign them a season. He bent over Johanna Frelonde's body.

Even in the uncertain light it was horribly clear how she'd died. Her face was swollen, her tongue protruded from her lips, and all, face, tongue, lips, was the color of a winter storm, an evil purplish black.

"She was a lovely lass," murmured Edith. "You should have seen her on her wedding day, fresh as the flowers she wore in her hair."

It is the spirit that quickens, Geoffrey told himself sadly, and the flesh profits nothing. Grimacing, he pulled one of the candlesticks closer so that the light fell on her neck. Yes, Johanna's skin was bruised and torn, all the way from the angle of her jaw down to the hollow in her throat. She must've fought and fought hard, causing her murderer to loose and tighten his grip repeatedly.

"She was a fine wife and a good mother to her son and her daughter, in happy times and sad as well."

"Of all things God has given for human use, nothing is more beautiful or better than a good woman." Geoffrey bowed politely to the corpse. "But what of Father Baldwin? Do you think he killed her?"

Edith's dried-apple face wrinkled even more. "Baldwin says the words of the sacraments well enough, but I doubt if he listens as he speaks them."

Well, no, Baldwin's kiss of peace had always tended to be a peck of condemnation. "He was—ah—said something about witchcraft."

"Witchcraft? Johanna could see beyond this world is all. So could her mother. She used her sight to help others. There was nothing in it that went against Holy Scripture."

But her sight must've discomforted the other villagers even so. Enough for one of them to kill her? Geoffrey lifted the cloth that covered the rest of Johanna's body, hoping to find some clue.

She'd been well into her years, but not yet old, and even in death looked strong and sturdy. Her hands were callused, the nails cracked and broken off short. She'd labored long and hard, but then as a widow she'd worked the land she inherited from her husband. . . . He looked closer. The nail on the forefinger of her right hand was a bit longer than the others, the end torn and dangling loose. She'd have taken the rest of it off herself, if she'd torn it in life.

And Geoffrey saw as clearly as he saw the body in front of him the pendulous cheeks of Baldwin de Lucy, hanging like empty saddlebags. On the left one was a raw red scratch extending from cheekbone to jawline—made perhaps by a fingernail whose owner had had no other defense.

"Thank you, mother." Geoffrey replaced the cloth over Johanna's bloated and discolored face. He genuflected before the altar cross, hastened outside, and stood in the church porch exhaling the scent of mildew and candle wax, incense and death. His duty demanded that he find and tell the truth, but if Baldwin had done the murder, there would be hell to pay. Not only for Baldwin in the hereafter but for everyone in this life caught between the hammer of the archbishop and the anvil of the king. A day of wrath indeed. . . .

The smith. The smith had discovered Baldwin bending over Johanna's body, yes, but there had to be another explanation.

Geoffrey plodded through the west gate in Canterbury's encircling walls and across the bridge over the river Stour. Another spattering of rain pocked the dull pewter surface of the water. The roofs of Estursete were colorless lumps bunched between the willow-choked bank of the river and the gates of the archbishop's manor house. A cow lowed mournfully. Geoffrey thought of the palace hall, a fire leaping in the fireplace and the table lined with trenchers, and his stomach rumbled.

A sudden rhythmic clanging sent blackbirds whirling into the sky. Ah, Wulfstan Smith himself. Geoffrey ducked beneath the thatched eave of the smithy.

Wulfstan's fire was a sullen lump of red, barely warm. The man himself was short but broad, hair and beard bristling like a boar's. He dipped an iron rod hissing and steaming into a bucket of water, then placed it in the fire. "What do you want?" he asked, his massive right hand tapping his hammer against his vast left palm.

"My name is Geoffrey of Norwich. I'm here on the archbishop's business. The murder of Johanna Frelonde."

"She was murdered all right. By that prig of a priest. I saw."

"What did you see?"

Wulfstan eyed Geoffrey's clothes, then peered beyond his shoulder, as though checking to see if he'd brought reinforcements. "Baldwin was shouting at Johanna, wasn't he? Calling her a witch and telling her to hold her tongue. She told him where to get off, she did. And not an hour later, I looked in her window and there she was, flat on the floor, him bending over her with his hands on her face."

"Her face? Not her throat?"

"He'd already done his worst, hadn't he? When he saw me looking at him, he rolled his eyes like a horse about to bolt and started babbling. In Latin, I warrant, but none of his fine words could take away what he did. And him always going on at us about sin and damnation."

"Baldwin called her a witch?" Geoffrey asked.

Wulfstan stirred the fire with the iron rod. Sparks flew upward and vanished into the cold air. "Johanna was simple, if you ask me. For all that, she was good with herbs. If you had a running sore or a pain in your belly she'd bring you a tonic or a poultice and you'd soon be right as rain. But she'd go on about things she oughtn't to know, things that were said and done in private, and things that were going to happen—I think she listened at windows, myself, although there're those here in Estursete who said she could see beyond this world. But then, some folk will believe anything."

The smith hadn't cared for Johanna, Geoffrey told himself. "Did she get on well with everyone? Except Baldwin, I suppose."

"No one gets on with Father Baldwin. He sees to that. As for Johanna, there're those who'd ask her help when they were in trouble and laugh at her when they healed. Godeswell, for one, he flattered her and Alice and got what he wanted, didn't he? Or Grene, he plowed for her and always praised her cooking to get himself a second helping. Neither of them had much use for her, though. Maybe old Edith treated Johanna like her own daughter, thought she could do no wrong. But I say Johanna stirred up trouble. I'll give that to Baldwin, he was right telling her to hold her tongue."

"Maybe you should try holding yours," said a smooth voice behind Geoffrey's back. He spun around.

A man and a woman stood watching him. Her face within the soft folds of her coverchief was pinched and pale, her shoulders rounded as though she carried a heavy weight. The man was of a good height, his chest beneath its fine linen tunic thrust as far forward as his chin. His eyes were the same color and temperature as the river.

Wulfstan jerked his head toward Geoffrey. "Archbishop's clerk. Asking after your mother. This here's Theoric Frelonde and his wife Alice," he added, his voice acid.

Geoffrey bowed. "I'm very sorry to disturb you, Master and Mistress Frelonde, but with Father Baldwin confined by the sheriff . . ."

"The archbishop's looking for an example, is that it?" Theoric took a step forward. "All he'd do is strip Baldwin of his holy orders, maybe shut him up in a monastery. Is that punishment for taking Mother away from us? For murdering her, and her with years yet to live, God willing?"

"My brother drowned before we were married and now Mother's gone, too," Alice said with a sniffle. "There's no one left but us. I don't understand why . . ."

". . . my lord the archbishop thinks there should be one law for the clergy and another for us," Theoric finished. "Aren't the priests supposed to be caring for us, not lording it over us like Norman nobles?"

"Baldwin's proud as any nobleman," Wulfstan muttered, "always making up to his betters."

"The ancient customs of England must be subject to God's will," Geoffrey pointed out.

"God's will?" asked Theoric. "Or Thomas Becket's will?"

"But the archbishop's a holy man," Alice murmured. "He won't stand for the buying and selling of offices. There's never been a hint of scandal with women or boys either, and he washes the feet of the poor every morning, just as Our Lord washed the feet of His apostles on Maundy Thursday."

Ostentatious humility, Geoffrey said to himself.

Theoric snorted skepticism. "That's as may be. What matters is whether Mother's murderer escapes justice. We have our pride, don't we?"

"But is Baldwin guilty of her murder?" Geoffrey asked.

"Who else?" demanded Theoric. "He was kneeling beside her body!"

Alice added, her voice barely above a whisper, "Mother may have been a bit simple, but she was a good woman. She meant to help folk with her warnings."

"Did she warn herself about her own death?" muttered Wulfstan. He picked up his hammer and the rod from the fire. Its tip was red hot. Geoffrey could feel its heat from where he stood.

"And you, master clerk," Theoric concluded, "can tell the archbishop he has no right to shelter a murderer from what he deserves, no matter how badly he wants to get up the king's nose!"

That was one message Geoffrey wasn't going to deliver. He contented himself by observing, "It's for God to say what we deserve, don't you think?"

"And when He does, some folk will find this little fire of mine as cool as spring water." Wulfstan began hammering, the muscles bulging beneath his sleeve.

Geoffrey's ears rang. He turned away from the shed to see Theoric and Alice also retreating, the man's hand resting comfortingly in the small of her back but his shoulders still square. Proud, yes, Geoffrey thought. As were most prosperous folk. Johanna had done well with her inheritance.

The day was failing, the already fragile light thinning further and further as the shadows streamed out from wall and tree. Rain began pattering down in earnest. Exhaling a long vaporous breath, Geoffrey set his face toward the town.

So the day ended in darkness and confusion. All he'd accomplished was to put Baldwin's head further into the noose. And to bring the sheriff and the justiciar and maybe even the sergeant closer to excommunication. Which was worse, to be stripped of one's life or one's immortal soul?

He dodged from eave to overhanging story to merchant's booth, but still he was cold and wet by the time he returned to the palace. And hungry. He had just enough time to pay a quick visit to Ivo in the kitchen.

Ivo waved him toward the fire blazing merrily on the great hearth. "Well, now—you're a sight, aren't you? Bread? Beef? Mutton?"

"Beef, thank you." Geoffrey took the strip of meat, bit, and chewed. Again he heard the cow lowing in the field at Estursete. Johanna's cow, probably, which now belonged to her son and his wife. "It's a cow when it's alive, isn't it, but *beouf* when it comes to the nobleman's table."

"And a sheep becomes *mouton*. The Normans brought England more than arms and armor. New names for old." Ivo dumped a bowlful of bread dough onto the table and began pummeling it.

Geoffrey remembered Johanna's doughy face and set the meat down. Outside the bells rang for Compline. In the heavy air, the notes sounded like the clang of Wulfstan's hammer.

Wulfstan had enormous hands and arms. He could have strangled Johanna. Accidentally, perhaps, intending only to quiet what he saw as her gossiping tongue. But why would the smith turn murderous—had Johanna "seen" something about him?

And what of Baldwin? Had he witnessed the murder? Then why not say so? And that scratch on his face needed an explanation.

Wiping his hands and mouth, Geoffrey thanked Ivo again. He hurried into the cathedral and took his place beside Edward. The monks were still filing into their seats in the choir. Thomas of London stood before them all, in pride of place, gazing at the high altar. The plain dark robes he wore made his fair skin look like alabaster. His hair was dark, too, if streaked lightly with silver. But his eyes weren't dark at all. In the light of the altar lamp they glowed like embers.

Just which truth, Geoffrey wondered, did Thomas want him to find? Not an easy one, he knew that much.

"How are you getting on?" whispered Edward.

"I'm not getting on," Geoffrey returned.

"The justiciar will be here soon, and the king behind him, breathing fire like a dragon." Edward nodded toward Thomas, his face sculpted like one of the effigies hidden in the side aisles. "And him cold as ice. Who'll give way first, do you think?"

"I'm not thinking, either," repeated Geoffrey. But he was, turning over images of Johanna's broken fingernail, Baldwin's scarred face, Wulfstan's big hands. Of well-dressed Theoric and Alice—*there's no one left but us*, she'd said. And who were Godeswell and Grene? Men who'd courted Johanna for their own purposes, it seemed, as Baldwin courted the prelates at the archbishop's table, as Thomas himself had once courted the king.

The voices of the monks soared into the far reaches of the cathedral. Harmony layered upon harmony until the great stone pillars and the rounded arches above trembled. It was in the fullness of word and sound that mortals praised the king of kings, Geoffrey thought, so that they might be heirs of His everlasting kingdom.

He looked curiously at the archbishop, who looked up to heaven, his face intense with a deep blistering hunger not of the flesh.

A CHILL MORNING FOG hung over Canterbury. The upper stories of the houses leaned like watching ghosts over the street. Even the voices of the merchants crying their goods were muffled. People materialized suddenly out of the street before him, and Geoffrey had to dodge again and again as he walked resolutely toward the castle.

There was the gateway, a dark-toothed rectangle in the expanse of the wall. It took Geoffrey only a moment to state his business and another to find himself in Baldwin's cell. At least the priest hadn't been imprisoned in the dungeon. And compared to the morning outside, the tiny chamber was warm, if redolent of a nearby latrine.

Baldwin huddled on a filthy pallet, a pitiful broken man. Hard to believe he'd ever sat proudly at the archbishop's right hand. He looked up at Geoffrey but said nothing.

His silence was reassuring. The scratch, a coarse red furrow on his unshaven cheek, was not. Geoffrey hunkered down beside him and asked, "How did you come by that scratch on your face? A willow branch, as you walked by the river?"

Baldwin's red-rimmed eyes turned toward the runnels of moisture on the opposite wall. "Guilt and sin will out," he said.

"Yes," Geoffrey prodded.

"I went to talk to Johanna about the fees due the archbishop. She was in one of her fey moods, chattering on about the son who drowned and her husband's death long years ago and Alice's pregnancy."

"Alice is expecting a child?"

"So Johanna said," Baldwin shrugged. "And then, and then— she started spouting nonsense about the archbishop himself."

"Did she?"

"I told her to watch her tongue before she strayed into heresy. But she went on like one possessed. Possessed of the demon who holds her soul now, I expect. She was a witch. How else could she foresee the future, unless she sold herself to an evil spirit?"

"But could she foresee accurately? If not, then she was only speaking idle gossip. If so—well, we won't know until the future comes, will we?"

"Maybe so," Baldwin conceded. "Maybe she was only a gossip making trouble for men, as Eve brought us all to the Fall. What is a woman, after all? Glittering mud, a stinking rose, sweet venom . . ."

"Virgin mother?" Geoffrey asked dryly. "What did Johanna say about the archbishop?"

The priest shook his head so quickly his jowls flapped. "I told you. Lunacies. Heresies. She holds her land from him, she mustn't say such things about him, she owes him respect and veneration and—and . . ."

Geoffrey almost asked, "Flattery?" but said instead, "Warnings?"

"Warnings, yes. Warnings of evil to come."

"There's not a soul in England who doesn't question the archbishop's present path."

"You don't understand!" Baldwin insisted, his eyes bulging. "I had no choice. I had to stop her. I had to shut her up. What if a demon heard her words and carried them out? I wrapped my hands around her throat and squeezed—be it on my head come the day of reckoning—but when she scratched my face it burned like a brand of shame, and I let her go. She was doubled over, choking, no longer speaking, but she was alive when I left her."

"You actually. . . ." Geoffrey's heart sank into his stomach and he grasped at a straw. "You're sure she was still alive when you left her?"

"Yes, as God is my witness, yes. It was when I came back to my senses and went back to her house that I found her dead. I touched her, hoping I could rouse her enough to make her last confession and save her soul, but she was already growing cold." Baldwin leaned back against the wall, shrinking like a deflated bladder. "She mustn't say such things about the archbishop. He's our lord and master. I had no choice but to shut her mouth."

No, thought Geoffrey, Thomas of London wasn't their lord and master, merely his representative. And he could imagine what Johanna's warnings were—Henry was quite capable of bringing Thomas to trial on some charge dating back to his days as Chancellor, simply to break his power as archbishop.

Groaning like an old man, Geoffrey stood, called for the jailer, and wended his way through the castle's corridors back to the street. Today he couldn't see the towers of the cathedral, only a few uncertain rooftops in the smoke-tinged fog. Although whether the fog was inside or outside his own mind he couldn't say.

No wonder Baldwin didn't want to take an oath that he hadn't harmed Johanna. He had. And Geoffrey had only the priest's word he hadn't killed her. He had to find someone else in the village—a human being, not a demon—who might want to see her dead. Who'd chanced upon Johanna weakened by Baldwin and who'd seized his opportunity, adding new bruises to those already on her throat.

What if Theoric, for example, wanted to hasten his inheritance? But as Johanna's son he already had use of the land and its income—why commit matricide? And with a child on the way who would in turn inherit. . . .

The thud of hooves and the jangling of armor shattered Geoffrey's deliberations. Four horses and their riders loomed over him. He skipped sideways. Ah, Hugh de Morville and his retainers. The nobleman was on his way to the bishop's palace, no doubt, there to contest his rank against Thomas's. At least the king and the archbishop—and Theoric Frelonde—agreed on one thing, that the arrogance of the nobles needed to be curbed. If the meek would inherit the earth, what would the proud inherit?

And Geoffrey answered cynically, large estates, entire counties, countries, and their crowns. "Sir Hugh," he called.

De Morville's craggy face peered down at him. "Gervase," he returned, his slight nod bracketing Geoffrey's rank between a bow and a push into the gutter.

"I'm Geoffrey. Geoffrey of Norwich . . ." The knight and his men disappeared creaking and clanking into the fog.

Rolling his eyes, Geoffrey strode on toward Estursete. Gervase, Geoffrey, it was all the same to de Morville. But then, what was a name? Some called the archbishop "Thomas Becket" after his father. And Wulfstan's children might well be "Smith" whether they were smiths or not. New names for old, as Ivo had said.

There was Saint Peter's church. This afternoon Johanna would be laid to rest beside its walls. What a shame that the entire family was gone, with Alice's brother drowned in the river before she and Theoric were married. . . .

Geoffrey stopped dead beside the church gate. Wait a minute. What would it matter to the Frelonde family if Alice's brother had drowned? A sad occurrence, yes, but—but . . . Edith said Johanna had a son and a daughter. Baldwin said Johanna was chattering about her son who drowned. Wulfstan said, *Godeswell, for one, he flattered her and Alice and got what he wanted, didn't he?*

Geoffrey bolted through the gate and wrenched open the heavy oaken door. Edith stood just inside, her hand extended as though she were about to push it open herself. "Well then, young man, you've come to see Johanna again. No hurry, she's not going anywhere."

"I beg your pardon, mother," Geoffrey blurted, "but I need to know which is the child of Johanna's body, Alice or Theoric Frelonde?"

"Why, Alice, of course. Theoric was born Godeswell in Suffolk."

"But since Alice is Johanna's only heir, Theoric took her name."

"Yes." The old woman nodded. "I never thought it was a love match—Alice needed someone to work the land, and since Theoric's people were merchants, he had no land. But he's been properly respectful of them, for all his talk of selling up and buying land in Suffolk. First Johanna and now Alice will have none of that, though. The farm at Estursete's belonged to the family since before the Conquest."

For one short second, Geoffrey was elated by his own cleverness. Then his elation plunged into cold water and steamed away. "Has Alice been here today?"

"No, only Theoric. He said Alice was dreadfully upset about Johanna, so much so she insisted on walking beside the river where her brother died. He's gone to fetch her for the funeral."

"Oh, no. No." Geoffrey grasped Edith's shoulders. Her frail bones felt like kindling. "Send someone to the castle. Give the sergeant my respects and ask him to bring his men to Estursete. Now."

"What?"

"Theoric killed Johanna. Finished killing her. . . ." He shook his head. But Baldwin had never been as important as he believed himself to be. "If both Johanna and Alice are dead—if Alice dies without issue—then Theoric can sell the land. And Alice is pregnant. I don't think she's gone for a walk by the river at all."

"Blessed Saint Peter," gasped Edith. She brushed past Geoffrey and hobbled down the walk. "Blessed Saint Dunstan . . . You, boy! Come here! I have an errand for you!"

Geoffrey sprinted the other way, caroming off passersby, and burst out of the city onto the bridge. The fog was thinning into mist. The roofs of Estursete solidified from nothingness even as he looked. Black birds circled overhead, like letters incised on the pallid sky.

He ran faster, the air icy against his feverish face. What did his own ambitions matter when a living soul—two souls—were at risk? He could see the scene, Theoric's hand resting on Alice's back, the smooth voice saying, "Look there, my dear, what's that in the water?" Then a splash, and Theoric crying to the village that he'd found his wife's body in the river, drowned just like her brother—of course she didn't take her own life in despair over her mother's death, not a good Christian woman like Alice.

Geoffrey burst into the smithy. "Smith. Come with me. Now."

"What the . . . ?" But Wulfstan was curious enough to follow. So were several other villagers. Geoffrey could hear their laughter behind him—an archbishop's clerk lurching clumsily through the mud was the best joke they'd seen in days. Normally, he'd cringe at the laughter, but not now.

A thin silvery mist hung over the river, veiling the tangled limbs of the willows. A path, yes, and there, the river rimmed with ice, the tips of the willow branches just etching the smooth surface of the water.

From the mist resolved the shapes of Alice and Theoric, standing on a bank above a still, dark pool. Even as Geoffrey inhaled to shout, the cold air burning his laboring lungs, Alice fell. Slowly, slowly, her coverchief waving like the wings of a butterfly, and Theoric's hand extended not to help her but to push.

Her body shattered the water. Droplets sparked in a sudden gleam of sun. "Theoric!" she shouted, but the name disappeared in a gulp. Theoric folded his arms and watched.

"God help us," gasped Geoffrey, and leaped.

The water was so cold it scalded his skin. The current pulled him under. He was powerless against it. His sight blurred, fog above, fog below—water plants waving and—Alice, billowing cloth, staring eyes, and open mouth still screaming, silently now.

No, she'd been cruelly used, but her mortal life wasn't yet over. Neither was his. And he had the strength of his youth, the stubbornness, the anger. . . . Geoffrey thrust himself toward Alice. Grasping her cold white hand, he struggled toward the distant glow of the sky.

His ears thrummed hollowly. A searing pain filled his chest and throat. The day of wrath, he thought, might just as well be cold as hot, frost instead of flame. His foot touched something solid. He heaved himself upward and his head broke through into air and light.

He heard Theoric's voice, ragged now, shouting, "The Normans took my family's land. I deserve my land. Back home in Suffolk, where it's always been. I deserve land."

Beside Geoffrey, Alice gasped and coughed. Wrapping his arm around her waist, he struck out for the bank. She was so slightly built it was hard to believe she'd soon be great with child. A child who would never know its father.

Wulfstan had Theoric's arms pinned behind his back. The man struggled and cursed but couldn't break free. And here came

the sergeant and his men, the now sober crowd of villagers parting before their weapons.

Geoffrey carried Alice out of the water and gave her up to
the other women. Again the sun came out, warm against his icy
skin, and the air he breathed seemed suddenly sweet.

BALDWIN BLINKED UP AT the clear blue sky like a mole. Gingerly,
he stepped across the mucky cobblestones at the castle gate. "So
it was Theoric?"

"Yes," Geoffrey replied. "It was Theoric who took advantage
of your weakness. I didn't tell the sheriff about your assault on
Johanna, but I shall certainly tell the archbishop."

"And I'll be lucky to spend the rest of my life in a monastery
in the wilds of Yorkshire," moaned Baldwin. "But better that than
a dungeon. Thank you, Geoffrey."

"I'm the archbishop's man, aren't I?" For now, Geoffrey added
to himself. His knees were wobbling, for all that he'd dried himself at the sheriff's fire waiting for Baldwin to be released. Impa-
tiently, he urged the priest up Castle Street. A quiet daily round
of prayer and devotion sounded very appealing just now. But even
in a remote monastery there'd probably be those who had ambitions. Geoffrey was beginning to think that simply doing right
was the greatest ambition of all.

And that's probably what Johanna thought she was doing.
"What did Johanna say to you, Baldwin? What did she foresee for
the archbishop?"

Baldwin shook his head. "Swords rising and falling in the red
light of the altar lamp like tongues of flame. The archbishop
hewed to the pavement and his blood a red pool around him. A
new and powerful saint elevated before the high altar."

My God, Geoffrey thought, and he stumbled over the cobbles. But he forced a laugh. "There you are. She was mad, wasn't
she? Not a witch at all, but one of God's most pitiable creatures."

"Yes. Yes, I'm sure you're right."

Am I? Geoffrey asked himself. If Henry was capable of bringing charges against Thomas, his all-too-powerful followers, eager to court his favor, might . . . No. Surely Johanna's vision was only symbolic.

They walked through the gates of the bishop's palace and parted, Baldwin trudging toward the monks' dormitory, Geoffrey to the archbishop's chamber. Over the roof of the cathedral peeked the scaffolding around Prior Wibert's new tower. Each man had to leave his legacy. And Theoric's legacy was a scaffold in the marketplace: an ugly and petty ending for a man who despite all his airs was just as ugly and petty.

Geoffrey found the archbishop alone, seated close beside his fireplace, a book open in his hands. He looked up from beneath his brows, and again Geoffrey felt small and weak in the heat of his scrutiny. "Well, then, Norwich, I hear you've acquitted yourself well."

"Yes, my lord," Geoffrey replied, and told the entire tale, concluding, "Theoric wanted the land. He thought he deserved it."

"So it was all a matter of greed for property and position," Thomas said. "But what is a man profited, if he gains the whole world and loses his soul?"

Had he found the truth Thomas wanted him to find? Geoffrey asked himself. Had the archbishop wanted to confront the king? Did he, too, feel himself carried away by currents beyond his control?

Truth seemed damnably elusive at the moment. "I wonder, my lord, if Theoric's crime was in not aiming high enough. How many noblemen have murdered their way into property and position and suffered nothing for their crimes?"

Thomas's brows angled wryly upward. "Many."

"The king's mother and her cousin plunged England into war, contesting property and position. Why do men commit mortal sins to get what they think they deserve? Why do men go to such great lengths to serve their ambitions? Scripture tells us not to lay up treasures upon earth, where moth and rot corrupt and where thieves break through and steal, but to lay up treasures in heaven."

"Not all men," answered Thomas, "have keen enough eyesight to see heaven before them. Thank you, Geoffrey. Oh . . ."

Geoffrey stopped his turn toward the door and turned back, almost losing his balance. "Yes, my lord?"

"Why did Baldwin try to strangle Johanna?"

He'd prepared himself for that question. "She meant to warn you, my lord, that your debate with the king may in time prove dangerous. Baldwin felt she was speaking nonsense verging upon heresy."

Thomas's smile was thin but not humorless. "On the contrary. She appears to have been quite clever and articulate. A pity she died trying to warn me of something I already know. Thank you. You may go."

But even truth was not as elusive as Thomas of London. Bowing, Geoffrey walked to the door, where he paused and glanced back over his shoulder.

Even though the room was dusky with shadow, Thomas himself sat in the circle of firelight, its rosy glow softening his stern, pale features. He gazed into the flames, but his eyes saw farther, beyond fire, beyond ice, to a place where fire and ice, dark and light, life and death themselves were as one.

With something between a chill and a thrill down his spine, Geoffrey shut the door and asked himself just how long before Johanna's vision came to pass.

Author's Note

In 1164 Thomas Becket was forced into exile in France. A few weeks after his return, on December 29, 1170, he was murdered in Canterbury Cathedral by four of Henry II's knights—including Hugh de Morville. None of them suffered any secular penalty. For almost four hundred years, until the reign of another Henry, the eighth, Thomas was England's greatest saint.

A Horse for My Kingdom

Gillian Linscott

Author's Note

Nobody kills a herald. No matter how hot the hatred or how fierce the fight, the herald is sacred. He goes from one army to the other to challenge, to parley, to arrange a truce or exchange of prisoners. Nobody—king, noble, or common soldier—raises a hand against him any more than they would against a priest. And yet at Mortimer's Cross, not far from the border where England becomes Wales, on a freezing cold morning the day after Candlemas in 1461, Bluemantle, the herald, was killed. England got a new king that day at the Battle of Mortimer's Cross, Edward, the fourth of that name, as anybody may read in the histories. But how and why Bluemantle died has not been told—until now.

Even in the muck and the cold, with night coming on and the enemy so close you could smell the wood smoke from their fires, men turned to watch as she went past. The ground was a paste of red-brown mud with a crust of frost over it just hard enough to take the start of a foot's pressure then crack and sink you ankle-deep in ooze. Yet she walked so cleverly her feet were hardly mired. The winter sun was down level with the tree trunks, with no warmth in it, and the cold river curling round their camp smoked vapor into the colder air. When a man pissed,

the heat went out of it in the time it took to splash against the toe
of his boot. But she glowed in the cold air as if she'd found the
trick of keeping her own private midsummer. Wherever she
walked, there was metal whirring and clattering, swords and axes
spluttering sparks on grindstones, scythes witter-wattering on
whetstones. She only paused for a moment, curious, eyes wide. A
man, feeling her sweet breath against the back of his neck,
stopped what he was doing and turned, smiling. But before he
could touch her, she moved on with that precise delicate walk,
haunches swaying.

"Fine horse," he said.

"Yuh."

"What's her name, then?"

"Flut."

Fillette was the chestnut's name to the young man who
owned her, but for the more-or-less man-shaped clod of rags and
mud that held the end of her halter rope, Flut did well enough.
Some names are made to travel a long way. Names like Edward
Plantagenet, Duke of York, and Earl of March. That one had to
ring out tomorrow in the herald's challenge across the frozen
fields to where the enemy, Pembroke's men, were waiting and
beyond that to the palace at Westminster where the mad king
lived. The name of the clod holding the end of the halter rope
only had to travel the length of a small stable yard at the most.
Because he went with the horse and if anybody called for him it
was because they wanted her, he answered to his version of her
name, Flut.

"Who does she belong to, then?"

"Master Thomas."

Which pretty well exhausted the few words Flut knew. He
and Fillette turned toward the corner of the field where their camp
was, but before they'd taken more than a step or two they had to
pull up to let a more important group pass in the opposite direction. At the center of it was a man riding a good bay, surrounded
by four servants on foot. He rode like somebody with authority
and wore a tabard quartered in Edward's colors of blue and red
embroidered in gold thread with lions and fleur-de-lys, with a blue
mantle hanging from his shoulders and spread out over the horse's

hindquarters. He had no armor or helmet and carried no weapons apart from a short hunting dagger at his belt. His face was stern, giving nothing away. When they saw him, the men went quiet and the whirr of weapon sharpening stopped until he'd gone past. The man who'd admired Fillette spoke in an undertone.

"Been sent for, Bluemantle has. Edward wants to tell him what to say tomorrow."

"Not much doubt about that, is there? Run back to King Henry and tell him to shift his arse and make way for young Edward."

"He won't put it like that."

"That's what he'll mean, though."

Somebody noticed Flut gaping after Bluemantle and explained.

"You never seen a herald, boyo? Nobody can't start fighting until he says so."

Flut's gape shifted from middle distance to the man speaking.

"Wasting your breath explaining it to him," somebody else said. "Stargazy, he is."

"He'll ride out there tomorrow, soon as it's light, through those trees and over the field to where they are, then out comes their herald and they sling words at each other for a bit, then off we all go."

The man flourished his pike. Flut and Fillette jumped backward and everybody laughed.

"Mares is no good for fighting," someone said.

Fillette and Flut ambled on, moving at exactly the same pace. Fillette was eight summers old. Flut, if anybody had been interested enough to ask, could have worked out that he must be quite a bit older because he'd been almost a full-grown man when she was born, but his existence, such as it was, dated from the spring morning when she slid out of her mother's womb onto a bed of dry bracken and he was told, "Lift her up boy. Get her round so the mare can lick at her." At night, he was ordered to sleep in the stable to make sure the wolves from the hills didn't come and get her. He couched in the bracken among the droppings and the sticky afterbirth, exchanging his smell for hers. It was a step up in life for him, who'd never slept between walls

before. The dried peas and nuts the foal's mother dropped while
she was feeding and he snatched up before the rats could get
them were the sweetest things he'd ever eaten. The milk he
sucked from her teats when the foal had finished was the warmest
thing that ever went down his throat. Since then, the only times
he and Fillette had been apart was when the master took her out
hunting, and even then he'd follow mile after mile in bare feet
over rocks and through brambles to be there when the riders
drew rein and then attach himself to her bridle. He was as much a
part of the horse as her tail and hooves.

THEIR BILLET WAS IN the far corner of the field because, apart from
the beauty of Fillette, they were some of the least important in
the whole of the army. The camp was arranged with Edward's
pavilion in the middle with his standard hanging from a lance
outside, men coming and going all the time, straw packed into
the mud around it to make the path easier, but mud still oozed
through. Next to it was the tent of his second in command, Sir
William Herbert, then of the other great men who'd brought
forces of hundreds, archers, foot soldiers, their own armorers.
The men were grouped round fires of logs dragged from the
wooded slopes behind the camp, cooking mutton and venison in
cauldrons, checking weapons. A stallion whinnied at the scent of
Fillette. She and Flut stepped out faster, got back to the patch of
muddy grass that had been home for three cold days of waiting.
    "Stand."
    The voice of Thomas Hindwell, owner of Fillette, so owner
of Flut, too. As they stood, an arrow swished past them and
twanged in a wooden target fixed to a willow. Then three more,
striking the target so close together that the feathers of their
flights touched. Thomas and his archers practicing, showing that
at least they could shoot as well as anybody else there, though in
this far corner there was nobody to watch. Thomas gestured to
the horse to walk on. He was young and tense, every gesture
larger than necessary, as if commanding a whole army instead of a

handful of men. Thomas Hindwell was a remote kinsman of Sir
William Herbert, so when the call had come he'd burnished his
father's sword and helmet, left his estate of a hundred rocky acres,
and marched the twenty miles to Mortimer's Cross with his entire
male household—nine all told. Three good archers, five servants
with pikes or axes, untried in war, a farm lad too young to be
much use, who might pass as a squire. That wasn't counting Flut.
Nobody counted Flut. He settled the horse in her shelter of
branches, fetched hay for her from the wagon, and stood by the
fire, watching as the archers unstrung their bows and checked
their arrow flights. They were in good humor. There was more
meat and ale, even in their small part of camp, than they'd seen in
three Christmases.

"You ready for the fight then, Flut boy?"

"A slummuck like 'im? When meat pasties grow on thorn
trees."

Flut just grinned and went to sit alongside the horse, cross-
legged on the cold ground.

"Thomas Hindwell."

A call from the edge of their trodden patch. A young man
waited, a few years older than Thomas and a head taller, warmly
wrapped in a cloak of russet-colored wool, a big white hound
beside him.

"Ralph."

Thomas gave his bow hastily to one of the archers, wishing
his rich cousin had found him with a sword, a gentleman's
weapon.

"Comfortable here, cousin?"

Ralph and his hound came to the fire without waiting to be
invited. A smoldering branch fell and smoke from damp wood
came pouring out like juices from a pudding. The household men
drew back from the fire, leaving their betters to talk.

"More comfortable tomorrow."

"After the battle."

"After the victory."

Six hours they'd have, at most. Six hours of winter daylight
to win all that Ralph had as a right, and Thomas had only learned
the lack of in a few bitter days in camp. Ralph had arrived leading

fifty men with helmets and good weapons, dressed in their master's livery, a wagon of silver plate to gleam in the firelight and make even a muddy field a feasting place. Above all, with a smile of greeting from Edward himself like the sun coming from behind a cloud: "Rejoiced to see you, Ralph, my cousin." Then an invitation to drink wine in the ducal, almost royal, pavilion. If Edward was declared king on the battlefield tomorrow, Ralph would rise with him. And Thomas? If everything went well in those few hours, then Thomas would rise, too. There'd be no need to trail back to the sheep-nibbled, furze-spiked acres, no need to waste life as his father had, not much better than a border farmer with sword and helmet rusting on the chimney breast and fingers curled inward from the joint-rot of the rainy borderlands.

"They're talking in there."

Ralph gestured over to Edward's pavilion, glowing in the dusk from the candles inside.

"Planning the battle."

Thomas said it like a man of the world, but his stomach lurched. Ralph gave him a sideways look.

"You think so?"

"What are they talking about then, if it's not the battle?"

Ralph smiled, teeth as white in the firelight as his hound's pelt.

"Peace, my dear cousin. Peace."

Thomas thought at first he was being told to keep quiet, hold his peace, but there was more than that in Ralph's smile.

"How can it be peace? Edward won't give way, not after what they did to his father."

"So the father's head is hacked off and the son has to bowl his own after it? Will that really seem a good game to him, do you think?"

"Edward can't give up his claim and march away, not after bringing us all here."

"Depends what the king's side's offering. If they were to promise to make him regent, say, declare him Henry's rightful heir, we might be laughing and drinking with those over there tomorrow night."

"You believe that?"

Ralph shrugged. "Pembroke's no fool. Winning or losing will hang on a hair tomorrow. Buy time. Bargain with us. That's what he'll try."

"And would Edward accept?"

Another shrug.

"Then what would we do?"

"Back to our fields, cousin, and keep our peaceful sheep."

Ralph could joke. He had friends, a fortune, a world before him. And yet Thomas sensed there was a purpose in the joke, a question he was supposed to ask.

"Is that what you wish for, cousin?"

"It is not. There are no reputations or fortunes to be won in peace, eating buttermilk cakes by the fire, and watching your old mother spinning."

They both laughed, and yet Thomas felt a cold hollow round his heart and a sudden wish to taste the warm doughy crumbs on his tongue and know that the whirring sound was his mother's spinning wheel, not blades on grindstones. He crushed it down.

"If he makes peace now, it's a mockery of us all."

Ralph's hand came down on his shoulder, warm through cloth and leather.

"Well said, Thomas. And yet when Bluemantle rides out tomorrow, it's quite likely a truce offer he'll be carrying. Think about that."

A horse whinnied from the other side of the field. Fillette replied, high and sharp. Ralph glanced toward her.

"Has that mare seen a battle before?"

Thomas shook his head.

"I thought not. Your Fillette's too fine and bright for work like this. I'll buy her off you now and breed from her back home."

"No." She was his only horse.

"Just as you wish. To tomorrow then, Thomas."

"To tomorrow." Ralph strode away, the hound at his heels, and Thomas stood so deep in thought that when the guest was gone and his men could move in to roast their collops of meat at the fire, they kept to the other side so as not to disturb him. Flut would get the rags of fat and gristle left when the other men had finished eating so he kept his distance, squatting on the dry bracken under the shelter of branches he'd built for the mare, listening to the men's talk as they waited for their meat to cook.

"Doesn't look too glad, does 'e?"

"Thinking about tomorrow?"

"What else?"

"Never been in a battle, 'e 'asn't."

"You neither."

"Tell us what it's like then."

"Not much."

"Not much what?"

"Not much to tell about. You wins, you walks away. You don't, you runs away."

"If you're lucky."

Fillette stirred and pawed at her bedding. Flut ran a soothing hand down her foreleg. Fighting he knew about, not battles. Fighting was men punching and wrestling over a woman or a stolen sheep, knocking teeth out or breaking bones. When they'd arrived at the field by the river and seen more people than he'd ever seen in his life before, more than he even knew existed, he'd pictured them all wrestling and writhing in the mud like rats in a rain barrel. Slowly, watching them at practice with their swords, axes, and arrows, he realized he'd been wrong.

"They've got Irish," one of the bowmen said, pointing with his chin over to the enemy fires. "Want looking out for, they do. Not as much armor between the lot of 'em as would cover a flea's arse but fight as if God had given 'em all ten lives to waste."

"About running . . . ," one of the untried men said.

"Don't think about it before you have to."

"If you don't think about it, 'ow do you know when you 'ave to?"

"You'll know."

"It's not our lot'll do the running tomorrow," an older bowmen said. "Pembroke's foreigners'll run so fast even she couldn't catch them."

He looked at Fillette, quietly nosing her hay.

"Wish I 'ad 'er. Safer up there on a 'orse with a good sharp gisarme."

The untried man mimed a blow downward with a battle-ax.
"That's not what it will be tomorrow. They'll ride up to the
front line, just—then get off and fight on foot like all the rest of us."
"Where's the sense in that?"
"More sense than sitting up there making yourself a target
for arrows."
The archer took up the mime, drawing a bow toward Fillette's heedless chest. Flut made a noise of protest, unregarded.
"Proper target she'll make, that bright in the sun. Won't last
an eye-blink."
The archer squinted toward her, released his imaginary
arrow. Another, sharper noise came from Flut. He jumped in front
of the horse, running his hands over her chest where the arrow
would have hit, glaring at the archer. The other men laughed.
"Gone and scared the poor gawby, you 'ave."
Flut, still glaring, squatted back in the bracken and didn't
take his eyes off them. They ate their meat, heated dagger blades
in the fire, and plunged them hissing into leather cups of ale,
heating it so that it soothed throats aching from the damp and
stored a little warmth to comfort the stomach in the night. The
stars came out and the frost came down so cold you could hear
the twigs and grass blades crackling as it caught them. The men
arranged small branches near the fire, spread baggage sacks over
them, and lay down wrapped in their cloaks. Fires across the
camp died to a red glow, but the lights in Edward's pavilion
glowed as bright as ever. Fillette finished her hay, sighed, and
folded herself down for the night. She rested neatly as a cat on
her side, long legs tucked up and Flut curled against her, letting
her warmth flow into him and his heartbeat and breathing slow
until they were indistinguishable from hers. One hand was still on
her chest at the point where the archer had aimed his imaginary
arrow. He slept and woke like that through hours of darkness. He
knew now that he'd die the next day. The proper men, who knew
battles, were sure that an arrow would let the warm life out of her,
so the life would go out of him, too. It wasn't grief or loyalty—he
didn't know about those—but simply a matter of fact, like a trout
dying when you took it away from the water. It was, after all, an
insecure bundle of warmth that a man carried round inside his

own skin. Just an arrow or lance prick would send it spilling into all that cold waiting outside. All he could do was lie there looking up at the stars through the branches of the shelter, hug her warmth while the night lasted, before the man they called Bluemantle rode out in the frosty morning and said the magic words that would start arrows flying.

Then, for the first time in his life, something started growing in his head that troubled him more than the thought of being dead. It was the thought that he might be able to do something about it. Things were done to Flut, not by Flut. The possibility that it might be otherwise turned the world upside down—as upside down as it would look to a trout flipped onto the bank and looking down at the water. And yet the trout twitches and tries with every fiber of its body to live. In the darkest hour of the night a twitch much like the fish's brought Flut upright and shivering. The horse stirred in protest. He bent just long enough to stroke her neck to quiet her then trotted away, feeling the warmth of her still on his hand, raising his fingers to his nostrils to sniff her comforting smell as his cloth-wrapped feet padded over frozen grass.

FILLETTE WITHOUT FLUT SLEPT uneasily, starting at the slightest noise. Then, with the sky deep black and even the voices of the watchmen gone silent, she untucked her legs and was on her feet in a moment, quivering.

"Easy girl, easy Fillette."

A man's leather gloved hand was on her neck, stroking and calming. She gave a little snuffling sound, quivering her lips, pushing against his chest. A hand came out from under his cloak and unclasped to offer her hazelnuts.

"Easy girl. Good girl." She ate and allowed herself to be led softly past the sleeping men and outside the enclosure to a willow tree by the river. A saddle and bridle were waiting there and although the man fumbled, fitting them with frozen fingers in the dark, she stood patiently. He got her to stand beside the tree so that he could mount from a knot in its trunk, then guided her along the river that ran black against the white grass. They followed it until they were past the watchmen's fire, then struck out over the pastureland toward where the enemy's fires glowed no more than a mile away across the fields, like a reflection of the camp they'd left. About halfway between the two lines, the rider made her stop behind a tangle of bushes and brambles on a bank overlooking three bare oak trees. They waited. Twice the noise of something moving near the oak trees made her prick her ears and tremble, but the man's hand calmed her, and she stood quietly until there was the faint stirring in the air that comes before daylight, and the eastern edge of the sky began to turn the same color as the frozen land.

As the light broadened, mist rose up from the river so that men moved in it as if wading, with only heads and upper bodies visible. They beat frozen hands against thighs or nursed them under armpits to supple them enough to cope with buckles, gulped bitter mouthfuls of ale from beakers that had necklets of jagged ice inside the rim. It was some time before Thomas's household realized that both their master and his horse had gone.

"Gone out already, 'e 'as. Wouldn't wait for us."

"Don't be a dunny. How would he go on his own with nobody to fettle the mare for him?"

"Where's 'e gone then?"

"Somewhere around he'll be. Just go and look for him."

Some of them looked all round the camp, but found no sign of him, and with the light growing everybody was too occupied with his own business to worry about an obscure man and his handful of followers. When the men who had gone to look came back to report failure to the others, even the battle veterans looked sick. You had to have a leader, somebody to fight around. Without that, it wasn't a battle, only a confusion. Thomas's men stood and stared at each other and at the Fillette's shelter, empty except for droppings and scattered bracken. As they stared, the sound of a trumpet drifted over from Edward's pavilion. Bluemantle was on his horse and had started his short and lonely ride toward the enemy lines.

MOVING IN THE DARK, moving near the ground were natural to Flut, who never expected to be far away from either. His chapped and callused fingers had never been nimble, so the cold was less of a clog to them than the fingers of quicker men. He did what needed to be done doggedly and slowly in the dark, by feel rather than sight, then huddled up between the tree roots, waiting. When he heard the bugle note drifting over from the camp, he got up, tightened the rags round his feet, and jumped for a low branch of the nearest oak. It took a lot of ungainly scrabbling, but at last he managed to wedge himself with his back against the trunk and his legs astride the branch, watching. Up on the bank, Fillette stirred again, hearing scrabblings from the oak tree.

"Easy, girl, easy. Only a pigeon waking up."

But the rider's voice was strained. He looped the reins over the pommel of the saddle, unhitched the longbow that was slung at his knee, thumbed the bowstring into its slot. It was morning now. Although the sun was not up, the sky above the mist was white and taut like the silk of a banner, and a man could have seen colors if there were any to see in the white and black landscape of rime and river. Then there was color, one patch of it coming quite slowly at easy walking pace, shining out against the black and white. Quarterings of blue and red, a gleam of gold, a blue plume on a hat, and the fall of a blue mantle. The rider took an arrow from the quiver on his back, notched it into the bowstring.

BLUEMANTLE'S BAY WENT AT a collected walk. It was against a herald's dignity to hurry, and nobody would want or expect fighting to start until the sun was well clear in the sky. For the next hour both armies would be waiting on the word of the heralds and, whether for war or peace, the thing must be done in proper order. The bay hardly needed guiding because there was only one sensible way between the battle lines—a causeway at

some distance from the muddy ground closer to the river, passing between oak trees. For most of the journey he kept his eyes
straight ahead to the line of pavilions and white and gold stan-
dards that marked the enemy camp of the Earls of Pembroke and
Wiltshire. Then at the last moment a gash of color much closer
and to his right caught his eye. Against the mist and standing on
ground a little higher than he was, Fillette seemed a gleaming
giant horse from legend, a horse out of the sun. Bluemantle
gasped in surprise, raised a hand. At that moment, the arrow
struck his throat, tumbling him backward out of the saddle with
the weight of the mantle pulling him to the ground.

THOMAS, DESPERATE WITH ANGER and humiliation, saw Bluemantle fall and the bay standing with the stolid puzzlement of a
horse that has unexpectedly lost its rider. Then, as his mind
tried to catch up with what was happening, he heard a whinny
that didn't come from the bay and looked up to see what Bluemantle had seen in the last moment of his life: a bright chestnut
horse gleaming against the mist. Fillette. He'd been looking for
her for hours, since he woke in the dark to find her gone and
faced the disgrace of being the only gentleman in the morning
who'd have to go into battle on foot. Without even rousing his
men, he'd rushed out to look for her all round the camp and, as
day broke, into the fields round the camp. Now there she was,
half a mile away from where she should have been, but with a
rider on her back and—unbelievably—Bluemantle on the
ground. Thomas shouted something, not knowing what. The
rider turned his face toward him then yanked the reins and
spurred Fillette at a canter down to the causeway. She almost
trampled the body of Bluemantle and tried to rear up, but the
rider dragged her head down and pointed her between the oak
trees at the enemy lines. Thomas gave chase, but before he
could even shout again or form any idea of what was happening,
there was a twanging sound, the rider was falling, and Fillette
was galloping on alone. Thomas tried to grab for her rein but

missed and fell sprawling over the obstacle in the path that was cousin Ralph's body.

FILLETTE CAME BACK. THE fact that she came back with Flut holding the end of the reins surprised nobody and wasn't even commented on, because that was where anybody would expect him to be. After a few panicking yards she'd stopped, seen him sliding down from the tree, and come to him questioning and trembling. Though he couldn't answer her questions, he could soothe her at least. Thomas couldn't help because he was facing angrier and more urgent questions from Sir William Herbert. Every eye in Edward's camp had been on Bluemantle as he rode out, everybody had seen his fall, and the army was buzzing with speculation and anger. Sir William had gone galloping down and found not only Bluemantle dead but his own kinsman Ralph dead, too, a few paces away, his head half off like a clumsily slaughtered hen in a poultry yard, and a more remote kinsman, Thomas, looking like a man who'd seen the devil.

"B . . . bowstring," Thomas stuttered. "There." He pointed to where the thin line was stretched across the causeway between two oak trees. "He rode into it. Ralph rode into it."

"Who put it there?"

"I . . . I think, sir, Ralph himself did. To kill Bluemantle in case he missed with the arrow."

"You are saying my kinsman killed the herald?"

"He was afraid, sir. Afraid Bluemantle was going to offer peace."

Sir William blinked then looked at Thomas for a long time. "Should I believe you?"

"On my soul's peril, sir. He stole my horse. She's well known in the camp. He wanted it to be thought it was my crime."

From Pembroke's camp a bugle sounded, then another. They were mocking sounds. The herald should have arrived by now and his lateness suggested Edward's side had no stomach for fighting. Sir William made up his mind.

"If you're innocent of these crimes, then prove it by giving every drop of blood in your body for Edward today. If not, you'll go to your God a perjured man."

"I'm innocent, sir."

Sir William nodded, more to indicate an end to discussion than belief and beckoned a servant to help him back on his horse. He looked down at Thomas.

"Say nothing of this. Bluemantle was treacherously butchered by enemy scouts who have no respect for heralds. Ralph was killed trying to save him. Do you understand?"

"Yes sir, I understand."

Flut held the rein as Thomas was helped into Fillette's saddle, then padded after them as they cantered back to their own lines. He'd have liked to get his bowstring back from the oak trees, since he'd stolen it from the pouch of one of the archers, but one of Sir William's men had taken it already.

THE NEWS THAT THEIR herald had been treacherously killed by the enemy infuriated Edward's men. They fought that day as if every man had a kingdom to win and by the time the mists curled back in the evening, the mud in the flat fields was even more red than nature had made it, the river was full of the bodies of Pembroke's soldiers, and every clump of bushes or dead bracken for miles around hid shivering, half-naked men hunted like rabbits at the end of harvest. There were men to bury on the winning side, too, but seven of Thomas's nine followers survived, and although Thomas himself couldn't have said with honesty whether he'd acquitted himself well or badly, he seemed to have done enough to be included in the general rejoicing. He'd shed some blood for Edward from a gash in his arm, although far from every drop as instructed, and when, as evening fell, Sir William came up to his fireside with a tall young man beside him, Thomas's heart dropped. It took him a few moments to recognize the tall young man with his plain cloak and muddied face, but when he did his heart seemed to slip further down, right to his stomach. He bowed and stammered "sir," then "sire."

Sir William said, "I have been telling the king." His voice caressed the last word like a man buffing a helmet. He turned to Edward. "If Thomas is telling the truth, then my kinsman Ralph was a horse thief as well as a murderer."

"If the penalty for stealing a horse is hanging, then he's paid that already."

Edward's voice was light, almost joking, but Thomas wasn't deceived by that and he knew that standing here by his fire he was nearer death than at any time in the battle. Edward had respected Bluemantle. If he believed Thomas had killed him there'd be just one more corpse to bury. Softly, desperately, he said, "Sire, it is the truth."

Fillette, still excited from the battle, whinnied from her shelter. Edward looked toward the noise.

"That's the horse, is it?"

"Yes, sire."

Edward strolled toward her, as if looking at her would decide the case.

"A fine mare."

At that point Thomas made his great decision, the one which not only saved his life but changed the fortunes of his family for generations to come. He stood at Fillette's head and looked straight into the face of Edward who, king or not, was much his own age.

"Yes, sire. Fine enough for a king to ride, if you'd accept her."

A little later, Edward sent his servant to lead Fillette over to his own pavilion. As usual Flut went too and stayed with her, as little noticed in the new king's stables as he was missed from his old yard, but aware that the quality of the hay was better.

The Simple Logic of It

Margaret Frazer

The April rain fell in a straight, soft veil from low clouds, sheening the lead-dull, slate-dark roofs of Westminster Palace and setting a cleansing gleam to the cobbles of the narrow back alleyway between the south gate and the blank rear wall of the Exchequer. It beaded finely on the dead man's face, turned open-eyed and unheeding upward, where he lay in a loose sprawl on his back, though the blood smeared on the stones near the foot of the wall and runneled between the cobbles showed where he had lain before someone turned him over. Probably the guard standing apart from his fellows, York guessed.

He guessed, too, from the guard's clay-colored, queasy face, that he must never have been to the wars in Normandy where dead men were a too-familiar sight for this one to have unsettled him, killed by what looked to have been simply a straight thrust through the body from behind and probably dead before he hit the stones.

"He's one of yours, isn't he?" Master Babthorpe demanded across the body.

"Yes." There was enough dawnlight now that York did not need the paling light from the guard-held torch hissing quietly to extinction in the rain to answer. "He's one of mine."

"He's not part of your London household, is he? What's he doing here?"

Being dead, York almost said but didn't; said instead, level-voiced, "He's one of my couriers between here and Normandy. Why he's here in particular, I don't know."

"Probably looking for you, though?" Master Babthorpe pressed and only belatedly added, without any particular courtesy, "your grace."

York brought his gaze up from Davydd's dead face to meet Master Babthorpe's hard stare, with several equally uncourteous answers coming to mind; but Babthorpe, as an officer of the royal household, had authority if not for his rudeness, then at least for his questions and, for that reason only, York answered his curtness with simply, "Yes. Very probably." Even though admitting it felt like walking by his own will into a trap.

But then he had had that sense of a trap waiting ever since he'd been asked from his breakfast to come here, because it was hardly necessary for the Duke of York to stand in a back alleyway in a drizzling rain identifying a dead man any number of other men could have named as well and apparently had, since someone had known to come for him with word he was wanted to view the body. It was when he'd seen that, besides the expected guards, there were a half dozen of the Earl of Suffolk's men to watch him acknowledge the man as his, that his unease had deepened to something more, because Suffolk had been main among those who had lately tried to bring him down with slanders he had mis-used his power as the king's governor of Normandy.

York wasn't supposed to know where the slanders had come from but he did, even if they had been so subtle—no open accu-sations against him, only a quiet, determined undermining of his reputation—that he'd not been able to name names with any proof, but been able only to demand he be vindicated publicly, in Parliament. The slanders had faded away then and Parliament been dismissed without the matter becoming officially open. He had thought—hoped—the thing was finished. But now . . .

"There was a letter found on him," Master Babthorpe said. "To you. From Normandy."

Already more chilled than the early hour and the rain justi-fied, York chilled more deeply but only said, making it seem it hardly mattered to him, "May I have it?"

"After my lord of Suffolk has." An effort not to smirk marred Master Babthorpe's dignity. "This whole matter—and the letter, too—must needs be put into his hands. You know that." Because while York was abroad, trying to keep England's hold on Normandy from disaster and going into debt while doing it, because somehow the garrisons had to be paid whether or not money for it came from England, and mostly the money had not, Suffolk had kept close to King Henry, gathering a great deal of power and a number of offices to himself, including Steward of the Royal Household, so that he had not only control over nearly everything that happened around the king but ready access to King Henry for himself and a strong say in who did or didn't come near the royal person.

York, despite—or because—he was the king's cousin and near enough in royal blood to be possibly King Henry's heir if King Henry died without issue of his own, was among those Suffolk preferred King Henry not to see often, and now Suffolk was who would have this letter and determine what to do about it, and York said, "Later then," as if it did not matter, while the questions ran behind his carefully blank face, beginning with why Davydd had been here in this back alleyway at all. As York's man, he had every right to come the main way into the palace, and if he'd come in the middle of the night, as he must have, a guard would have escorted him from the gate. So why had he been here in the black hour before dawn? Because it looked to be no longer ago than that that he was killed; his blood on the cobbles had started to dry before he had been rolled off of it, opening it to the rain, but had so far darkened only around the edges, enough to tell he had not lain here long. "Secret" and "urgent" were among the words coming to mind, seeing him here like this, but York, in the same, seeming-uncaring tone as before, asked, "Was he robbed?"

"His belt-pouch was empty except for the letter," Master Babthorpe answered.

York looked down at the pouch that hung from Davydd's belt. "Odd. You'd think a cutpurse, having killed him, would simply cut that loose and go."

Master Babthorpe shrugged. "Who knows how those kind of men's minds work?"

Usually more cleverly than that, York thought but did not say.

"My lord of York? Master Babthorpe?" asked a black-robed priest, come almost unnoticed to the fore of Suffolk's men behind Master Babthorpe. "I understand there's a man dead here and in need of prayers."

Belatedly, York realized that the man was no mere priest, despite his plain black gown and the bent shoulders of someone who spent more of his time over books than at anything else. He was the Bishop of Saint Asaph's, unlikely though that seemed, because even bishops of so slight a bishopric as Saint Asaph's were rarely as diffident as this man appeared to be.

But Master Babthorpe was making him a deep bow from the waist, saying hurriedly, "My lord bishop, there's no need of you here. A plain priest will suffice . . ."

Past him Bishop Pecock met York's slight bow of the head with one of his own, they being close enough to each other in rank as royal duke and God's bishop to exchange equal courtesies, and said, ignoring Master Babthorpe, "My lord of York."

"My lord bishop," York returned.

Raynold Pecock had been an Oxford scholar and then warden of Whittington College in London, nothing more, before he was made Bishop of Saint Asaph's for reasons unknown to York, abroad in Normandy at the time. Nor, since his return, had he ever had occasion to more than barely speak to this least of the bishops and never enough to build any thought of what sort of man he might be. Now, as he started toward Davydd's body, Master Babthorpe made to step into his way, saying with somewhat more impatience than respect, "My lord, I was shortly going to send for a priest. There's no need for you . . ."

Bishop Pecock did not pause, merely made a backward beckon of one hand to move Master Babthorpe out of his way, saying as he went past him, "Man dead by murder, gone without proper rites to judgment, is a man with his soul imperiled. A priest should have been sent for before anyone else."

Quietly, York revised his opinion of the Bishop of Saint Asaph's upward: he was not diffident at all, simply so confident of himself that he had no need to assert his place to anyone—unless

they were in his way like Master Babthorpe, now out of it and
standing in tight-lipped, disapproving silence while Bishop
Pecock stood looking down into Davydd's dead face before
finally shaking his head and saying, "This was evilly done." With
another sad shake of his head, he made the sign of the cross over
the body and raised his gaze to York. "I heard he was a Welshman, and being perhaps his bishop, I thought it well to come
myself. His name?"

Keeping to himself the thought that there seemed to be a
surprising amount known about Davydd to a surprising number of
people so soon after his death, York said, "He was Davydd ap
Rhys." Giving the name its Welsh form and sound. "Of Neath."

"Not of my diocese then, but Welsh nonetheless and in need
of prayers." And, even though the cobbles were both rain-wet and
back-alley dirty, Bishop Pecock knelt down and began a low murmuring of the Office of the Dead.

Over his bent head York said at Master Bapthorpe, "I hope
you've at least had sense enough to send for the crowner," and left
without waiting for an answer, his own three men who had come
with him parting from his way, then falling in behind him, their
presence at his back more of a comfort than it should need have
been, here in the palace where even to draw a weapon made a
man liable to arrest.

But here in the palace were his worst enemies, Suffolk and
the other lords of the royal privy council. What they wanted for
him was nothing so simple as his death, though he suspected
they'd not have minded if it came, so long as they could escape
any blame for it. Short of that convenience, what they most
intended was to cut off any chance of him having influence with
the king. Young King Henry VI reigned, but his royal privy council ruled, telling him what his decisions should be in most matters; and King Henry—being more given to piety than
kingship—mostly followed their bidding. York, too powerful in
his own royal right and too openly opposed to their ways, knew
himself to be a risk of which they wanted to be rid. They had
tried to cripple his governorship of Normandy when his success
in governing both the war and the uneasy peace had roused too
many discontented men's claims that he should have more hand

in England's government, presently troubled as it was under the royal privy council's rule with increasing disorders and ceaselessly rising debt.

And as surely as he knew all that, York knew that in some way Davydd's death and the letter he had carried was going to be used against him. But how? Who was it from and what was in it?

And how could he find out before too late?

TOO LATE, AS IT happened, came too soon, within two hours, before any of the men he had sent out with questions had returned with any answers. In the outer chamber of the rooms given to him in the palace, trying to pay heed to a bundle of account papers one of his clerks was showing him, he heard Bishop Pecock's Welsh-softened voice at the outer door asking a servant to ask if he might see the Duke of York. More than willingly giving over the accounts he had not been following anyway, York bade him enter and the clerk and other men to withdraw to the room's far end, then led Bishop Pecock to the room's other end, to the narrow window deep-set in the thickness of the stone wall with its sight over rooftops to Westminster Abbey, reared pale and huge against the washed blue of the clearing April sky and wind-drifting clouds. Even now, distracted as he was, the changeful play of sun and cloud shadows over its stonework and flaring buttresses gave him pleasure, but Bishop Pecock gave it not even a glance, and noting the red, curved marks on his cheek and over the bridge of his nose where the heavy wooden rims of glasses must have been setting until lately, York wondered if maybe that was simply because the bishop could not see it. But if Bishop Pecock's sight was poorly, it was quickly clear his wits were not as he began, directly to the point, "My lord of York, I've seen the letter that was found with your man."

"How?"

"There's been a meeting of the king's council." Bishop Pecock amended that. "Of some of the king's council." Then amended again. "Not really of the council but of those my lord of Suffolk thought would be of most use in dealing with the matters raised by the letter, as well as a few others of us to make the matter more credible, we being not suspect of being on one side more than another but expected to follow what we were told concerning conclusions to be drawn from the letter, you understand . . ."

With the suspicion that time would run out long before Bishop Pecock did, York interrupted, "What did it say?" Then more formally, to soften that rudeness, "I pray you, what was in it?"

Not seeming bothered to be interrupted, probably used to it, Bishop Pecock promptly shut his eyes and quoted, frowning at the words to make sure he had them, " 'Moleyns has the answers he sought. All is known. Do what you can.' "

The chill that had come on York beside Davydd's body deepened. A warning to him that "all is known" left far too many directions from which he might be attacked, beginning surely with whatever "answers" Moleyns had been seeking. Bishop Adam Moleyns of Chichester, Keeper of the King's Privy Seal, was Suffolk's creature first and last and always, and whatever he had been seeking would not be to York's good. Now, with this letter in hand, Moleyns could charge anything against him, and Suffolk would claim the letter as proof that the charges, whatever they were, were true.

"Is it signed?" York asked, annoyed to hear that his voice was trying to twist along with his stomach.

Bishop Pecock looked at him reproachfully. "Of course it's not signed. Put name to it of someone who could be asked and would not only deny it but maybe be able to prove the falsehood? Best to leave it with only your name and your denials to be dealt with."

The shape of the trap was becoming clearer by the moment and as yet York saw no way out of it. Who had been fool enough to send him such a letter?

"Except, of course, that everything about the letter is false," Bishop Pecock said as if stating an openly obvious truth.

York stared at him, then said, sharp with disbelief, "Why do you say that? How do you know? You have proof?"

"Assuredly." Bishop Pecock sounded surprised even to be asked.

"What?"

With the open pleasure of a scholar only too happy to present his thoughts, Bishop Pecock said readily, "To begin. I came to pray over your man because I heard Bishop Ayscough say as the household was coming out of morning mass that there was a murdered Welshman behind the Exchequer. Afterward, with thought upon that, it seems to me a strange thing for my lord bishop of Salisbury to know and be commenting upon there and at that hour. You see, even though it was something known, obviously, it was not widely known, the hour being still very early, or others would have been talking of it, too, and no one was, only my lord bishop, and why would he know of it before anyone else since, on the face of it, it was no matter that should come to him at all, let alone be first thing in the day, before even mass, yes?"

"Yes," York granted, having kept pace with that fairly well.

Bishop Pecock nodded, happy they were still together in it, and went on, "Now, if the premise is accepted that Reason governs all that happens—and we can surely accept that it does—then if a thing seems without Reason, there is nonetheless surely Reason behind it, and if one follows by Reason from what is presently known toward what is presently unknown, if, in other words, one follows with Logic the way that Reason leads, we can come to the understanding of anything, even of God, who surely gave us the gift of Reason for exactly that purpose."

Afraid there was little time left before Suffolk moved openly against him and remembering that one of the few things he had heard of Bishop Pecock was that he talked a great deal about things no one wanted to listen to, York cut short the explanation—if that was what it was—with, "Bishop Pecock . . ."

"Raynold," he said absently, his mind still mainly elsewhere. " 'Pecock' is a rather unlikely name, on the whole, don't you think? I like it better that my friends call me Raynold."

Letting it go by that he was disconcerted to be thought a friend, York asked, "How does Reason reckon in this?"

"Ah. Yes." Bishop Pecock veered easily back to where he had been. "Given the premise that it was unreasonable for Bishop Ayscough to take interest in this dead Welshman—or rather, that it seemed unreasonable but must not have been—I took closer look than I might otherwise have at this whole matter of your man being dead and the letter and found that there are certain things to be noted about both, but to begin with the letter . . ."

York held up a hand, stopping him because across the room Master Babthorpe had appeared in the doorway and was asking the servant there for leave to enter. York nodded permission and Master Babthorpe crossed the room and made a bow that included them both but with a curious look at Bishop Pecock, so that York said smoothly, unwilling for him to know anything he need not, "My lord of Saint Asaph's has just come to tell me what disposition is being made for my man's body. And you're here . . . ?"

He left the question hanging, bringing Master Babthorpe to answer, "My lord of Suffolk asks that you come to him in the lesser council chamber, if you would be so good, your grace. And you also, my lord," he added to Bishop Pecock.

"Only my lord of Suffolk?" York demanded.

"And a few others. They're presently there, so if you would come as soon as may be . . ."

"You mean now," York said bluntly.

Master Babthorpe agreed with another slight bow. "If you would be so good."

Be so good as to come and not so foolish as to refuse, York thought, but aloud said evenly, letting himself show nothing but confidence, "I pray you tell my lord of Suffolk and the others that I'm on my way."

THE LESSER COUNCIL CHAMBER was a room meant to impress, not large but well-proportioned, with a mullioned window looking out on the king's garden and the walls hung with painted tapestries showing the Judgment of Paris over the Golden Apple—perhaps not the best of choices for somewhere wise decisions were supposed to be made, York always thought—and the ceiling beams painted with patterns and mottoes concerning Justice and Truth—neither of which, York suspected, would have much place here today.

As expected, Suffolk, Bishop Ayscough, and Bishop
Moleyns were there: Suffolk at the head of the council table,
facing the door, the other two on the sides immediately to his
right and left. It was who else was there that mattered, and York
was not displeased to find, ranged down Bishop Ayscough's side
of the table, the Duke of Buckingham, Lord Cromwell, and Lord
Stourton. They were men who could, as Bishop Pecock had
said, be expected to follow what conclusions they were led to
about the letter, but they were also men who would be swayed
by facts rather than partisanship with Suffolk, and that gave
York at least a hope of fairness. It was a small hope but illogi-
cally somewhat grown because of Bishop Pecock, who had
probably been included as a make-weight. Three bishops and
three lords to judge between York and whatever Suffolk came
up with against him.

Now, as York crossed toward the table, one of Suffolk's men
pulled out the chair set by itself across from Buckingham,
Cromwell, and Stourton. To sit there would leave York facing
them much like a felon before a jury, with Suffolk, Ayscough, and
Moleyns as his "judges" at the table's head. Making no haste and
allowing no sign of unease, York made a small bow of his head to
his peers, then went deliberately to the high-backed chair at the
near end of the table, pulled it out for himself, and sat down to
face Suffolk along the table's length.

Coming in behind him, Bishop Pecock went to sit in the
pulled-out chair, thanked the man for it, and settled himself
comfortably, resting his clasped hands on the tabletop in front
of him.

Suffolk gave the briefest of frowns, then quickly smoothed it
away, returned to his usual gloss of good manners and ingrained
satisfaction with himself. He was a well-featured man and knew it
and used it and had charm enough and a sufficient degree of wit
to keep the king pleased with him and work other lords around to
seeing things his way. He would have willingly worked York
around, too, but York could not get past his own belief that Suffolk, regardless of charm and excellent good manners, was dan-
gerously shortsighted concerning the long-term consequences of
what he did.

In return Suffolk chose to consider him an enemy, to be shoved and kept from power as far as possible, and said at him now, "Well, York, we've a problem on our hands, it seems," without bothering to hide it was a problem that pleased him.

"Indeed?" York returned evenly. "I'm sorry to hear it."

Suffolk waited for more but was forced to go on without it, saying somewhat tersely, "It seems a man of yours has been found murdered . . ."

"Seems?" York cut in with mild surprise. "I thought it certain that he's found and equally certain that he was murdered."

Thrown out of his course, Suffolk fumbled, "Yes. Well. Be that as it may . . ." and lost track of where he was, and Bishop Ayscough put in sharply, "The point is that there was a letter on your man addressed to you with matter in it that raises troublesome questions."

York turned a cool look his way. The Bishop of Salisbury was a gray-featured, thrusting man, said to be more bane than blessing to his bishopric, and with no reason to expect his good will in any case, York said at him peremptorily, holding out a hand, "Let me see this letter I keep hearing about."

As quick looks and hesitation passed between Suffolk and Ayscough, Buckingham reached to take a paper lying open in front of Suffolk, saying, "Show it to him. It won't change anything," and shoved it down the table.

York took his time reading it despite there was only what Bishop Pecock had quoted: *Moleyns has the answers he sought. All is known. Do what you can.*

"Read the superscription, too," Bishop Ayscough said, and York turned the paper over to what had been the outside when the page had been thrice folded on itself and sealed. There, in dark ink and a firm hand, was written, *For the Duke of York, from Normandy, to be read in all haste.*

York looked at Suffolk, said, "Well?" and shoved the letter back along the table.

It was Bishop Pecock who put out a hand and took it. No one objected, probably no one heeded because, as Buckingham had said, it said what it said, no matter who had it.

"You see the difficulty?" Suffolk said, his course recovered. "Someone has seen fit to send you a strong warning that 'all is

known.' Now, as to the answers Bishop Moleyns has been seeking . . ."

York shifted his look coldly to the Bishop of Chichester.
"We all know what he's been seeking. We all know he had his
nose in places last year when he was in Normandy. And didn't
find anything." But that had been when York first understood how
deep Suffolk's distrust of him ran. No sooner had he come back to
England, than Moleyns had been off to Normandy, seeking some
evidence of York's ill-doing in either his governing or his finances
or preferably in both, to the point of offering to pay the travel-
price of anyone willing to come to England and give evidence.
No one had come.

"Questions have continued," Moleyns said with high-nosed
dignity. Small-built, he carried himself large and was beginning
to be the same around his middle, too, from deeply indulged
rich living. "Just of late we've had answers and not ones you'll
like."

"Such as?" York asked.

"Such as testimony . . ."

"Suborned," York said.

". . . and witnesses . . ."

"Bought."

". . . and documents . . ."

"Forged."

Moleyns's voice rose a little. ". . . of your abuse of the
moneys entrusted to you, your favoring of some men—Scales,
Oldhall, Ogaard, to be precise—over others in the matter of pay-
ments for no reason but your whim, your mishandling of both
men and funds to the point where presently Normandy is in
danger of being destroyed and lost by your doing!"

York could have told them exactly why Normandy was in
danger of being lost, and it had more to do with malfeasance here
than anything he had or had not done there. First and foremost was
the council's failure to send him promised funds to pay anybody
anything, followed by the support Suffolk and the others had given
to John of Somerset's harebrained, useless campaign into Anjou
when it was all English troops could do to hold the frontier as it
was and forcing York to hold the Normandy garrisons from revolt

by draining his own coffers to pay them at least something now and again . . .

"All this against you has been laid before the king," Suffolk said.

Damn, thought York, careful that his face showed nothing. He had hoped it wasn't gone that far yet.

". . . with promise that Bishop Moleyns' evidence to your wrongdoing will shortly be in his hands," Suffolk went on.

"Not that much in the way of evidence will be needed, what with this letter out of Normandy warning you of your danger," Bishop Ayscough said, arching a finger in disdainful point across the table to the paper lying under Bishop Pecock's hand. "What greater condemnation could there be than a secretly sent warning that all is known, do what you can?"

Especially when what they wanted to find out was not the truth but his supposed guilt, and a brief look at Buckingham, Cromwell, and Stourton's accusing looks back at him was enough to show how other men, even those more interested in fairness, would as easily believe what the letter "proved."

"Yes," Bishop Pecock sighed, paused, and then said, sounding regretful, "But then there's the trouble that this letter never came from Normandy, did it?"

Silence sharp as across a hawk-shadowed meadow fell the length of the table, and York doubted it was Bishop Pecock's poor eyesight that made him seem unaware that everyone was looking at him as he went on, holding the letter up, "It can't have. You see? There's no sign to it having been anywhere very long, in Davydd ap Rhys's belt-pouch or anywhere else. Though it's a little crumpled, the folds are fresh, nor is it marred as if long carried in bag or pouch or however, such as it must needs have been if it had indeed come from Normandy as it purports to. You see?" He turned the letter this way and that for everyone to view but seemed not to notice Suffolk thrusting out a demanding hand for it but instead laid it down again, his own hand firmly on it, and went on, "Therefore it follows that the paper was neither long-folded nor long-carried and therefore could not have been brought from Normandy, not by Davydd ap Rhys or anyone else. Yes?"

He asked the question generally. It was Buckingham, leaning forward over the table who answered, "Yes, but . . ."

"By your leave, my lord, if I might continue?" Bishop Pecock asked mildly and did so without pause for Buckingham's reply. "Therefore the letter must be from here, in England, not Normandy at all, and therefore at the very least the superscription is a lie."

"To mislead us," Bishop Ayscough said sharply, "into not realizing York has a secret ally here who passes word to him received from Normandy some other way."

"That's a little more complicated than need be, don't you think, my lord?" Bishop Pecock asked. "Though possible, I suppose," he granted. "But still, why shouldn't this ally simply speak to him directly rather than commit the matter to paper?"

"Because, whoever he is, he couldn't come to Westminster himself," Bishop Ayscough said. "The letter was his only way . . ."

"But the letter was written here in Westminster," Bishop Pecock said.

"That's a guess," said Suffolk.

"But it's not, my lord." Bishop Pecock sounded faintly scandalized by the thought. "It's a fact, proven by the fact that the paper bears a mark on its edge showing it came from the privy seal office, here in the palace."

York did not move but all his attention was sharply at alert now as Bishop Pecock held the paper edge on to them, turned it from Buckingham to Cromwell to Stourton to Bishop Ayscough to Suffolk to Moleyns and finally to him, saying, "You see here. That black mark on its edge. The privy seal office uses a great deal of paper which, while not so costly as parchment of course, nonetheless is costly enough not to be wasted or lost, which happens when people in need of paper sometimes take it for their own uses. To keep from such wastage, when paper is new-delivered to the privy seal's use, there is a black ink line drawn down the side of the stack, leaving a small black mark on the edge of every sheet, if you see what I mean."

Lord Cromwell demanded, "How do you come to know so much about the privy seal's paper?"

Bishop Pecock made a small, almost deprecating shrug. "One notices things, such as black marks on the edges of papers, and asks questions. I can't help it."

York, whose mind had been racing toward conclusions, said thoughtfully, as if to himself, "And Bishop Moleyns who 'has the answers he sought' is Keeper of the Privy Seal."

"Yes, indeed," Bishop Pecock said, as if that were a mildly interesting observation. "With access to as much privy seal paper as he wants, I suppose. But to return to where I was—if the letter shows no sign of having traveled far and was, in fact, written here in Westminster, it therefore did not come from Normandy. You see? Nor was it written by someone who would have to go so roundabout as to use one of York's couriers out of Normandy." He looked around the table earnestly. "You see how simple it is? Once a premise is granted—in this case, two premises, the first being that the paper is not far-traveled and the second, that it's from here—then a third premise derived from those must be granted—that the letter did not come from Normandy. Besides which, it would seem fair to consider the possibility that it was not meant for York at all, especially if no greater evidence to the contrary can be brought and I doubt that in this matter it can, so . . ."

York doubted he was the only one lost among premises, but it was Moleyns who protested, "That paper could have been stolen at anytime. Months ago even. There's no saying when or where that letter was written."

Bishop Pecock turned a benign gaze on him. "Is every stack of paper marked in the same place, time after time?"

"What? No. No one tries to do that. We just want them marked, is all."

"The mark on this sheet matches the mark on the supply presently on your head clerk's desk, to be given out as he deems necessary."

Bishop Moleyns gaped slightly, then demanded, "How do you know that?"

"I went to see, after our first meeting this morning."

"The mark proves nothing!" Bishop Ayscough said. "Not either way. Not any way. Not . . ."

He broke off, apparently well lost among Bishop Pecock's premises, but, "It raises doubts, though, where there weren't any," said Buckingham. He had a heavy-paced intelligence rather than quick, but he was fair-minded when he could manage it. For him, doubts were doubts and not to be ignored once they were raised, and York felt a stirring toward hope that this wasn't going to go all Suffolk's way after all.

"And then, of course, there's the trouble with how York's man died," Bishop Pecock said.

"There's no trouble there," Suffolk answered. "He was stabbed from behind by a thief who then robbed him and fled."

"Ah, yes. Well. I went with his body, you know, when it was taken for the crowner to view it because I thought it might be best to go on praying over him closely a while longer, his death being sudden and all. The crowner, of course, verified the cause of his death."

"It not taking much to verify a dagger-thrust from behind," York said bitterly.

"But there was more than that, you see," Bishop Pecock said. "There was also the large lump on the side of his head. The crowner commented on that, and I felt of it myself. He'd been struck very hard, I'd judge. And when he was stripped, there were large bruises to be seen around both his upper arms . . ." Bishop Pecock held up a hand, curving it as if around an arm, ". . . that large, as well as raw places rubbed into his wrists and both corners of his mouth. You see?"

At least some of them saw very clearly: Lord Stourton began swearing under his breath and York, sickened and angry, said harshly, "You're saying that the stabbing was only the last thing done to him. Before then, he was sometime hit on the head, maybe knocked unconscious, was also sometime gagged and his wrists tied. He fought against that hard enough to leave raw sores, and the bruises on his arms you're saying look as if they were made by someone holding roughly onto him."

"Or it might have been by two someones, one on either side," Lord Cromwell said.

Though he was holding it, York's anger tightened his voice. "Davydd was killed where he was found. That's certain, because of the blood. And the dagger-thrust looks to have come level at his back, as if he were standing when he was stabbed. But those other marks didn't come from any thief creeping up behind him to kill him. He'd been brought there, maybe unconscious, maybe only still gagged and bound and knowing what was happening, held up between probably two men while a third one ran him through from behind." York rose to his feet and leaned forward with fists braced on the table toward Suffolk. "His death was no chance killing. It was murder, for the sake of that letter supposedly for me being found on him here, where it could do the most damage to me."

Into the taut silence after that almost accusation, with Suffolk all too clearly naked of any reply, Bishop Pecock said mildly, "Judging by the facts as we have them, it would seem within the reaches of Reason to say so."

"Damnably right it does," Lord Stourton said forcefully. Lord Cromwell was nodding frowning agreement, his look along with Buckingham's glare turning toward Suffolk as Bishop Pecock went on, "The question then becomes . . ."

But Suffolk had regrouped enough to interrupt him warningly, "My lord bishop."

As if he suffered from deafness as well as poor eyesight, though York doubted it, Bishop Pecock went blandly on, ". . . how to close the whole matter with his grace of York cleared of the charges that I believe have already begun to spread through the palace, without making obvious what truly occurred?"

He ended on a question spread with seeming innocence among Suffolk, Ayscough, Moleyns, and the other lords, leaving it for Ayscough to say with forceful calm, "An excellent point, well taken. I think we should adjourn, though, for a time and take it up later, when we've all had time to think on it. Agreed?" he added at Suffolk, who said quickly, "Yes. Yes, I think so. This is definitely something we should take time to think on. My lords, until later?"

He was rising as he said it and on his own way out before anyone else was fully on their feet. Less hurriedly but no less firmly closing off the possibility of further talk, Ayscough and Moleyns followed him, and shortly, after a brief exchange of words with Buckingham, Cromwell, and Stourton to no particular purpose, York was alone with the Bishop of Saint Asaph's, the two of them still seated, regarding each other along the table in a full silence that finally ended with Bishop Pecock saying with soft, apologizing sadness, "There's nothing to tie them decisively to your man's death. You understand that, yes?"

"Yes," York agreed. While there was enough in all that Bishop Pecock had brought forward to discredit the letter, there was no way at all to bring Davydd's murder home to anyone— neither those who had planned it nor the men who had done it for them.

"It's your name must needs be fully cleared now, my lord, lest the taint of Moleyns's charges against you stick despite the facts being disproved. Not that they're actually Moleyns's charges against you. My lords of Suffolk and Salisbury have a large or larger hand in them, no doubt. It was simply that Moleyns has been most lately in Normandy, making it most reasonable to use his name in this, here and now. Therefore it's for him to refute what's said against you in his name, and from what little I've known of him, being myself but these two years a bishop and of the royal council but never of the most inner circles . . ."

"Raynold," York said.

Bishop Pecock broke off, blinked, gathered himself, and said, admirably to the point for a change, "Moleyns has no courage in himself. Present his charges against you in writing to King Henry. Forced to face you openly, Moleyns will dodge like a hunted hare."

York slowly nodded, seeing his point and that Suffolk and Bishop Ayscough would not say anything for risk of showing their own part in the matter too openly.

"But Davydd's death . . ." York said and stopped, frustrated.

"There's no way to bring anyone to trial for it that I can see," Bishop Pecock said with the clear feeling that if he could not see a way, there must not be one. "Countering their intents against you is the most retribution there can be."

Again York slowly nodded agreement. As vengeance went, it wasn't enough but it would have to be. They were stopped and he was safe.

For now.
Until they moved against him again.
Or he moved against them.

Author's Note

Of the named characters here, only Davydd ap Rhys is imagined. Both York's challenge to Bishop Moleyns and Moleyns's gibbered protest of innocence are on record. It was very few years afterward that Suffolk, Moleyns, and Ayscough were all murdered within a few months of each other. It was seven years more before Bishop Pecock proved too clever for other men's good and was brought down by the court faction who replaced them. Three years after that the Duke of York was killed in battle.

Plucking a Mandrake

Clayton Emery

The hunter's ears pricked to the gabble of ducks and bate of wings. From under an old blanket stuck full of sweet flag and canary grass, he watched the flock jitter across the sunset: teals, mallards, pintails, and fat graylag geese.

All afternoon Robin Hood had lain sopping wet amid tussocks of reeking marsh under his blind. With the caution of a hungry man, he nocked a bird arrow with steel spines like a hedgehog's. As he'd guessed, the weary ducks dropped toward this pond, for it was sheltered from the north wind, removed from foxes and badgers, and warmed by the southern sun. Slowly, Robin shrugged the itchy blanket from his shoulders, came to one knee, drew as he rose—

—and jumped at a cry of *"Yah yah yah!"*

Ducks exploded off the water, groping for sky, colliding and dodging and quacking. With his eye on the graylags, the outlaw loosed. Steel tines ripped the female's breast and she tumbled. Within seconds he dropped five more birds, but he'd hoped for twice that.

Cursing, Robin pushed through reeds. What bastardly fool blackguard had rousted his birds with that idiot croak?

He stopped. Dying ducks and feathers dotted the pond. Amidst them sloshed a bedraggled stick-man in a filthy smock and matted hair and beard. He seized a dying duck, stretched the neck, and bit to suck heart's blood.

117

Shocked, angered, and disgusted, Robin shouted, "Drop that, varlet! 'Tis mine!"

The man crouched, cringing, his mouth smeared with blood and feathers, eyes vacant. Robin saw a rude cross stitched to his smock: a cure for madness. The fool swatted water at Robin, hooting, "Yah, yah!" Clutching the duck, he floundered out of the pond and scuttled up the wooded slope toward the village.

Swearing, teeth chattering, Robin slogged through icy water to retrieve his ducks. Piercing the webbing on a string, he trudged up a twisted path between trees. He'd lay a few stripes on that madman. Even a dog knew better than to steal a man's game.

But shooting ducks was foolish, he decided: gigging hooks or drowning nets would gather more sooner. He needed many ducks. With Easter past and May Day looming, winter apples and rye and salt pork and herring were all eaten, and famine stalked the land. Food was so scarce in the Greenwood, he'd dispersed his band until fatter times. Not that that was why he hunted so far from home.

Muttering, dodging branches, stumbling over roots as dusk fell, absorbed, Robin bumped into a pair of dangling feet. In horror he snatched a handful of grass to scrub his face, then crossed himself repeatedly.

The dead man hung from an elm. Shrunken to a skeleton, neck stretched like a sausage, skin curdled a moldy gray, his lips were cracked, and his eyes picked out by crows and sparrows. The sockets glared at Robin in accusation.

Snatching his bow and birds, Robin Hood dashed up the trail toward the village.

SKEGBY MOOR WAS PONDS and fingers and rills and marsh and tall grass and brambles. Above the moor on low mounds rambled the village of Skegby, thirty cottages linked by muddy tracks and bridges of fallen trees. A fief of Tevershalt, a manor in the north, Skegby was old, squirreled away like a motte-and-bailey castle in the dark days of raids by blue-painted demons. The occupants

spoke in canted words and archaic idioms and had gaped at
Robin and Marian as if they were elephants from Egypt.

Yet the wattle-and-daub cottages were neat, the gardens and
patchwork fields tended. The air was ripe from privies and pigs,
yeast from the alehouse, coal smoke from the smithy, and incense
from the chapel. On the outskirts stood the cottage of a wise
woman, or witch. Robin Hood stopped running at her door.

The cottage was buried under vines and rosebushes, lapped
on all sides by a garden like a spring tide. Bees bumbled at a hive,
two brown goats rooted through chaff, and chickens scratched
for weevils. Indoors was just as crowded. Robin ducked hanging
herbs. The only furniture was a plank table crowded with pestles
and bowls and pots, a pair of stools, and a pallet that unrolled for
a bed. A white cat licked its paws by the hearth.

Fitful rushlight surrounded Marian's dark head like a halo.
She was dressed like Robin in winter-brown shirt and trousers and
greased deerhide boots. The witch was barrel-round in a faded
red gown and kirtle. A headscarf made her chapped cheeks
rounder. Her name was Rocana, an old name Robin had never
heard before.

"What's wrong, Rob?" Marian asked. "Why do you pant so?"

"Dead man." The outlaw gulped air. "On the path at the
bottom of the hill. Hanged. Walked right into him."

"Aye, a sad place to hang a man." Rocana's eyes crinkled in
sympathy. At the fireplace, she turned turnips buried in dock
leaves and ashes. "But that elm is traditional. I'm sorry, I should
have warned you. Ducks and a goose! Lovely!"

Robin shucked his sopping clothes and hung them near the
fire, then cleared a spot on the table for the ducks. Fingering a
diamond on a hen mallard's wing, Marian recited, " 'Touch blue
and your wish will come true.' "

They lopped off heads and winkled out innards while
Robin got his breath back. "What was he hanged for? Who is
he—or was he?"

"Ingram. Our local rake. Fathered half the bastards in the
parish. A poacher of sheep. The hills are full of deer and the moor
of ducks and eels, but Ingram wanted mutton. And I'd cook it for
him!" Rocana hooted. "But that half-Irish beast, Fedelm, the

bailiff, finally caught him. He always danced the Jack in the Green, too. Don't know who'll do't this year."

"It's almost May Day, isn't it?" Robin said. The first of May meant festivity, when a man donned the Jack in the Green, a cone of wicker and leaves for the forest spirit, the mythical tree man. Escorted by Green Men in face paint and leaves, and Morris dancers with sticks, and cloggers with swords, the Jack would caper while people danced after it, till the Jack was felled with swords to die and rise again, to show spring had arrived. It was Robin's favorite holiday, and he was suddenly homesick for the Greenwood.

Marian asked, "How long must he hang there?"

"Till he's ripe and falls. Like a pheasant."

"We'll have to tell our cousin, Will Scarlett. He's gallows fodder, too."

Robin carried guts to the back door to pitch them on the midden. A snuffling at the stoop jarred him. "What the hell?"

On hands and knees, the madman from the pond lapped from a wooden bowl.

"That's just Serle," Rocana called. "He drinks the milk we put out for the wee folk. They don't seem to mind."

Robin stepped around the madman, pitched the guts, and wiped his hands on mint leaves. Serle scuttled off. The outlaw huffed. Every village had an idiot: even he had Much the Miller's Son. Returning to pluck ducks, he asked, "What was Serle's offense, that God punished him so?"

Rocana seared duck breasts in a kettle, then added water from a red clay ewer. "I'll stew 'em to go farther. Serle abused his family. After a pot of ale he'd see in his poor wife and children all the demons of Hell. He pickled his brain. Now he's one with the beasts, and may God bless us all, I say."

"Beasts," Robin groused. "Better we lived like beasts. They follow God's will without questioning. Or meddling."

Marian sniffed. "Rocana says we needs stay a few days more."

"As you wish, honey," Robin sighed. "T'will let me lay in more ducks. If we can keep—Serle?—clear of the marshes."

"We can." The witch plucked herbs from the sheaves overhead and crumbled them in the stew. "I have a special way with him."

LONG AFTER DARK, THE cat lifted her head. Robin, an outlaw since boyhood, felt for his knife and checked the back exit. Something scratched at the door like a small dog.

Rocana admitted a young woman in faded brown. Her belly was swollen and her gown damp at the breasts. She carried a big baby, almost a toddler. She gasped at the witch's company and, timid as a deer, had to be coaxed inside. She sagged on a stool and relinquished her toddler to Marian, confessed that her child had stopped kicking, and was that right? While Rocana asked questions and ground herbs and seeds in a pestle, Marian cooed and kissed the baby's blonde head, inhaling its milky fragrance. Robin sat by the fire and fletched an arrow with a gray goose quill.

"Such a beautiful child." Marian touched the woman's swollen belly. "And another on the way. You're lucky."

The young woman smiled vacantly and touched her stomach. "This one's father is an angel."

"What?" Marian bobbled the infant.

The simple woman was sincere. "His father's an angel that comes in the night. He's tall and dark. This child will be doubly blessed."

"Yes . . ." Marian stroked the ash-blonde head. "I see . . ."

The cat picked up her head and scooted behind a sheaf of woodruff. Robin Hood laid his arrow on the hearth.

The door rattled and banged as a priest barged in. "Willa! You're not to come here! I've forbidden it!"

The young woman upset her stool, but Marian caught her. The priest offered no help. His dark cassock bore buttons from throat to hem and was girdled by a rosary with a wooden cross that banged his knee. His high brow, eagle's nose, and sharp cheekbones recalled a talking skull.

"And you, interloper," he snarled at Marian, "you'll not talk to this woman either!"

Robin Hood rose. "How is that your business?"

"Everything that transpires in this village is my business!"

The outlaw stifled a rising temper. Robin took clerics as he found them. Friar Tuck was poor as dirt, dedicated, and honest. The greedy Bishop of Hereford had been forced to dance in the Greenwood at arrow-point. Robin kept his voice level. "Not today."

Snorting, the priest grabbed Willa's arm. Robin Hood seized his, and the priest gasped. "Father, pray contain your zeal. The women discuss women's affairs. Men are not needed."

The priest could not wriggle free. "It's a sin to manhandle a cleric!"

Up close, Robin was distracted, for the glitter in the priest's deep eyes was somehow familiar. He brushed the thought aside. "It's man's nature to sin. I but do my part." Robin pitched the priest out the door. The man just missed rapping his head on the lintel. Robin shut the door.

Rocana swept her mix into a clay cup, then instructed Willa how to brew a tea. It took three tries. Marian surrendered the baby and Willa slipped into the night, tears of fear in her eyes. Fletching again, Robin asked, "Does the priest visit often?"

Smiling, crinkly, Rocana tidied her work table. "Alwyn's forbidden the women to come for my curings. They come anyway."

Robin licked a split feather. "What does he dislike?"

"Competition. We wrestle like boars for the same wallow. He's got his Latin and holy water and incense, I my Gaelic and magic water and herbs." She banged vessels as she worked. "We villagers are partial to harelips and webbed fingers, living on rabbits and ducks as we do, but you won't see Alwyn wield a needle or a knife! Yet he rails that I defy God's will with blasphemous magic! So when Young Gerald slashed his palm with a knife, Alwyn could only pray. I drew the blood poisoning with a sage and apple poultice and saved his arm and his life, thus defying God's will!"

The wise woman sighed. The cat rubbed against her hairy leg. "But it happens all over. Witches bein' driven out by churchmen. There're more of them, and better organized, with their bishops and councils and diets and edicts, while we're a handful of old women who pass on secrets from mother to daughter. And men are hungry as wolves. You know't, don't you, Marian? Men rule this world and women endure it."

Neither the Fox nor the Vixen of Sherwood denied it. Marian asked, "Why does Willa think her husband is an angel?"

"I let her think that. Her true husband is Serle, who's been mad more than a year. Better she's visited by an angel."

Robin Hood cleared his throat. "Rocana, if this village ever drove you out, you'd find a home in Sherwood."

The witch cocked her head like a girl. "Would I? That's very kind. But," she peered around at leaves and vines and flowers, "you can't grow a garden in the forest. And I'm rooted here the same way. Whate'er others may think, I'm part of this village."

FOR DAYS, THE WOMEN worked on Marian's "problem." Married more than a year, she had yet to conceive. Word was Rocana had cures. "Don't fret, dear. We can fix't. A good marriage is a prolific marriage."

The witch suggested many things. "Like cured like," so Robin set braided snares around clover patches, and Marian ate rabbit until she swore her ears grew. She drank tea of mugwort picked in May. For lovemaking, husband and wife slept outdoors under a rose arbor and the moon, yet with faces covered lest the moonshine drive them mad. Around their bed of blankets they scratched a six-pointed Seal of Solomon. Before and after making love, they prayed to Saint Anne. Rocana joked she had no pearls, or she'd grind one into Marian's food. And they eschewed green as unlucky for lovers.

Robin Hood chafed at probing questions. Did they have relations twice a week? Did he shed enough seed to fill the hollow of her palm? What of their families? Marian listed brothers and sisters while Robin had none, living or dead. Yes, it had taken his mother years to conceive, but how could that matter?

By day, unneeded, Robin hunted alone. Yet Marian was hopeful. One night, dreaming at the sky, she piped, "Look, Rob, a falling star! The soul of a child coming to be born! Maybe ours!"

ONE NIGHT, ROCANA WOKE Marian from their pallet, bid her dress, and gave her a knife and basket. The witch carried a frayed rope. Marian pressed her husband's shoulder to keep him abed. "Rob, stay and watch here, please?" Pleading and apologizing at the same time. Her husband neither nodded nor shook his head.

A full moon etched the world with silver light. The earth seemed blown of milky glass lit from below. The two women bustled to the dark garden, where the witch slipped the rope around the neck of a brown goat. Then the three hobbled off into the dark.

Catching up his bow and quiver, Robin followed the witch's creaking knees and wheezing. He couldn't hear Marian. They trod the path down the hill. Robin guessed their destination and muttered charms of protection, but wondered what they planned.

Like a lost scarecrow, the dead poacher Ingram hung from the elm. Under his dangling feet, Marian dug as Rocana instructed. Pressing alongside an oak, Robin watched and listened.

"I didn't think it grew in England," the young woman said. She grubbed in the soil some time. "I don't find it."

"Oh, dear. My memory's not what it used to be. . . . No, it don't grow in England. I planted it here before they hanged him. Ah, got it? Careful! Just uncover it, don't disturb it!" Rocana nickered to the goat and fumbled with the rope. "My rheumatism hates this spring damp. Slip the bight under a stub of it."

Robin hissed. Were they both mad?

"Stay! Stay! Move up the slope, dear. Stay!" Leaving the goat under the hanged man, the women backed past Robin's post without seeing him. A hundred feet up the slope, the witch warned, "Cover your ears."

Robin Hood clamped both hands to his head. Dark against dark in silver-splintered light, the goat tugged, then plodded up the slope toward its mistress. Gingerly, Robin uncovered his ears. He heard the witch reward the goat with a treat. She untied the rope and stuffed their prize into her basket.

"*Yah yah yah!*" The raucous blat split the night.

"There they are!" boomed a voice. Golden torchlight banished the silver moonlight.

Rocana muttered in Gaelic. Marian trilled, "Shall we run?"

"No, child. Stay put."

Through the trees came the priest, Alwyn, and three villagers, alike as stalks of wheat. They carried torches. Leading the pack like a dog shambled Serle, the madman. The priest's cassock and rosary flapped about his knees. Catching Serle's arm, he called, "Rocana! You dare defile the dead? You'll bring down the wrath of God with your doubly-damned blasphemy!"

"I've touched not the dead, Alwyn." The witch waved a crooked hand. "The lord's tree still bears fruit."

The priest ordered a torch held near the grotesque body. "If you don't trifle with the dead—and we may've interrupted your grisly work—what do you do at this witching hour?"

"It's none of your business," the witch snapped, "but we harvest by moonlight. Oak buds and cuckoo's pintle and such oddments."

Hidden in the dark, Robin Hood grunted. Those innocent plants were not what the goat plucked from the ground.

Unsatisfied, Alwyn refused to leave the women alone with the corpse. "Seize her! Drag her to the chapel! We'll see if she's innocent or not! Go on, grab her!"

Robin Hood startled everyone when he slipped to Rocana and planted his feet. The villagers balked, but the witch muttered, "No, let us go. We'll get this over with, once and for all."

Nonplussed, Robin didn't move. Marian tugged him away. "Watch and wait, darling. We'll make sure she suffers no harm."

The three men caught Rocana's elbows, gently, reluctantly, and avoided the basket on her arm. They escorted her up the slope after Alwyn.

Robin waggled his useless bow and squeezed his wife's hand. "I'm sorry I broke faith, honey, and spied. It's hard, but—"

His wife sniffled in the darkness. "We need help for me to conceive, Rob."

"Not that. I won't let you do it."

"Hush. We'll discuss it later."

Torchlight ringed the village chapel and common like fairy fire. Barefoot villagers streamed from their cottages, rubbing their eyes. Alwyn waved a Bible as he exhorted the crowd in a high singsong. The three men held Rocana, who waited, resigned and hardly terrified. Beside her stood the pregnant and confused Willa, wife of Serle. Beyond the crowd, in a disused byre, Robin saw the Jack, an eight-foot cone woven of wicker and thatched with prickly holly leaves for the dance on May Day.

Alwyn ranted against sin, and the villagers attended. A few men hollered agreement, some women vexed, but most just listened. This was neither sermon nor trial by ordeal but entertainment, another round in an ancient village feud. Robin Hood had seen grimmer football matches.

". . . Too long, witch, has this village tolerated your heathen interfering ways! Like the Witch of Endor, you've urged our women to wickedness! You've dealt out potions and salves that keep wives from conceiving even when visited by their husbands! You've dazzled the minds of good women and made them like drunks so men might ravish them in the fields! You've caused father to lie with daughter, brother with sister, and son with mother! You've stolen the bowels and members of babies to conjure flying potions . . ."

Rocana clucked her tongue. "Stop this rubbish, Alwyn! Everyone knows my healings, and everyone's profited by them . . ."

"Why not mount her on a horse again? Perry, fetch your cob!" a man joked. "Touch her brow with an iron knife!" jibed another. "Float her in the pond!" a woman shrilled. Even the jests were ancient.

The priest ranted, fulfilling his duty if not moving his audience. Robin Hood wondered if he were drunk. Or partly mad. Madness ran deep in this isolated hamlet . . . Suddenly, Robin gawked, realizing why the priest seemed familiar. "Marian, Alwyn is Serle's brother!"

"Yes, yes, Rob. Listen."

Robin Hood pouted. "Why do women always know these things first?"

"It demands in Exodus, 'Suffer not a witch to live!' Yet this village harbors a viper at our bosoms!" The priest raised a Bible as if he'd squash a fly, then thumped Rocana's brow. "Be condemned! Feel the fire of the holy word! Know the burning pits of Hell beckon!"

Rocana pushed at the book with feeble hands "Get that thing off me!" As she struggled, her basket upended. A knife and a dirty root thumped at the priest's feet. Alwyn pounced on the root, holding it up to catch the light. It resembled a triply forked carrot crusted with dirt.

Silence fell hard on peoples' ears. Alwyn's eyes grew feverish in the torchlight. "*This* you harvested under the gallows tree? You've done worse than *defile* the dead! You *use* them for purposes too foul to bespeak! You'll *burn* for this!"

Rocana bleated. The villagers murmured as the game took an ugly and unfamiliar turn. The priest wrung Rocana's shoulder. "There is no pit deep enough! No damnation strong enough—"

"Stop!" Rocana writhed in the priest's grip. "Unhand me, you rake! Must you paw every woman in this village—"

Quickly, Alwyn slapped her, then raised his hand again.

Quicker, Robin Hood's bow snagged the priest's wrist. "I'll break your arm, you black-bearded bastard! Don't you *dare* strike a woman!" Marian tugged her Irish knife loose in its sheath.

Maddened by his own ranting, Alwyn pointed at Marian. "You outlaw interloper! You'll suffer torments unimaginable when your wife conceives a *demon's child!*"

Growling, Robin Hood gripped the man's throat. The priest struggled as he waved the root in the air. Everyone saw it, and knew it.

Mandrake was the most ancient and mysterious of herbs. Its manlike shape let it breathe beneath the ground, where it stored up power for fertility and prophecy. Dangerous and jealous, a mandrake hugged the earth and hated to leave, so if carelessly plucked it screamed, loud and harsh to drive men mad. To harvest it, a witch tied the root to a dog or a goat, then whistled the animal from out of earshot to yank it from the ground.

"See you this?" rapped the priest. "A mandragon! A denial of God! She buried it under a dying man to soak up his seed that spilt upon strangling! And she'll compel *your* wife to purge *your* seed and insert *this* instead! Thus do *Christian* women birth *devils*—"

"Oh, no! Oh, *no, no, no!*" A soul-wrenching cry cut through even Alwyn's bellowing.

The deluded Willa pushed at her swollen belly with clumsy hands. "No, no! She said t'would make the child strong, t'would ward off the madness! Oh, get it away! Help me, Mother Mary! Get the devil child out of me!"

Villagers surged back as if from a mad dog. Rocana reached, but Willa lurched around the firelit circle, grasping at people, pleading. "Get it away, please, sweet Christ, get it away!"

No one could help, she saw. Her hand snatched at a man's belt for a knife. The blade flashed yellow in the torchlight.

"Stop her!" screamed Marian, and shoved at the crowd. Robin tangled with a man backing up. Rocana swiped at the young mother's hands.

All too late. Willa drove the blade into her low-slung belly. Transported by passion, unmindful of pain, she stabbed until blood and water gushed red and white and splashed in the dirt. She stabbed until she stumbled and fell. People screamed and howled and prayed as if the world ended.

Rocana flopped on her knees, clutched the dying woman's head, and wept. Willa's bloody hand floated toward Heaven.

Robin Hood hoicked Alwyn in the air by his cassock. "You—"

A man howled in the darkness. A woman screamed. "The Jack! It lives! It's Ingram come back! God have mercy!"

People shouted, screamed, pushed, ran. Robin fought to see and remember. What about the Jack? And who was Ingram? Then he saw.

Jerking and jigging, the Jack in the Green, a living dancing tree, thrashed and shivered as it dashed amidst the shrieking villagers. The cone's shiny leaves shimmered in the wild light as torchbearers ran hither and thither. Only Rocana kept her place, cradling the dying woman's head.

Alwyn squirmed from Robin's grasp. He fumbled his cross high to banish the evil apparition, then his nerve broke and he ran.

The crowd melted like a breaking sea wave. Despite fear and superstition boiling in his brain, Robin noticed bare feet stamped the turf under the green cone.

Sensing that the outlaws stood fast, the Jack rushed.

Shoving Marian aside, Robin snaked an arrow from his quiver, pulled to his cheek, and loosed.

The arrow slapped into the Jack, parting leaves at the height of a man's breast.

The spirit kept coming.

Superstition conquered reason. Robin hollered, "Run, Marian!" His wife had already bolted for sanctuary. Robin loped after. Marian dove into the chapel like a quail into a hedge. Robin grabbed the door and slammed it shut. In black stillness, their rasping breath was loud.

Visions whirled in Marian's mind: ghosts and fire and blood and wonder. But one picture stood out starker than the rest. "Robin—you missed!"

"What? No! I never miss!"

"He didn't go down!"

"*I never miss!*"

IT WAS HOURS BEFORE the outlaws dared peek. The moon was down, the common deserted, even the dead woman gone. The night was still, as if God had called home every man, woman, and child.

Close together and casting every which way, Robin and Marian crept down the path to Rocana's cottage. They had only starlight to see by, but they walked fast because they argued. They'd fought ever since coming to Skegby Moor, Robin reflected. What prompted all the anger in this village?

Robin's bow sliced the air as he whispered, "It's necromancy! I'll not have it, not mandrake! It goes against God's plan! It's criminal to put that—root up your—insides—"

"Women have used mandrake for centuries! It's in the Bible! Jacob's wife Rachel was barren until she asked Leah to borrow her mandrakes—"

"But plucking it under a corpse by the full moon!"

Marian hissed, "This is our only hope! Maybe the old ways—"

"You want the seed of a *dead man*? A living ghost? So you birth an imp or a changeling?"

"That's a man's help for you! Forbid everything and offer nothing in its place!"

"It's dangerous! You could go mad from the mandrake's scream! That priest was right about one thing! God's wrath has descended on us! You saw that poor woman kill herself—"

"That fool priest killed Willa, surely as if he plunged in the knife himself! Him and his wild accusations!"

"It wasn't the father, it was the witch! She duped that poor woman and the devil seized her! Retribution comes from crossing God's ways!"

"Oh, hush! You sound like these other ignorant sots! Men know more about breeding dogs than women!"

"That witch causes harm! She has a goat for a familiar—"

"A goat can't be a familiar!"

"Satan takes the form of a goat! Cloven hooves, a beard—"

"Satan's form is a *man*!"

"Oho! So it's *men* who—*Whoa!*"

Robin Hood spilled headlong over an obstacle across the path: a round springy mass of rustling leaves. Robin felt pricks along his arms and legs. "What the—These are holly—"

"It's the Jack!" Marian breathed. Now they could make out the shape, a long cone interwoven with leaves.

Robin huddled close to Marian. "Christ, look where it lies!"

Here the path split, one fork leading to Rocana's cottage, the other down the hill toward the marsh, passing under the gallows elm.

"Oh, Mother Mary . . ." squeaked Marian.

Both were reluctant to touch the fallen icon, but Robin's curiosity goaded. In the dark, he fumbled inside the wicker frame. "Nothing. Neither body nor blood. Nor arrow."

"It'd go through a ghost."

"A ghost couldn't lift this frame."

"A dead man, then."

"Then the arrow would stick him! Let's not talk of such things . . ." Robin sucked wind. "I'm going down the hill."

"I'll go with you."

"No. See if Rocana's returned. She might need guarding."

"Be careful."

"Oh, yes."

Crossing his breast, holding his bow foremost, Robin Hood wafted like a ghost down the path. In dead quiet, no night birds sang, no owls hooted. Robin crossed fingers on both hands.

Straining, he recognized the widened spot under the elm tree. The noose still dangled in place. Ingram was gone.

With a knife, the outlaw cut the rope's shank and tugged it down. The hangman's noose of thirteen turns was yanked almost closed. Robin Hood shuddered.

Noose in hand, he dashed up the slope.

The door of the witch's cottage hung open. A rush lamp flickered on the worktable, and he was grateful for the light and life. But something made him stumble at the threshold, a bad sign, and he snapped his fingers to dispel ill luck.

The place stank, he realized, rank and cold and brassy.

The worktable was bare. Pottery shards and herbs littered the floor. Ashes were scattered like snow. The stools were knocked over. The back door hung at an angle. Marian sat on the hearth, tears on her cheeks. Hard by the fireplace lay the squat shape of Rocana. Deep blue fingerprints marred her throat.

Wordlessly, the outlaw held up the noose. By rushlight they saw the tiny noose was foul with grime and sloughed skin.

"So it's true!" Marian breathed. "Ingram came back—"

"Hist! Don't say his name! You'll call him hither!"

Marian rose to shrink against her husband's chest. "The hanged man, then, the poacher! He got down off one tree and climbed into another! He donned the Jack to dance again! To take revenge on the village! The dead taunting the living! Oh, sweet Lord!"

Reaching under Robin's arms, Marian made the sign of the cross at the doors. "So much death in this village. It's in the air, like contagion. Maybe we should leave."

"Yes. With the dawn."

YET THEY STAYED, FOR with the sun came work to be done.

Father Alwyn refused to administer last rites for Rocana, or to hold a vigil, or to bury her in the chapel graveyard. Pagans could rot, he said, as offal for dogs. And he had Willa's funeral to minister. So Robin and Marian sank Rocana in the garden she'd loved, and entwined a wooden cross with yellow cowslips.

Warned off by the priest, most villagers stayed away. The few women who came crossed themselves as they talked. They'd all seen the abandoned Jack. They guessed dead Ingram murdered Rocana because she'd berated him for fathering bastards. And the dead resented the living. Ingram killed Rocana the same as he'd died, by strangling. At every Mass, Alwyn preached that "one sinner had fetched away another." No one, they reported, ventured out after dark.

Each night, as Robin barred the doors, he cut a fresh cross in the wood.

Ducks winged in, and Robin needed meat, so for days the archer netted and hooked and shot birds, then dressed them, smoked their breasts over a low fire, and packed them. The birds' numbers dwindled as the flocks nested in summer grounds farther north.

In spare moments, Robin returned to the common, to sight, pace, and crawl with his nose to the ground. Finally, he discovered his arrow buried in dirt lengthwise. It lay yards from where he'd shot it. When he plucked it free, he learned why. It lacked a red hen feather.

Back at the cottage, he showed Marian. "See? I didn't miss. This arrow passed through something that skinned off this fletch. That made it hook sharp to the right."

Marian pricked a chicken strung over the fire. "I see, Rob. I was wrong to think you'd missed. Yet the villain inside the Jack was dead. No arrow could stop him." She crossed her breast.

Robin grunted, but added, "Still, I didn't miss."

"Here. I've found something queer, too. I tried sorting herbs and seeds, but without Rocana's knowledge, they might as well be oak leaves. Yet I discovered this." She fetched a small stone crock that held a pale yellow dust. "Mandrake root."

"So?"

"Mandrake's rare, Rob. It only grows in the Holy Land. Rocana, may she find peace, claimed to have only a single whole root that she never cut. Yet here's a handful ground fine."

"Why would she lie?"

"I don't know. We all have secrets. Wash your hands."

They sat down to chicken roasted with sage and onions and a pitcher of goat's milk. "Drink up. It's the last. The bailiff collected the heriot and the mortuary, the death taxes. The best goat went to the lord and the second-best to the priest. We get the cat."

"She'll hardly make a meal."

"At least we don't need the milk. Serle hasn't returned for his bowlful since the witch died. He must scent death, like a dog."

"Or else he misstepped in the marsh and sank. Or was also killed by the vengeful dead man." Robin stopped chewing. "Do you suppose Serle might've killed Rocana, may she rest in peace? A madman can do anything."

"Why should he harm her? She fed him milk every night at the stoop. Even mad, he'd remember kindness."

"Poor dead Willa, may she rest easy, was his wife. She must have fed him when they were wed, but that didn't spare her beatings."

"I'd offer that Alwyn, the priest, killed her out of spite!" Marian threw chicken skin to the cat. " 'Like people, like priest,' and he's the most hateful man in the village!"

"Why should Alwyn kill her?" The outlaw plied his knife. "They feuded, but that went back years. And Alwyn wouldn't have wrecked the cottage."

"He's almost mad as his brother. The whole family's cursed by bad blood. And Alwyn has a temper. Once he saw that mandrake root, he turned vicious as a mad dog! He struck Rocana and bellowed about women birthing demons! The filthy hypocrite! Remember how he accused Rocana of bedazing women to be ravished?"

"I think so." Robin scratched his beard with a knife point. "He ranted about many things."

"What do you always say? 'A man accuses others of what he practices? A thief is quickest to say he's robbed, a cheat to say he's cheated'?"

"So . . . you think the priest bewitches women and ravishes them?"

"No, I think he promises Heaven and threatens Hell until they lie down."

"A woman shouldn't listen to a man," the husband mumbled. "Some reckon it's no sin to sleep with a priest. Some women think it's lucky!"

"How long has Serle been afflicted mad?"

"Hunh?" Robin's mouth was stuffed with chicken.

"More than a year, according to Rocana." Marian waved a drumstick. "Yet Willa bore only seven months. Serle didn't get her with child. And neither did mandrake root."

"So . . . wait. The *priest* bedded Willa? Christ on the cross, he can't do that! She's his brother's wife! That's incest!"

Marian nodded. "Another sin that he laid at Rocana's feet. He accused her of luring father to lay with daughter, and brother with sister, and mother with son."

"While Father Alwyn was lying with his sister-in-law!" Robin shook his head. "Pitiful Jesus, an incestuous priest! What would a bishop do? Castrate him?"

"Nothing. No one would tell. This village is like a family. It keeps it secrets close."

"Hang on. *Everyone* knows Alwyn fathered his brother's wife's child?"

"All the women know. 'Who's the father?' is the first question a woman would ask."

"*Incest?*"

"It's thick as fleas in this village, Rob. See you, how they all look alike? See the harelips and webbed toes and simple minds? Poor Willa, may she rest in peace, thought a dark angel visited her by night. Rocana, may she lie quiet, let her believe it."

"Still," Robin sighed, "men need a priest, same as they need a king."

"Men, yes. Women, no."

"Marian!"

"It's true! Men need a priest to absolve them of sins, but what can they do for women? When a woman's screaming in child-birth, can a priest put a knife under the bed to cut the pain or brew a broth of asparagus and chestnuts and fennel? Men work women harder than oxen. They kill them slowly with too many babies. The graveyards are full of three wives for every dead husband. Women cherish the old ways, because women don't need God! They need other women!"

"Jesus, Marian, you'll draw down lightning! I'll agree if you wish't. But a priest should tend spiritual matters and the witch secular ones. A wise woman shouldn't interfere in God's plans—"

"*It was God who made me barren! And with Rocana dead, I'll stay that way!*" Suddenly, Marian was sobbing. Robin reached to comfort, but she pulled away. "Just . . . leave me alone . . ."

Robin took his bow outside. The moonlit sky was strung with wisps blown from the north. "One way or another, we each dig our own grave."

DAYS LATER ROBIN SLOGGED knee-deep through tea-colored water after a dropped pintail. He stumbled against something lodged in duckweed.

A dead man bubbled up, gurgled, and belched gas. He had no head, just a gnawed stump tipped with the white dice of a spine.

Retching, Robin Hood slopped from the water and stumbled up the hill. The hell with ducks. He wanted out of this ghastly village. He and Marian had sought new life and found only death.

And nightmares that repeated. In back of the cottage, the madman Serle raided his smoking racks. The outlaw barked, "Hoy, get away!"

The madman clawed hair from his eyes and croaked, "I'm hungry! A man's got a right to eat!"

Robin stopped cold. Serle was filthy and ragged, but upright, pouty, and arrogant. His old self. "You're sane!"

"What of 't?"

Marian came to the doorway. Serle turned. Robin plucked a fleck of red from his coarse smock. "My hen feather! It was *you* in the Jack! You bent over and ran with it, so my arrow skinned your back! Why'd you do it?"

"The Jack saved Rocana from the trial by ordeal!" Marian was breathless. "Was that why, Serle? Because she'd been kind to you?"

"Hardly!" retorted Robin. "He dumped the Jack on the path to her cottage! My, God! *You* killed her!"

"I din't kill no one!" Dizzy and dazed, Serle sputtered. "I din't—"

Something flickered on the path to the gallows tree that caught Robin's eye. He saw Alwyn drop a sack and run. Wondering, Robin fetched the sack and found bread, cheese, and a jug of ale.

" 'The guilty flee where none pursueth.' " Robin ran after the priest. Marian caught up, loping like a deer.

Robin yelled, "That Alwyn is a two-faced lying hypocrite! That night, when everyone scattered before the Jack, he went searching for Serle and found he'd strangled the witch! He couldn't let his brother take the blame, so he dragged the Jack across the path to the gallows tree. He ripped down Ingram's body—popped the head right off!—and stuffed him in the pond to make him disappear! Then he shooed Serle into the marsh to hide! He's been taking him food, which is why Serle doesn't come sniffing for milk at the stoop. Alwyn blamed Rocana's murder on a dead man!"

They found the chapel barred and shuttered. Villagers clustered around twittering. Marian nodded at the door. "Break it down."

"What? A church?"

"Quickly, Rob."

Robin Hood handed Marian his bow. "Some men put faith in God, others in their wives." He ran shoulder-first and smashed the door, backed and bashed again until the bracket tore free.

Inside, Robin and Marian gasped. Another hanged man dangled, but this one wriggled and writhed.

Marian thrust the longbow at Robin. "Shoot him down!"

Alwyn, parish priest of Skegby Moor, swung by his neck. His hands clawed at a hemp rope sunk deep into his throat. A wooden cross lay tumbled on the dirt floor where he'd jumped off the altar.

The greatest archer in the England nocked, drew, and loosed. The arrow sliced the jerking rope. The priest crashed with a bone-jangling jolt. Robin and Marian knelt and tugged loose the noose, yet Alwyn remained blue. His hands flapped. Robin cursed. "His windpipe's crushed. He's finished."

"Strangled same as Ingram, same as Rocana." Marian called loudly, "Alwyn! You're dying! You needs confess! You killed Rocana, didn't you?"

The priest's eyes bugged at the ceiling, or Heaven beyond. He nodded.

"What?" Robin barked. "*He* killed Rocana?"

"And has hanged himself as punishment. Serle could tell the truth now. Alwyn made Serle hide in the marsh because Serle witnessed *Alwyn* strangle Rocana! But why did you kill her?"

"She drove—" a harsh whisper "—my brother—mad with— her witchments! Plucked—mandrake—when he was—nearby! The scream—drove him mad!"

"But now he's sane again!"

"I—saw."

From the doorway where villagers gaped, the scruffy brother shuffled up. Crying, he said, "Wyn . . ."

The childhood name tugged tears from the priest. His lips formed the word. "How?"

Marian began to cry. "It *was* mandrake root that drove Serle mad, but *not* by its scream. By milk. Women sip drams of mandrake when birthing because it fogs the mind and dulls pain. Rocana ground some root fine and fed it to Serle in goat's milk. One strong taste masks another. The potion banished Serle's reason."

"But *why* did she?" asked Robin.

Marian flung out a hand. "Serle terrorized his poor wife! He beat Willa without mercy! But he was shielded from justice by his brother's office. Rocana was just an old woman, but she had potions, so dosed him daily at her stoop. It rendered him harmless as a dog. But since Rocana's been dead these nine days, Serle's mind has cleared. You killed Rocana for the wrong reason, Alwyn, but it brought your brother back, damn him."

The priest sagged. "God—forgives."

Half-dazed by events, Robin Hood fetched a bowl of holy water. He knelt over the priest and dipped his finger to absolve the man—

Hissing, Marian slapped the bowl away. Holy water splashed and soaked into the dirt floor.

"Marian!" Robin was shocked. "He'll die unshriven!"

"Let him!"

"He confessed!"

"It's not enough! Look at him!" Tears spilled down Marian's cheeks. "He has no remorse! Never a word for poor Willa, his own sister-in-law, raped and deceived and degraded! Not a word for his bastard child, killed by his own words that made a deluded mother rip open her belly! No regrets for a harmless witch strangled! No regrets for the child I'll never have! Let him burn in Hell!"

Robin Hood stood tall over his wife, the back of his hand to his mouth. "God help us all, then."

Ⅎ Gift from God

Edward Marston

England, 1371.

Nobody had told him how beautiful she was. When he heard about her reputation as a weaver of spells, he imagined that she would be an ugly old crone who lived in some hovel, with only a mangy cat or a flea-bitten dog for company. Instead, much to his astonishment and pleasure, Catherine Teale was a handsome woman in her late twenties, alert, bright-eyed, and glowing with health. Her attire was serviceable rather than costly, but it enhanced her shapely figure. Hugh Costaine was duly impressed. As he reined in his horse, he gave her a smirk of admiration.

"*You* are the sorceress?" he said in surprise.

"No, sir," she replied with a polite shake of her head. "There is no sorcery involved in what I do. I have a gift, that is all."

"You have many gifts, as I can see."

Costaine leered at her. He was a tall, sharp-featured man, little above her own age but coarsened by debauchery that added a greyness to his beard and a decade to his appearance. As befitted the eldest son of Sir Richard Costaine, lord of the manor of Headcorn, he was wearing the finest array and riding a spirited black stallion. Catherine was about to go into the house when he accosted her. She had just returned from a walk across the fields to gather herbs. Costaine feasted his eyes on her.

"I need your help," he said at length.

"It is yours to command, sir."

"Prepare me a flask of poison. Something swift and venomous. Our stables are overrun with rats, and I would be rid of them."

"Then you must look elsewhere," Catherine suggested. "I do not make potions to end life, only to preserve it. I medicine the sick. That is my calling."

"If you can cure, you can also kill," he insisted. "I'll not be balked. Now, get into the house and mix what I require."

"I do not know how to, sir."

"Hurry, woman!"

"There is no point."

Costaine angered. "You deny my request?"

"It has been brought to the wrong person."

"But I heard many tales about you. They say that you practice sorcery. That you conjure spirits out of the air to help you."

"Idle gossip. Do not believe it."

"Too many mouths praise your skills."

"Skills of healing. Nothing more."

"Unnatural skills. Deeds of wonder. Magic. No more of this evasion," he ordered, dismounting to confront her. "I have ridden five miles on this errand. I need that poison forthwith. Fetch it at once."

He was close enough to appreciate her charms even more now. Her face was gorgeous, her skin luminous. Catherine exuded a scent that was almost intoxicating. Costaine inhaled deeply. Lust stirring, he gave her an oily grin and took a step nearer.

"You will be well-paid," he promised her. "Give me what I seek, and I will reward you with a kiss. A hundred of them." He reached out, but she eluded his grasp. He chuckled. "Do you find me so repellent?"

"No, sir."

"Then why keep me at bay? Is it to whet my appetite?"

"I would never do that."

"Not even to please me?"

"Not even then, sir."

"Do you know who I am?" he boasted. "And what I am?"

"Yes, sir."

"Well?"

"You are the son of Sir Richard Costaine, an honest gentleman and a courteous knight who would never show such a lack of gallantry."

"To hell with gallantry!" he retorted, snatching her by the arm. "You dare to refuse me? I'll have more than a kiss from you for that. When you have made my flask of poison, I'll have a sweeter potion from you in a bedchamber."

"But I am married, sir," she protested.

"What does that matter? So am I."

"You would take me against my will?"

"Of course not, lady," he said with a snigger. "I will woo you like any lovesick swain. Now, do as I tell you, and be swift about it."

As Costaine released her arm, a figure emerged from the house. Adam Teale was a big, broad-shouldered man in his thirties. He ambled across to them with an easy smile, but his eyes were watchful.

"What is the trouble, sir?" he asked. "I heard raised voices. Has my dear wife upset you in any way?"

"Yes," snarled the other. "She is trying to thwart me."

"Catherine would not do that without cause, sir. I am Adam Teale, the vintner, and I can vouch for my wife's good temper. There never was a gentler or kinder woman." He loomed over Costaine. "What is it that you want, sir? Perhaps I can help you."

"It's not wine that I'm after, vintner. It's poison."

"Then you've wasted your journey, sir. Only wholesome liquid is on sale here. Your father has been pleased to buy it from me on occasion."

"Enough of my father!"

"Does he know why you have come?"

"That is nothing to do with you," said the visitor, dismissively. He turned back to Catherine. "Will you obey me or will you not?"

She gave a shrug. "I have told you, sir. I do not concoct poison."

"It is true," her husband added. "Such gifts as my wife possesses are put to the relief of pain and sickness. You must search elsewhere."

Hand on the hilt of his sword, Costaine squared up to him, but Adam Teale met his gaze without flinching. He was not afraid of his belligerent visitor. Costaine was livid. Not only was he being turned away without the potion he sought, he was being deprived of the joys of ravishing the comely wife. They were two good reasons for his hatred to smolder. He vowed to exact revenge.

"A vintner, are you, Master Teale?" he sneered.

"And proud of my trade," Adam said.

"Take care your wine is not tainted by this sorceress you married."

"Catherine is a devout Christian."

Hugh Costaine let out a sudden laugh and mounted his horse.

"We shall see about that!" he cried.

As the visitor rode away, Adam put a protective arm around Catherine's shoulders. She planted a grateful kiss on his cheek.

"Did I arrive at the right moment?" he said.

"Oh, yes," she answered, fondly. "You always do."

AGNES HUCKVALE SAT DUTIFULLY beside her husband throughout the meal. He was in an expansive mood, loud, laughing, boastful, generous with his hospitality, and flushed with wine to the point where he kept shooting sly and meaningful glances at his wife. Agnes could no longer remember if she had ever loved Walter Huckvale. She had been struck by his wealth and impressed by his military feats, but she could not recall if her heart had really opened to him. It seemed so long ago. Agnes had been barely sixteen when she married a man who was well over twice her age. The gap between them had steadily widened and it was not only measured in years. Walter Huckvale pounded the table with his one remaining hand.

"More wine!" he called.

"You have already drunk more than your fill," warned his wife.

"I could never do that, Agnes." He looked around the empty tables through bleary eyes. "Where are our guests?"

"They retired to bed."

"So soon? Why did they not bid their host adieu?"

Agnes sighed. "They did, Walter, but you were too caught up in your memories to listen to them. When our guests took their leave, you were still fighting the Battle of Poitiers."

"And Crècy," he reminded her. "I won true renown at Crècy. It was at Poitiers that I lost my arm."

"You told us the story. Several times."

"It bears repetition."

The grizzled old warrior jutted out his chin with pride. A servant arrived with a jug of wine and poured some into his goblet. He did not offer any to Agnes. The servant bowed and left the room. Husband and wife sat amid the remains of the banquet, their faces lit by the flames of a hundred candles. Walter Huckvale sipped his wine and became playful.

"Let them go," he said. "I would be alone with my wife."

"I am tired."

"Then let me rouse you from your tiredness."

"It is too late an hour."

"Nonsense!" he announced, taking a long swig from his goblet. "I'll soon rekindle your spirits. Have you ever known me to fail, Agnes?"

He thrust his face close to her, and she caught the stink of his breath. There was no point in trying to contradict him. She had pledged obedience at the altar, and there was only one escape from that dread commitment. Agnes was doomed to suffer his bad breath, his coarse manners, his drunkenness, his bursts of rage, and his interminable reminiscences of military campaigns. Worst of all, she had to enjoy the random brutality of his love-making. It was an ordeal.

Huckvale remembered something, and an accusatory stare came into his eyes. Putting down his goblet, he reached out for her wrist.

"Where have you been all day?" he asked, sternly.

"Here."

"That's not true. I wanted you this afternoon, and you could not be found. You sneaked off somewhere, didn't you?"

"No, Walter."

"Yes, you did. Where was it?"

"You're hurting my wrist," she complained.

He tightened his grip. "Tell me, Agnes."

"I was in the garden, that is all."

"Where *were* you?" he roared.

But the question went unanswered. As the words left his tongue, they were followed by a gasp of sheer agony. Releasing her wrist, he went into a series of convulsions, his eyes bulging, his face purple, his whole body wracked with pain. Walter Huckvale put a hand to his stomach and looked appealingly at his wife. Then he pitched forward on to the bare wooden table, knocking his goblet to the floor with a clatter. Agnes drew back in horror. It was minutes before she was able to cry for help.

THE SHERIFF CAME TO arrest her with four armed men at his back, a show of strength that was quite unnecessary but which deterred her husband from any intervention. Catherine Teale was bewildered.

"What is my crime?" she wondered.

"Witchcraft," the Sheriff said.

"I am no witch, my lord."

"That remains to be proved, Mistress Teale."

"Who laid the charges against me?"

"Hugh Costaine. He traces the murder to your door."

"Murder?" echoed Catherine in alarm.

"Walter Huckvale was poisoned to death last night. It is alleged that you slew him by means of a venomous brew in his wine."

"How can that be, my lord sheriff?" Adam Teale asked. "I do not provide the wine for Walter Huckvale's table."

The Sheriff was sarcastic. "And why might that be?"

"He and I fell out over an unpaid bill."

"Yes, Master Teale. Harsh words were exchanged between you and Walter Huckvale. There were many witnesses. I can understand why you wanted to get back at him, but you lacked the means to do so." He turned to Catherine. "Your wife, however, did not. Because he refused to buy from you, she cast a spell on the wine he got elsewhere. She made him pay in the most dreadful way. He suffered the torments of Hell."

"That is a monstrous allegation!" Adam exclaimed.

"It is one that Mistress Teale must face. Be grateful that I do not arrest you on a charge of complicity. If I did not know you to be so upright and decent a man, I would suspect you had some part in this."

"No!" Catherine said firmly. "Take me alone, my lord. My husband is not implicated in any way."

"You confess your guilt, then?" demanded the Sheriff.

"I protest my innocence!"

"You will be examined by Bishop Nigel."

"So be it."

Catherine silenced her husband's protests with a patient smile. There was no point in incurring the sheriff's anger. Adam was as baffled by the charge as she was, but it was important that one of them remained at liberty. Catherine submitted to the indignity of having her hands tied then she was lifted onto the spare horse that had been brought for her. As the little cavalcade pulled away from him, Adam Teale bit his lip in exasperation. He remembered the parting words of Hugh Costaine. Evidently, their unwelcome visitor had spread his own brand of poison.

BISHOP NIGEL WAS A wiry little man in his sixties with a bald head that was covered with a network of blue veins and a pair of watery eyes. His voice was quiet but tinged with irritation. Several hours of interrogation had produced nothing but calm answers from the prisoner. Nigel was annoyed that he had not yet broken her spirit. They were alone together in a fetid cell, but it was the manacled Catherine Teale who bore herself with equanimity in the foul conditions. Perspiration glistened on the prelate's brow. He resumed his examination.

"Are you in league with the Devil?" he hissed.

"No, my lord bishop. I am married to the best man alive."

"Then your husband is part of this conspiracy."

"There *is* no conspiracy," she assured him.

"Adam Teale had a disagreement with Walter Huckvale."

"My husband has a disagreement with anyone who does not pay his bill. That is only right and proper. I seem to remember that he once had a mild altercation with your own steward when an account was left unsettled, but he did not wish to poison you, my lord bishop."

"Heaven forbid!"

"Adam had no *reason* to strike at Walter Huckvale."

"That is why you took retribution upon yourself. Do not deny it, Mistress Teale. Worrying reports about you have been coming in to me for several months now. I can no longer ignore them. You have been covertly engaged in sorcery." Bishop Nigel consulted the document in his hand, angling it to catch the light from the candle. "I have a full record of your nefarious activities here."

"Has anyone laid a complaint against me?"

"I lay a complaint," he snapped. "On behalf of the Church. I am enjoined by God to drive out the Devil."

"A worthy purpose but hardly relevant here."

"Is it not true that you cured an old woman from Pluckley of an ague that threatened to kill her? Is it not true that you brought a stillborn baby back to life in Marden by laying-on of hands? And is it not true that you helped to trace a man who had been missing from his home in Staplehurst for over a week?"

"I willingly admit all these things."

"Then your witchcraft is established!" he said, triumphantly.

"How?" she challenged. "A herbal compound cured the old woman in Pluckley. Such a mixture as any physician would prescribe. As for the stillborn child, it had never really been dead. It needed only some love and prayer to bring it fully to life. Most midwives would have done exactly as I did."

"And the man from Staplehurst?"

"He was a woodcutter, dazed when the bough of a tree chanced to fall on him. He wandered off, lost his bearings, and could not find his way back. I sensed that he had found his way to Maidstone."

"*Sensed?*"

"Yes, my lord bishop."

"What evil powers enabled you to do that?"

"They are not evil, or the result would not have been so good."

"Do not bandy words with me!"

"When people come to me for help, I give it to them."

"By means of sorcery."

"By means of my gift."

"And from whom does that come?"

"From the same source as your own—from God Almighty."

Her voice was so earnest and her manner so sincere that he was checked for an instant. Bishop Nigel had to remind himself that he was in the presence of a witch, clever enough to dissemble, cunning enough to assume whatever shape she wished. He was engaged in a tussle with the Devil and must not relax his hold.

"Hugh Costaine alleges that you know how to mix poison."

"My whole life is dedicated to healing."

"Unless you wish to strike at your husband's enemies."

"Adam has no enemies. Just one or two awkward customers. As it happens, your own steward was far more of a nuisance than Walter Huckvale. He claimed that the bill had been paid. And much more wine was sent to your palace than to—"

"Forget my steward!" barked the other. "He is immaterial."

"The point still holds."

"The only thing that holds in my view is the allegation from Hugh Costaine that you boasted about your skill in concocting vile poisons. You claimed that you could turn fine wine to foul simply by casting a spell. Why gainsay it? Hugh Costaine has sworn as much on the Bible."

"Bring that same Bible here and I will swear on Holy Scripture that I am innocent of this charge. I have nothing to do with this murder."

"But you do admit that you saw Hugh Costaine recently?"

"Yes, my lord bishop. He called at the house."

"And you discussed poison?"

"I made it clear to him that I had no means of making it."

"That is not what he says."

"Then it is a question of my word against his."

"His allegation is buttressed by this list of your crimes," said the Bishop, waving the document at her. "I have mentioned only three cases of your witchcraft so far. Over two dozen are recorded here."

"Have any of the people I helped spoken against me?"

"They dare not."

"Because they have no cause."

"Because you put the fear of death into them."

Bishop Nigel took a deep breath. He was about to launch into a recital of her alleged misdeeds, when a key grated in the lock and the oak door swung back heavily on its hinges. A tall, stately figure entered. Sir Richard Costaine was an older version of his son, but he had none of the latter's arrogance or marks of dissipation. Instead, he was a symbol of nobility, a distinguished soldier who had fought beside the Black Prince and a man who was renowned for his fair-mindedness. He glanced at Catherine with a mixture of apology and apprehension, not knowing whether to release her or accuse her of further villainy.

"Has your examination been completed?" he asked.

"Not yet, Sir Richard," said Bishop Nigel, airily. "The creature was on the point of capitulation when you interrupted us. Why have you come? Is something amiss?"

"I'm afraid that it is, Bishop Nigel. My son has disappeared."

"Disappeared?"

"He has not been seen all day. Nobody has any idea where he can be. A search has been organized, but there is no sign of Hugh." His eye traveled to Catherine. "I hope that this is not your doing, Mistress."

She was adamant. "I give you my word that it is not, Sir Richard."

"Do not be misled," warned the prelate, wagging a finger. "If she is capable of casting a spell on Walter Huckvale's wine, she has the power to work her evil on your son."

"When my hands are manacled?" she said, reasonably. "What sorcery can I practice when I am locked up here? You have been with me since this morning, my lord bishop. Your holiness would quell any evil spirits. Though, in truth, there are none here to quell."

Bishop Nigel snorted. "I beg leave to doubt that."

"How did Hugh mysteriously vanish?" Sir Richard asked.

"Not by any sorcery," returned Catherine.

"He should have been here hours ago. It is my wife's birthday. Nothing would keep him away from the celebrations. Hugh has his faults, but he loves his mother dearly. I suspect foul play."

"So do I," decided the bishop. "Hatched in this very cell."

Catherine Teale shook her head and gave a gentle smile.

"No evil has befallen your son, Sir Richard," she announced. "That I can tell you. Hugh Costaine is alive and well."

"Then where is he?" said the anxious father.

"I do not know. But I could help you to find him."

"How?"

"By using my gift."

"Do not trust her, Sir Richard!" warned the bishop. "The only gifts she possesses are for witchcraft and dissimulation."

"I find it difficult to accept that, Bishop Nigel."

"Look at the facts. Her husband argues with a customer, and the man's wine is poisoned. Your son accuses her, and she casts a spell on him. There are clear connections here. We are dealing with cause and effect."

"Are we?" Sir Richard said doubtfully. "I am not so sure. Could we not simply be looking at two coincidences?" He regarded Catherine with a mixture of curiosity and embarrassment. "I am sorry that you have been treated so harshly, Mistress Teale. When a serious charge is laid against you, it must be answered but I would have thought this interrogation could have been conducted in better surroundings than these." He wrinkled his nose in disgust. "You say that you can find my son."

"I can try, Sir Richard."

"By what means?"

"By sensing where he might be."

"*Sensing?*"

"That word again!" exclaimed the bishop.

"Let me touch something belonging to your son," she said. "A garment, a weapon, a personal item of some kind. It will help me in my search. Could you bring such a thing to me, Sir Richard?"

"I will do more than that, Mistress Teale. I will take you to my house and let you examine all of Hugh's wardrobe."

"But she is being held as a prisoner," complained Bishop Nigel.

"The sheriff will release her into my care when he understands the situation. We are in extremity here, Bishop Nigel. My wife is beside herself with fear. So is Hugh's own wife. They are both certain that he has met a dreadful fate. We want him back to celebrate what should be a happy occasion for the whole family. Hugh is missing. If Mistress Teale can find him for us," he added, soulfully, "we will believe that she really does have a gift from God."

GLAD TO BE RESCUED from her imprisonment, Catherine rode the short distance to Headcorn with Sir Richard Costaine at her side. The house was in a state of mild uproar when they arrived. Everyone was firmly convinced that Hugh was the victim of some attack. It was felt that he was such a strong and capable man that only violence could prevent his return. It was the hapless wife for whom Catherine felt most sympathy. The tearful Isabella Costaine still loved her husband enough to be blinded to his blatant shortcomings. When she heard that the visitor was there to aid the search, she begged Catherine to find her missing spouse soon.

Sir Richard calmed the household then led his companion off to the private apartments used by his son and his wife. Catherine was given ready access to Hugh Costaine's wardrobe. When she saw the apparel he was wearing at the time of his confrontation with her, she gave a mild shudder. Then she reached out to take the rich material in her hands. Closing her eyes, she let her fingers play with the mantle until she felt a distinctive tingle. She raised her lids once more.

"We must ride toward Sutton Valence," she said.

"But what would Hugh be doing there?" wondered Sir Richard.

"I do not know, but that is where I am being guided."

"By what? A voice? A sign?"

"By instinct."

Within a few minutes, their horses were cantering out of the courtyard. Four men-at-arms acted as an escort. Catherine was a good horsewoman, and they covered the ground at a steady pace. It was only when they reached the woods that she raised a hand to bring them to a halt. After looking all around, she elected to strike off to the right, nudging her mount forward so that it could pick its way through the trees. Sir Richard was directly behind her, trying to control a growing skepticism. Could a vintner's wife really have divine gifts? Or was he being led on a wild-goose chase?

When they came to a clearing, Sir Richard's doubts fled at once. Tethered to a bush was a black stallion, cropping the grass contentedly.

"It is my son's horse!" he said, dismounting.

Catherine nodded. "I expected to find a clue of some sort here."

"But what about Hugh himself?"

"We still have some way to go before we reach him," she said. "This is only the start. The first signpost, so to speak. But it shows that we are on the right track."

"Where do we go next, Mistress Teale?"

Catherine closed her eyes and was lost in meditation for a few minutes. When she came out of her trance, she spoke with certainty.

"We must continue on the road to Sutton Valence."

"How far?"

"I will know when we reach the spot, Sir Richard."

"And will Hugh be there?"

"Not this time."

Sir Richard Costaine mounted his horse then went back to rejoin his men, towing his son's stallion behind him by its rein.

Catherine paused in the clearing long enough to notice the little wine flagon that was all but concealed behind a bush. It was the sign she wanted.

The six of them rode on until they came to a fork in the road. Without hesitation, Catherine struck off to the left and followed a twisting track down a steep hill and on through a stand of elms. When they emerged from the trees, the track petered out beside a stream. Catherine indicated a tall pile of brushwood, a short distance away on the opposite bank.

"The trail leads to that dwelling," she explained.

"What dwelling? I see nothing but a heap of old wood."

"That is where he lives, Sir Richard."

"Who?"

"Thomas Legge."

"What manner of man would live in such a place?"

"A strange one."

"You know the fellow?"

"Only by repute."

They crossed the stream and headed along the opposite bank. As they got closer, they could see a thin wisp of smoke emerging from the top of the brushwood. A small dog suddenly leaped out and yapped at them. The noise brought Thomas Legge out of his lair. The entrance to his little home was so low that he had to crawl out on his hands and knees. The newcomers looked down at the bedraggled old man who peered up at them with suspicion. Thomas Legge seemed to be more animal than human, a misshapen creature with white beard and hair that were grimed with filth. He scrambled to his feet and kicked his dog into silence. His speech was slurred, his tone unwelcome.

"What do you want?" he growled.

"We need your help," Catherine explained. "This is Sir Richard Costaine, and we have come in search of his son."

"He's not here," Legge said. "Nobody's here but me."

"But I believe he came here." She pointed to the black stallion. "On that horse. Do you recognize the animal?" Legge gave a reluctant nod. "I thought so. He came in search of something, didn't he?"

"That's private," grunted the old man.

"Not if it concerns my son," Sir Richard said sharply. "Keep a civil tongue in your head, or you'll feel the flat of my sword. We want answers."

"I think I can give you one of them," Catherine ventured. "Your son came here to buy some rat poison. True or false, Thomas Legge?"

"True," Legge mumbled.

"He told you that his stables were overrun with rats, didn't he?"

"But they're not," Sir Richard said. "We keep too many dogs to have any trouble with vermin. Hugh knows that." He glared at the old man. "Is that what my son told you? We were plagued by rats?"

"Yes," agreed Legge.

"Did you give him the poison there and then?" Catherine asked.

"No. It took a long time to mix."

"So what happened?"

"He told me a man would come to fetch the poison that same afternoon. I had it ready. The man paid me."

"Who was the man?" said Sir Richard.

Legge gave a shrug. "No idea."

"Which direction did he come from?"

"I can tell you that, Sir Richard," Catherine said. "We have learned all that we can here. Follow me." She swung her horse around and led the party away.

Watching the group leave, Thomas Legge scratched his head in surprise. Why was he so popular all of a sudden? He could go for weeks without seeing anyone, yet he had had two visits already that day. He did not much care for the lady with her armed escort. His first visitor was much more preferable. Climbing back into his lair, he reached for the flagon of wine that the man had left him by way of reward. He took a long, satisfying swig.

IT TOOK THEM ONLY a short time to identify the man they sought. When they arrived at the house, they found it deep in mourning.

The body of Walter Huckvale still lay in the mortuary at the family chapel. His wife, the lovely Agnes, was bearing up well under her grief and was able to give her unexpected visitors a welcome. She was puzzled by their request.

"You wish to talk to my servants, Sir Richard?" she said.

"That is so," he replied, softly. "We have reason to believe that one of them may be able to help us. I was shocked to learn of your husband's untimely death. He and I fought together at Crècy and at Poitiers. Walter Huckvale deserved a hero's end."

Agnes nodded, showing a loyalty she did not really feel. She was clearly discomfited by Sir Richard's presence. Catherine believed that she could guess why.

"Let us get on with it," Sir Richard suggested briskly. "Perhaps you could have the servants sent into us one by one so that we can question them. We hope to throw new light on your husband's murder."

But the examination proved unnecessary. When the word spread among the servants, one of them took fright and bolted. Sir Richard's men had to ride for a mile before they ran him to ground. The man was dragged unceremoniously back to the house. He was squirming with guilt. Sir Richard was merciless.

"You helped poison your master," he accused.

"No, Sir Richard!" bleated the other.

"Do not lie to me!" A blow to the face knocked the man to the ground. "You served him that fatal draught of wine, didn't you?" The man shook his head. A kick made him groan. "Didn't you, you rogue?"

"Yes," confessed the servant.

"On whose orders?"

"I cannot tell you, Sir Richard."

"Do I have to beat the truth out of you, man?"

The servant looked up with a mixture of pleading and defiance.

"I wouldn't do that, if I were you," he said with a hollow laugh. "You might hear something that you wish you hadn't."

It was Catherine who once again led them with unerring accuracy to the right place. The cottage was on the edge of the Huckvale estate, small, comfortable, isolated, and well hidden by woodland. They found Hugh Costaine in the bedchamber, securely bound, gagged, and blindfolded. When he heard them enter the house, he kicked violently on the floor to attract their attention. Sir Richard was the first person to see him. He gazed down at his son with contempt before removing the blindfold and the gag. Hugh Costaine squinted in the light. He recognized the figure who towered over him.

"Father!" he exclaimed. "Thank heaven you came!"

"I can find no reason for thanks," the other said, grimly.

"Untie me so that I may pursue the rogue who attacked me."

"The only rogue I see is the one who lies at my feet. Whoever delivered you to me like this deserves a rich reward for he has solved the murder of Walter Huckvale."

"I did that!" ranted his son, nodding at Catherine. "There's the villain, standing beside you. That black-hearted witch put a spell on Walter Huckvale and struck him down with poison."

"Be quiet!" his father ordered. "We have caught the wretch who bought and administered the poison at your behest. He is under arrest and will hang for his crime. It shames me that my own son will hang beside him. What kind of birthday present is this for your mother? What kind of reward is it for your dear wife? You disgust me, Hugh. You and that heartless woman, Agnes Huckvale. She may have had no part in the murder, but she was ready to share a bed with you before her husband had even been consigned to his grave." He turned away. "Take him out. He offends my sight!"

Two men-at-arms hauled Hugh Costaine to his feet and hustled him out. Catherine ignored the vile taunts that were hurled at her by the departing prisoner. When Sir Richard looked at her, his face was ashen with despair. He tried to master his feelings.

"We owe you a huge apology, Mistress Teale," he said. "You were wrongly accused in order to throw suspicion away from the true villain. My son is the real sorcerer here. He knew that the only way to possess Agnes Huckvale was to remove her husband. You were unwittingly caught up in his evil design. There will be restitution for the way in which you have been cruelly abused."

"My liberty is restitution enough, Sir Richard."

"You have my heartfelt apology, and I will make sure that Bishop Nigel offers his words of regret as well. I will also insist on making some financial reparation. After all," he added with a sad smile, "you did find a missing son for me. I had no idea that you would solve a heinous crime in the process. It is a sorry day for my family."

Catherine put a consoling hand on his arm. She had no quarrel with Sir Richard Costaine. He had behaved honorably toward her and had made no attempt to shift the blame away from his son when the latter's villainy was exposed. The experience had aged him visibly.

"One of my men will take you back home," he offered.

"Thank you, Sir Richard."

"You were right, Mistress Teale. You do have a gift."

ADAM WAS WAITING FOR her in the house. After a warm embrace, he conducted her to the wooden bench and sat beside her with his arm around her shoulders. Catherine gave him a detailed account of all that had happened since her arrest. He listened patiently.

"It was that lie about the rats that betrayed him," he noted. "When you told me that Hugh Costaine came in search of rat poison, I knew that it was a ruse. A man like that would never run his own errands. He wanted that poison for a darker purpose."

"I counted on you working that out, Adam."

"I worked out much more than that, my love. Costaine would only stoop to murder for one reason. Lust. It seeps out of the man. Well, look at the way he tried to molest you. No," reflected Adam, "there had to be a woman involved and Walter Huckvale's wife was the obvious person. Then there was the poison, of course. If you would not provide it, there was only one person who would."

"Thomas Legge."

"I loosened his tongue with a flagon of wine, and he told me all I wanted to know. His testimony pointed me in the direction of the Huckvale estate. Hugh Costaine was not a person to bide his time. He wanted his reward immediately. When I saw his horse outside that cottage, I guessed that he was inside with his prize. Agnes Huckvale. I waited until the young widow slipped out then crept in to overpower Costaine and tie him up. That was how you found him."

"Delivered up to justice," she said. "Bishop Nigel would not believe me when I told him that I could sense things. For that is what I did. I sensed exactly what you would do to prove my innocence. You would go first to Thomas Legge to establish if and when he sold some poison. I knew that you would leave a sign for me and guessed where it would be."

"In a place very dear to both of us, my love."

"That clearing in the woods where you once asked for my hand." She gave a smile. "I did not expect to find a black stallion there, I can tell you. But it satisfied Sir Richard that we were on the right trail."

"Did you see the flagon?"

"Of course. It was certain proof of your success."

"My real success was getting wed to you, Catherine."

"I have been thinking the same about you," she admitted. "It has been a marriage of true minds. When I am being accosted by a foul-mouthed man like Hugh Costaine, you come to my aid at just the right time. When I am falsely accused, you spring to my defense. I love you so much," she said, kissing him on the lips. "You always know when I need you and how best to help me. That is my real gift."

"What is?"

"A husband called Adam Teale."

"Me?" he said with a grin. "Am I really a gift?"

"Oh, yes. A gift from God."

The Queen's Chastity

Tony Geraghty

"BY THE GRACE OF ALMIGHTY GOD, BE THIS SAD HISTORIE
NOT INCONTINENTLY REVEALED 'TIL YET TWO MILLENNIA
HAVE PAST—requiescat in pace"

Queen Eleanor's tomb at Llanthony, with its cryptic inscription, had long been an
object of speculation among scholars. Now that it was opened to reveal the remains
not of one, but three human skeletons, seven centuries after her presumed death,
medievalists revived a long-standing dispute. The matter was of little constitutional
importance now. Yet there was no shortage of academic dinosaurs ready to make
war about it on the Internet, from Honolulu to the London Library in Saint
James's. Both factions believed it was important to know the truth. To express the
matter somewhat indelicately, did the Queen of England cuckold her husband, the
future King Edward I, while he was crusading in the Holy Land from 1270 to
1272? Forensic science could only confirm that one skeleton was that of a woman
in her early forties. The other two—almost identical, apart from differences of
gender—were in their twenties and could have been twins. The skull of one of these
people was missing. In its place was that of a bird of prey. The younger skeletons
were, perhaps, her offspring (the DNA said as much), but to admit that would
have been to concede that the queen was indeed unfaithful, a theory peddled vigor-
ously by the Honolulu Faction and passionately opposed by the London Library
Faction, united by their belief in Eleanor's virtue. The London faction asserts that
Eleanor of Castille was with Edward all the way to the Holy Land and back.

159

I t is late afternoon in autumn. The forest air blends the odors of
   rutting deer, horse dung, and wood smoke from the charcoal
   burner, piled up irreverently at the center of a circle of standing stones.

"Did!"

"Didn't."

"Did!"

Two children, a boy and a girl, their faces and bare feet
blackened from a life built around the process of burning wood,
face one another like quarrelsome cats.

"How, then?" says the girl at last, a nervous finger curled into
her long hair. "How did he come back from the dead like you say?"

"It was a manacle," the boy retorts, one tiny fist punching
into the palm of the other hand, just as he had seen the priest at
Christmas. "Sweet Jesu came back through a manacle after they
nailed him to the tree."

"Well, I don't believe you," the girl says. She turns clock-
wise, pirouetting to show her nakedness beneath the worn
dress. "I believe in Green Man. I believe in the Old Religion."
Sticking her tongue out for good measure, she adds, "And the
Moon Goddess."

"Well, then," the boy shouts at her, his eyes glowing through
the smoke-dirt on his face, "you will go to Hell and be damned
for ever-and-ever-Amen."

Watching from among the clustered, conspiratorial sessile
oaks, a trio of women turn to one another. Two smile indulgently,
but the third, a peasant, casts her eyes down, murmuring, "They
shame me, Ma'am . . . If you wish to—"

"Not at all, Jenny Blackthorn." The Queen's smile does not
conceal her pallor or the deadly shadows beneath her tired eyes.
"Here,"—giving her a small bag of jingling coins—"take them to
the market and buy shoes for them. Soon it will be Hallowe'en."
Her hand shakes, but not because of cold.

Eleanor's companion, the taller of the two, buxom and glowing in a red gown that hampers her on horseback, even riding
sidesaddle, whispers, "Ma'am . . . We are far from home. Your
escort will wonder . . ." She touches the Royal arm, a breach of

protocol permitted only to a trusted lady of the bedchamber. Reluctantly, Eleanor allows herself to be led away, stifling what might be a cough or a sob, or both.

Browne to Long: Dear Long—What do you make of Queen Eleanor's deathbed confession?
                                                      —Browne, Honolulu.

Long to Browne: Dear Browne—Just another smear, started by Giraldus Cambrensis, working off his old grudge against Edward. He never forgave the King for refusing to confirm his election as Bishop of Saint David's. His way of hitting back was to tell the world that the King was a cuckold.
                                                      —Long, London.

"FATHER, FORGIVE ME, FOR I have sinned a mortal sin, a sin of impurity, and would be shriven now my hour is come."

The candle flickers. The rosary lies inert among the Queen's dying fingers.

"Be at peace, my child. Our Lord God is ever merciful. He died that we may live."

The voice of Bishop Gerald of Wales, lately returned from Ireland with young Prince John and preparing his great recruitment for the Crusade through the Welsh Marches, soothes Eleanor out of this life with a voice that is soft as the silk lining of her coffin. "But make your confession whilst there is yet time."

A little way off, a loose floorboard squeaks. Gerald raises a cautionary finger, silencing the intrusion. Two men—tall Prince John, his hooked nose scarred from jousting, and his inseparable companion and Clerk, Dark John, small and sinuous as a marmoset—strain to hear the words that follow.

"Father this is hard . . . hard. My husband Edward, having taken the Cross, was at Acre. Word came that he had died of a green wound. But it was false, a calumny, the work of the Evil One. I was comforted one night in my grief. Even now I dare not speak his name for it were mortal sin even were I in truth the widow I had thought myself to be."

She coughs. The side of her mouth stains pink bubbles, then smooth crimson as if an invisible artist has her as his paint pallet.

"So much blood there was. I was delivered a month before Edward disembarked at Southampton."

Her eyes roll back into her skull. Prince John, from the other side of the room, hisses: "The name! What is the Bastard's name? Is he a Pretender?"

Bishop Gerald's finger again ordains silence, though he, also, is disturbed by the political implications of this revelation. A Pretender? Where? Supported by what? An army of peasants, perhaps? These are dangerous times and Wales is still untamed.

The Queen's eyes open, fixed on the candle as if she sees hellfire looming.

"My son, my firstborn, was one of two. One son, one daughter, like puppies in a litter. John was later, the true son of his father.

"What became of them, child?"

"Jenny Blackthorn . . ."

The last flicker of life flows away as the candle gutters. Gerald closes her staring eyes, makes the Sign of the Cross on her forehead, and kneels to pray for her departing soul.

Browne, Honolulu, to Long, London: But Gerald wrote of twins, with the superstitious horror surrounding the phenomenon at that time. Why would he complicate a false story without cause?

Long, London, to Browne, Honolulu: Further evidence, in itself, that the Queen—and by extension, Edward—was cursed. He even hints at incest and suggests that the boy carried the "Mark of Cain" on his face (a single, linked eyebrow). All nonsense, of course.

THE MOURNING BELL TOLLS on a biting winter morning at Llanthony Priory, that huge, grey, graven emptiness that not even a host of gargoyles, nor even the gaping sheila-na-gig, can populate: a place that shudders under the perpetual storms that rage on the Black Mountain just above it. The choir sings its requiem for Eleanor. An angry Prince, his nose red with cold, his chain mail heavy with ice after the long ride from Gloucester, stamps stone flags either from frustration or cold, or both, ignoring the burial service.

The service over, he summons Bishop Gerald.

"Your Grace, lookie-here. Before our period of mourning is done, certes before our coronation, we will have the Bastard found."

Gerald notes with disquiet, but not surprise, that Prince John has already adopted the royal "We" instead of the humble, human "I."

"What is your advice?"

"This is not a matter for spiritual counsel, Sire. Perhaps"—he nods in his shrewd, political fashion toward Black John—"perhaps your loyal Clerk would know where to find Jenny Blackthorn if she yet live? Black John knew the Forest of Dean well as a boy, before the seminarians sent him to study in France to remove him from that sinister place of Devil worship where all who enter do so at risk to their immortal souls." Crossing himself, he continues: "In Gloucester it is rumored that one of that name succored twins: a boy and a girl, and that the same Jenny Blackthorn, the wife of a charcoal burner, was once visited by a fine gentlewoman who gave her money."

Browne, Honolulu, to Long, London: And what are we to make of "Black John," the Prince's confidant?

Long, London, to Browne, Honolulu: The Prince's creature, no more. European history is replete with witch-finders.

THE TUMBLED HAMLETS CLING to the edge of the Forest, as if afraid to venture far from it or enter the dark, unmarked green ways known only to the furtive people of the interior, the aboriginal

Celts. Doors shudder beneath blows of mailed fists. Dogs bark and babies scream and puke as the gnomic Black John and his posse storm like Norman centaurs into the huddled settlements. The villeins are arranged along one stone wall—or hawthorn hedge if no stone stands—the women at another. They face the wall to be kicked, pushed, or lashed if they complain.

"Where is Jenny Blackthorn?"

"Dead, sire, these ten years an' more."

"What of her brats?"

"The boy was taken by the Bishop's people to be priested, just before Jenny died of the red mushroom."

"And the girl?"

The villagers are silent, as if waiting. The posse turns, sensing something, as if stalked by a wood nymph. A slight, graceful woman dressed in faded green, her black hair wantonly about her shoulders, approaches them on bare feet. Her eyes are grey and the dark eyebrows meet above them. About her neck she wears a torque of gold. There are other marvels. On her left, gloved wrist rests a fine goshawk, its talons held in leathern jesses, the eyes masked by a hood.

"I am Cerridwen, daughter of Jenny Blackthorn."

The voice is surprisingly low. It carves patterns of sound that could make a man—and some women—drunk with the melody, most particularly the name, in which each syllable is spoken separately, like a drumbeat: "Cer-rid-wen."

"What would you want of me?"

Now the eyes are grey-green, changing, chameleonlike, with the shifting patterns of illusory light in an enchanted land. And they flash toward Black John with dangerous recognition. "T'were not love potions, I ween. Not twixt us."

Her laughter saws at the sinews of the centaurs about her. Black John, fear his companion, taps the arm of his giant escort. "Take her."

As they close on her, she slips off the hawk's hood and lofts the bird into the air. It circles over the posse, shrieking, and she responds: "Fly! Fly, my beauty!" With a last unearthly call, the sound of the very soul ascending, it soars, still circling, leather jesses still dangling from its legs, into invisibility. Later, they said this was no ordinary bird of prey, nor even a falcon of the hunting sort, trained by man, but one of her familiars. Certainly, she had a way with animals.

Browne, Honolulu, to Long, London: The real mystery here is the identity of this woman and what it was that made her so important. She was no possible threat to Prince John or his spurious claim to the throne.

Long, London, to Browne: Bread and circuses perhaps? As you say, there was no Pretender only the fear of one. But once the hunt was up and running, there had to be a quarry, even if it was some poor superstitious hag hauled out of her bed of cabbages to be hanged for the fun of it.

THE INQUIRY BEGINS. NO lack of witnesses this Beltane eve to attest that dark things have happened the year past in the gloomy Forest of Dean: babies stillborn and beasts aborting; agues and boils and the falling sickness afflicting the innocent; curdled milk and chimneys blocked by jackdaws. The procession of hard-luck stories through the echoing hall of Hereford Castle, beside the salmonful Wye, is a jolly romp, with mead and bread for all; a fair, my dear, with the hope of more entertainment to come and the start of better things after. Would they use the ducking stool? Or even swim the witch? Not yet, for no witness was found who had seen Cerridwen at her exercise . . . Not yet. Besides, she is here present, and who would denounce her to her face, she who has cured so many with her magic? What might befall if we did?

"I cannot swear on my oath it was her doing, Sire."

Black John twists restlessly in his seat. It is a fine wooden seat, almost like a throne, that elevates him above the common people. "Tell it to me again, your history," he orders the witness. Cerridwen, her wrists bound before her and legs tied likewise, squats with her back to a pillar behind him, out of his eye. The witness repeats his story as he faces her, avoiding her gaze.

Long, London, to Browne: There was also a genuine fear of "Sathan" and his works including sorcery, heresy, and what the writer Perkins described later as "the damned Art of Witchcraft." Witchcraft was tolerated through much of Christendom until Rome linked it to heresy for internal, political reasons at about the time this trial took place.

Browne to Long, London: Or even earlier in some places. Remember the "Canon Episcopy"? All that stuff about "some wicked women are perverted by the Devil so they believe they ride out at night on beasts with Diana, the pagan goddess and a horde of women." That was A.D. 900.

ON THE FOURTH DAY, the Ecclesiastical Court hears the testimony of one Symonds, wheelwright, red of hair and quick of temper. Symonds for years past has sought to bed Cerridwen, and always did she stifle his lust with laughter. Now comes his revenge.

"I have heard the woman say to others of her persuasion, 'May the injured Lucifer greet thee.' I have seen her at full moon trip naked and consort with things not of this world."

Consort? How, "consort"?—"In her body. Couple with Sathan in the form of a black dog, sire."

A sigh of horror mixed with satisfaction—a catharsis—overcomes those present. They cross themselves piously even as they revel in its sinfulness. Black John's "Hah!" breaks the silence that follows. Then, turning to face Cerridwen, he puts the Question:

"Art thou a witch?"

She, looking him in the eye, replies, "I am thy mother's childe, John."

What's this? A buzz of interest fills the room like the drone of a blowfly on the King's meat before it be covered with tansy.

Black John touches the crucifix that rests upon his chest. "You talk in riddles, woman. The demon within you it is that speaks. You are possessed of the Evil One."

Why yes, of course . . . The congregation nods its assent. Only the Prince, watching from a high place, out of sight of them all, does not nod. His grip tightens on the dagger at his waist, the knuckles white with sudden anger.

"Put her down," Black John says. "Let her see the instruments. Return her to us tomorrow, and we shall examine her body for the customary marks." With that, he sweeps out of the room, almost invisible behind his screen of armed men.

THAT NIGHT, UNDER A waning moon, three figures in the habit of the Brown Monks, their faces in the obscurity of their cowls, unlock the door and enter her cell. Without ado, two of them suppress her struggles whilst the third opens a leathern vessel, enters his hand therein, and, like unto a boy taking eggs from a plover's nest, plucks forth a small sponge. She feels the finger enter her privy parts. Her last, living experience on this plane is a spreading warmth from her arse, from where the sponge passeth its deadly, drowsing benison into her very vitals.

Browne, Honolulu, to Long, London: The record is unclear at this point. The woman they called "Cerridwen" is found dead on the fifth day of her trial, her body unmarked. There is no sign of violence, no evidence of poisoning. She leaves a long, written confession in good Latin, although it seems unlikely she was literate in any language, including her own.

"THE CONFESSION IS QUITE clear, Sire," says Black John.
    The Prince, whittling a cross-stave with his knife, spits.
    "How do I know that? Am I a Clerk? Am I to spend my time learning letters? I script my name. That is enough. But show me the document."
    The Prince touches the manuscript with his fingers as if willing the symbols to obey his will and answer to him, yet they remain inert on the page like the closed eyes of Cerridwen.
    "I will read it again, Sire," Black John says.

" 'I, Cerridwen, natural-born daughter of Jenny Blackthorn of
Crabtree Hill within the Forest of Dean in the County of Gloucester, doe declare on my dying breath and in the full knowledge I
am about to face my maker the Lord God Jesus Christ, and doe
confess as follows:

'This night the Angel of Death appeared unto me and called
upon me to repent my life of wicked apostasy, to renounce Satan
and all his works and that I did. I die a Christian.

'In my infancy a Great Ladie visited my mother and brought
with her a baby she must conceal because of some great shame.
The baby died of a fever and was buried eftsoons in unconsecrated ground in the deepest part of the Forest. The grave was
uncovered by hogges and the body eaten by the said hogges and
other carnivorous beasts. Jenny Blackthorn, fearful of the Great
Ladie's wrath and hoping for preferment, adopted a male child of
the same age, her sister's tenth-born, her sister now being out of
her wits. The Great Ladie did visit us once and was persuaded
that the son of my mother's sister was in truth her own beloved
infant. She sent us many a groat to keep us fed, and may she be
blessed for her Christian charity.

'I was seduced by Satan when young and was his bride 'til
taken by the Clerk they call "Black John." The son of my mother's
sister I called "Jack," that some also say is known to be "John." I
know not what was his fate after he sailed to France from the port
of Gloucester with John of Salisbury, but 'twas malice and the
Anti-Christ that spoke when I told to the congregation here at
Hereford that we were kin, Black John the Clerk and I.

'Signed in her own blood . . . Cerridwen, daughter of Jenny
Blackthorn. The sixth day of June 1290.' "

The Prince, a very Apollo, shines upon Black John and
embraces him. "So ends our search for the Bastard. You did well,
coz." Yet his eye, over the shoulder of his Clerk, meets the eye of
Bishop Gerald and things unsaid pass between them.

"How shall we end this business, dear heart?" the Prince asks
Black John. "Shall we bury the witch and have done? What says
our good Bishop?"

"Sire, if she be truly a disciple of Satan, she may not be laid
in consecrated earth for 'twould be blasphemy. Nor if she be a

suicide, for 'twould be the only sin without release, it being the sin of despair and therefore renunciation of Our Lord's grace."

"Why then, Bishop, do you and your physicians and herbals examine the woman's body forthwith for the usual blemishes, the teats, the suckling-marks, the strawberries and hirsute moles, and the rest? Now to horse! The deer run and my hounds have need of exercise and I be no Acteon for turning from hunter into hunted stag even by the sorcery of a dead Diana."

Roaring with laughter at his own wit, he exits the castle.

Long, London, to Browne, Honolulu: Yet it is clear that something happened as a result of this woman's death that had considerable implications for the main players in the drama. What is your theory?

Browne, Honolulu, to Long, London: I believe she knew too much. But who was at risk from the knowledge she concealed?

IN AN UNCONSECRATED BELL tower that stands alongside but detached from the Church of Saint Dubricius at Pembridge, beyond the spite-filled eyes of the Forest and the wagging tongues of Hereford City, they bare the corpse of Cerridwen and seek signs of the incubus . . . without success. The skin upon this form is so white as to be transparent; the body hairless as a childe's. Black John, ordered to attend the hunt, is not present. Gerald, his hirsute hands and arms bare, still wears his ecclesiastical ring and Holy Cross for his soul's sake. His eyes seek heaven but see only the oaken beams above and the bell they call Big Tom . . . and perched upon one of the beams, a goshawk with loose jesses about its legs, an unnatural bird that gazes contumaciously upon him with human intelligence through lambent yellow eye.

"The privy parts," he says. His assistants, heads covered, open the legs. And turn their backs. Gerald's fingers delve and probe as they have done many times before to uncover the signs, the guilty teats and warts but always 'til this day upon a still-living body. He reflects that he must write a careful treatise concerning this matter for the scholars of the Holy See . . . But what is this? Inside the rear orifice, like a fledgling within the nest, a sponge which, when removed from its place of concealment, exudes an essence the herbalist knows is not Self-heal nor Saint John's Wort but tincture of mandrake, hemlock, and poppy contained within that tiny angel of oblivion favored by midwives and called by some "the soporific sponge." And there is something more: monkshood, that seductive blue-and-white flower shaped exactly like its sacerdotal namesake. It is a delight to behold on a fine summer's day in the hedgerow yet, like wolfbane, the most perfect poison.

The herbalist has a sad mien, like a dog that be kicked daily or the oft-whipped Ass that Apuleius became when bewitched. His nose affrighted, the herbalist says: "Your Grace, this poor creature did not die naturally nor of her own hand, but incontinently at the hand of another. Never have I seen the sponge thus used against a mortal body. This be the Devil's work."

Long, London, to Browne, Honolulu: The end of Black John was equally enigmatic. One fragment attributed to John Dee quotes an earlier source, now lost, to suggest that in this case the body was discovered in a gown that had been worn by Cerridwen and that so dressed, he was her very double.

Browne, Honolulu, to Long, London: This fragment I had not traced. Could it be that there are still some significant manuscripts to be found in England rather than more safely in the air-conditioned libraries of Texas? It is an interesting anecdote. We know for sure only that Dark John disappeared from the history at this point.

THE HUNT RETURNS, SPATTERED with gore but not yet sated with blood. Bishop Gerald waits at the Keep. He has a secret for the Prince's ear alone that cannot wait the morrow. The Prince's eyes darken at the disclosure. That night, they banquet on venison and nightingale, the Prince and his bosom companion Black John. Also here present are the Bishop, the hunt, the Master of Hounds, and

sundry others. Last to enter is the bearded Penhebogyd, Master of
the Hawks, for whom even the Prince must needs rise to welcome,
by ancient custom, as he takes his place at table, the fourth in
precedence. But not even Penhebogyd observes the jessed goshawk
that perches patiently upon a windowsill high above the room.

The feast nears its end. The lutenists make musicke, and the
Prince murmurs to Black John, "I would entertain Lady Katherine
in my bedchamber this night, when the last candle be out."

Black John makes his preparations: doth paint his face like a
girl's; color his lips cherry; adorn his head with a wig of rich hair
that touches his shoulders; his body with sweet oils and a gown
that transforms him from man to woman as if Circe herself were
his wardrobe mistress. The Court well knows of Lady Katherine
but speaks not of the matter. This night, for the last time, though
she wit it not, she walks the long, silent gallery to the Prince's
bedchamber, lifting her skirts delicately as she steps daintily over
the Irish wolfhound that guards the door.

Next morning she is discovered facedown in the castle moat,
still gowned, a green ribbon that was in her hair now about her
neck, her eyes and tongue protuberant. The court jester capers.
Others do likewise. But only he dare lampoon that Black John was
privily impaled even before they removed the head for treason.
"Forsooth!" he rejoices. "Treason in the head without doubt but
otherwise, and otherwhere, faithful unto death, ah-hah!"

The head of Black John upon its pole faces down the rebel-
lious West from the city walls of Hereford through a long, dry
summer but no carrion molest it, for it is guarded night and day
by a goshawk. The skull shrinks, desiccates, and when the wind
blows it shifts and moves on its pole, and the lower jaw snaps
open and shut as if to speak. Undevout, superstitious country folk
say it has a secret message for them that the Prince would keep
from their ears as he increases their tithes most cruelly.

*Browne, Honolulu, to Long, London: We do know, however, that some six
months after the death, the Forest of Dean rebelled.*

Long, London, to Browne, Honolulu: That was a pathetic protest by a rag-tag rabble. According to Giraldus, the Prince suspected that his Clerk was financially corrupt. So, arbitrarily, he doubled local taxes to generate the income he believed was on tap already. That was a serious mistake.

THE REBEL ARMY HAS straw for armor and a few Welsh mountain cobs for cavalry; bows and slings for skirmishing; pikes, sickles, and even scythes for the combat. The Prince laughs, his visor raised carelessly, battle-ax honed to a glittering niceness. The first head he will take is the rebel leader's. The leader is an inconsequential, moonstruck baker. The Prince spurs his horse forward, without waiting for his escort, into the narrow forest trail, where the uncommitted spectators mock him with arses exposed and turned in his way. His ax swings in his right hand and in rhythm to the canter of the horse as he closes on his opponent. The baker, riding a cob, flinches and endeavors to turn away, but he is no horseman and gives the wrong aid. His animal swings into the Prince's thundering path; rears up in fright, hurling him to the ground where he lies gasping for breath. The Prince turns back, comes in for the kill, still smiling as a pair of goshawk talons lash his face, blinding him with his own blood.

The hawk, shrieking vengeance like a banshee forewarning of death, flies off a short way, returns, and attacks again. Now its beak removes first one eye, then a second. The newly blind Prince spurs his horse, holding his seat, but crashes into an overhanging branch in his sightlessness. The peasants with their pikes finish what the bird has miraculously begun, then melt like kernes or sprites into the green gloom among mocking crickets as the Prince's men carry home the corpse of their leader.

Browne, Honolulu, to Long, London: Did the Prince die as Gerald suggests, pursued by some demon or familiar owing its allegiance to Cerridwen?

Long, London: I think not, unless you count his own folly as something that was supernaturally inspired. If that be so, we are all bewitched at some point in our lives. But dare we admit that?

The Reiving of Bonville Keep

Kathy Lynn Emerson

Bonville Keep lay two days' ride from Edinburgh. Driven by his desire for revenge, Sir Gavin Dunnett and his men made the journey in one. Only the temporary truce between England and Scotland prevented them from laying siege to the castle. An act of war against an English baron would have angered the king of Scots, to whom Gavin now owed allegiance. He was obliged to employ more devious means to gain entry.

At dusk, he donned the full, black gown of a Benedictine and entered enemy territory alone. What he found inside the curtain wall astonished him. The place was ripe for reiving. Guards lazed at their posts. Half the servants were far gone in drink. Even the steward seemed lax in his duties. New to the Borders, Gavin decided. From the bleary look in his watery blue eyes, the fellow had also imbibed a considerable quantity of ale.

"We are about to sup," the steward said. "Will you join us, brother?"

Careful to keep his hood raised to hide his lack of a tonsure, since a full head of black hair on a monk would raise far too many questions, Gavin accepted the invitation.

"A pity monks cannot perform marriage ceremonies."

"You wish to wed?" Gavin asked as they entered the great hall. "Who is the lucky woman?"

The steward gestured toward the raised dais at the far end of the room. "Lady Bonville is a new-made widow and ripe for the plucking."

It was as well the steward did not have all his wits about him, for Gavin could not control his start of surprise. Lord Bonville was dead? Then who had sent him word of Isabella's death?

The logical answer to his question sat in regal splendor at the table on the dais. Beatrice Bonville, Gavin's old nemesis. His eyes narrowed as he stared at her. Seven years had passed since he'd last seen her, but she still possessed an exotic beauty. Sleek, glossy, raven locks contrasted with milk-white skin. For a woman whose husband had recently died, she seemed most merry. In spite of losing him? Or because he was no longer alive?

As Gavin watched from a place at a lower table, Lady Bonville smiled and flirted with her flaxen-haired steward and with the black-avised man who seemed to be the husband of one of her stepdaughters. Three of them shared the dais. With their distinctive Bonville hair, its color so pale a shade of yellow that it was nearly white, Gavin had no difficulty picking them out. Two of them looked enough alike to be twins.

A waiting gentlewoman, small of stature with a plain face and drab brown tresses, stood just behind Lady Bonville. Without warning, her mistress turned and boxed her ears. She had been too slow to refill a goblet with wine. The pockmarked servant lad, who stumbled and sloshed the sauce as he set a platter full of steaming food on the table, received a hard pinch on the forearm for his carelessness.

"Heartless bitch," muttered the burly halberdier seated to Gavin's right.

"What has Lady Bonville done to you?"

"Refused to pay our quarterly stipend. Says there is no money at all. None to pay her servants. None to attract husbands for Bonville's three youngest daughters. There's talk she means to send them to be brides of Christ at Holystone Priory."

Gavin had a hard time believing Lord Bonville had died penniless. There must be some gold left. Some of *his* gold. He had sent enough of it here over the years, he thought bitterly.

"There is the child to be dowried, too," the halberdier said.

Gavin dipped his venison in pepper sauce. "What child is that?"

"The half-Scots wench. The old lord's granddaughter. Just seven years old is Mistress Isabella, but they do say she's been ill, nigh unto death, mayhap." He crossed himself piously before draining another mazer of ale.

Gavin scarce noticed if the taste of the sauce on his tongue was fierce or merely pungent. He felt his heart contract. His breathing became labored. His daughter was still alive? What trick was this?

"From what illness does she suffer?" he asked cautiously.

"No one knows."

"How long has she been ill?"

After a moment's computation, something which seemed to tax the fellow's inebriated brain, he answered. "Nearly a month now. 'Twas shortly after Lord Bonville's death. To keep any possible contagion from spreading, the widow had her moved to the north tower."

Gavin scowled at the dais. Beatrice Bonville had exiled a sick child. Left her to die alone. He drank deeply of his own ale and tried to make sense of what he'd just heard.

Two days earlier, after he'd sent word to Bonville Keep that he intended to reclaim Isabella, he'd received a missive, signed by Lord Bonville, telling him that his daughter, his only child, had died in infancy.

But it was Bonville who was dead. That meant Lady Bonville must have dispatched the messenger. Gavin frowned. Even if she'd expected Isabella to die before he arrived, he could not imagine why she'd lie about the matter.

Far from keeping him away, the widow's callous message had spurred Gavin into action. He'd jumped to the conclusion that Lord Bonville had robbed him, taking under false pretenses the generous sums Gavin had sent to England to defray the cost of Isabella's upbringing.

His daughter had been a newborn when Gavin had last seen her. He'd left England the same day he'd buried Mariotta Bonville, his beautiful young English wife. Since then, he'd gained fame and fortune fighting in tournaments on the Continent and hiring out as a mercenary. He'd given little thought to Isabella. Indeed, when he'd heard the child was dead, and had been all along, he'd felt more anger than grief. Enraged at what he'd seen as Bonville's duplicity, Gavin had vowed to reive Bonville Keep and take back all that hard-earned gold from the man who'd dared deceive him.

He should have known, Gavin thought, that Beatrice would be the real villain in this. She was the one who had objected, eight years earlier, when he'd asked Lord Bonville for his daughter's hand in marriage. Beatrice had told her husband that Gavin was not worthy to wed Mariotta. She'd denounced him for being a Scot and called undue attention to his poverty. At the same time, behind her husband's back, she'd tried to get Gavin into her bed.

When he'd declined this dubious honor and threatened to expose her wanton ways if she did not withdraw her objections, Beatrice had been furious. They'd avoided each other throughout his brief marriage to Mariotta. Afterward, blinded by his grief for the wife who'd died in childbirth, Gavin had accepted Beatrice's show of sympathy at face value.

What a fool he'd been to leave his daughter here! A belated sense of guilt fanned the flames of Gavin's resentment toward Beatrice, even though he knew he'd had little choice. In truth, he'd have been no fit caretaker for an infant.

Lord Bonville, on the other hand, had seemed an ideal person to look after the child. Mariotta's father had possessed more experience than any man in England when it came to raising up young gentlewomen. In hope of a son to inherit after him, he'd married four times. The first three wives had been fertile but had produced only girls. Twelve in all. The last Lady Bonville, Beatrice, had been barren.

Staring at the woman on the dais, Gavin felt his anger at her intensify until a red haze seemed to form in front of his eyes. He blinked hard to regain control of his emotions, but his desire for revenge did not dissipate. The monk whose robes he'd borrowed would have advised him to forgive Beatrice. Gavin was more inclined to make the wicked woman pay for her sins.

Supper and the revelry that followed continued deep into the night. During those long hours, Gavin bided his time, listening and learning as much as he could from the conversations around him. It seemed to be the popular belief that Lord Bonville had spent all his money marrying off the first nine of his daughters.

Most people also knew that the steward, Michael Barlow, was Beatrice Bonville's lover. So was James Maplett, her step-daughter Marion's husband, the dark-haired man on the dais. No one said much about the other Bonville sisters, or about Isabella.

Gavin waited until Beatrice retired for the night, then slipped quietly out of the great hall. He started toward the north tower, then stopped. He had time, he realized, to carry out part of his original plan. He could still assuage his desire for revenge. Afterward, he would reclaim Isabella.

EXHAUSTION DULLED ALISON BONVILLE'S usually sharp reflexes. Despite her best efforts to stay awake, she'd fallen into a fitful doze and was slow to realize the significance of a rush of cooler air into the tower chamber.

A faint shuffling sound—leather-shod feet on the rush-covered floor—had her eyes popping open in alarm. At the same time, she caught a whiff of spilled ale and damp wool. Almost too late, a sense of imminent danger engulfed her.

Alison sat bolt upright on the window seat, reaching for the knife that hung from her belt as she searched the dimly lit room for an intruder. Rage and fear in equal parts filled her heart, when she saw a dark shape bending over her niece's bed. Her only thought to protect the defenseless child, she launched herself at this threatening figure.

She attacked just as he started to lift Isabella into his arms, but some small, inadvertent sound on her part was enough to warn him of another presence in the chamber. At the last possible moment, he released his burden and started to turn. Instead of finding its target in his back, where Alison had hoped to damage some vital organ, her blade struck his shoulder and stuck there as he turned to face her fully.

Heedless of the danger of reaching across the breadth of his massive chest to grasp at the hilt of the knife, she tried to retrieve her weapon. Her fingers barely grazed it before he seized her wrist in a crushing grip. To cut off any outcry, his free arm clamped down with bruising force across her back, pressing her face into the muffling folds of his robe.

Instinctively, she struggled, but it was impossible to break free. Even breathing became difficult once her nose and mouth were tight against his chest. She dimly realized, too late for it to matter, that even had her aim been true, she'd have done little damage. She could feel the thick padding of a quilted gambeson beneath an outer covering of wool. Her small, sharp blade was imbedded in naught but cloth.

A child's whimper penetrated the haze of Alison's desperation when her captor's soft-spoken command to be still could not. The moment she stopped fighting, he loosened his grip sufficiently to allow her to gulp in much-needed air.

"Isabella," she whispered in a hoarse croak she scarce recognized as her own voice.

His hesitation lasted no more than an instant. As soon as his hold on her eased, Alison dashed to the girl's side, all thought of calling for help banished by her need to assure herself that Isabella was no worse.

The forehead beneath her palm was cool and dry. Isabella responded to the familiar touch with a little sigh and sank once more into drugged sleep. With loving fingers, Alison brushed a wisp of hair away from her niece's face. Only then did she realize that the intruder had moved silently to the other side of the bed. Belatedly, she recognized his outer garb as that of a monk.

Confusion held her motionless as he knelt, his attention fixed on the child's pale face. The man was no Benedictine, no matter how he was dressed. Only moments earlier, she had been certain that he was a murderer bent on killing Isabella, but watching him now, Alison experienced an odd sense of familiarity. Inexplicably, she no longer feared him.

Without looking at her, he spoke in a soft, deadly voice. "If you cry out, I will kill you."

"At this hour of the night, the servants are all asleep and what guards may have been posted are most likely deep in their cups, their wits addled." Even sober, they'd have been loath to bestir themselves. None of them felt much loyalty to the Bonvilles these days. Why should they when they had not been paid for months?

As if surprised by her comment, the man lifted his head. For the first time, Alison saw the face of the man she'd tried to kill.

Recognition sent her reeling.

She had been right. This was no monk. Nor was he a brigand or a border reiver, as she had supposed. He was no stranger, either. The man kneeling opposite her was Isabella's father. It might have been years since she'd last seen him, but she'd never forgotten his eyes. They were the color of a stormy sea at dusk.

"What is wrong with her?" He indicated his daughter.

"Lady Bonville tried to kill her."

The moment the words were out, her hands flew to her lips. Even if this was Isabella's father, it had been passing foolish of her to make such a claim.

He stared at her without speaking, the angry flare of his nostrils the only indication of his feelings. Then he reached again for the sleeping child, lifting her into his arms as he stood. "She will never hurt Isabella again." He started toward the door.

"Wait."

"Silence, woman, or I'll bind and gag you."

His tone made Alison realize that he had taken her for a servant. It was an understandable error. To nurse Isabella, she had put off the trappings of a noblewoman. The cote-hardie she wore over her linen chemise, its full skirt short enough to clear the ground but long enough to hide her flat, leather slippers, was made of plain russet-colored wool, bereft of decoration save for the belt that held the now empty sheath for her knife and an undecorated leather bag.

Gavin Dunnett had no reason to think her one of his wife's little sisters. She'd been a child of eleven when he'd last seen her. Moreover, Alison's distinctive Bonville hair, of the pale blonde

color some poets called "silver-gilt," was covered by a simple
linen coif.

"Isabella is my daughter," he said.

Alison had no wish to challenge his rights. The girl would
be far better off with him.

So would she.

"She needs warm clothing," Alison told him. "And someone
to look after her. Give me but a moment, and I will pack her
belongings and mine, too."

It was the perfect solution, Alison thought. She could not
bear the idea of being separated from Isabella, to whom she had
long been more mother than aunt. And after what had happened
earlier tonight in Beatrice's chamber, escaping across the border
into Scotland had undeniable appeal.

She had been dreading the new day, but until Gavin Dunnett appeared, she'd given no consideration to flight. She'd had
no place to go. Now, in spite of all the unknown danger that
might lie ahead, she felt like a condemned prisoner who'd just
been offered a pardon.

"Make haste," he said.

Within minutes, Alison had Isabella bundled into layers of
wool and camlet and had retrieved her own warm outerwear. The
child was stirring when Gavin once again lifted her.

"Who are you?" she asked in a sleepy voice.

"I am your father."

Isabella looked around for Alison.

"He is your father, Isabella. We are going to go with him
now. We must be very quiet."

Her eyes wide and solemn, Isabella nodded.

Alison followed Gavin Dunnett down the narrow, winding
steps cut into the thickness of the wall and along the passageway
that led to the cavernous, vaulted kitchen that occupied the
ground floor of the north tower. They passed through, mere
shadows, unseen by any of the servants sleeping there, and
exited by way of a heavy wooden door. Gavin paused just outside, at the top of a flight of worn stone stairs. Below them was
the inner bailey, an open space they'd have to cross in order to
reach the postern gate.

Nothing seemed to be stirring. No one challenged their progress as they went past the kitchen garden and the fish pond stocked with trout and pike. They made it safely across a small wooden bridge and reached the high stone wall without mishap.

"I've a currach hidden a short way downstream," Gavin whispered as he unbarred and opened the oaken gate. Just on the other side, a path descended to the riverbank.

Alison turned to take one last look at her home. To her horror, she saw armed men streaming toward her across the little bridge.

"Stop her!" one shouted. "Do not let her escape!"

Alison pushed hard at the door in the wall, slamming the postern gate closed before the rapidly approaching guards could catch sight of Gavin or Isabella. She turned back toward the castle, calling out, "I have no intention of going anywhere. Can a lady not enjoy a moonlit walk in her own garden without causing such a to-do?"

Rough hands seized her. Alison recognized Michael Barlow, the steward. The others were men-at-arms under his command.

"Release me, sirrah! What have I done to warrant such treatment?"

"Murder," Barlow said.

"Who has been murdered?"

"You know the answer to that question, Mistress Alison, else why would you try to run away? Your stepmother is dead. Stabbed through the heart."

He shoved her into the arms of one of his men.

"Lock her up for the crowner to question! No one is to talk to her until he arrives."

MISTRESS ALISON?

FROM HIS place of concealment on the other side of the postern gate, Gavin Dunnett absorbed the shock of this revelation. The young woman who'd fought him to protect Isabella was no mere nursemaid. She was Alison Bonville. One of Mariotta's sisters. Isabella's aunt.

She could not have killed Beatrice.

In spite of the fury with which she had attacked him, he did not believe her capable of murder, but his opinion, Gavin realized, would not save her. She had been in the wrong place at the wrong time. Now that she'd been taken into custody while trying to escape, no one at Bonville Keep would trouble to look elsewhere for a killer.

She'd gone quietly so he and Isabella could get away.

There could be no other explanation for her silence.

When the tramp of boots had receded and it was safe to move, he set Isabella on her feet and hunkered down until their eyes were level. "Who cares for you, Isabella? Who looks after your needs."

"Mine Aunt Alison."

He was not surprised by the answer. "Not some servant?"

Isabella shook her head. "Is it true you are my father?"

"Aye."

"Mine Aunt Alison has told me stories about you. She said you are a brave and honorable knight."

Gavin had men and horses waiting at an encampment only a short distance downstream. He could take Isabella there and set out for Scotland at first light. Once she was certain Isabella had time to get safely away, Alison could accuse him of the murder, thus regaining her own freedom.

But would she? And would they believe her if she did? Gavin frowned.

With Beatrice dead, he supposed there was no need to kidnap his daughter. As long as no one learned of this visit to the castle, he could return in daylight and claim her openly. If he did so, he would also be able to help Alison, who out of love for his child had sacrificed herself.

He sighed.

A brave and honorable knight, she'd called him.

She had been listening to too many ballads, tales of knights with pure hearts and noble intentions. What she'd seen here on the Border should have given the lie to such fancies. Real knights served whatever man paid for their services. They cared little for honor and less about those who got in their way. No matter who won any of the wars between England and Scotland, the folk who lived in the Debatable Land were the worse for it. Man, beast, and crops, all were trampled under the hooves of knights' horses and the bootheels of foot soldiers.

After seven years, Gavin had grown tired of fighting, tired of killing. He'd had no interest in finding employment in another endless, futile war. He'd had enough of innocent people dying. He'd returned home to Scotland to purchase a modest and remote estate. There he'd hoped to settle down, raise his daughter, and with God's blessing find a new wife to give him more children.

In a quiet voice, he told Isabella what they must do.

SEVERAL HOURS LATER, HIS black armor polished so that it gleamed in the sun and his black warhorse lifting him above the head of his squire, who rode upon a mule, Sir Gavin Dunnett once again entered Bonville Keep. This time the steward came out to greet him with a wary look upon his face.

"We are in mourning here," he announced. "We cannot offer hospitality."

"And you are?"

"He is Michael Barlow, Lady Bonville's *former* steward," another voice interrupted. "Now that she is dead, I am the one who will decide who is welcome here."

Although Gavin recognized the speaker as James Maplett, husband to Marion Bonville, he inquired as to his identity. When he received the answer he expected, he asked by what authority James laid claim to the castle.

"I am the husband of the eldest of Lord Bonville's heiresses."

"Is that all it takes, then? To be the eldest daughter's husband? You would yield your authority to the husband of an older sister?"

Caught off guard by the question, Maplett conceded that he would. "But there are none here," he pointed out.

"In that you are mistaken. I am Sir Gavin Dunnett. My wife, Mariotta, was older by a year than your Marion."

The smug look on Maplett's face was replaced by one of chagrin. Barlow gaped at Gavin in shocked disbelief.

Ignoring them both, he caught the eye of the halberdier with whom he'd supped and tossed the fellow a pouch heavy with coins. "Use that to pay back wages," he commanded.

His generosity stilled any protests guards or servants might have made. The arrival of the rest of his men silenced belated objections from Barlow and Maplett.

Once he had control of Bonville Keep, Gavin closeted himself with his daughter, who had done as he bade her in the wee hours of the morning and returned to her bed, saying nothing to anyone of her father's nocturnal visit. After reassuring her that all would be well, he entrusted her to the keeping of Alison's two younger sisters. Then he ordered Alison released from captivity and brought to him.

GAVIN DUNNETT REMINDED ALISON of a caged beast as he paced back and forth in the tower chamber. At last he turned on her. "Did you kill Beatrice Bonville?"

"I was about to ask you the same thing. You have certainly profited by her death."

"I did not kill her, either. Oh, I thought about it." In a few pithy words, he told her of Beatrice's claim that Isabella had died in infancy and his intent, when he'd believed that lie, to reive the castle. "I deemed it a just revenge to liberate a few of Beatrice's favorite pieces of jewelry before coming for Isabella."

So, Alison thought, he'd broken into the castle treasury. She did not begrudge him any of the trinkets he'd taken. Indeed, she would not have blamed him if he *had* killed Beatrice.

"Does it matter who stabbed my stepmother?" she asked. "I can think of no one here who mourns her passing."

"It rests with me, as temporary caretaker of this castle, to discover who killed Lady Bonville, if only because the crowner has

already been sent for. In search of the king's share of the criminal's estate, he'll want someone to blame. Being English, he'd
delight in finding evidence against a Scot."

"So you propose to give me to him instead?"

"I propose that you help me discover the real killer. If you
did not murder her and I did not, then it only makes sense that
we work together to find the truth." Taking Alison's agreement for
granted, he barked another question at her. "You accused Beatrice
of poisoning Isabella. What did you mean?"

"Why, what I said. Two days ago, I returned early from an
errand on which Beatrice had sent me and caught her dosing
Isabella with a substance I did not recognize. Soon after, Isabella
suffered a relapse. She became violently ill. I feared she would
die, even though I treated her with nettle, and goat's milk, and
honey water, and even mustard seed. All the antidotes I knew of."

"She first sickened hard upon her grandfather's death, or so I
have been told. Was that the result of poison, too?"

"I think so. When she fell ill, no one knew the cause, just as
no one knew what caused my father's sudden demise."

"Do you mean to say Lord Bonville was murdered?"

"I cannot prove it. He was not a young man, nor in the best
of health."

Gavin seemed to read her mind. "You think Isabella saw something . . . heard something . . . but would she not have told you?"

"Not if Beatrice threatened her. I think she did. And then, to
make sure of Isabella's silence, she tried to kill her, too. There is
henbane missing from the stillroom."

"A poison?"

"Aye. Oh, there was reason for it to be there. My father suffered from gout. Henbane leaves, stamped with populeon oint-
ment, are used in its treatment. But the juice, if enough be taken
internally, can kill in a matter of minutes."

"A dangerous poison, then."

"Aye. Just smelling the flowers can make one drowsy. A small
dose cures insomnia. A larger one causes an unquiet sleep that ends
in death." She did not add that some superstitious folk believed the
plant could also be used as a love charm—if it were gathered in the
early morning by a naked man standing on one foot.

"Did you tell anyone of your suspicions?"

"Only my sisters."

"Which sisters?"

"The two who are younger than I am. I was born tenth, Tertia eleventh, and Ysende twelfth."

"The three Beatrice meant to send to Holystone to be nuns."

Alison bristled. "If you think that would be reason enough for one of us to kill her—"

"Can you account for their whereabouts every minute of last night? For that matter, can you prove you were here with Isabella when Beatrice was murdered?"

Alison was unable to school her features in time. One look at the expression on her face and his suspicions about her returned. "What is it you have not told me, Alison?"

"Nothing to do with murder." She sighed. Better Gavin hear the truth from her than wonder if she'd committed a much greater crime. "I searched my stepmother's chamber while she was still at supper. I was looking for the missing container of poison. I found nothing. I dreaded the morrow—today—when Beatrice would take me to task for my actions, but I did not kill her to prevent being scolded."

"How would she know you'd been in her chamber?"

"Christiana saw me creeping away."

"Christiana?"

"Beatrice's waiting gentlewoman. I was certain she would tell Beatrice, but I meant to brazen it out. It is not as if I stole anything." She sent him a pointed look. "But then you came, and I did not want to lose Isabella, and I saw a chance to get away from Beatrice's wrath, besides."

"Or a chance to escape punishment."

It hurt to think he still did not trust her. And angered her. Hands on her hips, Alison glared at her accuser. "Ask Christiana. She can swear nobody was in Beatrice's chamber, dead or alive, when I left it."

Where else, she wondered suddenly, had Gavin gone before he came to the north tower for Isabella? He'd been in the great hall, disguised as a Benedictine monk. That much she'd surmised. But that left several hours unaccounted for. _Could_ Gavin have killed Beatrice? The possibility turned her almost as cold as her fear that he would continue to suspect her of the crime.

Gavin heaved a gusty sigh. "I believe you, Alison. I need no confirmation. Let us go, together, and talk to Isabella."

IN THE INNER CHAMBER in which his daughter had slept before her banishment to the north tower, a room she'd shared with Lord Bonville's three unmarried daughters, Tertia and Ysende kept their niece company. So did Christiana Talbot. Gavin did not notice her at first. It was easy to overlook the plain-faced waiting gentlewoman when she was in the company of a flock of tall, slender, fair-haired Bonvilles.

"This chamber adjoins the one where Beatrice was struck down," he said to Alison's sisters. "Did you hear anything?"

"We slept soundly," one of the sisters told him. They looked too much alike for him to tell which one she was.

"I heard naught until Christiana screamed," the other said.

"You found the body?" He turned to stare at the gentlewoman. His intense gaze seemed to fluster her.

Before he could pose his next question, Alison asked one of her own. "Did you see anyone near Beatrice's chamber after I left it?"

"Only Lady Bonville herself," Christiana replied. "She'd ordered me to sleep on the truckle bed, in case she wanted something fetched in the night."

Gavin lowered his voice in deference to his daughter's presence, although the child seemed intent on a piece of embroidery and was paying no attention to their conversation. "She slept alone?"

"Aye, Sir Gavin. For once."

Gavin frowned. "But if you were in the room, how did the killer reach her without waking you?"

"I went out to use the privy," Christiana mumbled. "I was only gone a few minutes. When I came back, I noticed that the bedcurtains were askew. Then I saw the blood."

"Could one of her lovers have killed her? For jealousy? For revenge? Because she rejected him?"

"She never rejected anyone," Alison muttered.

Christina looked discomfited, but after a moment her face brightened. "I have remembered something! She did have a falling-out with one of them. A Scots emissary visited here a month ago. Lady Bonville seemed most taken with him at first, but he left in anger."

Another lover? "Before or after Lord Bonville's death?"

"He left the day after. But he might have come back!"

Clearly, she hoped he had. Better, to her mind, that the killer be an outsider.

"I thank you for this intelligence, mistress. It may be most significant."

Christiana bobbed a curtsy and fled the chamber.

Gavin let her go, but he could not so easily dismiss the disturbing possibility she had raised. If Bonville's death, or Beatrice's, had been motivated by some political intrigue between England and Scotland, then he might never discover the truth.

After a few more questions, which yielded no new information, Gavin sent Alison's sisters away. Then, in a gentle, coaxing voice, he spoke to his daughter. "Lady Bonville can no longer harm you, Isabella," he said. "She is dead."

The child looked up from her embroidery, her small, pinched face too somber for her years. "Dead? Like Grandfather?"

He nodded.

"Is the man dead, too?"

"What man, Isabella?"

Although she stabbed her needle into the cloth with more force than necessary, Isabella did not answer. She was stitching a rose, Gavin saw, in blood red silk.

Alison knelt beside the girl's low stool. "Your father speaks true, sweeting. No one will hurt you ever again. But you must tell us everything you know."

A single tear dropped onto the fabric. "I wanted to keep Grandfather company."

Gavin settled himself on the floor, tailor-fashion, the better to hear his daughter's soft-spoken words. With one hand, he reached out to her. The other sought Alison's fingers until, with the kneeling woman and the seated child, he had formed a circle. He could not be certain how the others felt, but the contact rendered him calmer and more hopeful.

"You did nothing wrong, Isabella," he said.

"Lady Bonville told me to stay away."

"She banned you from your grandfather's sickroom?"

Isabella nodded.

"And you disobeyed?" Alison dried Isabella's tears.

"Yes."

"Tell us, sweeting. What happened then?"

With a final sniff, Isabella glanced at Gavin, then set aside her embroidery and turned to her aunt to confess. "I crept back to sit with him. He did not wake up, but I think he knew I was there."

"I am sure that comforted him," Alison said.

"Then I heard someone coming, so I hid myself behind the screen."

"What screen?" Gavin asked.

"It conceals the close stool," Alison told him. "Go on, Isabella. What did you hear?"

"Lady Bonville. She said—" Isabella broke off and looked about to weep again.

"What did she say?" Alison now held both of Isabella's hands in hers. Their eyes were locked.

"Hold him down while I make him swallow it."

Alison's gaze shifted to meet Gavin's, then away. Even though they had suspected as much, it was a shock to hear Beatrice's guilt so clearly revealed. He could only imagine how his daughter had felt.

"Did the man say anything?" Gavin hated to force Isabella to go on reliving that terrible day, but there was no choice. Beatrice might be dead, but her accomplice was not.

"I heard noises," Isabella whispered. "Choking and sputtering."

Her grandfather's death throes.

"And the man? Did he say anything when the noises stopped?"

"He said all this would be his now that Bonville was dead."

"Did you recognize his voice? Think, Isabella. Had you ever heard it before?"

"He whispered."

Alison wrapped the girl tight in an embrace. It seemed the most natural thing in the world for Gavin to shift his position so that he, too, could fling one comforting arm around their shoulders. Neither of them objected. Alison even managed a faint smile of approval.

"What happened after Beatrice and the man left?" he asked.

Isabella's eyes filled once more. "I came out of hiding and I saw him. Dead." A choked sob all but obscured the word. "I ran away, back to mine own chamber, but she saw me."

"Beatrice saw you leave the room?"

"She caught me and shook me till my teeth rattled. She said if I ever said a word about what went on in Grandfather's chamber, she'd kill me. I promised not to tell anyone, ever." Isabella turned wide, confused eyes to Gavin. "Why did she still hurt me when I promised not to tell?"

If Beatrice had not been dead already, Gavin thought, he'd kill her now for what she'd done to his daughter. He rose stiffly when Isabella dissolved once more into tears, and went to stand by the chamber window, while Alison calmed her.

He was still there some time later when, exhausted by her weeping, Isabella finally fell asleep.

"She is not yet out of danger," Alison whispered as she came up beside him.

"Aye. It stands to reason that the same person who helped Beatrice murder Lord Bonville also killed Beatrice."

"A falling-out among criminals?"

He nodded. "And if he knows what Isabella overheard, if he believes there is any chance she can identify him, he will try to silence her."

"Then we must discover who he is," Alison said. "One of Beatrice's recent lovers, that much seems certain. That narrows the field to three."

"Two, unless you think the Scots emissary returned to the castle in disguise."

She sent him a speaking glance. If Gavin had done so, someone else could have. Aloud, she asked, "Which one seems more
likely? Michael Barlow or James Maplett?"

"Barlow wanted to marry Beatrice. It is not unheard-of for a
steward to wed his . . . mistress. In that way he'd have gained
power and, perhaps, wealth. *All this would be his.* But if that was his
goal, why kill her? With Beatrice dead, he'd have nothing."

"A lover's quarrel?" Alison suggested. "A crime of passion?"

"Maplett had a better motive. He expected by Beatrice's
death to gain the Bonville estates, by virtue of being the husband
of your sister Marion. But any fool should have known his reason-
ing was faulty. He is no more the Bonville heir than I am."

Alison looked thoughtful, but she had no more to con-
tribute. She went off to question the servants while Gavin talked
to the Bonville men-at-arms.

A FEW HOURS LATER, they were no closer to a solution. Gavin
swallowed the last of the ale in his mazer and contemplated the
dregs. Would that he could read the truth in their pattern. 'Twas
as good a method as any.

Word had come just before they sat down to sup that the
crowner would arrive on the morrow. Gavin was determined to
present him with a murderer and be on his way soon after. Truce
or no, it was dangerous for a Scot to linger long on the English
side of the border.

Old Lord Bonville had known that. It had been, in truth, his
only objection to Gavin's marriage with Mariotta. Kinship, he'd
said, made for a strong bond, but an outsider would always find
acceptance hard to come by. A pity, he'd joked, that Gavin did
not have the look of a Bonville.

Gavin blinked. Could the answer be that obvious?

He turned to Alison, with whom he shared a trencher, and
whispered a question in her ear.

After giving him a startled look, she nodded. "There has scarce been time for word of my father's death to reach the cadet branch of the family. They settled in Cornwall generations ago."

"Motive for murder." He started to rise.

Her hand on his forearm stayed him. "Which murder?"

"Both."

But she shook her head. "I do not think so, for I have remembered something, too. And yet, I do think that if you accuse my father's poisoner of murdering Beatrice, you might just startle her killer into speaking."

Gavin did not ask for an explanation. He trusted Alison's instincts. Abruptly, he stood, scattering the remains of his meal, and called for more light.

When every sconce boasted a torch, every candlestick a taper, Gavin's gaze went first to Maplett, then moved on to Michael Barlow. "You are an impostor," he said to the latter, "and a murderer. You will hang for your crimes."

Before he could enumerate his reasons for accusing Barlow, Christiana Talbot cried out in distress. Everyone turned to look at her.

"You must not harm him. He did not kill Lady Bonville!"

"How can you be so certain?"

Christiana sent Barlow a glance filled with painful longing, then squared her shoulders and faced Gavin. "Because I killed her."

"Did you, by God?" In spite of Alison's prediction, Gavin had not expected this. "Why?"

"To keep Michael from marrying her." As if that confession sapped all her bravado, she dissolved into tears.

It was some time before Gavin could extract a coherent story. Details emerged in fits and starts, punctuated by much wailing and many loud lamentations.

Michael Barlow had promised to marry Christiana, but when Lord Bonville died, he'd told her he intended to wed the widow instead. He'd have it all, he'd bragged. Desperate to win him away from Beatrice, Christiana had confronted the other woman in her bedchamber.

"I told her she could not have him." Tears flowed freely down Christiana's pale cheeks. "He was mine! But she laughed at me. Made sport of me. Said I was too plain of face to take him away from her."

In a moment of overwhelming rage, Christiana Talbot had used the knife with which she cut her meat to stab Lady Bonville to death.

Gavin felt sorry for the woman, even as he ordered her taken into custody. "Seize Barlow, too," he added.

"You cannot arrest me," Barlow protested. "She's just told you she acted alone. She killed the woman I meant to marry. I had naught to do with it."

"But you had everything to do with another crime. You helped Beatrice Bonville kill her husband."

Barlow began to sputter a denial. Gavin held up one hand to silence him, then told the gathered company what Isabella had overheard.

"Arrant nonsense," Barlow declared. "You say yourself that the child did not recognize the voice of Lady Bonville's accomplice. He could have been anyone. That Scots emissary—"

"There might be more than one man willing to kill at Lady Bonville's bidding," Gavin interrupted, "but only one had an inheritance to gain. By law, the Bonville title and much of the estate goes to the last baron's closest male relative. A distant cousin, I believe. Distant enough that church and state would permit him to marry the widow if he chose to."

"No. No, I—"

"You carry the proof of your inheritance with you, Master Barlow. If that is your name. You are the only man here who could be the Bonville heir, for you are the only man here who has the Bonville hair."

At a signal from Gavin, the men-at-arms pulled Barlow out of the shadows. His flaxen locks shone silver-gilt in the candlelight, rendering futile any further denials.

As the prisoners were led away, Gavin turned to Alison. "How did you guess Christiana was guilty?"

"She slept that night in the same chamber with Beatrice, the same chamber where my father died. That meant there was no reason for her to leave the room to visit the privy. That chamber is furnished with a perfectly good close stool, behind the screen where Isabella hid."

"But why did you think she'd confess to save Barlow?"

Alison looked surprised he should ask. "Everyone in the castle knew about Christiana's unrequited passion for my stepmother's lover."

THE NEXT MORNING, AFTER the crowner had accepted Gavin's evidence and ridden away with two murderers in custody, Gavin came to collect his daughter and her belongings. Alison was waiting with the girl, her own possessions packed and ready.

"I will accompany Isabella to Scotland," she informed him. "I am certain that whatever distant male cousin is next in line to inherit cares not a whit what I do or where I go."

To her surprise, Gavin did not argue. He merely pointed out, lest she have any false hopes, that under English law a man could not marry his deceased wife's sister without a papal dispensation.

"I am not interested in marriage," she informed him in a haughty voice. "I am content to be Isabella's companion."

"Better than life in a nunnery," he agreed.

Dusk was falling by the time they crossed the border. Gavin turned to Alison and smiled down at her through the open visor of his helmet.

"Then again," he said in a conversational tone of voice, as if there had been mere minutes instead of most of a day's ride between his last remark on the subject and this one, "Scots law on marriage differs from the English."

"In what way?" she asked.

His smile widened into a grin as he produced the Bonville betrothal ring, the one piece of jewelry he'd not returned to the castle treasury. "In Scotland it is a much simpler matter for a widower to marry the sister of his late wife."

She smiled back at him, a twinkle in her bright blue eyes.

"I know," she said, and extended her hand.

For the Love of Old Bones

Michael Jecks

The sudden violence was a shock: swift and devastating. They came at us from all sides, and what were we supposed to do? We couldn't run; we couldn't hide. There was nowhere to conceal ourselves on that desolate damned moor.

I was struck down early. When I came to, it was to find my head being cradled in the lap of a rough countryman, a shepherd from the rank smell of him, holding a leather bottle of sour-tasting water to my lips that I drank with gratitude. All about me, when I felt able to gaze around, were my companions: resting, holding broken heads, or wincing as their bruised limbs gave them pain. It was all I could do to pull away and kneel, fingering my rosary as I offered my thanks to God for delivering us from our attackers.

"The Abbot is dead!"

The cry broke in upon my devotions and I had to stifle my gasp of horror. I saw Brother Charles at the side of Abbot Bertrand's slumped figure and hurried over to them as fast as my wounded head would allow.

Abbot Bertrand de Surgères, my lord, lay dead; stabbed in his back.

IT IS DIFFICULT ALWAYS to try to recall small details after a horrible event. I and my English brethren have suffered much in the years since the great famine of 1315 to 1316. As peasants lost their food, so there was less for us monks; the murrain of sheep and cattle that followed devastated our meager flocks and herds, and now, late in the year of our Lord thirteen hundred and twenty-one, I had myself taken my fill of despair.

With the pain in my head from the crushing blow, I was in no state to assist my brothers in tidying the body of our Abbot. I sat resting while they unclothed him and redressed him in fresh linen and tunic; others walked a mile or more northward to a wood, from where they fetched sturdy boughs to fashion a stretcher. The horses had gone, of course. For my part, I could not help them. I knew only pain and sadness as I watched them work.

It was a cold, quiet place, this. The sun was watery this late in the year, and its radiance failed to warm. We were on the side of a hill, with a small stream gurgling at our feet. A few warped and twisted trees stood about, but all were distorted, grotesque imitations of the strong oaks and elms I knew. The grass itself looked scrubby and unwholesome, while the ground held a thick scattering of rocks and large stones, giving the scene a feeling of devastation, as if a battle had raged over it all. It felt to me like a place blasted with God's rage. As it should, I thought, with one of His Abbots lying murdered on the ground.

The shepherd disappeared soon after I awoke, but while my companions set the Abbot's body on the stretcher and began gathering together the few belongings that the robbers had scattered, I sat quietly. I saw Brother Humphrey pick up the Abbot's silver crucifix. He saw my quick look and smiled weakly. In our little convent there have been occasions when odd bits and pieces have gone missing, and he knows I suspect him. The cord of the cross was broken, although the cross and tiny figure were fine; nearby, Abbot Bertrand's purse lay on the ground. Humphrey picked up both and passed them to me with a puzzled expression.

As he stood there, I heard hoofs. Looking up, I saw three men at the brow of the hill. One was the shepherd, the other two were on horseback. They were unknown to me; indeed, I could hardly make out their features for the low, autumnal sun was behind them, and it was hard to see more than a vague shadow. Now, of course, I know Bailiff Puttock of Lydford and his friend Sir Baldwin of Furnshill near Cadbury, but then they were only strange, intimidating figures on their horses, staring down at us intently while the shepherd leaned on his staff.

At the sight of them Humphrey let out a cry of despair, fearing a fresh attack; a pair of servants grabbed their staffs and advanced, determined to protect us. The three remaining brothers began reciting the *paternoster*; me, I simply fell to my knees and prayed.

THE MEN RODE DOWN the incline and I could make them out. It was soon obvious that one of them was a knight—his sword belt and golden spurs gleamed as the sun caught them. His slow approach was reassuring, too. It gave me the impression that we were safe: he hardly looked like one of the predatory knights who might conceal robbery by making demands in courtly language. In any event, such a one would have brought a strong party of men-at-arms to steal what they wanted.

"Brothers, please don't fear us," the other man said as he neared the staffman. "I'm Bailiff Puttock under Abbot Champeaux of Tavistock Abbey and my friend is Sir Baldwin, the Keeper of the King's Peace in Crediton. This shepherd told us of the attack and we have already sent for the Coroner to view the body. May we help you?"

I heaved a sigh of relief. There was no fearing men such as these. "Godspeed, gentlemen! It is an enormous relief to meet you. Now at least we need fear no footpads while on the moors."

It was the knight who spoke first, studying me with an oddly intense expression, like one who has no liking for monks. He was tall, with heavy shoulders and a flat belly to prove that he practiced regularly with his sword. Intelligent dark eyes glittered in a square face with a thin beard that followed the line of his jaw. One scar marred his features, twisting his mouth. "Your name, Brother?"

"I am Brother Peter, from Launceston Abbey. My Abbot sent me to help our brethren on their arduous journey to France and back. We were on our way to Launceston when this happened."

"It's a long way to go without horses, Brother," the other man pointed out.

"We had horses until last night, when they were taken."

"You were robbed? God's teeth! The thieving bastards!" Bailiff Puttock burst out. "How many were there? And which way did they go?"

"I was knocked down early on," I grimaced, gingerly feeling the back of my tonsure. The skin was broken slightly and there was a large lump forming that persuaded me not to prod or probe too hard.

"There were six of them. They appeared like devils as the sun faded, running straight at us . . ."

As I spoke I could recall the horror. Screaming, shrieking men, all wielding staves or clubs, springing down from the surrounding rocks, belaboring us, holding us off while two young lads, scarcely more than boys, took our horses. And a short while later, nothing: they had clubbed me.

The knight was silent, but the Bailiff cocked his head. "None of them had a knife?"

"I don't recall. My head—I was unconscious."

"What was their leader like?"

"Heavyset, bearded, with long dark hair."

"I have heard of him."

"They took most of our provisions as well as our mounts."

Sir Baldwin walked off a few yards, bending and studying the ground. He went to the stream and followed its bank a short distance, then round the curve of the hill, disappearing from sight.

His friend appeared confused. "You say these men attacked and took your horses—but only your Abbot was stabbed? It seems odd. . . ."

He would likely have added more, but then his friend called, "They went this way. Their prints are all over the mud at the side of the stream. It looks like they have gone westward."

"Which is where we should go as well," Bailiff Puttock said. "If there are thieves on the moors we should warn the abbey. We can send a second messenger to the Coroner explaining where we have gone."

"And it would be a good place for these good brothers to recover from their ordeal," Sir Baldwin agreed.

"IT SEEMS CURIOUS THAT the thieves should have left such wealth behind."

We were resting in a hollow on the old track to Tavistock. All of us were tired after our ordeal and needed plenty of breaks. The knight was squatting, studying the crucifix and purse.

The Bailiff shrugged unconcernedly. "They grabbed what they could."

"But they killed an Abbot."

"So? In the dark they probably didn't realize he was an Abbot, nor that they had killed him. It was a short, sharp scuffle in the gloom."

"Hmm."

I could see that the knight wasn't convinced. The Bailiff, too, for all his vaunted confidence, scarcely seemed more certain. Both stared down at the items. I cleared my throat and held up the cold meat in my hand. "Could one of you lend me a knife? My own was still on the packhorse."

With a grunt the knight pulled a small blade from his boot and passed it to me.

"I've known thieves leave behind goods after being scared off," Bailiff Puttock continued after a while.

"And I have known Bailiffs who have left wine in the jug after a feast—but that does not mean I have ever seen you behaving abstemiously. No, these robbers planned their raid. Two things are curious: first, that they bothered to kill the man; second, that they left his wealth at his side."

"Who were these robbers, Sir Baldwin?" I interjected.

"We may never catch them, Brother," he said with a smile. "There are so many who have been displaced since the recent

wars in Wales. They have swollen the ranks of the poor devils
who lost everything during the famine."

"Poor devils, my arse!" Puttock growled. "They should have
remained at their homes and helped rebuild their vills and towns,
not become outlaw and run for the hills."

"Some had little choice," Sir Baldwin said.

"Some didn't, no, but this gang sounds like Hamo's lot again."

"They've never killed before," Sir Baldwin said slowly.

"True, but the leader sounds like Hamo and the theft of the
horses is just like his mob."

Sir Baldwin rose. "This is not helping us. You saw nothing of
the death of your Abbot, Brother Peter?" I shook my head. "Then
let us ask your friends. Could you introduce us?"

I nodded. "Brother Humphrey is another Englishman like
me, but Brother Charles comes from France. He is the shorter of
the three. The third, the handsome young one, is Brother Roger,
who is also French. He comes from the Abbot's own convent."

"What was the reason for their visit?" the Bailiff asked.

"There has been debate for many years about where certain
relics should be stored. The fingerbone of Saint Peter is held at
Launceston and I was sent to the Abbot to explain why we felt it
should remain," I told him sadly.

My head throbbed again with the recollection of that dreadful
meeting. It was held by Abbot Bertrand in his chapter house, and
the place reeked. The fire's logs hadn't been properly dried and the
hearth in the middle of the room smoked foully, filling the place
with an acrid stench; censers competed with it, with the result that
all of us were coughing by the end of the meeting—if it could be so
termed. We discussed the ins and outs of sites for the bones, but the
decision had already been made. That was made abundantly clear.
Our carefully thought-out arguments were overruled or ignored.

"They could think of taking such a relic back to France?" Sir
Baldwin asked with frank astonishment.

I allowed a little acid into my voice. "It's the way of the
French. Now that they have installed the Pope in Avignon they
feel that they can win any argument they wish."

"But to take the bones from a place like Launceston! It is not
as if there is much else for the people to venerate there!"

"No, indeed. Launceston is far from civilization. It is an out-post on the fringes of society; without the few items we have, how can we hope for God's grace to protect us?"

Bailiff Puttock watched the men. "And you say that this Brother Charles is French? Let's ask him about last night."

MY FRIEND BROTHER CHARLES was a short, thickset man of maybe five-and-twenty years. Originally from the southern provinces of France, near the border with Toulouse, his tonsure was fringed with sandy colored hair. Upon being called to meet with the knight and his comrade, Brother Charles appeared nervous, as if he feared their presence.

Bailiff Puttock spoke first. "I hear you're from a French Abbey, come here to remove English relics?"

Brother Charles threw me a helpless look. "I was com-manded to join my Abbot, it is true."

"To take away bones from Launceston?"

"That was the plan. The mother-abbey has need of them."

"So does Launceston," the Bailiff snarled gruffly.

"My Abbot decided. I was ordered to join him together with my friend Brother Roger and these other good monks, Humphrey and Peter, from the monastery of Launceston."

"Very well. What happened last night?"

"My Lord, I was preparing some pottage for our evening meal when I heard a shout. It was one of the grooms. I looked up and saw him toppling over. A great bear of a man stood behind him, grasping a heavy staff. It was awful! I was about to rush to help the groom when I realized there were more attack-ers. I thought it better to go to the Abbot's side and help defend the camp."

"Where was everyone else?" Sir Baldwin asked.

"I can hardly recall, Sir Baldwin. It is all so confused in my mind. The men attacked so swiftly . . . I was at the fire when I heard the first scream. When I turned I saw Brother Peter crum-ple. Abbot Bertrand still had Brother Humphrey and Brother

Roger with him. There was so much shouting—so many cries and screams. One of our servants was felled and then I realized a man was near me, the same gross fellow who had hurt Brother Peter. I avoided his club and went to my Lord Abbot's side.

"But when I got there, two men rushed at us, and I only had time to grab a stick and thrust at them, but missed, I fear. I was knocked back, driven toward the fire again, fearing all the time that the big man who had knocked Brother Peter down could strike me from behind. The Abbot fell. I saw him, I think. It was all so confused! Then they were pulling away, and we heard the sound of our horses cantering away. The men laughed as they scurried off. And I saw my Abbot on the ground."

"Did he say anything?"

"No. He was dead. The blade that struck him down killed him instantly. He made no sound."

"How close was he to you?"

"He was only a few yards from me." Brother Charles belatedly realized that the questioning was focusing unpleasantly upon him. "But we had all gathered close to each other!"

Sir Baldwin held up his hand. "Do not worry yourself. We only wish to see the place through your eyes. Tell me, what was the Abbot like?"

Brother Charles threw me a confused, desperate look, and I interjected, "Sir Baldwin, what has this to do with his death? Surely, it would be better for us to continue on our way and warn others of these thieves before they can harm other travelers?"

"Yes, but please humor us. This Abbot of yours—was he a generous, kindly fellow?"

I gave a brittle smile. One should hardly speak ill of the dead, but . . . I chose the path of least trouble. "He was deeply religious and devoted to his abbey."

Sir Baldwin eyed me with a faint grin. "He was not your friend, then."

There was no need for me to say anything. I merely hung my head.

"Was it the bones?"

I met his eye with stern resolution. "Sir Baldwin, I feel that your questions are bordering upon the impertinent. You are questioning me about a matter that is of little, if any, concern of yours. An Abbot has been murdered and that offense falls under Canon Law. It is not within your jurisdiction. However, we do have a responsibility to others to see to their protection. For that reason I should like to hurry to Tavistock. In addition, I have to take the good Abbot's body to the abbey for burial. Should we not continue on our way?"

THE WAY WAS HARD. Devonshire has few good roads. All of them involve climbing hills and dropping into rock-strewn valleys with few good bridges over the chilly, fast streams. It was a miracle that none of us broke an ankle on the treacherous soil or fell into one of the foul-smelling bogs.

The knight and his friend were good enough to lend their horses, one to me, one to poor Brother Roger. He, too, had been struck down in the attack, and he rode slumped, his head rocking as if he were dozing. Once I had to hurry to his side and hold him upright when he all but fell from the saddle.

After that I felt I had little option but to accede when the Bailiff suggested that we should stop again. It led to my feeling fretful and irritable, but I could see no alternative.

We had come to a pleasant space in which strange buildings of stone abounded. They might have been ancient huts for shepherds like the man who had helped us and who now traipsed along gloomily. He had been told that he should join us so that his evidence could also be given alongside our own.

Many men worked the moors, I reflected. Miners scrabbled for tin, copper, and arsenic on the wildlands; farmers raised their sheep and cattle; builders dug quarries. All lived out there, in the inhospitable waste.

Yet none could be seen from here. The moor stretched five leagues, maybe, north and south of this point, and was at least four leagues wide. That was why gangs of thieves and outlaws could easily lose themselves. Even now they could be up there watching us, laughing as they sat astride our own ponies.

The thought made me shiver with anger. Knaves like them deserved to die!

THE BAILIFF AND THE knight approached Humphrey almost as soon as we had stopped, and I pursed my lips with annoyance. It was obvious that they intended to question him as they had Brother Charles, and I wasn't going to have it. Instead, I called Brother Humphrey to me, asking him to join me in prayer.

He did so with alacrity, and I smiled, glad to have rescued him. I also caught sight of the speculative expression on the knight's face. It was suspicious, as if he thought I was behaving oddly, but I didn't care. I took Humphrey's hand and led him away, sitting with him on a stone and murmuring the prayers for the office of Sext. It was surely about noon.

While we prayed and offered ourselves once more to God, I saw Brother Roger walking away to fetch water. It was a relief, for I was sure that as soon as they could, the knight and the Bailiff would be after him as well with their questions.

Finishing our prayers, I patted Humphrey's arm and he gave me an anxious smile in return. Poor Humphrey was plainly scared. His pale grey eyes were fearful, darting hither and thither like those of a hunted animal. The affair was taking its toll on the nineteen-year-old, and I gave him a reassuring grin.

I was about to offer him some advice when he stopped me. "Last night—I have to tell someone . . ."

"Shh!" I hissed. I could sense the two pests approaching. Their shadows loomed.

"Brother Humphrey, we'd like to ask you what you saw last night," Bailiff Puttock said.

The knight hunkered down beside us. "It's hard to understand why the Abbot should have died. Especially since he had money on him, money that was not taken but was instead left at his side. Did you see him stabbed?"

"No, Sir Baldwin. I could scarcely see anything."

"You weren't knocked unconscious?" the Bailiff asked.

"No."

"You came from Launceston with Brother Peter here, didn't you?"

"Yes. We were both sent to persuade the Abbot against taking our relics."

"But he decided to in any case?"

"They wouldn't listen to us!" Humphrey stormed. "It wasn't fair! They'd already decided to steal our . . ."

I interrupted hastily. "This was no theft, Humphrey. It was their right and their decision."

"The relics are ours! They should remain in Cornwall!"

"Did you like the Abbot?" Sir Baldwin asked.

Humphrey looked at me, and I glanced at the knight with an annoyed coldness. "Sir Baldwin, what has this to do with anything? The Abbot—God bless his soul!—is dead. What good can raking over other people's feelings for him achieve?"

"Brother, you were unconscious and couldn't have seen much," Bailiff Puttock said easily, "but we have to find out as much about these robbers as we can because we have to catch them. All we want is to gain a good idea of exactly what happened last night."

Before Humphrey could answer, I peered over my shoulder. Brother Roger had not returned. "Go and seek Brother Roger. I fear he could have become lost. God forbid that he should be swallowed in a mire."

When he was gone, I faced the two once more. They exchanged a look.

"Brother Humphrey is well known to me, and I would prefer that you didn't question him too deeply. It could harm him."

"What's that supposed to mean?" the Bailiff demanded. "The man's fine, but you seem determined to protect him from our questions. Why?"

"Because he is not well," I told him harshly. "Good God! Can't you see? The fellow is a wreck."

"Because of the attack?"

I took a deep breath. "No, because his father was a clerk in Holy Orders who raped a nun. Humphrey is convinced that his whole existence is an affront to God."

"Christ's bones!" the Bailiff gasped. "The poor bastard!"

"So I would be most grateful if you could leave the poor fellow alone. He needs peace, and the attack itself has severely upset him. I should have thought that you would have been able to see that!"

The two apologized handsomely. It was plain that the Bailiff was shocked by what he had heard. And who wouldn't be? The story was one to chill the blood—being born as a result of the rape of one of Christ's own brides was hideous. It had marked out poor Humphrey from early on: the product of a heretical union.

"Did the Abbot know of his past?" Sir Baldwin asked.

"Yes. Naturally. Abbot Bertrand knew about all of us."

I saw the knight's attention move behind me and turned in time to see Humphrey leading Brother Roger back into the makeshift camp. The Frenchman looked confused and happily took his seat on a satchel, while Humphrey solicitously spread a blanket over his knees and patted his hand. I called to him sharply and asked him to fetch a wineskin. We could all do with some refreshment.

Only a few moments after the knight and Bailiff had risen, they began to move in the direction of Brother Roger. I followed them, pointing out that the poor lad was dazed still from his wound.

"I understand that, but I would still like to ask him a little about the attack," the knight stated in what I can only call a curt manner. He was growing testy.

"There seems little need. I have told you what I saw, and you know who the killer is."

"You have told us that you did not see anyone stab him," the Bailiff said. "We still have to see whether anyone might have seen who actually did."

"Good God above! I told you about our attackers—what more do you want?"

"A witness who saw him shove a knife into your Abbot's back," he said shortly.

I could feel the anger twisting my features as I trailed after them toward the sitting monk, and I was forced to pray for patience in the face of what felt like overwhelming provocation.

Brother Roger was young, only perhaps twenty-two. Looking up with a mild squint against the brightness of the day, he
had to keep closing his eyes as we spoke, as though the sun's light
was too powerful for him.

"My friend, these men wish to ask you about the attack last
night to find out whether you saw the leader of the outlaws stab . . ."

The knight interrupted me. "Brother Roger, you were yourself knocked on the head. When did you waken?"

"This morning. I was unconscious for some hours. And my
head!" He winced. "It was worse than the headache after an
evening drinking strong wine!"

"What do you remember of the attack?"

"I was near the Abbot, and when the first cry came to us, he
was on his feet and rushing for the horses, but he was stopped. A
group of the felons appeared, and we ran to the Abbot's side to
protect him. I was there at his right hand," he added with a hint
of self-consciousness.

"Did you see anyone stab him?"

"No."

Brother Charles had approached and now he interrupted. "I
saw him crumple like an axed pig. One moment up and fighting;
the next, collapsed in a heap. It was as if he had been struck by a rock."

"You are sure of this?" the knight pressed him.

"Oh, yes," Charles said emphatically. "He fell because he was
struck on the head."

"One of the outlaws could have heaved a stone at him," the
Bailiff said pensively.

"Perhaps," Sir Baldwin said. "Tell me, Brother Roger: the
Abbot, was he always a bold man?"

"Very brave and courageous. He would always leap to the
front of any battle. He had been a knight, you see. He was Sir
Bertrand de Toulouse before he took Holy Orders."

Now Baldwin's brow eased. The frown that had wrinkled his
forehead faded. "So that is why he was so keen to be at the fore-
front of the fighting!"

"Yes. He would always go to a fight to protect his own. And,
of course, he saw a man attacking Humphrey," he added with a
faintly sneering tone to his voice.

"Humphrey was sorely pressed?" Bailiff Puttock asked.

I shot the loathsome Frenchman a look of warning but he met it with sneering complacency. "No, Bailiff. Abbot Bertrand was a sodomite; he wished to preserve the life of the man he adored."

AFTER HE HAD LET it out, there was little more for me to say. I walked away and left the knight and his friend still talking to the Frenchman, but I wished to hear no more of their inquiry. If they wanted more, they could come and find me.

I left the camp, seeking the stream that Roger had apparently discovered. It was a short distance away. Some twenty yards farther up was the corpse of a sheep, and as I drank I saw that it had horns still attached to its skull. As soon as I had drunk my fill, I walked up and pulled them off. They would decorate a walking stick.

It was relaxing here, listening to the chuckle and gurgle of the water. I rested upon a rock and stared at the water for a time, considering. So much had happened recently: There was the horror of finding that the Abbot wanted our relics, to help him persuade gullible peasants and townspeople to give him more money in exchange for prayers said within the church. The shock of learning that he had made up his mind before the arguments could be put before him. And last there was the terror in Humphrey's eyes when the Abbot had fondled and caressed him after the meeting, promising him wealth and advancement should he agree to share the Abbot's bed.

Humphrey had lost the veneer of calmness he had developed over such a long period. It had been appalling to him to discover that the Abbot was corrupt—*perverted!* How could he respond, he asked, and I told him: simply refuse and walk from the Abbot if he tried it again.

But now I had to cover my face in my hands at the result.

I AROSE, PREPARING TO return to the camp, when I heard the scream. Eerie, it seemed to shiver on the air as a gust wafted it toward me. It was as if a hand of ice had clutched at my heart. A trickle of freezing liquid washed down my spine, and I felt the hairs of my head stand erect.

All at once I remembered the stories of ghosts and demons on the moors. This grim wasteland was home to devils of all kinds who hunted fresh souls with their packs of baying wishhounds. This shriek sounded like that of a soul in torment, and my hand grabbed at my crucifix even as I mouthed the *paternoster* with a shocked dread.

Before I could finish, Sir Baldwin was at my side, his sword in his hand. "Where did it come from?" he rasped, staring north-ward from us.

For the second time that day, I was glad to see him, and for the second time I could tell him little. "Up there somewhere."

He gave me a twisted little grin. "This is hardly what a monk should be used to."

"I'm not!" I said grimly. The sight of his unsheathed sword had recovered a little of my courage. The blade was beautiful, fashioned from bright peacock-blue steel.

He motioned with it. "Shall we see what caused that noise?"

"Very well."

I had no desire to see this, but equally I had no wish to appear a coward. Also, if it were a human or mortal beast creating that unholy row, I would be safe enough with the knight; while if it were the noise of a devil seeking a soul, I should be as safe out in the moors as I was in the camp. Either way, I knew that how-ever strong my faith *should* have been, I would feel happier with this armed man at my side.

"I've told the servants to guard the camp," Bailiff Puttock said, striding toward us. He carried a coil of rope over one shoulder.

"Good," Sir Baldwin said absently. "Brother Peter thinks the noise came from over there."

The Bailiff chuckled. "I'm afraid not. The wind can do odd things to sounds out here. No, it would have come from there." He pointed, and soon was leading the way.

THE SCREAM CAME AGAIN as we clambered over rocks and tussocks of loose grass. It was also damp. "What could that noise be?" I asked.

Bailiff Puttock cast me a smiling glance. "Haven't you got bogs near Launceston? It's the sound of a desperate man bellowing for help after falling in one of our mires. Not a nice way to die, that."

I realized then what my eyes and feet had been telling me. The ground here trembled underfoot as I placed my feet upon it, and the grasses each carried an odd, white pennant at the tip of their stems: this was no grass, it was a field of rushes.

"Watch my feet and step only in my own footprints," the Bailiff commanded.

I was happy to obey him. When I lost concentration for a moment, my leg slipped up to the shin in foul, evil-looking mud. I muttered a curse, and as I pulled my foot free, there came another cry. It scarcely sounded human.

We scrambled up to the top of a ridge, and upon the other side we had a clear view for some miles. There, at the edge of a field of white rush flowers, we saw a man's head. His arms were outspread and one gripped at something, a bush or twig.

"He's further gone than I'd thought," the Bailiff muttered before springing down the gentle incline, the knight, his sword now sheathed, and I stumbling along as best we could. At the base of the hill was a kind of path made of stepping-stones and we had to hop from one to another until we came close to the mire.

"Christ Jesus; praise the saints! Thank you, thank you, thank you!"

"My God!" I said. "It's him!"

The Bailiff grinned. "Meet Hamo!"

It took time to persuade the moor to give up its victim. When we finally hauled him from the filthy mud, he lay sprawled like a drowned cat rescued from a rain butt, as if he were already dead. Bailiff Puttock bound his arms with his rope. Soon Hamo gave a convulsive gasp, almost a sob, his face red and fierce after his struggle.

"The *bastards*," he wheezed. "They threw me there to die, God rot their guts!"

"You," Sir Baldwin said mildly, "are arrested."

"What for?" the man demanded suspiciously.

"The murder of Abbot Bertrand," Bailiff Puttock said, firmly binding his hands. "You stole his horses last night and stabbed the Abbot when he lay on the ground."

Hamo shrugged expansively. "I'll hang for the horses, and you can only hang a man the once, but I never killed him. That was why my gang threw me in the mire to die, the bastards! Because they heard a rumor that an Abbot had been killed; but it wasn't me. I saw him fall like he'd been struck dead while we fought, but then there were two other men to worry about. I didn't have time to stab him. Do you know where the gang lives? I can take you there if you want to kill them." He shivered, casting a glance back at the mire.

"We'll think about it. Do you swear on your soul that you didn't kill the Abbot?" the Bailiff asked.

"I swear it on my soul and on my mother's soul. I never hurt the man. He fell before I could strike him."

IT WAS CLEAR THAT the two were impressed by his assertions. Sir Baldwin prodded him with his sword while the Bailiff gripped the rope's end, and I wandered along cautiously in their wake.

Returning we took a longer path, one which was, I am glad to say, less soggy than the one we had taken on the way to find this barbarous fellow. Before long we had got back to the camp and had bound our captive to a tree. He nodded and grinned to the men gathered there, but he was refused any wine or water from our stores. Since he had stolen our stocks, we reasoned it was hardly reasonable that he should take a share in what was left us.

"Why didn't you take the Abbot's crucifix?" the Bailiff asked.

"I didn't even see it. Look, there was a fight, right? I waded in quickly so that our boys could cut the horses free and lead them away. I stood against the Abbot, but he suddenly fell; when he did, I was beset by two more men." He grudgingly nodded toward Roger and Charles. "I didn't have time to feel the man's body. Almost as soon as he fell there was a shout and we withdrew. That's all I know."

"What of these others?" Sir Baldwin said, indicating Humphrey and me.

"I saw that one," he said, nodding toward me. "I hit him early on. Not hard, but he dropped. The other one—I don't remember."

"So you, Brother Humphrey, are the only one who is not accounted for," Sir Baldwin said softly.

"Sir Baldwin, that is outrageous!" I roared. "Dare you suggest . . ."

"Quiet, father, let me . . ."

The Bailiff's jaw dropped. "You . . . *you* are his father?"

I sank wearily to a rock and passed a hand over my forehead. "Yes," I admitted. "I was the evil fool who raped his mother, may God forgive me! And I murdered the Abbot."

"Father, no! It was me he insulted!"

"Bailiff, I know what I am saying," I said again. In truth, it was a relief to end the anticipation. "My son was in danger from the Abbot. I had to protect him. The Abbot wanted him to go to his bedchamber. He told me, and I sought to defend him as best I could." I stood and patted my son's shoulder. "When I saw the fight, it was as if I saw the means. I threw a stone at the Abbot hoping that he would falter and be struck down, killed. He fell, and I then went and stabbed him when no one else was watching."

"Interesting," Sir Baldwin said. "Yet you were yourself unconscious during the attack."

"I fell, but I was only bewildered for a moment. As soon as I came to, I saw what was happening. There was a rock by my hand and I hurled it at him."

"And?" Bailiff Puttock asked.

"What do you mean, 'and'?"

"You threw the stone at him, jumped to your feet, and hurled yourself across the camp to stab him?"

"Yes," I said.

"Where is your knife?"

His words made me blink. I hadn't thought of that. I don't wear a knife. My eating knife was on the packhorse. I had already told them that. "My knife . . . I dropped it after—"

"Father, stop it!"

I couldn't restrain him, my boy threw himself at my feet. "I didn't kill him and neither did you! You never threw a rock. You had collapsed! I saw you."

"So who did kill him?" I asked, and now, I confess, I was too astonished to be more than a little bemused by the course of events.

"Him!" Humphrey spat, pointing at Brother Roger. "When I saw you had fallen, I cried out. The Abbot thought I had been hurt and leapt to my side. Roger knocked the Abbot down in a fit of jealousy, and I think he stabbed the Abbot later when no one was watching."

"Me? Why should I do this?"

"Because the Abbot had thrown you over. He thought you pretty when you were a choirboy, and I suppose he loved you in a way, but then he wanted me instead, and you couldn't cope with that, could you?"

"I was fighting with him, and I fell, just as did your father."

"My father has blood on his head and a lump—what do you have?" Humphrey sneered.

It was with a sense of—I confess it—disbelief that I realized what my son had noticed. The Frenchman had said that he was dreadfully knocked, had taken a horse because of his supposed pain, and yet he had no bruise, no lump, no blood. And he could stand and debate with Humphrey.

As the thought came to me, I saw him stand, white-faced with rage. Suddenly, he whipped a hand beneath his robe and pulled out a knife. He launched himself on my boy.

I suppose I didn't think of the danger. All I knew was that my boy was at risk. Did I realize I was risking my own life? I don't know. Perhaps there was an awareness, but no matter. I would do it again if I had the opportunity.

You see, all my son's life I had seen him walk in shame, paying the debt that I had created for him. This at least I could do for him: I could protect him, and hopefully prove that his father was himself forgiven by God for his great sin.

Yes, I jumped forward and threw my arms about Brother Roger. The first stab was nothing, a thud against my breast as if he had clenched a fist and thumped me with it; the second made a huge pain which is with me still, and my left arm was made useless. Still, I could hold on with my right, and this I did. I held him until Bailiff Puttock struck him smartly with the pommel of his sword, and Brother Roger collapsed with me on top of him.

This is the truth, as I believe in the life to come. Oh, Holy Lady, take me and heal me from the sins and pain of this world!

My son, farewell!

SIR BALDWIN WATCHED AS Brother Humphrey finished the dictation and set the paper aside, sniveling, dropping his reed. The knight's attention went to the frankly bemused expression on the face of the outlaw. Near him lay the knife that had fallen from Brother Roger's hand. Baldwin stared at it a long moment, then at the felon. Slowly, he turned away and faced the group again.

"We must take the body of Brother Peter with us. Perhaps we could put it on the stretcher with the Abbot," he said, walking around the group.

Simon kicked the unconscious Brother Roger. "We have to get this shit back to town as well. And then organize a posse to get the rest of the outlaws."

"They'll be long gone by now," Sir Baldwin said. He looked toward the outlaw. There was a profoundly innocent expression on Hamo's face. "You! Where will your gang be tonight, do you think?"

"They said they were going to head down toward Dartmouth. There're always women to be bought in a sailor's town."

"There you are," Baldwin said. "Now, I know it is not within our jurisdiction to arrest a monk because he falls under Canon Law, but do you think we could tie this fellow and ensure he doesn't try to run away?"

Bailiff Puttock was about to answer when a scrabbling of feet and a gasp made him turn. Where the felon had squatted bound to a tree, there remained only a coil of rope. Hamo was pelting away over the coarse grass.

As the Bailiff made to chase after him, Sir Baldwin put a hand to his arm. "Leave him, friend. There have been enough deaths already. Let's allow one man to remain alive."

"But he and his gang started all this!"

"Yes, I know. But under Canon Law no monk or cleric can be hanged. This man murdered his Abbot, an act of treachery as well as homicide, but can't swing; that felon didn't kill anyone, but he would be hanged as soon as he appeared in a town. Is that justice? Let him go."

The Bailiff watched the man disappear among the thick rocks of the moors. "So long as the damned cretin doesn't fall into another mire again," he said with resignation. "I'll be buggered before I save him a second time!"

The Wizard of Lindsay Woods

Brendan DuBois

I n the year of our Lord 1296 and in the fourteenth year of the reign of Edward the First, in the village of Bromley, the parish priest of the village, one Father Stephen, was preparing for his early evening vespers in his tiny home near the church, when there was a pounding on the door. He got up from the stained wooden table and walked over the dirt floor, past the small, smoldering hearth, and called out, "Who be there?"

"If you will, Father, do open up," came the familiar voice. "It is Gawain, of your brother's manor."

Father Stephen undid the door and let the large man in. It was a warm afternoon in April, on the feast day of Saint George, and dusk was approaching. From the door he could make out the small stone church where he serviced the people of this village, and the fields where he did his other work as well, to feed himself and whatever visitors he might have. He had one weak tallow candle burning in the center of the table, and as Gawain took one of the stools, his sword clanking at his side, Father Stephen went to a shelf on the wall and removed a small bottle of ale, a wooden goblet, and a flat piece of bread. He set the food before Gawain, who eagerly began eating. The bearded Gawain was broad in shoulders and in girth and was one of the knights under the guide of Lord Henry, who ruled this village and others in the area.

Lord Henry. Butcher of Isle-sur-la-Sorgue. The man who ruled these villages and fields with a heavy and bloody hand. He had many knights and men in his service, and Father Stephen felt a small bit of comfort at being visited by Gawain. While a rough and crude man, Gawain did not quite share the blood taste that many of his fellow travelers at Lord Henry's manor shared.

Father Stephen sat down across from Gawain and asked, "And how I can be of assistance on this day, Gawain?"

The burly man drew a hand across his face, swallowed the last of the ale. "Two matters have arisen that require your service, Father. The first is the death of Thomas, son of Atwood. He died yesterday and his body needs to be shrived. Tonight, if possible."

Father Stephen nodded, not letting his disquiet show on his face. Thomas had been a bright young lad, son of the local tanner, who had a head for numbers and an interest in Latin. Father Stephen had wanted to see the boy enter the priesthood or the monastery, but Thomas was built like a bull, with wide shoulders and strong arms. So he had been called into knightly service, to put his arms under his lord, and now he was dead. Another young man with such promise, now growing cold. And for what? To be in service of those who kill. Now he is nothing, a body to be shrived, to receive penance.

Aloud, Father Stephen said, "I see. I will be ready to travel shortly. And what is the other matter of which you speak?"

Gawain belched and began picking at bread crumbs along the tabletop, wetting his thumb, picking each crumb up, and noisily sucking the morsel off. "The manner of his death, Father. I saw it myself. He was killed by a wizard, a wizard who lives in Lindsay Woods."

He folded his hands. "A wizard? In Lindsay Woods? And why were you there anyway? Are those woods not the property of Lord Mullen?"

Another satisfied belch and Gawain hooked a thumb in his sword belt. "True, those woods at one time did belong to that drunken fool. But there was a hearing at court, some complex thing that makes my head ache just thinking about it. A dispute between Lord Mullen and Lord Henry. All I know is that those woods now belong to our Lord Henry." He grinned. "Lord Mullen had been boastful, when he last saw Lord Henry. He said you may have those woods, but you will never possess them. A wizard lives there, and he will not let you nor anyone that belongs to Lord Henry pass on through. Any such shall die in those woods, and Lord Henry replied that while Normans no doubt believe in such tales, as a good Saxon he believes in cold iron and nothing else."

Father Stephen nodded. "I see. And Thomas was killed by this magical man yesterday, was he?"

Gawain now looked fearful, as he remembered the day. "Yes. There were three of us. William of deNoucy, myself, and Thomas. The young boy was eager, so I allowed him to ride first. It was late in the morning, almost at the noon sun, and we were riding along the trail. You pass over three streams along the way. The third stream is the boundary to Lindsay Woods. As we were riding up a slight hill, a tall man came out, in black robes bordered with red. The tallest man I had ever seen. He held up his hand and a staff, and said he would not allow us to pass."

Outside there were the sounds of crows, as they circled the fields being worked, seeking to pick at some scrap. "Then what happened?"

Gawain shuddered and crossed himself. "He seemed to be such an old man. I told Thomas to ride ahead and to push the man aside. I told him not to kill the old man, just to show him that Lord Henry was now the ruler of these woods. So Thomas laughed and drew his sword, and rode toward the man. That . . . that's when it happened."

Silence came into the small hut, and the flickering candle made Gawain's features seem to dance. Father Stephen looked into the fear of those eyes and felt a taste of disquiet. Gawain was known as one of the most fearless of all the knights and men at Lord Henry's manor. It was not a good thing to see, to see such a man frightened.

Gawain's voice seemed to tighten. "On my honor, Father, I swear that I am not telling a tale. This is what I truly did see, as did William of deNoucy. As Thomas rode toward the wizard, he raised his staff and uttered some words loudly, words I did not recognize. Then the end of the staff burst into flames and lightning, and Thomas fell from his horse. Our own mounts reared and tossed us both onto the ground, Father. When we got back on our own feet, all three horses had fled back down the trail. The wizard had disappeared. William and I were not severely injured, but Thomas . . . he was dead, Father. In an instant."

"I see," he said. "And did the wizard reappear?"

"Nay, he did not."

"And what did you and William do then?"

"We carried Thomas between us, and led him to a small home that belongs to a woodcutter named Harold, just outside of Lindsay Woods. Along the way we found all three of our horses, including Thomas's mount. All three were still shaking and foaming with fear. I then went to Lord Henry, where he then commanded me to retrieve you, to give the Last Rites for Thomas's immortal soul."

Father Stephen got up from the stool and went to another shelf, where he took down a small leather satchel that held his vestments and sacred oils. "For that I will do. And that is all."

Gawain shook his massive head. "I fear not, Father. For Lord Henry also demands that you vanquish the wizard."

He felt his throat tighten up at the thought of Lord Henry. "Our lord did, did he? And did he say how I was to vanquish this wizard?"

Gawain now looked embarrassed. "I know not, Father. Lord Henry said . . . well, he said that you would be able to do so."

Father Stephen returned to the table. "What exactly did our lord say about me?"

The knight said shyly, "He said that Father Stephen is known widely among these lands as a particularly holy man, and if wizards are in the employ of the devil, then Father Stephen should have no difficulty banishing him from Lindsay Woods."

"I see," he said, looking into the man's disturbed face. "Tell me, Gawain. Do you believe in spirits, in witches, in the life of wizards?"

Gawain answered. "I am a simple man, Father, who believes in the end of the sword, and not much else. Yet I have seen and heard things that strike fear into me. Lights in the sky. Screams in the night. Stories from my fellow knights of odd things that have happened in the woods. And this wizard, killing Thomas with a staff, some distance away. I know the legends and the tales. I know not if all of these tales are true. But I do know what I saw with my own eyes. I saw this wizard and what he did." There was a pause, and Gawain spoke again. "And you, Father? What do you believe in?"

Father Stephen said, "I believe in our Lord God and nothing else. Let us depart."

GAWAIN RODE ON HIS black horse, called Shadow, while Father Stephen made do with his donkey, called Job, which he kept in a small stall built on the side of his house. Along with his satchel he brought along a simple wool blanket, rolled up. Gawain sighed heavily as he slowed his horse's gait to match the plodding stride of Job.

"Cannot Lord Henry supply you with a horse?" Gawain asked. "One would think a priest of your stature would . . . well, you think he would supply you with a mount better than your donkey."

"A donkey such as Job brought our Lord Jesus into Jerusalem," Father Stephen said, looking out on the fields and woods surrounding his stone church, Saint Agatha's. "I deserve no better. I am just a simple priest."

Gawain kept silent for a half dozen gaits, and said softly, "Father, you know you are more than just a simple priest. A man such as yourself, Oxford learned and the brother of Lord Henry himself, a man who once carried arms, you could do better. You should at least be a bishop."

Father Stephen saw the stooped-over figures of the men and women and children of his church, whom he blessed and married and baptized and buried. His people, his flock, his responsibility. "God's work needs to be done, and I am a better man for doing it here."

"Is it God's will, then?"

"No," he said sharply. "It is mine. And we will speak of it no further."

IT WAS DARK WHEN they reached the hut that belonged to the woodcutter Harold and his family, and the family of the dead knight Thomas was there as well. The man's body was laid out on a table outside, clad only in a shroud, and as the people about him sobbed and cried out, Father Stephen went through the rituals of the Last Rites. _Quid quid delquisti_ . . . Though he had not been here at the time of Thomas's death, this was the best he could do, and as he said aloud the Latin phrases, he looked down at the young man's face.

My poor Thomas, he thought, how did you come to this? A chance to inhabit the world of learning and books and knowledge, the true path of God's work, to learn more about you and your world, and you turned it down. You chose the easy path, the path of fame and wealth and honor and death, of course, death all about you. Men with swords and shields and armor, spreading death among the simple people, his flock. Burning homes and fields for coin and honor, bloody swords rising up and down, the stench of smoldering hay and wooden beams, the harsh cries of the men, the screams of the women, and the piercing cries of the children, newly orphaned. . . .

He stopped, his mind awhirl. He could not remember what to say next. In the dim light of the torches, the people looked toward him, looked toward their shepherd in this world to lead them to the light, to lead them from the darkness. For just a moment the old memories came back and he felt like a fraud, an impostor. What was he doing here? What could he possibly do for these people? He was terrified for an instant, at being uncovered for what he was.

But only for a moment. The eyes of some of the children up front were looking at him, trusting in him, knowing that he spoke for God. He went on and completed the services, if for no one else, then at least for the children. *In nomine Patris, et Filii, et Spiritus sancti.* Amen.

LATER HE SPOKE TO Gawain and said, "I have need of you, and a torch, and nobody else."

"What for, Father?"

"I wish to look at Thomas."

Gawain gulped audibly. "In what manner, Father?"

Father Stephen said, "He was killed by a wizard. I wish to see if I can learn how this deed was done. You will agree there is no wizard here among us. I cannot talk to him. But the wizard's work remains. I wish to see it."

"But Father . . . I mean . . ."

He grasped the man's shoulder. "Have no fear, Gawain. For we are doing God's work this evening, and God will not allow us to fall into any harm. Our brother Thomas is gone. Only his body remains. We will not disturb his flesh or bones. We will only look. Do come with me."

They were outside again, and Gawain spoke briefly with the family of Thomas, who all crossed themselves and went into the woodcutter's hut. The night sounds of frogs and crickets filled the cool air and Father Stephen stepped closer. Gawain was behind him, as if seeking comfort from having the priest move in first. "Bring the torch up behind me, if you will," he said, and as Gawain did so, he saw that the features of the young man were beginning to change. He would have to be buried early on the morrow, before the rot set in. He said a brief prayer and then undid the shroud, and the torchlight began to quaver.

He looked back and saw that Gawain's hand was shaking. "Be strong, Gawain," he whispered. "Be strong."

When the shroud was lying aside, he bent over and examined the flesh. There were old marks and scars along the shoulders and wrists and legs, from even such short service as a knight, but there was a fresh wound that intrigued him.

"Here," he said, "bring the torch in closer to the chest."

The light flickered some more, and Father Stephen heard Gawain murmuring a prayer, the Latin words nearly meaningless in the rush to be said. He looked at the wound, which was in the center of the chest. It was almost round in its shape, and about as wide as his thumb.

"Look there," he said. "Gawain, have you ever seen such a wound?"

"Nay, Father, I have not." The knight's voice sounded strained.

"Nor have I." He went around to the side and grasped the dead boy's shoulders, and pulled him to his side. The dead boy's flesh was cold and stiff and he murmured a quick prayer, asking for forgiveness for disturbing him such as this. His view was blocked and Father Stephen said, "Gawain, do you see anything on his back? Another wound?"

"Father, aye, I do. But this one is bigger and has torn his flesh so. Father, please, I am disturbed. Are we finished here?"

He gently lowered the boy's body down and blessed him yet again. "Yes, Gawain, we are."

DINNER WAS BREAD AND ale and seasoned cold venison, and he and Gawain slept in the rear barn on a pile of hay. The woodcutter had offered to let him sleep in their tiny home, but that would mean putting some of the children out in the barn, and that he would not do. He would not disturb the children. They made their beds as well as they could, as they heard the rustle of rats among them. Gawain extinguished a small oil lamp that they had borrowed from the woodcutter and he rested his head back in his hands, staring up at the darkness.

"Gawain?" Father Stephen asked, resting there in the night.

"Aye, Father."

"Did you know Thomas well, before he died?"

He could hear the crackling of hay as Gawain shifted. "No, not really, Father. I just knew that he was young and eager, and quite strong."

Father Stephen sighed. "Did you know that he had a taste for learning? That for a while he was eager to learn how to read and write? Did you know that?"

"No, Father, I did not."

Of course not, Father Stephen thought. You and your kind, all that matters is the moment, the manner of death and honor, and blood being spilled. Always and always, blood being spilled.

"The day of his death," Father Stephen said.

"Yes?"

"What was he wearing? What kind of armor?"

"Why, none, Father. He was just wearing a cloak, his hose, and a leather jerkin. For we feared not that we would encounter any men of arms on our trip to Lindsay Woods."

"No, just a wizard, am I right? An old man who could be pushed away or killed without much work on your part."

"Aye," came the sad voice. "You are right."

He thought for a moment longer and said, "Gawain, after the burial tomorrow of Thomas, we must travel."

Gawain's voice was troubled. "To Lindsay Woods?"

"No, to Lord Henry's manor. We must see him, and I must talk to him."

The knight's voice was cautionary. "He will not be pleased, to see you without news of the wizard's death."

"His pleasure is not my worry," Father Stephen said. "Now, I bid you a good night's sleep, Gawain."

"And you, too, Father."

Father Stephen pulled his old wool blanket over him and turned over, soon listening to the whistling snore of Gawain and the squeaks and rustles from the rats sharing their quarters.

The morning meal was old bread, dried apples, and another small piece of venison, and in a cleared area near the path, they laid Thomas's body to rest. It was not a churchyard but it would have to do, and later, Father Stephen would come back to consecrate this ground. The hole had been dug and Thomas's body had been wrapped in the shroud, and as his body was lowered into the ground, Father Stephen said the Latin prayers again, commending Thomas's soul unto the Lord. The boy's family and the family of Harold the woodcutter watched on, and some of the children—bored at what was going on—played in the distance. Life, Father Stephen thought, life does go on. No matter what the men at arms say.

When the services were done and the last of the dirt had been shoveled over the body by Harold and the boy's uncle, Father Stephen got onto his donkey and said to Gawain, "Now, we travel."

"Aye, Father. Whatever you say."

The midday meal was eaten along the way, more dried apples and stale heels of bread, and as they approached the large, cultivated fields around the manor house of Lord Henry, Gawain said, "There are many things that I do not understand, Father."

"Then do not fret," he said. "For that is the way of the world. And what is the matter for which you do not understand?"

Gawain waved a hand about their surroundings. "You could be here, Father. Either at your brother's side or serving your church, but you could be here. In warm quarters, eating meat every day. Meeting with travelers and lords who read and write as you do, and who speak Latin as well. Educated people, traveled people. Yet you stay in Bromley, in a muddy house with a leaky roof, eating food that is no better than what the villains eat. Why is that?"

"Because that is what I have chosen," he said carefully.

Gawain glared at him from his high perch on his saddle. "That is no answer, Father, and you know it."

"Then that is the best answer you can have. Look, we near my brother's manor. Let us not talk of it any more."

As their mounts were led away, Father Stephen looked with a critical eye at the manor, the place where he had been born and had been raised. There were a few happy memories here but not too many. His older brother had been his father's son, and he had been his mother's. While Henry learned the ways of armor and battle and fighting, he had learned to read and write and had memorized the old tales and songs. He had even done some learning at nearby Oxford. They had been brothers but had been rivals, right from the start. Their three sisters—all now married off, and one, Celeste, living in Burgundy—had stayed within their own manors, and he had not seen them for years.

But it had not been a bad life, not until their mother and father had taken ill and had died, within a week of each other. Henry had been thrust into the head of the family, and in some complicated plot to increase his power and his holdings, he had traveled to France, to fight for King Edward, old Longshanks. And Stephen had gone along as well, as a frightened yet eager young knight, to show his older brother that he, too, could fight for their family, even if he was book-learned and knew how to read and write Latin.

He shook his head at the memories, looked again at the manor. Henry had done well. Part of the manor had been expanded, and it looked like some of the windows had been replaced with real glass. The large door to the manor opened and a tall man came out, bowed in their direction. It was Ambrose, Lord Henry's head servant. "Father, Lord Henry bids you welcome, and invites you to join him."

Father Stephen bowed back. "As he wishes."

As they dismounted Gawain said, "And how did Lord Henry know we were approaching?"

"These are my brother's lands," he said. "No doubt we were spotted some distance away, and the news came here quickly. My brother does not like to be surprised by unwelcome guests."

Shortly they were in the manor hall, where tables were set up on the stone flooring. Tapestries hung along the wall and even some music was being played, by a player of the fiddle and a player of a pipe in one corner. Dogs wandered about, snarling and biting at each other over scraps tossed at them by the well-dressed men and women sitting at the long tables. Lord Henry—and my, how his brother had gotten heavy and his beard gray—sat at the table at the head of the room, laughing loud at something. Next to him was a thin girl, Lady Catherine, a young girl not yet thirteen, and who had been betrothed to Henry to settle some land dispute.

Father Stephen murmured a quiet prayer as he advanced across the room. That laughter from his brother brought back memories of their time in France, the laughter as he bounded into battle and slaughtered the inhabitants of a village whose only crime was that they pledged their loyalty to a French king.

"Come, come," his brother yelled out. "Look who approaches." He belched and swayed in his great chair, and Father Stephen realized Lord Henry was drunk. His brother yelled out, "My holy brother comes to greet me. Do you bring me good news, then? Has the wizard been vanquished? Did you bathe him in Holy Water? Did you strike at him with a relic of Saint Agnes? Did you bid him farewell by tossing phrases at him in Latin?"

Lord Henry laughed and the other people in the great hall laughed as well, and dogs barked some more as scraps were tossed to them. Father Stephen thought of the hungry families in his village, who would gladly get on the floor to wrestle the scraps away from the dogs, and he stepped closer to his older brother.

"No," he said, speaking clearly and plainly. "The wizard has not yet been vanquished. And if he is to be vanquished by my services, then I demand payment."

From behind him he listened to the gasp of anguish from Gawain, and then the sudden silence, as the laughter and the jeers from the guests quieted. Even the musicians had silenced themselves. There was snarling from two battling dogs by the doorway and no other sound. Lady Catherine sat very still, her thin hands in her lap. Lord Henry's face grew redder and he said, his voice no longer booming and full of laughter, "What nonsense is this?"

"There is no nonsense," Father Stephen said. "Just fair compensation, for ridding your new possession of Lindsay Woods of a wizard, a wizard who has killed one of your knights."

Lord Henry stared right at him. "You are a servant of the church. You will do your duty."

"Aye, but I am not a servant of you, Lord Henry. I serve a greater master. To fight against a wizard who is not in my village, who has not harmed anyone of my parish, is something that I must be compensated for. It is only fair."

"I shall not pay you, or any other meddlesome priest, by God," he growled. "For I will take care of this matter myself. You can go back to your muddy village and starve for all I care."

"Really?" Father Stephen said, looking about the faces of the men among the guests. "Which one of your knights or compatriots wishes to ride against a wizard, a man who strikes death from afar? I have seen what he has done. I have held Thomas's own body in my hands, have seen the dreadful wound that this wizard has caused. I can vanquish the wizard easily, my Lord, but to do so, I demand payment. It is only fair. You know that well."

Lord Henry stared at him again, and Father Stephen willed his legs not to quake. The look from those eyes was similar to what he had seen in battle in France, when Henry was approaching his enemies, and Father Stephen knew that was what his brother now considered him: an enemy, nothing else.

"A compensation, then," Lord Henry said. "What price does a servant of God place upon destroying a wizard?"

He took a deep breath. "One-third of Lindsay Woods to be given to the Church of Saint Agnes, for service to the poor and our parish. That is all."

"All?" Henry shouted. "That is all? One-third of my property to a useless man of the cloth? One-third of my property to one who will not raise arms against my enemies? Who will not perform his rightly duties for his family?"

By now Henry was on his feet, and his young wife was trembling as she listened to his shouts. Even the dogs had run away from the inside of the hall, and Father Stephen saw how all the guests were now looking away, as if afraid that by looking at Lord Henry, they, too, would incur his wrath.

Father Stephen clasped his hands before him in a prayerful gesture, but one that he knew was only being done to prevent his hands from shaking. Trying to keep his voice level, he called out,

"My lord, my duties are now to the Church and to God. I have taken a sacred oath, one that cannot be broken, even by a man as powerful as you. While I no longer raise arms against your enemies, I am a loyal subject to our king and to you. Yet I am not a slave nor a serf. I ask for compensation fairly, not for my own purse, but to aid the Church and the people whom she serves."

"One-third," Lord Henry muttered, looking around the room. "One-third . . ."

"With all respect and graciousness, my lord, you know as well as I do that with the wizard in those woods, and the death that he can incur in the snap of a finger, that those woods of yours will forever be useless. It is better to have two-thirds of something, my lord, rather than three-thirds of nothing."

A few brave souls at the rear of the manor hall—who could not readily be identified—chuckled in appreciation at his comments, and Lord Henry sat heavily down upon his great chair. Lady Catherine tried to hide a tiny smile with a handkerchief. He pulled up a goblet of ale and emptied it in a few large swallows, and then tossed the empty goblet upon the stone floor.

"Is this how you repay your older brother?" he said. "I called upon you to rid me of this wizard, to bring yourself fame and attention in these parts. Nothing else. And you come to me, filled with impertinence, demanding payment. I think, younger brother, it would have been better for all of us if you had not come back to Bromley from France."

Father Stephen bowed slightly. "I came back from France due to God's will, and nothing else."

Lord Henry raised a hand dismissively. "If the wizard is vanquished, then you will receive your one-third of Lindsay Woods, priest. And may those woods be cursed to you and whoever from your church who gains to profit from them."

A little voice inside of him said, You won, you've actually won, but Father Stephen pressed forward. "There is the matter of two more items, my lord."

Lord Henry managed to smile. "Two more subjects, you slippery toad? And what might they be?"

"When I left this manor years ago, I left behind a trunk of some of my possessions. I wish to examine this trunk."

"What, so you can charge me with theft?"

"No, my lord. It is just a matter that I must attend to."

Lady Catherine stroked her husband's arm and whispered into an ear. He said, "Yes, yes, you may examine the trunk. My servant Ambrose will tell you where it is. And what is the second matter, and be quick about it."

"I plan to ride out and meet with the wizard tomorrow," Father Stephen said. "I wish to be accompanied by one of your knights. Gawain. And none other."

Father Stephen thought he heard the knight's low moan from behind him. His older brother scowled and said, "And what for? So he may kill this wizard if you lose your nerve?"

"No," Father Stephen clearly said. "So that he may come back and tell you if I have failed, and that the wizard has indeed killed me."

Lord Henry's smile was quite wide. "That will indeed be worth the time of one of my knights. So it shall be done. Now, leave me and this room. You bore me, priest."

He nodded and quickly walked out, hoping his legs would not quite give out until he had passed through the door.

THE STALL AT LEAST had some clean hay, and Father Stephen made his bed again among the dry grasses. This barn was large, and there were the grunts and whinnies of some of the lord's horses to keep him company. He knew that as a brother of Lord Henry and a son of the man who had first built this place, that he could have demanded better quarters. But when Lord Henry's head servant Ambrose had directed him to these stables, he had not protested. Nor had he protested when Ambrose had said the kitchen servants were no longer available, so no evening meal could be provided. Father Stephen would give his older brother these tiny victories. He had gained one much greater.

He pulled his wool blanket about him and tried not to think of tomorrow, but only the here and now. He said his evening prayers and ate a dried apple that he had saved from their midday meal, and when he had closed his eyes, he tried to go to sleep.

But sleep would not come. There was someone else in the stable, someone coming in his direction. He could hear the steps upon the stone walkway leading past the main stables. A cold touch of fear stirred in his chest. He knew his brother well. His brother had been bested and humiliated today in front of his peers. Perhaps that was not worth the eventual use of a portion of Lindsay Woods. Perhaps the death of an impertinent younger brother would make Lord Henry a pleased man this evening. There were many knights and men at arms who would come in this stable tonight with a sharp blade, to do their Lord's bidding, as knights did Henry II's bidding in killing Saint Thomas á Becket in Canterbury so many years ago. The flickering light of a small lamp was now visible.

Father Stephen spoke up. "If you mean to see me and do me harm, then do approach now, and waste not either of our evenings."

A familiar voice came to him in reply. "That is an odd thing to say, Father Stephen, to one who is trying to bring you a meal."

From the darkness Gawain emerged and sat down heavily on the hay next to Father Stephen. He held a wooden bowl that he passed over and which Father Stephen bent to. There was a hunk of cheese, some ham, and soft, freshly baked white bread. He ate the feast and offered some to Gawain, who declined.

"No, Father, I've had my fill of the lord's hospitality tonight. When I heard where they had placed you and how they had not fed you, well . . . it did not seem right. So here I am."

"Bless you, Gawain, for your thoughtfulness," he said earnestly.

"Bah," he said. "What kind of blessings have you brought upon me, to demand that I accompany you tomorrow to meet the wizard?"

He finished the last of the bread. "What I said earlier to my brother was true. I do not require your presence to fight the wizard. I will do that on my own. I require you to be a witness, that is all. You need not put yourself in any harm."

Then, Father Stephen was surprised when Gawain grunted in reply and blew out the light. Gawain shifted his weight in the hay and Father Stephen could make him out, lying down next to him.

"Why are you here?" he asked. "Should you not go back to your own quarters?"

"Aye, you are right," the knight said wearily. "I should go back. In fact, there is a new serving girl who has looked at me with interest, and I feel sure that I would not be spending my night alone if I had spoken to her earlier. But still . . . it is not right that you be in the stable alone, Father. I decided to come here and share your quarters, as poor as they are."

"That is noble of you, Gawain."

"Bah, nobility has nothing to do with it," he said. "I wanted to speak to you, Father, about you and your brother. His lordship said something earlier, about your not returning to Bromley from France, and about your not taking arms to defend your family. What was the meaning of those words?"

In the darkness, now, in the dark it was easy to remember. With no light, with nothing to look at but the blackness, it was easy to recall all those memories. Not only the sights of what he had seen in France, but the sounds as well. The creak of leather. The clang of swords against shields. The gurgling cries of the wounded, drowning in their own blood. The dark growls of the horses, riding in fear. The snapping sounds of timber and thatch burning. And the scents, as well. The strong smell of spilt blood. The stench of sweat and tears. The musky odors of villages and bodies being burnt.

"It is no secret," Father Stephen said slowly, "that I was not always a priest. That I once raised arms in defense of my family and for our king. That is all. That is no secret."

"But what happened, then, to change everything?" Gawain asked, pressing on. "What happened?"

And then he surprised himself, by letting go, by telling tales that he had only shared with his confessor. "I was young when I was with my brother in France. It was a glorious adventure, at first. To serve your family, to serve your King, and to serve your God. It all seemed destined, all seemed right. The first few battles, knights against knights, they were desperate battles, but they had a . . . well, a righteousness about them. But later, then, we pressed a siege against a French town. The town belonged to the King of England, but they pledged their loyalties to the King of France. My brother would not let this happen. We laid siege to the village and when we finally broke through their walls, the killing started. The burning of the homes and farms. The slaughter not only of the men at arms, but the women as well. And the old men. And the children."

Oh, the cries of the small children, as the knights chased them along the muddy paths, screaming for their mother, screaming for their father, screaming for the Lord God to save them all. . . .

"When I saw all that happened, I threw away my sword and left the battle," he said. "I could not stand to see what I had done, in aiding my brother and our family and our King. I swore then on that bloody soil, that if I survived getting back to England, that I would enter the priesthood and serve the poor, the people who have no arms nor men to defend them. That is what I swore, and that has angered my brother ever since."

Gawain spoke softly to him. "But you were in the service of your King, and your God, when you were in France. There was nothing wrong in what you did, you must know that."

"Hah," Father Stephen said. "What I do know is that the King of England and the King of France and all the people they rule, they all worship the same God, and that God must shed tears of anger and sorrow at what those Kings do in His name. And when I witnessed this by own eyes, and I saw what I had joined in doing, I knew that I could no longer raise arms, nor support those men who raise arms as well. And that is what I have done."

"And what will you do tomorrow, against the wizard?"

Father Stephen rolled over in the hay. "I will do the bidding of my God, to help my people. Nothing else."

If Gawain said anything in reply, Father Stephen did not hear it. Soon, Gawain was snoring, loud enough to drown out the sounds of the horses in their stalls, and the ever-present rustling of rats in the stored hay.

MORNING DAWNED COLD AND wet, with a heavy mist over the fields of Lord Henry's manor. Today was the feast day of Saint Mark, the Evangelist. Father Stephen had gotten up the earliest and had examined his old trunk, given to him as a young boy by his parents, and where he had stored his old memories and possessions of his previous life. The chest had been in a crowded cellar and when he was done, he had been glad to get out into the morning light.

He had clambered up on his donkey, Job, his chest feeling heavy and slow, and he joined Gawain out in the front of the manor. And to his surprise, they were not alone. Lord Henry was there, in simple clothes, sitting astride a huge white horse, his face scowling yet again.

"Ah, so the priest is still here and has not run away, his bowels and bladder loose with fear," he said, holding the reins of his horse tightly in his beefy hands.

Father Stephen nodded. "I have pledged to you that I will vanquish this wizard today. Just as you have pledged to pass over one-third of Lindsay Woods to my church when this deed is done."

Lord Henry managed a smile. "Ah, priest, but perhaps I do not recall making such a pledge. Perhaps the drink I had last night loosened my tongue and my wits. Perhaps there is no such pledge."

Again, he nodded, in polite deference. "My lord, of course, is correct. Perhaps there is no pledge. Yet I remind him that he uttered such a pledge in front of numerous lords and ladies yesterday in his manor hall. To back away from such a pledge . . . well, my lord knows all too well what would happen to his reputation and standing among his peers and subjects."

His brother's face was glaring again, and even his horse shifted anxiously, stomping one hoof and then another. "Be gone, priest, and be quick. The King has called a council, about a campaign upon Scotland, and I need not to burden my mind with the problems of a wizard and poor priest. Go on and do what must be done."

"So I shall, my brother, so I shall."

But before Lord Henry went to return to the manor, he leaned over his mount and spoke quietly to Gawain, who nodded at the words told to him. Then Gawain moved on, spurring his horse, Shadow, to the open road. When Father Stephen started out to the trail, he looked back, knowing somehow that he would never again see his brother or the manor.

THE TRIP WAS SLOWER this time, as the weight about his chest and shoulders seemed to grow heavier with each passing step. Even his donkey, Job, seemed burdened by all that had occurred, and Father Stephen could sense the frustration of Gawain, riding next to him.

"By God, Father," he growled, "could we at least pick up our pace? I do not want to face this wizard at dusk or at dark. I want this awful job done as soon as possible, in the brightness of noon, if possible."

Father Stephen replied, "We will be there when we get there, and not any sooner. Be patient, Gawain, be patient."

Eventually, they were in the fields near Lindsay Woods, and they crossed the first of the three streams, and then the second. When they approached the third stream, Gawain crossed himself and halted his horse next to Father Stephen. The stream was wide and seemed deep, and it moved with ferocity, raising white-caps and spumes of spray.

"There, Father," he said, his voice lowered. "To the right is a ford, which even your donkey should be able to traverse. Then, the trail goes up this slight hill. Near the top of the hill is where we saw the wizard."

Father Stephen stayed quiet, his chest and back aching with the weight he was carrying. The sounds were of their animals breathing and the rushing of the stream. It seemed like all of the animals of the woods had disappeared, as if the wizard had bade them to run away and not witness what was about to occur. He, too, crossed himself. He was sure earlier of what he was to do and what would happen, but he was no fool. He felt the taste of fear, a taste that was even stronger than when he was in the muddy fields of France, fighting for his life against another swordsman.

He spoke up. "I will go first, Gawain. Please do follow me, but do not be reckless or bold. This is my matter, not yours. I will approach the wizard and face him down, no matter what magic or fiery staff he may possess. God rides with us both, this I promise. Be not afraid."

Gawain pulled out his sword and laid it across the spine of his horse. "I am afraid, this I do admit. But I will follow you, Father. Do lead on."

Father Stephen pulled on the reins, and Job reluctantly stepped into the water. Job was not one to hesitate, no matter how stubborn he could be, and he wondered if perhaps the poor dumb beast could sense the danger that was ahead. The water wet his feet and legs but then he was on the other side, in Lindsay Woods. He turned and saw Gawain splashing across, to join him. Father Stephen smiled at him, then reached into his robes, and took out a small crucifix.

He started saying the Our Father as he went up the hill. *Pater noster qui es in coelis.* . . . As he approached the top of the hill, the fear that had been there earlier returned with a vengeance, like a mid-winter storm. An old man with a white beard was at the top of the hill, clad in robes of red and black, holding up his hand as to halt them both. The man was tall, quite tall, possibly the tallest man he had ever seen. In his other hand, he held a long staff of wood and metal. Just like Gawain had said.

The wizard of Lindsay Woods.

Father Stephen raised up his crucifix and pressed on.

IT WAS THE WIZARD who spoke first. "Get ye away from here. These are my woods, my home. Ye have no right here. Get away before I kill thee all."

His donkey, Job, seemed to start at the sounds of the old man. His voice was raspy and low, as if he had shouted for many days as a young lad.

Father Stephen swallowed, noting how dry his mouth had become. He raised up his crucifix. "I bid you to leave, old man.

These woods belong to Lord Henry. You have no right of owner-
ship. Let us pass and then be on your way, before any harm comes
to you."

The wizard laughed. "A priest, are ye? I have traveled long
and far in this world, priest, to learn that your religion is no more
the true religion than any other. There are many places and
people who have never heard of you and your God. Ye have no
power over me. So leave, now, damn ye, before I smite ye down."

He held up the crucifix again and spurred on Job, who was
breathing hard and struggling against the reins. But move on the
donkey did, and Father Stephen spoke aloud, "Move away,
wizard, before harm befalls you. I command you in the name of
God and Lord Henry to depart this place forever."

As he spoke, he saw something on a rock near the wizard's
lance. Something was smoldering there, a wisp of smoke rising
up. The wizard cackled again and said, "I warned ye, and now ye
shall die!"

The old man moved quickly for one so aged, for he grasped
some smoldering stick and brought it up in his left hand. With his
right hand he held out the staff of metal and wood, and Father
Stephen saw another V-shaped stick there as well, now holding
up the staff. He spurred on Job and then the wizard cackled
again, started shouting in a strange tongue, and he brought the
smoking stick against the side of the staff.

What happened next happened almost as fast as the blink of
an eye, for there was a loud thunderclap, like a sudden appearance of a rainstorm, and the end of the staff spew forth a cloud of
smoke and fire, and then something hammered at his chest, and
Father Stephen fell to the ground, unable to breathe, unable to
move, unable even to pray.

EVERYTHING WAS GRAY, FOR what seemed to be a long time. Then
Father Stephen coughed and sat up. His chest throbbed and
ached, and before him were two figures. He wiped at his eyes
and saw Gawain standing over the figure of the wizard, cursing,

and raising up his sword. Father Stephen shouted, "No, do not kill him, I forbid it!"

With sword raised, Gawain turned to him in astonishment. "By all the saints . . . Father, you are still alive?"

He grabbed at his chest and stumbled to his feet. Job and Shadow were nowhere to be found. "I am. I may be in some pain, but I am alive. Pray to come over here and assist me."

Gawain came to him as Father Stephen removed his outer robe, and Gawain again looked at him in amazement. Underneath the cloak Father Stephen wore a dull-colored breastplate, a piece of armor he had not worn since returning from France during those cold and bloody days, and which had been stored in the trunk back at the manor. The armor still fit him well and was in good shape, save for the deep dent now in the center. Though now aching and dizzy, he felt good at having guessed right about the true nature of the wizard's power. He had no doubt there were witches and wizards in this world. But he found it easier to believe in the actions of man. He undid the straps and let the armor fall to the ground, and then strode uneasily over to the wizard.

Gawain followed, saying, "When he smote you down, Father, I had to come and strike at him, no matter what the consequences. Bad enough that he killed the young Thomas in my presence. I could not allow him to kill you as well without replying in kind."

Father Stephen knelt down to the old man. His staff was on the ground, some distance away. There was a stench in the air, of decay and sulfur. Blood was on the wizard's lips, and soiled the side of his robe. The robe had also fallen across the man's thin legs, and Father Stephen noted the small stilts he had been standing on. Stilts, hidden by his robes, and which made him that much taller.

"He has been injured," Father Stephen said.

"Aye," Gawain said. "I struck him a blow after you fell, and I was to strike again before you stopped me. Yet I believe my first blow may be enough."

The wizard's eyes fluttered open, and he coughed, and smiled again. "The strong man is right, he is, and I fear I am mortally injured."

Father Stephen bent closer. "Who are you, then, old man? A friend or relative?"

"A friend or relative of who, do you ask?"

"Of Lord Mullen, the previous owner of these woods. The tale of the Wizard of Lindsay Woods came to pass only after these woods were taken from him and given to Lord Henry. Not before. The wizard who supposedly haunted these woods has only been here for a short while. So, who are you, then?"

Another cough. "I am his older brother, I am. William."

Gawain shook his head. "That cannot be true. William is believed dead. He left for one of the last Holy Crusades, years ago."

The old man cackled. "That is true, that is true, and here I am, back among our family estates, though everyone thought I had died, years ago. I did go on the Holy Crusade, and the places I went and the things I saw . . . such poor peasants as yourself would never believe what I saw, what I did."

Father Stephen eyed the wizard's staff. "Is that where you got your staff, the one that makes so much noise and propels a stone with such speed that it can kill?"

"No, not stone," William said, his voice growing softer. "A piece of soft metal. I stole the staff from a merchant from Cathay, where I served as a slave for years. I also stole some of the soft metal and a bag of the powder that ignites so easily. . . . Cathay, a place where the men and the women dress in such luxuries, yet their eyes are like cats . . . Cathay . . ."

Gawain said, "So why were you here, playing at being a wizard?"

Father Stephen answered him. "So the woods would be thought to be haunted. So that all travelers would avoid it. So that sometime in the future, Lord Mullen could get it back from Lord Henry, at a pittance. Am I right, William?"

A slow nod, as blood started trickling down into his beard. "You are a smart one, priest. A smart one. You outfoxed me by wearing that armor under your cloak. . . . If I had put more of the fire powder inside the lance, you might not have lived. . . . "

"But I did, William, I did."

Gawain started to say something but Father Stephen held up his hand, as the old man murmured something. Father Stephen bent over and said, "Please speak again, William."

A soft, breathy voice. "I meant not what I said earlier, in insulting you, Father. Would you . . . would you . . . give me the Last Rites? Please?"

Father Stephen nodded. "Of course."

And as he began the prayers, the old man died.

THEY BURIED HIM IN the woods, and when they went out into the open, Gawain picked up the staff and examined it. "Now I can see how it works," he said. "There is a small hole here at the base, where that small stick that was burning was placed. It ignited the powder inside and propelled that metal that killed young Thomas and knocked you from Job."

Gawain looked up. "Yonder is the bag that contains the fire powder. I must bring these back to Lord Henry. His alchemist can determine what is in the powder, and his smithy can see how this fire lance was made. Imagine how powerful his knights will be once they have weapons such as these."

Father Stephen picked up the small bag that contained a black, gritty powder, and lumps of metal. "You are right, of course, Gawain. May I examine the staff, as well?"

Gawain handed over the tube of metal and wood, which felt heavy. There were elaborate carvings along the wooden base, showing dragons and other creatures. He looked up at Gawain and said, "My friend, is that your horse, coming down the hill?"

When Gawain turned Father Stephen tossed the bag with the powder into the stream, and then smashed the fire staff once and then twice against the near boulder. After the metal and wood had been bent and broken, and before the bellowing Gawain could get any closer, he tossed the destroyed lance into the raging waters of the stream as well.

"Father!" Gawain shouted. "What in the name of the Blessed Mary and the Saints did you do that for? Do you know what you've just done?"

Father Stephen's chest ached and his throat still was dry, but he pressed on. "Earlier today, what did my brother tell you, before we left?"

Gawain glared at him. "I cannot say."

"Ah, you cannot say, but I can certainly guess. He told you that if the wizard was just a man, and nothing else, that after I vanquished him you should find out what his weapon was and bring it back to him. Am I right?"

Gawain still looked angry. "The old man was right. You are a smart one. But why, Father?"

Father Stephen felt his chest, felt the tender area that had been hurt by that hurtling piece of metal. "Why? You need to ask me that question, why? It's a weapon of barbarism, that is why. You see how much blood men armed only with swords and bows spill on this good earth, day in and day out. Can you imagine the slaughter that can occur, if each knight, if each man of arms, can kill with such a weapon as this staff? Who can kill from afar? What that can mean to the villages and people of this land?"

Gawain said, "That may be true, Father, but you saw with your own eyes. This weapon exists. It is from Cathay. One of these days it will come back to this island, will come back to men such as Lord Henry."

Father Stephen nodded, and went over and picked up his robe. "Perhaps you are right. Perhaps it will come next year, perhaps next century. And perhaps in that time, men on this island will finally come to listen to the words of God, learn to love each other, and put down the tools of killing."

Gawain sighed and bent down to pick up his sword. "That day may never come, Father."

"True, but only if we let it happen," Father Stephen said. "Only if we let it happen, and I intend to do my best not to see it happen. That is my calling. To work for my people and to work for peace."

LATER, AFTER THEY HAD recovered both Shadow and Job and began riding out of Lindsay Woods, Gawain said, "What do you intend to tell Lord Henry?"

"Me?" Father Stephen said. "I intend to say nothing, and to return to my parish. It is up to you to tell him what happened this day, that we were successful in killing the wizard and freeing Lindsay Woods for his lordship. Two-thirds to him, of course, and one-third to my parish."

Gawain said, "He will complain."

"Aye, he will complain, but he will proceed. He must, to preserve his name among his peers. And it will also be up to you, Gawain, on what you will say—or won't say—about the fire staff."

The knight laughed. "Say? I will say nothing, Father, since I have nothing to show. Who would believe me, that a weapon exists that would allow a serf or slave to kill a knight from afar, without even touching him?"

As they rode away, the image of the old man William bothered him for a while, the older brother, trying to protect the lands of his younger brother. That is all. A sad thing, to die in defense of one's brother, after having traveled across Europe and to Cathay. Yet noble. Father Stephen imagined it must be a pleasurable thing, to have such a brother.

Still, a sad thing, all the same, but Father Stephen soon thought of other things, as well. A new roof for the church. More land for himself, to grow more food to help those families who nearly starved each year. More peace for the people of the village of Bromley, and of course, a future—and if God willed it, not too far off—when men of arms turned their swords into plowshares, so that the villages would no longer burn and that the children would no longer cry.

God willing, he would live long enough to see that day.

Improvements

Kristine Kathryn Rusch

W hen the strange woman appeared, Maude was in the buttery, speaking with the clerk of the kitchen about his latest round of purchases. He went to market too often, she thought, and was too extravagant for the types of meals he produced. She would, if he did not modify his expenditures, have to fire him.

He would be the first servant she fired since her husband died.

The very idea filled her with dread. She had run the household since her marriage ten years before, but her husband had handled the money, the hiring and firing of servants, and the overall management of the large estate.

Now she managed it in trust for their only child, a son who was still in swaddling. Still, some duties made her hands shake.

The clerk of the kitchen was a large florid man whom her husband had hired shortly before the baby was born. She had had misgivings about him then but had been too tired to speak of them. Then her husband became ill, the baby had been born, and her husband had died, all within half a year's time. She felt as if she woke up only recently to find herself in a life that only resembled the one she had once had.

The buttery was a small room off the kitchen. Beer and candles sat on the shelves. The stairs from the beer cellar descended down one side, and the main door of the buttery opened into the hall. She had sent the yeoman of the buttery—he was such a gossip—into the garden for a brief rest. Not that he needed one. His services were rarely used this early in the day.

The clerk of the kitchen was explaining, in his condescending voice, how some foods tasted poorly without the proper ingredients. She had her hands folded inside her sleeves, her wimple pinching her chin. She had been listening to him for too long, but she didn't know how to make him stop.

And that was when they heard the screams, coming from the kitchen.

The clerk looked at her as if he had never heard such sounds before. She pushed past him into the Hall, through the Court, and into the kitchen.

It stank of grease and smoke and roasting meat. Even though no one was yet cooking the evening meal, the smell from last night's lingered.

The kitchen staff was huddled near the outside door. One of the kitchen maids had her hands over her mouth. She was doubled over away from the door, as if she had seen something horrible.

Maude hurried past the work table to the door. The servants parted as they saw her, all but the chief cook who blocked her way with his large body.

"Milady," he said. "This is not for a lady to see."

"Move aside," she said.

He stared at her a moment, his blue eyes red-streaked from smoke, his lips thin and pursed as if he had tasted something bad. Then he stepped away from the door.

A woman lay on the flagstones leading into the garden. Her ragged clothes were blood-covered as were her face and hair. When she saw Maude, she raised a thin hand as if beseeching her.

"We shall take care of this, Milady," the chief cook said. "It is nothing that should bother you."

But they hadn't taken care of it so far, had they? Besides, how could she leave a creature in such obvious distress?

"It is simply a beggar woman," the chief cook said. "We see many of them at the kitchen. She was probably beset by thieves."

"A beggar woman beset by thieves? That does not seem likely." Maude stepped outside. She knew why the staff was protecting her. The woman wore garments that Maude recognized from the town's stew.

"She is a harlot, Milady," the chief cook hissed. "Please. It is not right for you—"

"Enough!" Maude said. She crossed the flagstones and crouched beside the woman.

The woman smelled of sweat and fear. She was so thin that all the bones in her hand were visible. Her face was swollen and bruised, her teeth blackened and nearly gone. Yet Maude was certain the woman was younger than she.

Her surcoat had once been a rough wool, but time and use had worn it to nothing. There were several tears in it, recent tears, that rendered it nearly useless. She wore nothing underneath, and Maude could see scars beside the fresh bruises.

"Milady," the woman murmured.

Maude put a hand on the woman's forehead. No fever. She could not see where the blood came from. "Who did this to you?"

The woman touched her bloody garment. "Not mine." She spoke so softly that Maude could barely hear her. "Anne's."

Maude felt a shiver run through her. "Where is Anne?"

The woman looked toward the forest beyond, and the road that led back into town. "I could not help her any longer . . ."

It was then that Maude looked at the woman's feet. She wore no hose and no shoes. Her right arm, Maude suddenly realized, was twisted in an unnatural way

"Help me get her inside," Maude said to the chief cook.

"No, Mistress," the woman said, but Maude ignored her.

The chief cook crossed his arms. "Milady, she is—"

"One of God's children," Maude said. "We shall take care of her."

The chief cook sent out scullions and the indoor grooms. Apparently, the cook was too good to help a woman in need.

The men slipped their arms beneath the woman and she moaned. Maude wondered how many other bones had been broken.

"Place her in the servants' quarters and send for the wet nurse," Maude said. Her wet nurse knew potions and herbs and healings. She had cursed the doctors when she saw what they had done to Maude's husband, saying that if Maude had brought her in sooner, she could have saved him.

Considering that she saved the steward, who later fell to the same disease, Maude believed her.

The quarters where she had them take the woman were for the greater servants. They had rooms of their own, with cots stuffed with straw, instead of mattresses on the floor. This room had been empty since her husband died. She had lost a few servants and hadn't had the energy to replace them.

The men laid the woman on the bed. She was paler than she had been before, and her eyes were glassy with pain.

"What are you called?" Maude asked.

"Mistress, your man, he is right about what I am."

"Do not argue," Maude said. "You are here now. What are you called?"

"Joan."

"Joan," Maude said. "Who did this?"

Joan closed her eyes. At that moment, the wet nurse appeared. She held a towel as if she had just left the young lord, and her surcoat was not properly fastened.

When she saw the woman on the bed, her gaze met Maude's. "Milady, you know—"

"I know," Maude said. "See what you can do. She's been badly beaten and her arm is broken."

The wet nurse nodded. She came inside, put a hand on Joan's forehead, and then began to examine her. Maude stood.

The men were still crowded inside the room. It was as if they saw Joan as a curiosity and nothing more.

"Come," Maude said. "We shall find this Anne."

HALFWAY TO TOWN, THEY found what remained of Anne. She lay in a crumpled heap beside the road, her limbs bent at unnatural angles. Her face was bloodied, as if her nose had been broken, but that was not where all of the blood came from.

She had knife wounds on her hands and arms, and another through her belly. The dry road contained a black trail, as if she had lost blood the entire way.

Joan had carried her on a broken leg, until she could come no farther.

Maude turned to the head groom who had accompanied her. She took one of Anne's cold, damaged hands, and held it out to him.

"What do you think of this?" she asked.

He shrugged. He could barely look at her. "This is not your concern, Milady."

"Of course it is," she snapped, startled at the tone that came out of her mouth. Had she ever spoken to anyone so harshly? "This is my land."

He looked at her then, and it seemed as though there was pity in his eyes. It made her bristle.

"What becomes of these women," he said, "is their choice."

"I doubt anyone would choose to die like this," Maude said. She ran her fingers over the deep wounds. The skin had parted so far that she could see muscle. "I believe she was trying to defend herself."

"Be that as it may, Milady," the groom said, "she knew what such a life would bring."

Did she? Did anyone? Maude remembered the day after her marriage, as she rode in her husband's carriage to her new home, the estate she now ran. Had she known that day how many miscarriages she would have? How the first babe born to them would die three days later in so much pain that his little wails broke her heart? Had she known then that she would love her surviving son so much that it hurt?

Of course not. And the greatest surprise of all had been how badly she missed her husband, now that he was gone.

"You know something of these women then?" she asked her groom.

He flushed. "Only what I have overheard in taverns, Milady."

She narrowed her eyes, not believing him. "They are from the stew, are they not?"

He nodded.

"Is such treatment common there?"

His flush grew deeper. "Milady, I am not—"

"I am a woman married and widowed," she said. "I am not unfamiliar with such things."

"There are perversions, Milady, that I cannot speak of to a gentle-born lady."

She raised her eyebrows. "Perversions that would result in this?"

He looked away from her. His skin was the color of dark wine. "There are men who enjoy inflicting pain."

She shuddered once and decided that perhaps he was right; she was not ready to hear such things. Still, a woman had died on her land and another had come to her for help.

"What do you think they were doing here?" she asked. "Where do you think they were going?"

He shook his head. He knew, as well as she, that no one would have taken the women in.

The hand did not feel human. It was too cold, the flesh hard.

"We shall give her a Christian burial," Maude said.

"Milady! She deserves no such treatment."

"Did you know her then?" Maude asked.

He shook his head.

"Then you do not know who and what she was. Like me, you can only guess. And I choose to guess that she was a godly woman. You shall send some men to bring her back to the house. We shall place her in the chapel, find her suitable clothes before the priest arrives, and have him say a few words over her."

"He will not like this, Milady."

"He will not know," she said.

"How will he not learn of it?" the groom asked. "So many have seen her, so many already know."

She raised her head, anger making her feel stronger than she had for almost a year. "If anyone speaks of this," she said firmly, "he will be fired."

The groom's eyes widened. She had never been this cold before.

He nodded once. "As you wish," he said.

BECAUSE OF HER DUTIES to young Henry, the wet nurse enlisted the aid of two kitchen maids and a chambermaid, all of whom, the wet nurse said, also had knowledge of healing.

Maude was amazed that she knew so little of her staff. They bowed to her when she came into the room. It now smelled of wine and camphor. While Maude was gone, Joan's sore feet had been cleaned and bound with cloth, her bruises rubbed with hot stones, and her broken arm set and splinted.

But she was awake, her eyes dark against her pale face.

"Leave us for a moment," Maude said to the servants.

They bowed again and slipped through the door. Maude took Joan's hand. It was fragile as a bird's wing, but at least it felt alive, warm and callused, the bones delicate against her palm.

"Anne is dead," Maude said.

Joan closed her eyes for a moment, and nodded. It was as if Maude's words made the death real.

"I am giving her a Christian funeral," Maude said. "She is in the chapel. If you are well enough, you may attend."

Joan bit her lower lip. "You do not want me there."

"Of course I do," she said.

" 'Tis not a place for me." Joan bowed her head.

"Our Lord did not think so," Maude said. "Mary Magdalene was of your profession, yet she was at his side."

Joan squeezed Maude's hand. "You are a good woman. I did not mean to burden you."

"It is no burden." Maude put her other hand on top of Joan's. "Who did this to you?"

"Milady, it is not for you to hear."

"I am so tired of everyone telling me what I may and may not hear," Maude said. "I have lived more than a score of years, and I know of the stew and the men who frequent it. Now, stop protecting my dainty ears and tell me who did this to you."

"A man," Joan whispered. "I do not know his name."

"Is he the same one who killed Anne?"

A tear eased out of Joan's right eye. "No."

"Yet you left together."

"She would not have been hurt if not for me."

"Tell me," Maude said, and so Joan did.

THE STORY CAME OUT in fits and whispers, sometimes lost beneath the choking sound of Joan's heavily drawn breath. A man—a customer—had ill used her, and Anne, seeing how badly Joan was hurt, went to William, the stewholder, asking him to send for a doctor. He refused and demanded that Joan, who was popular, finish her night's work.

Anne returned to Joan's room and bundled her up, taking bread from the kitchen, and rolled it and some clothing in two blankets. Anne had heard of nunneries that took in Daughters of Eve—the Order of Saint Mary Magdalene—and they would travel until they found such a place.

Anne was helping Joan out of the stew when William found them. He accused Anne of stealing, and he drew a knife. He cut her, and that brought him to a frenzy. He attacked her like a madman, and did not stop. Joan could not help her.

Blood spattered her face, and then his, and that seemed to awaken him from his fit. He left them in the road outside the stew; left them, Joan believed, to die.

She managed to lift Anne over her shoulder, holding her in place with her good hand. Somehow she managed to make it to the middle of the forest before she fell, unable to go on. There she realized that Anne's eyes were open and unseeing, that Anne was not drawing a breath.

She remembered no more.

"I do not even think I saw your manor," she said. "I was just walking because I did not know what else to do."

MAUDE DID NOT KNOW what to do either. She sat in her private chamber, head bowed. But she did not ask for God's aid. Somehow she felt that God's presence was in none of this.

The stewholder, she knew, had rights over his women. He could prevent them from leaving. He could punish them for an obvious theft. But Maude did not believe the theft of bread and blankets was sin enough for this. She did not believe that women who sought to better themselves deserved to die by the side of the road, to be left there like discarded clothes.

It took her an hour to come to her decision.

And then she sent for her steward.

HE WAS A MAN of some years, thin after his illness, his hair gone except for graying tufts at the sides. Her husband had trusted him implicitly and Maude had trusted him as well. His advice had been sound, his care for the estate excellent.

He seemed uncomfortable to be in her private rooms. He waited, with the door open, for her instruction.

"Have the sheriff arrest the stewholder," she said. "His name is William."

"Milady," the steward said. "Since your husband's death, we have had no magistrate."

She nodded. "I will sit in judgment," she said.

He stared at her for a long moment, as if she were not someone he recognized.

"What would be the charge, then?" the steward asked.

"Murder," she said.

SHE HELD THE HEARING the next day. She sat in her hall as the sheriff brought in William the Stewholder. He was a portly man whose scarlet tunic was made of an expensive serge and whose shoes were lined with fur.

He looked as if he could afford the loss of a blanket or two.

His hands were shackled, but his feet were not.

When he saw her, his face flushed the color of his tunic. "I'll not sit before a woman!" he cried.

"You have no choice," she said in her new voice, the voice that had been born of this experience. "I am the trustee of my husband's lands, and until my son comes of age, I am the one who runs them."

"That means she's the magistrate," the sheriff said, shaking William.

"Did you," she asked, "stab a woman named Anne?"

"She stole from me."

"Enough to warrant two dozen wounds?" Maude asked.

"The price of theft is death!" he shouted, spittle coming from his mouth. Apparently, he felt that she would only understand him if he yelled.

"I determine the price of theft on these lands," Maude said, amazed she could sound so calm. "Those women were injured. They wanted medical care."

"Only one was injured," he said.

"Yet you wanted her to work."

He shrugged. "She'd done it before."

Maude stared at him for a long moment. He stared back, unrepentant.

"I sentence you," she said, "to a pilgrimage. You shall visit holy sites until you learn the meaning of humility."

"How shall that be judged?" the sheriff asked.

"I believe it will take many years," she said. "Perhaps your pilgrimage shall be eternal. I shall think on it and come to that decision by the morrow, when you shall be shipped out."

"You cannot do this," he said.

"We've already established that I can."

"Those whores you're so worried about will have no one to manage them."

She felt cold. She hadn't thought of that. She looked at the sheriff. "You shall bring them here. They shall learn useful work."

"Milady, they may leave, but that will not stop someone else from opening a stew," the sheriff said.

"I am aware of that," she said. "But at least it will not be William here." She waved in dismissal. "Take him away."

THAT EVENING, SHE SAT alone in the chapel as the priest sent Anne's soul on its way. Joan had been too ill to come. It would take many weeks for Joan to heal.

By then, Maude hoped the men she had sent to find the nearest Order of Saint Mary Magdalene would have returned with good news.

For it did not matter how a woman was born, as a daughter of Eve, or a daughter of Mary, she deserved to live a life free of brutality and pain.

Maude lived such a life, but she had not known it until now. And it had taken a sight that most would have shielded her from to teach her that she had strengths she had never expected.

She would hold these lands in trust for her son. And when he came of age, she would give them to him gladly, better than they had been when she came to them.

Better, because she had made them so.

A Light on the Road to Woodstock

Ellis Peters

The King's court was in no hurry to return to England that
late autumn of 1120, even though the fighting, somewhat
desultory in these last stages, was long over, and the
enforced peace sealed by a royal marriage. King Henry had
brought to a successful conclusion his sixteen years of patient,
cunning, relentless plotting, fighting, and manipulating, and
could now sit back in high content, master not only of England
but of Normandy, too. What the Conqueror had misguidedly
dealt out in two separate parcels to his two elder sons, his
youngest son had now put together again and clamped into one.
Not without a hand in removing from the light of day, some
said, both of his brothers, one of whom had been shoveled into a
hasty grave under the tower at Winchester, while the other was
now a prisoner in Devizes, and unlikely ever to be seen again by
the outer world.

The court could well afford to linger to enjoy victory, while
Henry trimmed into neatness the last loose edges still to be made
secure. But his fleet was already preparing at Barfleur for the
voyage back to England, and he would be home before the
month ended. Meantime, many of his barons and knights who
had fought his battles were withdrawing their contingents and

making for home, among them one Roger Mauduit, who had a young and handsome wife waiting for him, certain legal business on his mind, and twenty-five men to ship back to England, most of them to be paid off on landing.

There were one or two among the miscellaneous riffraff he had recruited here in Normandy on his lord's behalf whom it might be worth keeping on in his own service, along with the few men of his household, at least until he was safely home. The vagabond clerk turned soldier, let him be unfrocked priest or what he might, was an excellent copyist and a sound Latin scholar, and could put legal documents in their best and most presentable form, in good time for the King's court at Woodstock. And the Welsh man-at-arms, blunt and insubordinate as he was, was also experienced and accomplished in arms, a man of his word, once given, and utterly reliable in whatever situation on land or sea, for in both elements he had long practice behind him. Roger was well aware that he was not greatly loved, and he had little faith in either the valor or the loyalty of his own men. But this Welshman from Gwynedd, by way of Antioch and Jerusalem and only God knows where else, had imbibed the code of arms and wore it as a second nature. With or without love, such service as he pledged, that he would provide.

Roger put it to them both as his men were embarking at Barfleur, in the middle of a deceptively placid November, and upon a calm sea.

"I would have you two accompany me to my manor of Sutton Mauduit by Northampton, when we disembark, and stay in my pay until a certain lawsuit I have against the abbey of Shrewsbury is resolved. The King intends to come to Woodstock when he arrives in England and will be there to preside over my case on the twenty-third day of this month. Will you remain in my service until that day?"

The Welshman said that he would, until that day or until the case was resolved. He said it indifferently, as one who has no business of any importance anywhere else in the world to pull him in another direction. As well Northampton as anywhere else. As well Woodstock. And after Woodstock? Why anywhere in

particular? There was no identifiable light beckoning him anywhere, along any road. The world was wide, fair, and full of savor,
but without signposts.

Alard, the tatterdemalion clerk, hesitated, scratched his
thick thatch of grizzled red hair, and finally also said yes, but as if
some vague regret drew him in another direction. It meant pay
for some days more, he could not afford to say no.

"I would have gone with him with better heart," he said later,
when they were leaning on the rail together, watching the low
blue line of the English shore rise out of a placid sea, "if he had
been taking a more westerly road."

"Why that?" asked Cadfael ap Meilyr ap Dafydd. "Have you
kin in the west?"

"I had once. I have not now."

"Dead?"

"I am the one who died." Alard heaved lean shoulders in a
helpless shrug, and grinned. "Fifty-seven brothers I had, and now
I'm brotherless. I begin to miss my kin, now I'm past forty. I never
valued them when I was young." He slanted a rueful glance at his
companion and shook his head. "I was a monk of Evesham, an
oblatus, given to God by my father when I was five years old.
When I was fifteen, I could no longer abide to live my life in one
place, and I ran. Stability is one of the vows we take—to be content in one stay, and go abroad only when ordered. That was not
for me, not then. My sort they call *vagus*—frivolous minds that
must wander. Well, I've wandered far enough, God knows, in my
time. I begin to fear I can never stand still again."

The Welshman drew his cloak about him against the chill of
the wind. "Are you hankering for a return?"

"Even you seamen must drop anchor somewhere at last,"
Alard said. "They'd have my hide if I went back, that I know. But
there's this about penance, it pays all debts, and leaves the record
clear. They'd find a place for me, once I'd paid. But I don't know
. . . I don't know . . . The *vagus* is still in me. I'm torn two ways."

"After twenty-five years," said Cadfael, "a month or two
more for quiet thinking can do no harm. Copy his papers for him
and take your ease until his business is settled."

They were much of an age, though the renegade monk looked the elder by ten years, and much knocked about by the world he had coveted from within the cloister. It had never paid him well in goods or gear, for he went threadbare and thin, but in wisdom he might have got his fair wages. A little soldiering, a little clerking, some horse-tending, any labor that came to hand, until he could turn his hand to almost anything a hale man can do. He had seen, he said, Italy as far south as Rome, served once for a time under the Count of Flanders, crossed the mountains into Spain, never abiding anywhere for long. His feet still served him, but his mind grew weary of the road.

"And you?" he said, eyeing his companion, whom he had known now for a year in this last campaign. "You're something of a *vagus* yourself, by your own account. All those years crusading and battling corsairs in the midland sea, and still you have not enough of it but must cross the sea again to get buffeted about Normandy. Had you no better business of your own, once you got back to England but you must enlist again in this muddled mêlée of a war? No woman to take your mind off fighting?"

"What of yourself? Free of the cloister, free of the vows!"

"Somehow," said Alard, himself puzzled, "I never saw it so. A woman here and there, yes, when the heat was on me, and there was a woman by and willing, but marriage and wiving . . . it never seemed to me I had the right."

The Welshman braced his feet on the gently swaying deck and watched the distant shore draw nearer. A broad-set, sturdy, muscular man in his healthy prime, brown-haired and brown-skinned from eastern suns and outdoor living, well provided in leather coat and good cloth, and well armed with sword and dagger. A comely enough face, strongly featured, with the bold bones of his race—there had been women, in his time, who had found him handsome.

"I had a girl," he said meditatively, "years back, before ever I went crusading. But I left her when I took the Cross; left her for three years and stayed away seventeen. The truth is, in the east I forgot her, and in the west she, thanks be to God, had forgotten me. I did inquire, when I got back. She'd made a better bargain and married a decent, solid man who had nothing of the *vagus* in him. A guildsman and counselor of the town of Shrewsbury, no less. So I shed the load from my conscience and went back to what I knew, soldiering. With no regrets," he said simply. "It was all over and done, years since. I doubt if I should have known her again, or she me." There had been other women's faces in the years between, still vivid in his memory, while hers had faded into mist.

"And what will you do," Alard asked, "now the King's got everything he wanted, married his son to Anjou and Maine, and made an end of fighting? Go back to the east? There's never any want of squabbles there to keep a man busy."

"No," said Cadfael, eyes fixed on the shore that began to show the solidity of land and the undulations of cliff and down. For that, too, was over and done, years since, and not as well done as once he had hoped. This desultory campaigning in Normandy was little more than a postscriptum, an afterthought, a means of filling in the interim between what was past and what was to come, and as yet unrevealed. All he knew of it was that it must be something new and momentous, a door opening into another room. "It seems we have both a few days' grace, you and I, to find out where we are going. We'd best make good use of the time."

There was stir enough before night to keep them from wondering beyond the next moment or troubling their minds about what was past or what was to come. Their ship put into the roads with a steady and favorable wind, and made course into Southampton before the light faded, and there was work for Alard checking the gear as it was unloaded, and for Cadfael disembarking the horses. A night's sleep in lodgings and stables in the town, and they would be on their way with the dawn.

"So the King's due in Woodstock," Alard said, rustling sleepily in his straw in a warm loft over the horses, "in time to sit in judgment on the twenty-third of the month. He makes his forest lodges the hub of his kingdom, there's more statecraft talked at Woodstock, so they say, than ever at Westminster. And he keeps his beasts there—lions and leopards—even camels. Did you ever see camels, Cadfael? There in the east?"

"Saw them and rode them. Common as horses there, hardworking and serviceable, but uncomfortable riding and foultempered. Thank God it's horses we'll be mounting in the morning." And after a long silence, on the edge of sleep, he asked curiously into the straw-scented darkness, "If ever you do go back, what is it you want of Evesham?"

"Do I know?" Alard responded drowsily, and followed that with a sudden sharpening sigh, again fully awake. "The silence, it might be . . . or the stillness. To have no more running to do . . . to have arrived, and have no more need to run. The appetite changes. Now I think it would be a beautiful thing to be still."

THE MANOR THAT WAS the head of Roger Mauduit's scattered and substantial honor lay somewhat southeast of Northampton, comfortably under the lee of the long ridge of wooded hills where the King had a chase, and spreading its extensive fields over the rich lowland between. The house was of stone, and ample, over a deep undercroft, and with a low tower providing two small chambers at the eastern end, and the array of sturdy byres, barns, and stables that lined the containing walls was impressive. Someone had proved a good steward while the lord was away about King Henry's business.

The furnishings of the hall were no less eloquent of good management, and the men and maids of the household went about their work with a brisk wariness that showed they went in some awe of whomever presided over their labors. It needed only a single day of watching the Lady Eadwina in action to show who ruled the roost here. Roger Mauduit had married a wife not only handsome but also efficient and masterful. She had had her own way here for three years, and by all the signs had enjoyed her dominance. She might, even, be none too glad to resign her charge now, however glad she might be to have her lord home again.

She was a tall, graceful woman, ten years younger than Roger, with an abundance of fair hair and large blue eyes that went discreetly half-veiled by absurdly long lashes most of the time, but flashed a bright and steely challenge when she opened them fully. Her smile was likewise discreet and almost constant, concealing rather than revealing whatever went on in her mind; and though her welcome to her returning lord left nothing to be desired, but lavished on him every possible tribute of ceremony and affection from the moment his horse entered at the gate, Cadfael could not but wonder whether she was not, at the same time, taking stock of every man he brought in with him, and every article of gear or harness or weaponry in their equipment, as one taking jealous inventory of his goods and resolved to make sure nothing was lacking.

She had her little son by the hand, a boy of about seven years old, and the child had the same fair coloring, the same contained and almost supercilious smile, and was as spruce and fine as his mother.

The lady received Alard with a sweeping glance that deprecated his tatterdemalion appearance and doubted his morality, but nevertheless she was willing to accept and make use of his abilities. The clerk who kept the manor roll and the accounts was efficient enough, but had no Latin, and could not write a good court hand. Alard was whisked away to a small table set in the angle of the great hearth, and kept hard at work copying certain charters and letters, and preparing them for presentation.

"This suit of his is against the abbey of Shrewsbury," said Alard, freed of his labors after supper in hall. "I recall you said that girl of yours had married a merchant in that town. Shrewsbury is a Benedictine house, like mine of Evesham." His, he called it still, after so many years of abandoning it; or his again, after time had brushed away whatever division there had ever been. "You must know it, if you come from there."

"I was born in Trefriw, in Gwynedd," Cadfael said, "but I took service early with an English wool merchant and came to Shrewsbury with his household. Fourteen, I was then—in Wales fourteen is manhood—and as I was a good lad with the short bow, and took kindly to the sword, I suppose I was worth my keep. The best of my following years were spent in Shrewsbury. I know it like my own palm, abbey and all. My master sent me there a year and more, to get my letters. But I quit that service when he died. I'd pledged nothing to the son, and he was a poor shadow of his father. That was when I took the Cross. So did many like me, all afire. I won't say what followed was all ash, but it burned very low at times."

"It's Mauduit who holds this disputed land," Alard said, "and the abbey that sues to recover it, and the thing's been going on four years without a settlement, ever since the old man here died. From what I know of the Benedictines, I'd rate their honesty above our Roger's, I tell you straight. And yet his charters seem to be genuine, as far as I can tell."

"Where is this land they're fighting over?" Cadfael asked.

"It's a manor by the name of Rotesley, near Stretton, demesne, village, advowson of the Church and all. It seems when the great earl was just dead and his abbey still building, Roger's father gave Rotesley to the abbey. No dispute about that, the charter's there to show it. But the abbey granted it back to him as tenant for life, to live out his latter years there undisturbed, Roger being then married and installed here at Sutton. That's where the dispute starts. The abbey claims it was clearly agreed the tenancy ended with the old man's death, that he himself understood it so, and intended it should be restored to the abbey as soon as he was out of it. While Roger says there was no such agreement to restore it unconditionally, but the tenancy was granted to the Mauduits, and ought to be hereditary. And so far he's hung on to it tooth and claw. After several hearings they remitted it to the King himself. And that's why you and I, my friend, will be off with his lordship to Woodstock the day after tomorrow."

"And how do you rate his chances of success? He seems none too sure himself," said Cadfael, "to judge by his short temper and nail-biting this last day or so."

"Why, the charter could have been worded better. It says simply that the village is granted back in tenancy during the old man's lifetime, but fails to say anything about what shall happen afterward, whatever may have been intended. From what I hear, they were on very good terms, Abbot Fulchered and the old lord, agreements between them on other matters in the manor book are worded as between men who trusted each other. The witnesses are all of them dead, as Abbot Fulchered is dead. It's one Godefrid now. But for all I know the abbey may hold letters that have passed between the two, and a letter is witness of intent, no less than a formal charter. All in good time we shall see."

The nobility still sat at the high table, in no haste to retire, Roger brooding over his wine, of which he had already drunk his fair share and more. Cadfael eyed them with interest, seen thus in a family setting. The boy had gone to his bed, hauled away by an elderly nurse, but the Lady Eadwina sat in close attendance at her lord's left hand and kept his cup well filled, smiling her faint, demure smile. On her left sat a very fine young squire of about twenty-five years, deferential and discreet, with a smile somehow the male reflection of her own. The source of both was secret, the spring of their pleasure or amusement, or whatever caused them so to smile, remained private and slightly unnerving, like the carved stone smiles of certain very old statues Cadfael had seen in Greece, long ago. For all his mild, amiable, and ornamental appearance, combed and curled and courtly, he was a big, well-set-up young fellow, with a set to his smooth jaw. Cadfael studied him with interest, for he was plainly privileged here.

"Goscelin," Alard said by way of explanation, following his friend's glance. "Her right-hand man while Roger was away."

Her left-hand man now, by the look of it, thought Cadfael. For her left hand and Goscelin's right were private under the table, while she spoke winningly into her husband's ear; and if those two hands were not paddling palms at this moment Cadfael was very much deceived. Above and below the drapings of the board were two different worlds. "I wonder," he said thoughtfully, "what she's breathing into Roger's ear now."

What the lady was breathing into her husband's ear was, in fact: "You fret over nothing, my lord. What does it matter how strong his proofs, if he never reaches Woodstock in time to present them? You know the law: If one party fails to appear, judgment is given for the other. The assize judges may allow more than one default if they please, but do you think King Henry will? Whoever fails of keeping tryst with him will be felled on the spot. And you know the road by which Prior Heribert must come." Her voice was a silken purr in his ear. "And have you not a hunting lodge in the forest north of Woodstock, through which that road passes?"

Roger's hand had stiffened round the stem of his wine cup. He was not so drunk but he was listening intently.

"Shrewsbury to Woodstock will be a two- or three-day journey to such a rider. All you need do is have a watcher on the road north of you to give warning. The woods are thick enough, masterless men have been known to haunt there. Even if he comes by daylight, your part need never be known. Hide him but a few days, it will be long enough. Then turn him loose by night, and who's ever to know what footpads held and robbed him? You need not even touch his parchments—robbers would count them worthless. Take what common thieves would take, and theirs will be the blame."

Roger opened his tight-shut mouth to say in a doubtful growl, "He'll not be traveling alone."

"Hah! Two or three abbey servants—they'll run like hares. You need not trouble yourself over them. Three stout, silent men of your own will be more than enough."

He brooded, and began to think so, too, and to review in his mind the men of his household, seeking the right hands for such work. Not the Welshman and the clerk, the strangers here; their part was to be the honest onlookers in case there should ever be questions asked.

THEY LEFT SUTTON MAUDUIT on the twentieth day of November, which seemed unnecessarily early, though as Roger had decreed that they should settle in his hunting lodge in the forest close by Woodstock, which meant conveying stores with them to make the house habitable and provision it for a party for, presumably, a stay of three nights at least. It was perhaps a wise precaution. Roger was taking no chances in his suit, he said; he meant to be established on the ground in good time, and have all his proofs in order.

"But so he has," said Alard, pricked in his professional pride, "for I've gone over everything with him, and the case, if open in default of specific instructions, is plain enough and will stand up.

What the abbey can muster, who knows? They say the abbot is not well, which is why his prior comes in his place. My work is done."

He had the faraway look in his eye, as the party rode out and faced westward, of one either penned and longing to be where he could but see, or loose and weary and being drawn home. Either a *vagus* escaping outward, or a penitent flying back in haste before the doors should close against him. There must indeed be something desirable and lovely to cause a man to look toward it with that look on his face.

Three men-at-arms and two grooms accompanied Roger, in addition to Alard and Cadfael, whose term of service would end with the session in court after which they might go where they would, Cadfael horsed, since he owned his own mount, Alard afoot, since the pony he rode belonged to Roger. It came as something of a surprise to Cadfael that the squire Goscelin should also saddle up and ride with the party, very debonair and well armed with sword and dagger.

"I marvel," said Cadfael dryly, "that the lady doesn't need him at home for her own protection, while her lord's absent."

The Lady Eadwina, however, bade farewell to the whole party with the greatest serenity, and to her husband with demonstrative affection, putting forward her little son to be embraced and kissed. Perhaps, thought Cadfael, relenting, I do her wrong, simply because I feel chilled by that smile of hers. For all I know she may be the truest wife living.

They set out early, and before Buckingham made a halt at the small and penurious priory of Bradwell, where Roger elected to spend the night, keeping his three men-at-arms with him, while Goscelin with the rest of the party rode on to the hunting lodge to make all ready for their lord's reception the following day. It was growing dark by the time they arrived, and the bustle of kindling fire and torches, and unloading the bed linen and stores from the sumpter ponies went on into the night. The lodge was small, stockaded, well furnished with stabling and mews, and in thick woodland, a place comfortable enough once they had a roaring fire on the hearth and food on the table.

"The road the prior of Shrewsbury will be coming by," said Alard, warming himself by the fire after supper, "passes through

Evesham. As like as not they'll stay the last night there." With
every mile west, Cadfael had seen him straining forward with
mounting eagerness. "The road cannot be far away from us here;
it passes through this forest."

"It must be nearly thirty miles to Evesham," Cadfael said. "A
long day's riding for a clerical party. It will be night by the time
they ride past into Woodstock. If you're set on going, stay at least
to get your pay, for you'll need it before the thirty miles is done."

They went to their slumber in the warmth of the hall without a word more said. But he would go, Alard, whether he himself
knew it yet or not. Cadfael knew it. His friend was a tired horse
with the scent of the stable in his nostrils; nothing would stop
him now until he reached it.

It was well into the middle of the day when Roger and his
escort arrived, and they approached not directly as the advance
party had done, but from the woods to the north, as though they
had been indulging in a little hunting or hawking by the way,
except that they had neither hawk nor hound with them. A fine,
clear, cool day for riding, there was no reason in the world why
they should not go roundabout for the pure pleasure of it—and
indeed, they seemed to come in high content!—but that Roger's
mind had been so preoccupied and so anxious concerning his lawsuit that distractions seemed unlikely. Cadfael was given to thinking about unlikely developments, which from old campaigns he
knew to prove significant in most cases. Goscelin, who was out at
the gate to welcome them in, was apparently oblivious to the
direction from which they came. That way lay Alard's highway to
his rest. But what meaning ought it to have for Roger Mauduit?

The table was lavish that night, and lord and squire drank
well and ate well, and gave no sign of any care, though they
might, Cadfael thought, watching them from his lower place,
seem a little tight and knife-edged. Well, the King's court could
account for that. Shrewsbury's prior was drawing steadily nearer,
with whatever weapons he had for the battle. But it seemed rather
an exultant tension than an anxious one. Was Roger counting his
chickens already?

The morning of the twenty-second of November dawned, and
the noon passed, and with every moment Alard's restlessness and

abstraction grew, until with evening it possessed him utterly, and he could no longer resist. He presented himself before Roger after supper, when his mood might be mellow from good food and wine.

"My lord, with the morrow my service to you is completed. You need me no longer, and with your goodwill I would set forth now for where I am going. I go afoot and need provision for the road. If you have been content with my work, pay me what is due, and let me go."

It seemed that Roger had been startled out of some equally absorbing preoccupation of his own and was in haste to return to it, for he made no demur but paid at once. To do him justice, he had never been a grudging paymaster. He drove as hard a bargain as he could at the outset, but once the agreement was made, he kept it.

"Go when you please," he said. "Fill your bag from the kitchen for the journey when you leave. You did good work, I give you that."

And he returned to whatever it was that so engrossed his thoughts, and Alard went to collect the proffered largesse and his own meager possessions.

"I am going," he said, meeting Cadfael in the hall doorway. "I must go." There was no more doubt in voice or face. "They will take me back, though in the lowest place. From that there's no falling. The blessed Benedict wrote in the Rule that even to the third time of straying a man may be received again if he promise full amendment."

It was a dark night, without moon or stars but in fleeting moments when the wind ripped apart the cloud covering to let through a brief gleam of moonlight. The weather had grown gusty and wild in the last two days, the King's fleet must have had a rough crossing from Barfleur.

"You'd do better," Cadfael urged, "to wait for morning and go by daylight. Here's a safe bed, and the King's peace, however well enforced, hardly covers every mile of the King's high roads."

But Alard would not wait. The yearning was on him too strongly, and a penniless vagabond who had ventured all the roads of Christendom by day or night was hardly likely to flinch from the last thirty miles of his wanderings.

"Then I'll go with you as far as the road, and see you on your way," Cadfael said.

There was a mile or so of track through thick forest between them and the high road that bore away west-northwest on the upland journey to Evesham. The ribbon of open highway, hemmed on both sides by trees, was hardly less dark than the forest itself. King Henry had fenced in his private park at Woodstock to house his wild beasts, but maintained also his hunting chase here, many miles in extent. At the road they parted, and Cadfael stood to watch his friend march steadily away towardsthe west, eyes fixed ahead, upon his penance and his absolution, a tired man with a rest assured.

Cadfael turned back toward the lodge as soon as the receding shadow had melted into the night. He was in no haste to go in, for the night, though blustery, was not cold, and he was in no mind to seek the company of others of the party now that one best known to him was gone, and gone in so mysteriously rapt a fashion. He walked on among the trees, turning his back on his bed for a while.

The constant thrashing of branches in the wind all but drowned the scuffling and shouting that suddenly broke out behind him, at some distance among the trees, until a horse's shrill whinny brought him about with a jerk and set him running through the underbrush toward the spot where confused voices yelled alarm and broken bushes thrashed. The clamor seemed some little way off, and he was startled as he shouldered his way headlong through a thicket to collide heavily with two entangled bodies, send them spinning apart, and himself fall asprawl upon one of them in the flattened grass. The man under him uttered a scared and angry cry, and the voice was Roger's. The other man had made no sound at all, but slid away very rapidly and lightly to vanish among the trees, a tall shadow swallowed in shadows.

Cadfael drew off in haste, reaching an arm to hoist the winded man. "My lord, are you hurt? What, in God's name, is to do here?" The sleeve he clutched slid warm and wet under his hand. "You're injured! Hold fast, let's see what harm's done before you move . . ."

Then there was the voice of Goscelin, for once loud and vehement in alarm, shouting for his lord and crashing headlong through bush and brake to fall on his knees beside Roger, lamenting and raging.

"My lord, my lord, what happened here? What rogues were those, loose in the woods? Dared they waylay travelers so close to the King's highway? You're hurt—here's blood . . ."

Roger got his breath back and sat up, feeling at his left arm below the shoulder, and wincing. "A scratch. My arm . . . God curse him, whoever he may be, the fellow struck for my heart. Man, if you had not come charging like a bull, I might have been dead. You hurled me off the point of his dagger. Thank God, there's no great harm, but I bleed . . . Help me back home!"

"That a man may not walk by night in his own woods," Goscelin fumed, hoisting his lord carefully to his feet, "without being set upon by outlaws! Help here, you, Cadfael, take his other arm . . . Footpads so close to Woodstock! Tomorrow we must turn out the watch to comb these tracks and hunt them out of cover, before they kill . . ."

"Get me withindoors," snapped Roger, "and have this coat and shirt off me, and let's staunch this bleeding. I'm alive, that's the main!"

They helped him back between them, through the more open ways toward the lodge. It dawned on Cadfael, as they went, that the clamor of furtive battle had ceased completely, even the wind had abated, and somewhere on the road, distantly, he caught the rhythm of galloping hooves, very fast and light, as of a riderless horse in panic flight.

THE GASH IN ROGER Mauduit's left arm, just below the shoulder, was long but not deep and grew shallower as it descended. The stroke that marked him thus could well have been meant for his heart. Cadfael's hurtling impact, at the very moment the attack was launched, had been the means of averting murder. The shadow that had melted into the night had no form, nothing about it rendered it human or recognizable. He had heard an outcry and run toward it, a projectile to strike attacked and attacker apart; questioned, that was all he could say.

For which, said Roger, bandaged and resting and warmed with mulled wine, he was heartily thankful. And indeed, Roger was behaving with remarkable fortitude and calm for a man who had just escaped death. By the time he had demonstrated to his dismayed grooms and men-at-arms that he was alive and not much the worse, appointed the hour when they should set out for Woodstock in the morning, and been helped to his bed by Goscelin, there was even a suggestion of complacency about him, as though a gash in the arm was a small price to pay for the successful retention of a valuable property and the defeat of his clerical opponents.

IN THE COURT OF the palace of Woodstock the King's chamberlains, clerks, and judges were fluttering about in a curiously distracted manner, or so it seemed to Cadfael, standing apart among the commoners to observe their antics. They gathered in small groups, conversing in low voices and with anxious faces, broke apart to regroup with others of their kind, hurried in and out among the litigants, avoiding or brushing off all questions, exchanged documents, hurried to the door to peer out, as if looking for some late arrival. And there was indeed one litigant who had not kept to his time, for there was no sign of a Benedictine prior among those assembled nor had anyone appeared to explain or justify his absence. And Roger Mauduit, in spite of his stiff and painful arm, continued to relax, with ever-increasing assurance, into shining complacency.

The appointed hour was already some minutes past when four agitated fellows, two of them Benedictine brothers, made a hasty entrance, and accosted the presiding clerk.

"Sir," bleated the leader, loud in nervous dismay, "we here are come from the abbey of Shrewsbury, escort to our prior, who was on his way to plead a case at law here. Sir, you must hold him excused, for it is not his blame nor ours that he cannot appear. In the forest some two miles north, as we rode hither last night in the dark, we were attacked by a band of lawless robbers, and they have seized our prior and dragged him away . . ."

The spokesman's voice had risen shrilly in his agitation, he had the attention of every man in the hall by this time. Certainly, he had Cadfael's. Masterless men some two miles out of Woodstock, plying their trade last night, could only be the same who had happened upon Roger Mauduit and all but been the death of him. Any such gang, so close to the court, was astonishing enough; there could hardly be two. The clerk was outraged at the very idea.

"Seized and captured him? And you four were with him? Can this be true? How many were they who attacked you?"

"We could not tell for certain. Three at least—but they were lying in ambush; we had no chance to stand them off. They pulled him from his horse and were off into the trees with him. They knew the woods, and we did not. Sir, we did go after them, but they beat us off."

It was evident they had done their best, for two of them showed bruised and scratched, and all were soiled and torn as to their clothing.

"We have hunted through the night but found no trace, only we caught his horse a mile down the highway as we came hither. So we plead here that our prior's absence be not seen as a default, for indeed he would have been here in the town last night if all had gone as it should."

"Hush, wait!" the clerk said peremptorily.

All heads had turned toward the door of the hall, where a great flurry of officials had suddenly surged into view, cleaving through the press with fixed and ominous haste, to take the center of the floor below the King's empty dais. A chamberlain, elderly and authoritative, struck the floor loudly with his staff and commanded silence. And at sight of his face silence fell like a stone.

"My lords, gentlemen, all who have pleas here this day, and all others present, you are bidden to disperse, for there will be no hearings today. All suits that should be heard here must be postponed three days and will be heard by his Grace's judges. His Grace the King cannot appear."

This time the silence fell again like a heavy curtain, muffling even thought or conjecture.

"The court is in mourning from this hour. We have received news of desolating import. His Grace with the greater part of his fleet made the crossing to England safely, as is known, but the *Blanche Nef*, in which his Grace's son and heir, Prince William, with all his companions and many other noble souls were embarked, put to sea late, and was caught in gales before ever clearing Barfleur. The ship is lost, split upon a rock, foundered with all hands, not a soul is come safe to land. Go hence quietly, and pray for the souls of the flower of this realm."

So that was the end of one man's year of triumph, an empty achievement, a ruinous victory, Normandy won, his enemies routed, and now everything swept aside, broken apart upon an obstinate rock, washed away in a malicious sea. His only lawful son, recently married in splendor, now denied even a coffin and a grave, for if ever they found those royal bodies it would be by the relenting grace of God, for the sea seldom put its winnings ashore by Barfleur. Even some of his unlawful sons, of whom there were many, gone down with their royal brother, no one left but the one legal daughter to inherit a barren empire.

Cadfael walked alone in a corner of the King's park and considered the foolishness of mortal vainglory, that was paid for with such a bitter price. But also he thought of the affairs of little men, to whom even a luckless King owed justice. For somewhere there was still to be sought the lost prior of Shrewsbury, carried off by masterless men in the forest, a litigant who might still be lost three days hence, when his suit came up again for hearing, unless someone in the meantime knew where to look for him.

He was in little doubt now. A lawless gang at liberty so close to a royal palace was in any case unlikely enough, and Cadfael was liable to brood on the unlikely. But that there should be two—no, that was impossible. And if one only, then that same one whose ambush he had overheard at some distance, yet close enough, too close for comfort, to Roger Mauduit's hunting lodge.

Probably the unhappy brothers from Shrewsbury were off beating the wilds of the forest afresh. Cadfael knew better where to look. No doubt Roger was biting his nails in some anxiety over the delay, but he had no reason to suppose that three days would release the captive to appear against him, nor was he paying much attention to what his Welsh man-at-arms was doing with his time.

Cadfael took his horse and rode back without haste toward the hunting lodge. He left in the early dusk, as soon as the evening meal was over in Mauduit's lodging. No one was paying any heed to him by that time of day. All Roger had to do was hold his tongue and keep his wits about him for three days, and the disputed manor would still be adjudged to him. Everything was beautifully in hand, after all.

Two of the men-at-arms and one groom had been left behind at the hunting lodge. Cadfael doubted if the man they guarded was to be found in the house itself, for unless he was blindfolded he would be able to gather far too much knowledge of his surroundings, and the fable of the masterless men would be tossed into the rubbish heap. No, he would be held in darkness, or dim light at best, even during the day, in straw or the rush flooring of a common hut, fed adequately but plainly and roughly, as wild men might keep a prisoner they were too cautious to kill, or too superstitious, until they turned him loose in some remote place, stripped of everything he had of value. On the other hand, he must be somewhere securely inside the boundary fence, otherwise there would be too high a risk of his being found. Between the gate and the house there were trees enough to obscure the large holding of a man of consequence. Somewhere among the stables and barns, or the now-empty kennels, there he must be held.

Cadfael tethered his horse in cover well aside from the lodge and found himself a perch in a tall oak tree, from which vantage point he could see over the fence into the courtyard.

He was in luck. The three within fed themselves at leisure before they fed their prisoner, preferring to wait for dark. By the time the groom emerged from the hall with a pitcher and a bowl in his hands, Cadfael had his night eyes. They were quite easy about their charge, expecting no interference from any man. The groom vanished momentarily between the trees within the enclosure, but appeared again at one of the low buildings tucked under the fence, set down his pitcher for a moment, while he hoisted clear a heavy wooden bar that held the door fast shut, and he vanished within. The door thudded to after him, as though he had slammed it shut with his back braced against it, taking no chances even with an elderly monastic. In a few minutes he emerged again empty-handed, hauled the bar into place again, and returned, whistling, to the hall and the enjoyment of Mauduit's ale.

Not the stables nor the kennels, but a small stout hay store built on short wooden piles raised from the ground. At least the prior would have fairly snug lying.

Cadfael let the last of the light fade before he made a move. The wooden wall was stout and high, but more than one of the old trees outside leaned a branch over it, and it was no great labor to climb without and drop into the deep grass within. He made first for the gate, and quietly unbarred the narrow wicket set into it. Faint threads of torchlight filtered through the chinks in the hall shutters, but nothing else stirred. Cadfael laid hold of the heavy bar of the storehouse door, and eased it silently out of its socket, opening the door by cautious inches, and whispering through the chink: "Father . . . ?"

There was a sharp rustling of hay within, but no immediate reply.

"Father Prior, is it you? Softly . . . Are you bound?"

A hesitant and slightly timorous voice said, "No." And in a moment, with better assurance: "My son, you are not one of these sinful men?"

"Sinful man I am, but not of their company. Hush, quietly now! I have a horse close by. I came from Woodstock to find you. Reach me your hand, Father, and come forth."

A hand came wavering out of the hay-scented darkness to clutch convulsively at Cadfael's hand. The pale patch of a tonsured crown gleamed faintly, and a small, rounded figure crept forth and stepped into the thick grass. He had the wit to waste no breath then on questions, but stood docile and silent while Cadfael rebarred the door on emptiness and, taking him by the hand, led him softly along the fence to the unfastened wicket in the great gate. Only when the door was closed as softly behind them did he heave a great, thankful sigh.

They were out, it was done, and no one would be likely to learn of the escape until morning. Cadfael led the way to where he had left his horse tethered. The forest lay serene and quiet about them.

"You ride, Father, and I'll walk with you. It's no more than two miles into Woodstock. We're safe enough now."

Bewildered and confused by so sudden a reversal, the prior confided and obeyed like a child. Not until they were out on the silent high road did he say sadly, "I have failed of my mission. Son, may God bless you for this kindness that is beyond my understanding. For how *did* you know of me, and how could you divine where to find me? I understand nothing of what has been happening to me. And I am not a very brave man . . . But my failure is no fault of yours, and my blessing I owe you without stint."

"You have not failed, Father," Cadfael said simply. "The suit is still unheard and will be for three days more. All your companions are safe in Woodstock, except that they fret and search for you. And if you know where they will be lodging, I would recommend that you join them now, by night, and stay well out of sight until the day the case is heard. For if this trap was designed to keep you from appearing in the King's court, some further attempt might yet be made. Have you your evidences safe? They did not take them?"

"Brother Orderic, my clerk, was carrying the documents, but he could not conduct the case in court. I only am accredited to represent my abbot. But, my son, how is it that the case still goes unheard? The King keeps strict day and time, it's well known. How comes it that God and you have saved me from disgrace and loss?"

"Father, for all too bitter reason, the King could not be present."

Cadfael told him the whole of it, how half the young chivalry of England had been wiped out in one blow, and the King left without an heir. Prior Heribert, shocked and dismayed, fell to praying in a grieving whisper for both dead and living, and Cadfael walked beside the horse in silence, for what more was there to be said? Except that King Henry, even in this shattering hour, willed that his justice should still prevail, and that was virtue in any monarch. Only when they came into the sleeping town did Cadfael again interrupt the prior's fervent prayers with a strange question.

"Father, was any man of your escort carrying steel? A dagger, or any such weapon?"

"No, no, God forbid!" said the prior, shocked. "We have no use for arms. We trust in God's peace, and after it in the King's."

"So I thought," Cadfael said, nodding. "It is another discipline, for another venture."

BY THE CHANGE IN Mauduit's countenance, Cadfael knew the hour of the following day when the news reached him that his prisoner was flown. All the rest of that day he went about with nerves at stretch and ears pricked for any sensational rumors being bandied around the town, and eyes roving anxiously in dread of the sight of Prior Heribert in court or street, braced to pour out his complaint to the King's officers. But as the hours passed and still there was no sign, he began to be a little eased in his mind, and to hope still for a miraculous deliverance. The Benedictine brothers were seen here and there, mute and somber-faced; surely they could have had no word of their superior. There was nothing to be done but set his teeth, keep his countenance, wait, and hope.

The second day passed, and the third day came, and Mauduit's hopes had soared again, for still there was no word. He made his appearance before the King's judge confidently, his charters in hand. The abbey was the suitor. If all went well, Roger would not even have to state his case, for the plea would fail of itself when the pleader failed to appear.

It came as a shattering shock when a sudden stir at the door, prompt to the hour appointed, blew into the hall a small, round, unimpressive person in the Benedictine habit, hugging to him an armful of vellum rolls and followed by his black-gowned brothers in close attendance. Cadfael, too, was observing him with interest, for it was the first time he had seen him clearly. A modest man of comfortable figure and amiable countenance, rosy and mild. Not so old as that night journey had suggested, perhaps forty-five, with a shining innocence about him. But to Roger Mauduit it might have been a fire-breathing dragon entering the hall.

And who would have expected, from that gentle, even deprecating presence, the clarity and expertise with which that small man deployed his original charter, punctiliously identical to Roger's according to the account Alard had given, and omitting any specific mention of what should follow Arnulf Mauduit's death—how scrupulously he pointed out the omission and the arguments to which it might give rise, and followed it up with two letters written by that same Arnulf Mauduit to Abbot Fulchered, referring in plain terms to the obligatory return of the manor and village after his death, and pledging his son's loyal observance of the obligation.

It might have been want of proofs that caused Roger to make so poor a job of refuting the evidence, or it might have been craven conscience. Whatever the cause, judgment was given for the abbey.

Cᴀᴅꜰᴀᴇʟ ᴘʀᴇꜱᴇɴᴛᴇᴅ ʜɪᴍꜱᴇʟꜰ ʙᴇꜰᴏʀᴇ the lord he was leaving, barely an hour after the verdict was given.

"My lord, your suit is concluded, and my service with it. I have done what I pledged, here I part from you."

Roger sat sunk in gloom and rage, and lifted upon him a glare that should have felled him, but failed of its impact.

"I misdoubt me," Roger said, smoldering, "how you have observed your loyalty to me. Who else could know . . .' He bit his tongue in time, for as long as it remained unsaid, no accusation had been made, and no rebuttal was needed. He would have liked to ask, How did you know? But he thought better of it. "Go, then, if you have nothing more to say."

"As to that," Cadfael said meaningly, "nothing more need be said. It's over." And that was recognizable as a promise, but with

uneasy implications, for plainly on some other matter he still had
a thing to say.

"My lord, give some thought to this, for I was until now in your
service and wish you no harm. Of those four who attended Prior
Heribert on his way here, not one carried arms. There was neither
sword nor dagger nor knife of any kind among the five of them."

He saw the significance of that go home, slowly but with
bitter force. The masterless men had been nothing but a children's tale, but until now Roger had thought, as he had been
meant to think, that that dagger-stroke in the forest had been a
bold attempt by an abbey servant to defend his prior. He blinked
and swallowed and stared, and began to sweat, beholding a per-
ilous gulf into which he had all but stumbled.

"There were none there who bore arms," said Cadfael, "but
your own."

A double-edged ambush that had been, to have him out in
the forest by night, all unsuspecting. And there were as many
miles between Woodstock and Sutton Mauduit returning as
coming, and there would be other nights as dark on the way.

"Who?" asked Roger in a grating whisper. "Which of them?
Give him a name!"

"No," Cadfael said simply. "Do your own divining. I am no
longer in your service, I have said all I mean to say."

Roger's face had turned grey. He was hearing again the plan
unfolded so seductively in his ear. "You cannot leave me so! If you
know so much, for God's sake return with me, see me safely
home, at least. You I could trust!"

"No," said Cadfael again. "You are warned, now guard
yourself."

It was fair, he considered; it was enough. He turned and
went away without another word. He went, just as he was, to
Vespers in the parish church, for no better reason—or so he
thought then—than that the dimness within the open doorway
beckoned him as he turned his back on a duty completed, invit-
ing him to quietness and thought, and the bell was just sounding.
The little prior was there, ardent in thanksgiving, one more creature who had fumbled his way to the completion of a task and the
turning of a leaf in the book of his life.

Cadfael watched out the office and stood mute and still for some time after priest and worshippers had departed. The silence after their going was deeper than the ocean and more secure than the earth. Cadfael breathed and consumed it like new bread. It was the light touch of a small hand on the hilt of his sword that startled him out of that profound isolation. He looked down to see a little acolyte, no higher than his elbow, regarding him gravely from great round eyes of blinding blue, intent and challenging, as solemn as ever was angelic messenger.

"Sir," said the child in stern treble reproof, tapping the hilt with an infant finger, "should not all weapons of war be laid aside here?"

"Sir," said Cadfael hardly less gravely, though he was smiling, "you may very well be right." And slowly he unbuckled the sword from his belt and went and laid it down, flatlings, on the lowest step under the altar. It looked strangely appropriate and at peace there. The hilt, after all, was a cross.

PRIOR HERIBERT WAS AT a frugal supper with his happy brothers in the parish priest's house when Cadfael asked audience with him. The little man came out graciously to welcome a stranger, and knew him for an acquaintance at least and now at a breath certainly a friend.

"You, my son! And surely it was you at Vespers? I felt that I should know the shape of you. You are the most welcome of guests here, and if there is anything I and mine can do to repay you for what you did for us, you need but name it."

"Father," Cadfael said, briskly Welsh in his asking, "do you ride for home tomorrow?"

"Surely, my son, we leave after Prime. Abbot Godefrid will be waiting to hear how we have fared."

"Then, Father, here am I at the turning of my life, free of one master's service, and finished with arms. Take me with you!"

ℳuthors' Biographies

Peter Tremayne is the pseudonym of Peter Beresford Ellis, a professor of law who lives in London, England. He conceived the idea for Sister Fidelma, a seventh-century Celtic lawyer, to demonstrate for his students that women could be legal advocates under the Irish system of law. Sister Fidelma has since appeared in eight novels, the most recent being *The Spider's Web*, and many short stories that have been collected in the anthology *Hemlock at Vespers* and *Other Sister Fidelma Mysteries*. He has also written, under his own name, more than twenty-five books on history, biography, and Irish and Celtic mythology, including *Celtic Women: Women in Celtic Society* and *Literature and Celt and Greek: Celts in the Hellenic World*. A native of Coventry, England, he has written a column for the *Irish Democrat* since 1987.

Doug Allyn is an accomplished author whose short fiction regularly graces a year's best collections. His work has appeared in *Once Upon a Crime*, *Cat Crimes Through Time*, and *The Year's 25 Finest Criman and Mystery Stories*, volumes 3 and 4. His stories of Talifer, the wandering minstrel, have appeared in *Ellery Queen's Mystery Magazine* and *Murder Most Scottish*. His story "The Dancing Bear," a Tallifer tale, won the Edgar Award for short fiction for 1994. His other series character is veterinarian Dr. David Westbrook, whose exploits have recently been collected in the anthology *All Creatures Dark and Dangerous*. He lives with his wife in Montrose, Michigan.

Lillian Stewart Carl writes what she calls "gonzo mythology" fantasy novels, as well as mystery and romantic suspense novels. While growing up in Missouri and Ohio, she began writing at an early age and has continued all her life, even while traveling to Europe, Great Britain, the Middle East, and India, among other places. Her novels include *Dust to Dust*, *Shadow Dancers*, and *Wings of Power*. Her short fiction has appeared in *Alternate Generals* and *Past Lives, Present Tense*. She lives in Carrollton, Texas.

Gillian Linscott lives a few miles from the site of the Battle at Mortimer's Cross, where she took inspiration for her story. Known for her Edwardian novels featuring radical suffragette Nell Bray, she has also written five novels about Bray. A former Parliamentary reporter for the BBC, she has also written a historical mystery set in Alaska as well as a contemporary mystery series featuring ex-policeman-turned-physical-trainer Birdie Linnett. Her short fiction appears in such anthologies as *Murder, They Wrote*. She lives with her husband, nonfiction author Tony Geraghty, in England.

Margaret Frazer is the pseudonym of Gail Frazier, who has been writing mystery novels for years, formerly with Mary Kuhfield. She has since taken the pseudonym of Margaret Frazer to continue the medieval murder mysteries featuring Sister Frevisse, a great-niece of Geoffrey Chaucer. The series spans nine novels, with *The Maidens' Tale* and *The Prioress's Tale*. She lives in Minnesota and is hard at work on more Sister Frevisse mysteries.

Clayton Emery has been a blacksmith, dishwasher, schoolteacher in Australia, carpenter, zookeeper, farmhand, land surveyor, volunteer firefighter, and award-winning technical writer. He's forty-four years old, an umpteenth-generation Yankee, a Navy brat, and an aging hippie. He lives in New Hampshire with his doctor wife and son Hunter, who keeps him apprised of the latest computer games. He spends his spare time restoring a 1763 house, gardens, and stone walls, and reenacting the American revolution in a kilt. He has written in every genre from children's books to mystery to fantasy to science fiction. Other short stories featuring Robin Hood and Marian have been published in *Ellery Queen's Mystery Magazine*. Read more of his stories at www.claytonemery.com.

Edward Marston is the prolific author of plays, short stories, and novels, with his historical mystery *The Roaring Boy* being nominated for the Edgar Award for best novel in 1995. He is currently writing two series, one featuring Nicholas Bracewell, a stage manager for an acting company in Elizabethan England, the other with Ralph Delchard and Gervase Bret, two men who travel England investigating land claims in the eleventh century. His latest novel is *The King's Evil*, another mystery, set in Restoration England. A former chairman of the Crime Writer's Association in the United Kingdom, he lives in rural Kent, England.

Tony Geraghty is the respected author of the nonfiction military books *Who Dares Win*, a history of the British Special Air Services Regiment; *March or Die: A New History of the French Foreign Legion*; and *Brixmis*, the story of England's spying role during the Cold War. A veteran paratrooper, he lives with his wife, fellow author Gillian Linscott, in England.

Kathy Lynn Emerson has enjoyed great success with her Lady Appleton–Face Down series. Her latest, *Face Down Beneath the Eleanor Cross*, has just been released. She has written in just about every genre, including romance, children's fiction and nonfiction, biography, and history. Recently, the Face Down series was optioned for film. She lives and writes in rural Maine with her husband of more than twenty-five years and a large calico cat.

Michael Jecks worked as a computer salesman until 1994, when an industry sales slump forced him to consider a new career. He wrote *The Last Templar*, the first of nine medieval mystery novels, found an agent, and then a publisher who offered him a three-book deal. Of his novels, he says, "I guess I'm like many people who love books—for many years I thought I should try writing, but with a mortgage to support, there never seemed to be time. My stories are based on extensive research, which has persuaded me that people haven't changed at all in seven hundred years. The same motivations lead to murder: jealousy, infidelity, greed, and so on. I try to show where our ancestors were different. How did the law work, how did people generally view government and justice? How did they live? It's not easy to show what life was really like, but it's a challenge I enjoy." Recent novels in his Medieval West County series include *The Abbot's Gibbet* and *Belladonna at Belstone*.

Brendan DuBois, primarily known for making the New England countryside come alive in his novels and short stories, has written several dozen critically acclaimed short stories, and has had his work appear in several best year's anthologies. One of his latest stories, "The Dark Snow," was nominated for the Edgar Award for best short story of 1996. Recent novels include *Shattered Shell*, the third mystery featuring contemporary magazine writer-sleuth Lewis Cole, and *Resurrection Day*, a techno-thriller extrapolating what might have happened if the Cuban Missile Crisis had turned into a full-fledged war. He lives in Exeter, New Hampshire.

Kristine Kathryn Rusch won three Reader's Choice Awards in 1999 for three different stories in three different magazines in two different genres: mystery and science fiction. That same year, her short fiction was nominated for the Hugo, Nebula, and Locus Awards. Since she had just returned to writing short fiction after quitting her short-fiction editing job at *The Magazine of Fantasy and Science Fiction*, she was quite encouraged by this welcome back to writing. She never quit writing novels, and has sold more than forty-five of them, some under pseudonyms, in mystery, science fiction, fantasy, horror, and romance. Her most recent mystery novel is *Hitler's Angel*. Her most recent fantasy novel is *The Black Queen*.

Ellis Peters (1913–1995) wrote more than seventy novels during her forty-year career as an author, but she will always be remembered as the creator of the twelfth-century Benedictine monk Cadfael, arguably the most famous of all medieval sleuths. The Cadfael novels were successful worldwide, eventually translated into twenty languages, and adapted into a BBC series starring Derek Jacobi. The series was also critically lauded, and she won a

Crime Writers Association Silver Dagger for the novel *Monk's Hood* and was nominated for an Agatha Award for the novel *The Potter's Field*. She also won the Edgar Allan Poe Award from the Mystery Writers of America for her novel *Death and the Joyful Woman*, featuring her earlier series characters, George, Bunty, and Dominic Felse, a sleuthing family that lived in Shropshire, England. She was awarded the Order of the British Empire in 1994, just before the last Cadfael novel, *Brother Cadfael's Penance*, was released.

Introduction:
John Helfers is a writer and editor living in Green Bay, Wisconsin. His fiction appears in more than a dozen anthologies, including *Future Net*, *Once Upon a Crime*, *First to Fight*, and *The UFO Files*, among others. His first anthology project, *Black Cats and Broken Mirrors*, was published by DAW Books in 1998, and it contains the Nebula Award–winning short story "Thirteen Ways to Water." Recent books include the published anthologies *Future Crimes* and *Alien Abductions*, as well as a novel in progress. Born in Lombard, Illinois, he moved to Green Bay in 1990, where he attended the University of Wisconsin–Green Bay, graduating in 1995 with a degree in English. Currently, he writes and edits full time.

Copyrights and Permissions